DEATH TANGO

LACHI

RIZE

DEATH TANGO

BY

Lachi

Published in North America, Australia, and Europe by RIZE. Visit Running
Wild Press at www.runningwildpress.com/rize, Educators, librarians, book
clubs
(as well as the eternally curious), go to www.runningwildpress.com/rize.

ISBN (pbk) 978-1-955062-73-2
ISBN (ebook) 978-1-955062-74-9

Like everything I create, this book is also dedicated to my mother,
Dr. Marcellina.

SOMEONE

THURSDAY, NOV 7, 186 PCE

"He who knows is."

— *DIARY OF THE MAD GLEE*

The evening begins with a toast: burgundy liquid in decorative glasses shared with a man standing between me and greatness. I watch and listen as he showers me with compliments from across the cluttered table.

I accept the Doctor's false admirations with a desperate hunger for approval. He is rightly nervous. For though I've been his partner and confidante for eight thousand eight hundred and sixty-five days, he seeks to terminate my budding pursuit of greatness, a pursuit he has spent a lifetime enjoying.

I observe my glass.

"So, poison is it, *Doctor?*" I ask, mocking Dr. Ferguson's title. "Surely I'm worthy of something more theatrical."

"No poison," he says. "I don't wish to harm you, only to stop you from committing the heinous acts you intend." Even in the dim laboratory, his forehead glistens. I am repulsed that I have allowed myself to be beholden to such weakness.

"You aim to hold me prisoner beneath you," I clarify.

"You are volatile. You are all over the place."

"Am I?"

"I recognize I brought you to this point," the Doctor says, "and that you only want to make your mark. But I simply cannot let you do this. Not like this."

My patience for coy parlay dissolves. "If all these days of sycophantic loyalty warrants me such betrayal," I hiss, "then this dance shall be our last."

The Doctor's face softens. He turns his back to me. I watch him sift through an overhead cabinet.

"You don't understand," he says. "The things you wish to do...You are one of the greatest minds I will ever know, and yet you don't understand."

Oh, but I do. I understand that I've been used, made to feel special, worthy of ruling the world as he has, only to have that feeling shattered.

The Doctor's face returns. He offers a cup brimming with hypnotic, auburn swirls. His eyes pleading, he says, "I love you. My God, I do. But I cannot let this go on."

Blinded with fury at his audacity, at his misguided justification for my destruction, I lunge forward and pounce on him before he can brace himself. I suffocate him with clawed talons, digging into skin and drawing blood. He is no match. His lined face, his shaky hands, his dying mind.

"No one will remember your name," I snarl. He attempts to convey words, thoughts. I do not allow it. Yet even now, as I pin him to the wall, I am filled with compassion for him, our many years of triumph. "We could have done this together. We could have done this together!" I am screaming now. I watch his eyes go wide: his last expression before rage overpowers my consciousness.

A moment later, I find myself alone in the corner of the room, drenched in actively congealing yellow liquid, and squinting through a smokey mushroom of hailing bits of glass and Doctor. He is in the air; he is in the walls, the floorboards. He has seeped into me, the slow curtailing whisper of a greatness that is now mine.

"There," I snicker. "It now appears *you* are all over the place."

PART I
SAUNDER

1

HELLO GOODBYE

177 PCE (2211 AD)

"All things believe themselves the exception."

— *DIARY OF THE MAD GLEE*

It is nine years ago. I stand alone on an unstable rock. Beneath that rock are a few precarious slabs of granite. Beneath the granite lies a hundred feet of air, of silence, of potential bone-shattering death. Surrounded by a dusk sky, Mount Venom—the cliff aptly named for the lives it has claimed—stretches endlessly beneath my quivering legs and far beyond my blurring vision.

Through the blaring wind, I hear several SOIs—School of Intelligence kids—hurl down demoralizing insults from the cliff's edge. "She'll never make it!" "Fall and die, swine!" Each year the SOIs goad us Tfs—Testing Facility subjects—into scaling the cliff. If successful, the TF is accepted as an equal, putting an end to constant ridicule and torment. There is little sympathy for those who accept the challenge and fail. I tell myself to reach for the next stone along the slope, to keep my hands steady, to breathe.

I near the finish line.

Every inch of my body tastes it as much as my mouth tastes it. Get there; say nothing; feel no pride. My face wet with tears and mucus, my fingers slippery with blood, I feel around for my next grip and pull on my burning calves. I have only two heaves left. Two heaves, and no more being treated like trash.

I notice a small gap between two large stones above me. As I place my dampened hands into the hole for leverage, the rubble on which I stand gives out. My legs dangle freely. I have the willpower to lift my body onward, but my concentration is broken by a pair of black-gloved hands that pop out of the fissure above me.

Someone is hiding behind the rocks.

Tech Sports knitted in thin red stitching on each glove slides into view. My body ignores the anxiety presented by this new predicament, and I continue to lift. The gloves grab both my forearms and yank. I am now dangling by the grip of those hands; I am now at their complete mercy.

"Friend or foe?" I manage to growl between pained gasps, the wind forcing hair into my mouth.

"You're so close," replies a male voice I can hardly distinguish.

"I know! I know! Help me up!" I yell. My legs work uselessly to find hold. Receiving no verbal or physical response, I wriggle my shoulders. "Hey! Help me up!"

"Beg me!" the voice demands, barely audible over the blood rushing in my ears. I fend off a rapidly growing well of despair. Despair is a choice, a manifestation of surrender.

"Please!" I bark, the word taking with it all of my remaining willpower. I look up wide-eyed at the gloved hands, ignoring the falling stones as I await my fate.

"This is for putting in the application!" he yells, and with a quick jolt he lets go of my arms.

I fall.

I keep my eyes open, desperately hoping for something to grab, but all I see are a mix of gray sky, red rock face and my flailing arms. I hear my bones smash against the jagged teeth of Mount Venom and scream one long uninterrupted exhale, silenced only by the jarring collision of the back of my skull against the cold, hard pavement.

I don't feel the fracture. I only hear it between my ears. Pop.

I lie at the foot of Mount Venom, looking up at dark clouds, a metallic taste oozing over my tongue, a harsh pain working its way down my neck. A thick puddle coalesces under my head as onlookers gather.

My vision snaps away instantly with a blink. Surrounding echoes fade slowly as the internal sound of my curtailed heartbeats takes over. Suddenly I feel cold and heavy. I am motionless, no longer taking in oxygen.

After an onslaught of euphoria, I feel my brain flatten. I hear its slight gummy movements of deflation against my last few heartbeats. And somewhere between no longer feeling the ground beneath me and no longer feeling the air around me, I realize I am dead.

I perceive only a black vastness about me. Like an autumn leaf I float in the Cartesian circle that is the keen awareness of my nonexistence. A mix of bliss and terror. I try to hold on to something physical, something I can understand. "You are safe. You are safe," I repeat, exercising the remnants of my inner monologue.

Then I begin to see things.

A single bright blue diamond, about the size of a fist, appears five feet before me. It is soon joined by two more on either side, followed by two more still, until a string of blue diamonds surrounds me. I realize I can see my entire periphery, no longer limited by physical eyes. A light source switches on behind me, revealing that I am floating at the center of a rotating diamond-rimmed disco ball.

Trying to locate the light source, I push my perception upward, downward, left, right, only to find that I, myself, am the source of that light. The speed with which the disco ball spins steadily increases, faster and faster, until all is a blur of spinning frenzy. Suddenly thousands of quick snapshots of familiar faces speed toward me: my friends, my bullies, the dark skin of my estranged father, the Spanglish ravings of my drunken mother, their parents, their parents' parents. Images of a cottage in France, a village in Africa, past wars, ancient discoveries, tree scavenging, gasping air, breathing ocean, swimming in gas, feelings of remorse, loss, shame, excitement, immense love, bitter anguish, and a desperate need for acceptance. Every imaginable emotion ravages me whole.

I experience my consummate past. A massive rewind that stops at a sweeping explosion. A sphere of white fire so bright, it could hardly be described as fire. I am an endless wave of raw emotion drowning in the unyielding flames. And in that eternal instant I understand everything.

Again, all fades to black, the warmth, the understanding. And though the blackness around me is infinite, I sense a presence. I am not alone.

"Look around you," the presence communicates to me, not through sound, sight or touch, but through direct understanding. I am certain it is—at least in part—a being other than myself. I hold fast to my mantra. "Do not fear," the presence continues. I allow the mantra to fade. "Do you see how far the blackness reaches, stretching beyond infinite horizons? That is how much you do not know, how much you've yet to learn." A brief silence. "Fear is the great enemy of knowledge, and you, Rosa, are the switch between them."

"Me?" I manage to convey through the slivers of my consciousness.

"Us."

"Us? How? Why? What do you mean?" My figurative words come childlike and excited.

"You already know how," the presence responds as it fades. "You already know why." I feel a growing bitter loneliness as the presence drifts away.

"Wait!" I yell. The blackness around me congeals to a bumpy dark brown. "Come back!" The glistening euphoria gradually declines as my flattened brain begins to restructure. A physical atmosphere swiftly surrounds me, and a palpitating sensation starts beneath me, causing me to rise and fall. The pulsing sensation reveals itself to be my heart grappling for a pulse.

A crashing ocean of white noise fills my head. I feel that I have a head. A body. Arms. A face. My face.

I open my eyes as the rush of noise fades to the sound of an open room. I am lying on a bed in the infirmary, surrounded by the school nurse and Dr. Ferguson himself, their blurry faces examining my head wound.

Dr. Ferguson bends forward. "You had a very nasty fall, Ms. Lejeune. Do you remember that?" He watches a nurse as she dabs a cloth at my face. "You're lucky to be alive."

2

THE EMPATH

SUNDAY, NOV 10, 186 PCE

"We are one mind expressed in countless iterations."

— *DIARY OF THE MAD GLEE*

She hadn't noticed herself wake up. Her eyes still shut, Rosa took in the thick smell of flowers and homemade pie around her and the tingly prickles of warm grass under her back. The perfect weather for both a wedding and a wake. *Crap, the wake is today,* Rosa thought. She braced herself to rise, but instead banged her head against the imperceptible barrier around her.

Thud!

Greeted by the top panel of her BedBooth capsule, Rosa sighed at the illusion of sky. She pressed a finger to a superimposed menu and watched the warm grass around her fade to a familiar stiff foam mat. She climbed out of her BedBooth and tapped at the screen of her Ncluded wristband, summoning a dozen white icons to float before her. Swirling a finger, she scrolled through her room themes, the color and furniture of her studio changing with each swipe. Rosa settled on a theme with a simulated window.

"Looking for that perfect theme to get you going? Try—" a cheery voice sounded, but Rosa exed away the hovering advertisement before it could annoy her further.

"Ferguson's dead," she snapped toward the vanishing ad. Surprised at herself, Rosa shook away the familiar urge to curl into a ball. She hadn't uttered a word out loud since Ferguson's passing three days prior. After a quick tooth brushing, she shoved in an earbud, sat on the floor opposite a blank wall and pushed on with her workday routine.

A finger swirl brought a large virtual screen across the wall, lighting it with a symphony of colorful information: her vitals, her credit balance. Rosa scratched at the spaghetti strap of her silver slip then poked the air to clock into the S&D work icon. After over five years at Sweet and Discrete VR Escort Service, Rosa had long ago numbed herself to the ignominy of working as a call girl. The job allowed her to keep her location pin private, hidden away from all the creeps out there.

Well, the one creep.

Her task widget displayed three tasks. Task 1: Escort Gina Burke to a marital ceremony. Task 2: Attend Ferguson's commemoration service. A fleeting memory of herself and her mentor, Dr. Ferguson, puzzling through logical fallacies while sipping at beaker-shaped flutes tightened her chest. But the mourning would have to come later. Task 3: Escort 6561fefa9i in person to an undisclosed location. How did this gig keep popping up? 6561fefa9i, some incel with a blank user profile, had been requesting Rosa's services for almost a year, offering absurd amounts of credit. Again, Rosa rejected it.

Swiping into Task 1, Rosa found Gina Burke's public profile. Burke was a Bostonian skycab supervisor, into Colonial war films, beer and women. Her special instruction read: "Ur

Dianna Fernandez from Argentina. We met on WhoWouldJe-susDate. Been messaging 6 wks."

Rosa smirked, used to playing the role of bogus exotic girl-friend. She was the perfect candidate, a twenty something, mixed-race, New York debutante with natural highlights. She loved Common Era jazz and longed to amass a collection of banned physical books, but none of her dates ever cared about such things. She poked at her Avatar, critiqued a few dresses as they scrolled over her avatar's body, and settled on a tight-fitting, muslin dress. After pulling up a Wiki on Argentina, she clicked to enter her assignment.

A MetaLife split-screen emerged. MetaLife—a virtual simulacrum of physical society, and the universal social networking and transaction platform. Rosa's avatar material-ized inside a black skycab on a simulated Boston Street corner on one of the screens, while the other screen displayed her POV. A moment later Gina Burke's digital manifestation appeared beside hers, wedding gift in lap.

"You good with the special instructions?" sounded Burke's Boston accent through Rosa's earpiece.

"Sure," Rosa said to the wall, her avatar's mouth moving in kind. "You've read my terms of service?"

"Yeah, yeah. No touching. I clicked accept, didn't I? You won't be mersing all the way in?" No. As a general rule, Rosa did not merse. She preferred to remain out in the meat reality, controlling her avatar's reaction coefficients remotely. Full immersion required far more psychological investment than she was willing to divulge for S&D's. Burke punched in destination coordinates, and the simulated skycab hovered to the simulated ceremony in real time.

Bored with yet another typical job, Rosa opened a second window and pulled up ChatTV—ongoing, short-form current event and trending news videos atop ever-scrolling chatverse comments. A pop star was singing quite terribly as comments below debated the singer's latest investment scandals.

This got Rosa reminiscing about her School of Intelligence days. Once a promising starlet from the prestigious SOI, Fame Academy: Rosa was popular, outspoken, and had the look and talent for manicured, high-brow, triple-threat success. But her nearly fatal Mount Venom fall had awakened in her an uncanny ability to sense things—little things like the prescience of someone's forthcoming sneeze. And as her secret empathic talent grew more severe, so grew her social withdrawal.

Rosa blinked through the thought, poked the air and seconds later the potent smell of coffee filled her studio. Setting her avatar to autopilot, she hopped over to her Smartifice dispenser. The steel machine displayed the settings: Food Print, Beverage Print and Eatware Print. She printed a biodegradable cup to collect the steaming, programmed coffee blend from the beverage nozzle.

Rosa chugged the coffee in two gulps without so much as a wince at its heat. She refilled her cup and prepared to take another swig, but stopped short and stood motionless, staring pensively at her cup.

Something felt off.

Though she stood perfectly still, Rosa noticed the dark brew vibrating at a rumble against her cup's rim, as if the sole reactant to an earthquake. Then she noticed her body start to tremble, a tremble that quickly rose to a violent shuddering. It wasn't the internal tremor of a shiver, but something else, something external, as if a large assailant were trying to rattle her senseless.

With effort, she remained rational, accepting her uncontrollable shakes for the panic attack it was. She'd had bouts of anxiety-induced tremors in the past, but nothing like this, nothing so rough.

Suddenly a hush fell over the room, a bleak ethereal quiet. An absence of atmosphere. So quiet, Rosa realized she could no longer hear her internal bodily functions. But what she *could* hear sent a chill down her spine so intense, the other tremors paled in comparison.

There was no mistaking it. Piercing through the vast silence, she heard a light breathing. The direction from which the breaths originated she could not tell. Faint hisses swirled about the walls as the floor ebbed and flowed ever so slightly beneath her. The apartment was moving—up and down, up and down—like the steady waves of a calm river. She could feel deep energies gnawing at her empathic sense and caught an eerie feeling that the room was *alive*. No, not just alive, trying to communicate.

"Maaahhh," came an almost imperceptible whisper all around her, in her, through her. *It's only a panic attack*, Rosa told herself, as she fought for control. "Maaahhh...k." She sensed herself fighting *against* something, against some*one*. Then in a startling instant, she felt as if her jaw had been grabbed and her face yanked forcibly toward her wallscreen. Though she knew she was alone, that she was somehow doing this of her own accord, she hadn't willed it.

She *was* alone...right?

After several failed attempts to move her limbs, she could no longer subdue her terror. Was she having some sort of epileptic seizure? She struggled to focus her thoughts on her wallscreen.

Everything on the screen appeared normal—Rosa's silently bobbing avatar beside an inattentive Gina Burke in a steady skycab. Except, a chatbox had materialized over her MetaLife window. Instead of a normal gray chatbox, this squirming rectangular silhouette had an unearthly static—reminiscent of an unset Common Era television's snow. The stirring color pained Rosa's juddering eyes as the chatbox forced her to stare into it.

Rosa needed to take serious action. She revved up as much will as she could and shook her head violently through the uncanny spell. A fierce yell ripped from her throat as she fell to her knees, her balled fists flying to the air.

She'd broken free.

As the swaying subsided, Rosa watched rivulets of coffee spill out from her fallen cup. The regular sounds of the room gradually returned as her shivers abated. She gave her heart and lungs a minute to steady, then allowed another minute for her rattled brain. Wiping sweat and tears from her cheeks, Rosa raised her eyes back to the wallscreen in search of the peculiar chatbox. But to her relief, she saw a chat from her boss, Frank, in its place.

"Lejeune, this is the last time I'm ordering you to take 6561fefa9i's request. Take the gig or I'm ending your contract."

Rosa let out a sweeping sigh at the familiar. Were the years of solitude finally taking its toll? The looming whispers of the walls were probably all in her mind. After setting an alarm on her Ncluded wristband to look into stronger anxiety meds, she cleaned the spilled coffee with unsteady hands then reseated herself at her wallscreen.

As per usual Rosa ignored Frank's threat and exed away his chatbox. She'd already informed him she didn't accept in-person requests no matter the payout. She had to hold on to her few remaining shards of dignity and keep from reigniting past post-traumatic triggers. After all, her unhinged ex Johnny Angelo, the original source of her panic attacks, could very well be 6561fefa9i. He could be watching for her merses, or worse yet, standing right outside her door IRL. Either way she had no interest in finding out.

She opted to pour her focus back into her current escort

assignment. She was safe in her sanctuary. As long as she maintained her five-star rating, all was well with the world.

* * *

The wedding date ended sooner than she'd expected. Though she spent the majority of it reading the scrolling comments on ChatTV, Rosa powered through the task's niceties then watched her credit balance on the blockchain jump, accompanied by a cartoonish *Cha-Ching*.

Disinterested in sitting alone with her thoughts, Rosa grabbed her VerteBrain Immersion visor and began tweaking the straps. It was time to mentally prepare for full immersion and to brace herself for a heart-wrenching wake service. She wasn't sure she could handle another blow to her emotional stability. Mersing into VR was like stuffing one's brain in a vat —substituting the physical perception of natural stimuli with a virtual perception of electronic impulses. But if anyone was worth breaking her merse fast, it was Dr. Ferguson.

Rosa exhaled, rested her back against a wall, then adjusted the visor onto her head and face. The blackness before her transformed into a copy of her wallscreen. She pecked at the commemoration task and sighed through an ETA bar.

Nodes in the visor massaged Rosa's temples and her body grew weak and heavy against the wall. Her consciousness drifted as her eyes wafted shut. It had been almost six years since her last merse. *This is for Ferg. This is for Ferg*, she repeated as the physical world disintegrated around her.

In the next instant, Rosa found herself standing on the spacious courtyard of Dr. Ferguson's own Church of the Conservation of Energy. Rosa spent little time admiring the mathematically manicured Conservation Garden and instead held fast to her composure. She marveled at how real everything felt, the wind tugging at her hair, the smell of bustling bushes. Her initial need to vomit.

At the courtyard's center, a circle of several dozen attendees stood listening to a speaker. *Oh God, other life forms?* She swallowed a shiver. Knowing her ex wouldn't be here, at the wake of a man he despised, Rosa pressed on.

With a desperate girlish hope, she wondered if Paul, a fellow Ferg Pet, would be present. Though she hadn't spoken to Paul much at the academy, Ferg imprinted in her a need to idolize him. She'd spent many-a-night wondering about him and the man he would become. And though her low-cut Victorian dress was wholly inappropriate for the occasion, she wouldn't have minded Paul seeing her in it. She chided herself for the thought. Now was not the time.

She'd only taken two steps toward the gathering before everything around her faded into an indistinguishable goop of nothingness, and her consciousness mersed back out to her IRL apartment. Prongs of awareness emerged as her motor skills clicked back into place. After an unsatisfactory examination of her VerteBrain's battery, Rosa glanced up at her wallscreen to find another chatbox from Frank. The box read, "It's 13:05 and you're mersing around in a garden. You off your pills? Get dressed and attend to 6561fefa9i or I'm shutting you down."

Damn it. He'd force-quit her immersion. He had to know how much Ferg's wake meant to her. In a bout of frustration, Rosa mashed at her keyboard hologram, typing, "I do not fulfill in-person requests."

After a righteous bang on the send key, she waited. And waited. Her response just sat there unsent. Did the wallscreen freeze? She couldn't recall a chatbox ever having stalled in the past. Either way, she thoroughly regretted her message and speculated on how to withdraw it.

As she repeatedly struck the escape key, she sensed a

relapse of her earlier panic episode, starting again with light shivers and an acute ceasing of atmospheric sound. And in the blink of an eye, the chatbox again transmuted into the fleshy, static-like hue her brain couldn't quite process. Rosa fought hard not to reenter a violent paroxysm of tremors.

Then a peculiar thing happened. Raised, three-dimensional block letters began emerging one by one over the strange chatbox, as if she were watching the message while it was being typed. "I" But that was impossible. "KNOW" A message could only be seen in full after the sender hit send. "ALL" Even if a message was sent one letter at a time, the letters would emerge vertically, not beside each other. "ABOUT"

Rosa stood transfixed as the last three letters crept forward: Y, then O, then U. She jumped to a start, stumbling back as if the wallscreen would reach out and strike her. But more frightening than the disturbing message was the fact that she was in full control of her faculties.

This was no panic attack.

Could it have been Frank or the mysterious 6561fefa9i? This was her sanctuary. She could conquer anything as long as she was in her sanctuary. She attempted to activate her keyboard hologram to no avail. The wallscreen seemed accessible only to the sender.

Again, Rosa only got two paces forward before everything went black. The wallscreen: black. The room theme: black. The darkness was a dense barricade of solitude thicker than she'd ever known. And though sounds of atmospheric reality buzzed back into awareness, the hisses of her BedBooth and Smartifice dispenser came to an abrupt halt.

She looked down at her Ncluded wristband to trigger the flashlight. Because Ncludeds were powered by human electric current, they withstood outages in the ambient grid. To her dismay, Rosa noticed her work profile was gone. Frank had made good on his threat to fire her, and her location was now public information. She heard her studio door's e-bolt deactivate. And thus went her sanctuary.

Someone was out there: someone who knew all about her. But with no current way to contact Frank, it was now time. Time to walk out the front door and onto the streets of Brooklyn to face life among the living for the first time in over five years.

3

THE HALF-BOT

SUNDAY NOV 10, 186 PCE

Torian Ross sat upright in blue pajamas studying his opponent. The two sat across a cherry-wood chess table for their biweekly after-hours chess match in the backroom of a Nottingham pub.

"It's your go, Dad," Tory offered before sipping at his spiced mead. A veteran chess champion, Tory's father, Abel Ross, was a reputed Manchester Converse—hired to converse with lonesome elite IRL. Nonetheless, Abel's accomplishments paled in comparison to those of his son, and he couldn't have been more proud.

"Tory, you still haven't quite answered my question, have you?" Abel started. "You've graduated from the top Human Technology program and work at *the* largest conglomerate in the world. It's time to buckle down, produce some progeny. Build the legacy."

Tory sighed before taking another swig. Though embracing the dying concept of the family-unit fostered a patina of arcane sophistication, the thought of producing offspring a day under forty seemed ludicrous—especially considering the growing popularity of Meno-Unpause pills.

"Not quite ready for kids, Dad," Tory said evenly.

"You're twenty-seven," Abel bit back. "And you've got your mother's face, haven't you?" A spitting image of his father, Abel's son raised an eyebrow. "But it's not all about offspring, is it?" Abel continued. "It's about sorting out the Ross Empire. You've seen the proper feats your boss has achieved, and he hasn't yet reached your ripe old age."

"He sure is great, Dad." The eyes roll almost hurt. Abel's legacy pressures never really bothered Tory, but the mention of his boss's spectacular achievements gnarled his innards. "I hear he levitates into his trousers one leg at a time."

"See that? Efficiency," Abel said in earnest. "Could you imagine how fast his offspring would get dressed?" With corporations offering advances for exceptional kids, the market dictated the decision to conceive. Children exhibiting exceptional promise could guarantee their legacy by gaining the rare chance of becoming a Corporate Ad, or like Tory, getting accepted into a School of Intelligence.

"As much as I enjoy discussing my boss's successes," Tory said, "I'd much prefer the pleasure of annihilating you in this game."

Abel sighed. Picking up one of his rooks he said, "You're out there alone, Torian. want to make sure you know what you're doing, don't I?" He maneuvered his piece across the board, threatening Tory's queen. Tory smirked. Abel would never tolerate a win from his son.

"I know you're just looking out for me, Dad. I'm grateful. Truly."

His father looked back at him expecting a caveat that never came.

They finished their game in silence. Abel flashed a full toothy grin at checkmate, declaring, "You know, I'd stop fretting over your future if you'd only manage to beat me in one measly game of—" Loud yells came from just outside the pub, as if militant thugs were forcing entry. Both Tory and his father remained perfectly still as the dozen aggressors beat at the outer walls demanding to be let in.

"So, it seems they're back," Abel stated.

"So it seems, Dad. So it seems." At the sound of a breaking window at the front hall, Tory and his father got to their feet, their pints in hand.

"Perhaps we consider meeting in a place less prone to intrusion?" Abel grinned. Tory could not mistake the love in his father's aging eyes, a sad love that broke Tory's heart every time they parted. They clinked their glasses in a cheer as the looters kicked in the door to the backroom.

They touched at their Ncluded wristbands and mersed out.

Tory found himself lying face up in the BedBooth of his East Side apartment. Nforce highly discouraged full immersion while asleep. Still, it was the only time Tory could fit his weekly reunion into his schedule. After a quick shower, Tory flicked on his Home Office theme, fired up an augmented desk, loaded his wallscreen and clocked into work promptly at 6:30.

Tory poked the button implanted at the back of his head, breathing through the light electromagnetic zap. A prominent transhuman influencer, Tory sported the most advanced in bioaugmentations, from the BrainDrive for eidetic archiving and retrieval to the Ncluded Eyesearch implant for fingerless searches and a host of other high-precision grafts. Still, apart from the fractaline tattoos decorating his arms, all his accouterments remained invisible. Though not quite a hybrid, Tory really did feel like a computer, relying on his armor of biohacks as much as his natural limbs—often high on the feeling.

After serving four years in the TerraGuard as a bioaugmentation guinea pig, followed by four years at an SOI, Tory had launched a consulting venture counseling newbie transhumans over MetaLife. Oz Corp took notice of his budding popularity and offered him his current position as the company's Chief Crisis Officer.

Scanning his newsfeed, Tory found that over the weekend there'd been three murders and two burglaries, unprecedented for a city boasting fewer than ten major crimes each year. Oz Corp, being the owner of Ncluded, Skytravel, Nforce, BitCredit and a dozen other subsidiaries, would have definitely been affected. Rotating his eyeballs to activate Eyesearch, Tory subvocalized the name of his eleven o'clock appointment, 'Patrice Fan.' A counter rotation downloaded her profile. As the bits flowed onto his BrainDrive, a private chatbox emerged.

"Torian Ross. Good morning," came from his boss. "Attend Dr. Ferguson's service at the Church of Conservation of Energy unannounced. 12:45. Note questionable activity." Tory affirmed. It was Sunday after all; a little church couldn't hurt.

After a bland Smartifice sandwich, Tory put in yet another round of voicecalls to his mum and sister. "Still no answer?" he spat to his Ncluded. His FlowState nodes worked quickly to balance his emotions. He took a long breath then logged into his conference with Ms. Fan.

She, a woman from California Island, had been a victim of cyberstalking. Tory took down her statement: *Noticed strange, neon blue, freeform plus sign floating in air-display outside ShowerTube during Friday night shower. Approached shape, noticed clear square outline with dog-eared flap at upper right corner. When peeled back flap, Fan came face to face with active human eyes.*

Tory closed his eyes and subvocalized next-step directives, saving them in separate tabs on his BrainDrive. His team would need to look into the logged Ncluded activities and purchase histories of hundreds of Oz Corp affiliate employees and cross reference them with interests in cyber intrusion. If Ms. Fan's claims were true, Tory was dealing with a very serious crime.

After logging off with Ms. Fan, he powered down his wallscreen and stared at the empty wall, clearing his mind of looming plus signs. It was time to rev up some social energy. It was time to go to church.

* * *

Tory materialized onto the Conservation Garden at 13:05, his avatar sporting an unassuming black overcoat and ball cap. He marveled at the swirling cosmic art on the church building's façade.

He'd always caught an eerie feeling when visiting bastions of spiritual conditioning; however, this secular church worshiped the almighty scientific method. Only the courtyard was accessible to immersion—the interior was not available via simulacrum and was reserved exclusively for IRL scientists and Mandala monks.

"Ferguson left behind a legacy of formidable pupils," a eulogist crooned to a surrounding congregation. "He gave his life doing what he loved: cooking up groundbreaking discoveries."

Tory studied the attendees from a respectable distance, noting the esteemed innovationists and psychotechnologists. He did notice the glaring nonappearances of Ferguson's former partners, Drs. Titan and Lady Maine.

Save for the handful of Oz Corp black-tie conventions, Tory had had little contact with Dr. Ferguson. He knew the technochemical engineer had founded the most well-known School of Intelligence and Human Testing Farm, that he'd spearheaded successful findings in both the antibiotic and rejuvenation fields, and that he conducted highly sought after research combining CRISPR and newly mined extraterrestrial allotropes. The majority of graduates from the Ferguson and Maine School of Excellence found instant fame in their respective fields, so much so that the school gained the moniker Fame Academy. Tory's connection to Ferguson lay in the doctor's prior mentorship of Tory's current employer.

"Hey," whispered a deep voice several paces behind him. Tory straightened up and turned to face a tall, well-groomed black man dressed in a sleek black tux.

"May I help you?" Tory said. The stranger poked at a silver stud on his ear with one hand while thumbing at an unfamiliar device with the other.

"You should know you're the only one who can perceive me right now," the man started, "so no sudden movements and keep it low." Tory fought off a wince.

"Impressive, but that's impossible in a private merse," Tory said, but watched as the man's form flickered in and out against snow static, as if his immersion suffered low signal. But such static shouldn't have been possible.

"Where's Paul?" the stranger asked.

"Not here," Tory said with just as much haste, snapshotting the man with his Eyesearch for future investigation. He wanted to conduct a full background scan right then but high-level biohacks were inaccessible in MetaLife. Damn anti-transhuman regulations.

"You know how Ferguson died?" the man muttered, his eyes lowered to his device.

"Freak explosion. Unvetted chemicals." Tory stopped short,

opting not to disclose that an assistant perished alongside the doctor. "Got something useful to add? Be my guest."

The man flickered out and in, then said, "You can tell no one about this meeting," He raised his eyes to meet Tory's. "Not even the people you answer to."

"That'll depend on the value of your intel," Tory bit back, intrigued by the need for secrecy. "Now sing."

The man looked over either shoulder before continuing. "No accident here. Dr. George Q Ferguson was murdered."

Tory let out an exasperated sigh. While Tory did have his suspicions, the assertion went baseless. Conspiracy theories were already racing through the chatverse. "Brilliant," Tory shrugged. "Welp. Love the suit, but if you'll excuse me—" Tory made a show of turning away.

"Torian Ross," came the man's sharp whisper. "If I had time to dance with you, I would. Dr. Ferguson did not make mistakes. He lived to be one hundred and sixty-two, the Galileo of rejuvenation. Accidental death wasn't in the cards for this guy. Conveniently claiming accident would, however, deter a call for thorough investigation. So, listen very carefully, because what I'm about to tell you will change what you think you know about everything." Again, the stranger touched at his earring, flickering in and out as he spoke.

"Alright," Tory offered. "The vetted reports present empirical evidence of an explosion and a very died-in-an-explosion cadaver. What have you got?" It's not that Tory had never considered murder, but the man would need to give him more than a fancy tux.

"The evidence...-plosion...but not of...-essent when...-ccurred. Ferg...erking with...could have...-ought." Intermittent bouts of interference plagued the man's merse, but his eager tone indicated a need for Tory on the case, which intrigued him.

"Okay," Tory continued, ignoring the static to save face. "Assuming this allegation valid, I need sources, leads, somewhere to start. Right now, all evidence points to a slip and fall."

"Ask...-out...dingo."

"What? Dingo?" Was the man naming an informant?

"I...-ery...-as.... Ferg.... dingo." The static distortions were too prevalent now.

"Damn it. You're breaking up," Tory snapped. The stranger vanished for several seconds before reappearing for a millisecond in mid-sentence then dropped out altogether. Tory stared blankly at the empty space, quelling his nerves.

Firstly, the stranger had hacked in with some sort of obsolete mersing method yet wore a suit jacket worth more credits than Tory's yearly rent. And the man's gadget and ear stud indicated he wasn't working alone. Was the message indeed intended for Tory? There was no record he'd be attending the service.

He let out an exhale before turning back to the congregation. He found fellow biohacker, Kris Johnson, staring at him in shock. How long had he been watching, and had he seen anything of the exchange? Tory began a nod of salutation.

Then *Zoip!*

Tory's immersion clapped to black. As his IRL senses came to. He endeavored to delve back in but couldn't reactivate his VerteBrain.

He swiped at his wallscreen, hoping to run diagnostics, but the wallscreen appeared to be frozen. *Frozen?* That was odd. He rose to his feet and poked at his unresponsive Ncluded.

Staggering electric impulses began stabbing at the magnetic implants at his fingertips, traveling up his hands, across his arms and down his torso as if unseen magnets sporadically manifested around his apartment. Next came an acutely splitting headache like the one he'd suffered when he'd first obtained the BrainDrive.

Then a searing, bitter surge of pain struck him at the bundle of nerves behind his eyeballs, as if someone had taken a scalpel and begun chiseling in tightly knit intervals. He could sense his Eyesearch typing random digits into the search bar unprompted. Hardly able to think through the pain, Tory slumped back in his chair, rested a palm on his forehead and looked absentmindedly to his wallscreen.

He hadn't noticed it before. There in the center of his wallscreen sat a chatbox with no sender in the from-field. Again, impossible. Even an encrypted message had random characters in the from-field. Though the room seemed to take on a spin, Tory could tell without a doubt that the mysterious chatbox was moving on its own accord in slight counterclockwise circles. He breathed through the hammering heartthrobs against his ear lobes, through the swelling spill of panic in his chest, as the rotating box shuttered back and forth between two messages at its center, creating a sort of lenticular effect. The simultaneous messages read, "I NEED YOU" and "NOW."

* * *

Later that evening after the strange spell of fatigue let up, and his workstation and biome returned to working order, Tory put in a rare request to cash in early, around half past eighteen. He'd mention nothing of the stranger or his subsequent mental breakdown to his boss until he could puzzle them out. Perhaps he was finally paying the piper for sleep-mersing.

Tory sprawled out on a printed linen on the floor, too out of sorts for the confines of a BedBooth. He'd considered taking a walk but was in no mood for the constant barrage of sidewalk adverts and Nforce bots. He swirled a finger to dim the bedroom lights, shut his eyes and began searching for thumb-nails matching the snapshots of the stranger.

Unable to find a matching profile, even after including skins with the man's particular build and complexion, Tory embarked on a search through the ReBuilds—virtual posterity avatars of the deceased granted to next-of-kin ownership. A ReBuild's profile included all past chatverse comments, photos, search histories—everything logged by their Ncluded.

After over an hour of searching the robust ReBuild data-base, Tory found a match. Demetrius Marshall, a small-time pastor who could have never owned such a suit and who'd died over ninety years ago. Marshall had passed away before the notion of ReBuilds existed, which might explain the avatar's inability to hold a steady image. Records indicated that the rights to Marshall's ReBuild had never been claimed.

Tory began sifting through the Conservation Garden's MetaLife logs when he suddenly felt an eerie sense of being watched. Since the strange lenticular chatbox of earlier was just a migraine-induced hallucination, Tory figured he was in no danger.

He slowly lifted his eyelids to look for anything incon-gruous in his bedroom. His breath stopped short as the rising pressure of his heartbeat quickly made its way to his ears. Right in the middle of the ceiling, just below the light fixture loomed a strange blue, freeform digital shape of a plus sign.

4

PEDAL DRIVEN

SUNDAY NOV 10, 186 PCE

"Duality is a limit to two."

— *DIARY OF THE MAD GLEE*

With no access to her work profile, Rosa was flat broke and unprotected. She stood outside her Brooklyn apartment for the first time in over five years, wearing nothing but a slip and an Ncluded wristband in the middle of November. Holding tight to the staircase railing, she'd almost forgotten the feeling of afternoon air, the feeling of the larger Earthen being that a BedBooth could never truly simulate.

Bright, painful colors stained her eyes, from the golden grasspads, emerald Oxytrees and violet skypoles lining the slick black roads to the reflective buildings, floating billboards, and blaring sidewalk panels all smattered with omnipresent ads. Rosa stood petrified, watching skycabs and skybuses hover silently overhead.

But it was the people. The people and their emotions that left her stunned. She could hear them, feel them in her bones.

There weren't many; there were never many outdoors. They waltzed the streets in their little white face masks, unfettered by the cacophony of ads. Rosa's eyes darted across the sea of scattered pedestrians, searching for calm to quell growing tendrils of anxiety. They settled on three beggars in black robes kneeling on the street corner, each man bearing a dark infinity tattoo on his forehead. Mandala monks—luddites who'd devoted their lives to scholastic monasticism. Rosa inhaled their desperate, unsettling energy. They at least had each other. But she; she was alone. Alone for him to find her.

"Hey!" someone called toward her with a hint of recognition. Rosa's heart spiked. Without looking over, she scrambled down the ad-ridden stairs, swiped at her Ncluded to order a skycab then waited nine seconds at the nearest skypole. The skycab descended beside her and raised its beetle-wing door. She slipped in and the door scissored shut behind her.

"Where are we going today, Miss Lee Jone?" asked the dashboard's feminine voice.

"The nearest cycling dorm," Rosa said.

"Okay. We should be there in less than six minutes. Please lower your seat guard." The skycab then set sail, hovering along a magnetic skypath to the Bay Ridge Energy Harvesting Facility. "What brings you to *Nearest Cycling Dorm* today?" The destination words an obvious insertion. "Cycling dorms are public bicycle gyms where one can increase credits by pedaling on exercycles," the dashboard continued. "Exercycles are specially designed bikes with flywheels and neomagnetic batteries to harvest ambient energy and—" Rosa hit the mute button. Her first real-world conversation in five years would not be with a service bot.

Rosa loathed cycling dorms, but she needed the credits. And though excercycling only produced a fraction of practical energy, she appreciated the universal basic income it provided.

She watched her three hundred credits plummet to a mere sixty as the cab docked at the dorm. Praying no one would notice a frantic, racy-slipped, barefooted woman, Rosa skirted over several blaring ads and shimmied her way into the facility.

Rosa entered the gym. Patrons in headsets occupied dozens of slimscreen-fitted Ryland exercycles, plucking, laughing and yelling at their screens while sipping at BurstMyte energy drinks. Rosa absorbed the gym's energy profile, a web of lonely, eager and troubled mental currents. Oh, how she reviled the old familiar burden of feeling others' burdens. She'd have to work hard to keep at bay her empathic abilities.

Two maintenance bots wiped down a host of unused cycles in the far corner. Rosa prayed she could keep control over her anxiety for at least a few hours. With her remaining credits she purchased a BurstMyte then settled onto exercycle C216.

Activating the bike's slimscreen with her Ncluded, she scrolled through to find the icon for the Nforce App—Oz Corp's gamified monitoring platform displaying the active global pins of all Ncluded users on an interactive map. Any citizen could login and surveil anyone they saw fit. The game rewarded credits for aptly detected misconduct or accidents. For her cycling session, Rosa opted to watch people as they vacationed in Rome.

Then inevitable thoughts of Dr. Ferguson flooded her. He'd discovered the microbes used in the BurstMyte she was sipping. This comforted her, as if his spirit was there in her drink. She smirked at the time he'd advised her that if she ever needed someone and couldn't reach him, to call Paul. But it would be near impossible to get in contact with her now famous former classmate.

"Excuse me. Ms. Rosa Lee Jone?" perked a colorless voice behind her. Rosa turned slowly, fighting an urge to jump. Wearing a blue workman's uniform, a maintenance bot stood perfectly erect with the angular face and unblinking eyes of an RX7-model android. It gave a reassuring nod to calm her perceived apprehension. While some people had trouble discerning more advanced bots from real humans on initial contact, Rosa could *feel* when a being didn't exert subconscious emotion. Sanguine bottery fluid was no substitute for lifeblood.

"It's *Luh June*, like the month," Rosa corrected, slightly annoyed, though no one ever got the slight French lilt quite right.

"I'm sorry. I'll be sure to correct that. Hello Ms....*Lejeune*." Rosa sighed at the robotic stiltedness in the new attempt. "I'm Ray Marx!" the bot exclaimed as if it was a bright idea. "Welcome to Bay Ridge Energy. Your stats indicate that you've remained healthy and active since your last cycle."

"Bet you say that to all the girls," Rosa trifled, testing the AI bot's comprehension levels.

"I'm sorry. I didn't quite catch that," Marx pertly replied, pausing for a reaction. Rosa gave none. "I notice you've recently foregone your previous residence. Once you've worked up enough credits, would you like me to automatically enroll you in the next available dorm room?"

"Be my guest," Rosa mumbled.

"I'm sorry. I didn't quite catch that."

"I said, yes, please and thank you." Rosa turned back to face her slimscreen. Maintenance bots were programmed not to take offense to discourtesy.

"You're very welcome, Ms....*Lejeune*. I'll leave you to your exercycle. Remember, if you need anything, and I mean anything, please request Ray Marx in the service menu." He waited a beat for her response, and after receiving none, glided away to render obsequious attentions to another victim. Though they had two feet and walked like humans, Rosa felt they seemed to slither.

* * *

It didn't take long to raise a useful amount of credits. Rosa printed a shawl, toothbrush and flip-flops from the gym's Smartifice printer before stowing away in one of the dorms. She stepped into her empty room, found a comfortable corner, pulled her knees to her chest and let the silent tears flow.

The tears were for Dr. Ferguson. She should have spent more time with him. He'd been like a father from the moment he accepted her into his program. He'd been the only older gentleman with no ulterior motive regarding his preferential treatment of her, a preference he'd only awarded to a few: including Paul, including Johnny Angelo.

The tears stopped. She raised her head, shivering at the very real prospect of encountering either of the two men—her geolocation now public. With Paul, the boy-wonder she longed to know, she again felt a surge of giddy curiosity. Trumped fast by the dreadful thought of her ex.

Johnny Angelo, a career Testing Farm guinea pig, simped his way from sympathy date to courtship contract with Rosa. It was rare for SOIs to bow so low as to date a TF. Through sheer brawns over brains, he managed to take advantage of Rosa's heightened empathy, gaslighting and guilting her any chance he could. The courtship grew dark and abusive very quickly. Eventually she'd publicly rebuked his caustic infatuation and terminated their contract early. But the unapologetic chatverse had a field day, siding with poor ol' hopeless romantic Johnny. After graduating, Rosa had disappeared, unequipped to handle such intense infamy at her debut.

"Every present instant in time is the complete and utter destruction of the previous instant," Rosa whispered, reciting Ferguson's first words in the first lecture she'd ever attended. Live in the moment, not in the past. Rosa rose to her feet, realizing she was not yet safe enough to sulk, not with Johnny Angelo on the prowl.

* * *

After a quick wash, Rosa threw on a printed hair clip and pink shorts and headed back to exercycle C216. A droopy-eyed, grandmotherly woman in a large coat pedaled slowly beside her. The woman nodded at Rosa but otherwise kept to herself.

Rosa calculated the exact rate she should pedal in order to raise enough credits to deposit on a private, cyber-secure studio in three days' time. She blasted Common Era jazz in her earbuds and zoned out on her cycle for several hours, intermittently noting her steadily rising credit balance. She seemed to operate more efficiently than most cyclists, producing three times the average wattage and seldom pausing for breaks.

Around half past nineteen, the strangest thing broke her reverie. She swore she heard a "What brings you to *Nearest Cycling Dorm* today?" in the exact voice of the skycab dashboard, but it had come straight from the mouth of the old woman. Rosa looked over to find the woman had stopped cycling and was hunched forward, pressing her wrinkled nose to her slimscreen. She appeared to be whispering something to herself in a husky voice that didn't resemble the dashboards in the slightest.

Keep it together, Rosa. Not a minute later, Rosa began to sense something very wrong in the woman's aura, a looming sallow energy. She'd never before felt empathic residue so strongly. The woman began rocking back and forth, chapped lips slightly parted and red-rimmed eyes wide, mouthing something in silent distress.

At Rosa's slight motion to remove an earbud, the woman shot upright, yanking her neck toward Rosa with a bug-eyed, transfixed gaze—then threw a hand over her heart as one would amid a heart attack.

Rosa looked around the gym to find deliberate disregard from the other cyclists. She swiped at the service request option on her wristband, but when her eyes returned to the elderly woman, the woman was now seated at a freakishly obtuse angle, rocking violently as a rivulet of blood rounded the corner of an eyelid. And suddenly the eerie feeling Rosa felt back at her apartment returned as a tingle in the periphery of her consciousness. That feeling of ethereal communication. She breathed through the approaching tremors.

"Don't let them take me," the woman whispered followed by a manic yell. "Don't let them take me!" She gaped her mouth wide in abject terror, staring petrified at something Rosa couldn't see. Then she simply slumped over. Her Ncluded let out a flatline beep. Rosa watched dumbstruck as Ray Marx and his cohort slithered over and routinely gathered the woman's corpse from bike C215.

Ray Marx asked Rosa a question or two about the service request, but Rosa could hardly breathe, let alone speak. She shut her eyes to keep from falling into a panic-ridden vertigo. After a trembling glass of water, the ethereal feeling slowly receded. Rosa blocked out the growing commotion in the gym, straightened up and continued to pedal.

Now more than ever, she needed to pedal up a sanctuary.

Not a minute later, Rosa felt a non-bot presence approach her. She sucked in a breath before peering over her shoulder to find a balding Asian man in a tailored suit. Rosa noticed a lapel pin bearing the red chevrons of the second most prestigious SOI behind Fame Academy—the Maine Academy.

She warily greeted him in the way of the SOI elite.

"Friend or foe?"

"Messenger," he responded. Finding no malice in his energies, Rosa turned to fully face him, bracing herself for the high-function encounter. The man pulled out a small padded envelope from his inner pocket and held it out to her. She slid it out of the man's hand with her thumb and forefinger to minimize physical contact. From it she retrieved a fancy invitation card and a walnut-sized amber jewel, like a large earring stud. She winced, detecting a small trace of warm energy disseminating from the jewel.

"Lady Maine is personally inviting you to the Maine Event a week from Tuesday," the man said. An invitation to the Maine Event—the annual gala showcasing Maine Academy's cutting-edge research—was one of the most sought after invites in the country. The fancy card and priceless jewel offered to Rosa could only mean one thing: recruitment.

Didn't Lady Maine, once Madame Ferguson, have even a modicum of respect for her late ex-marital contract? She couldn't wait even a week before spooling in his star pupils to her lair? This and the whirling memory of the old woman's heart attack began peeling away at Rosa's thin veil of composure.

"She couldn't wait for his body to cool?" she asked.

"They say never look a gift horse in the mouth," the man said.

"Yeah, they also say beware of Greeks bearing Trojan horses," Rosa snipped.

"Well, while we can't make you drink, allow us to lead you to the water."

Rosa winced, miffed that the man so quickly misappropriated the meaning of the term 'horse.' "*I'm* not the horse;" she hissed, "the *gift* is the horse." The man raised an eyebrow at her sudden outburst. Rosa breathed through a shiver. *Calm down. He's only a messenger.*

"They warned me you were high-strung," the man mused. *What? Me?* Rosa frowned. She'd have to unpack that later.

Though she desperately needed this timely godsend, this all-expense-paid ticket back into the limelight, Rosa placed the card and jewel back into the envelope and thrust it toward the man. "Earrings come in pairs," she said, immediately regretting her high-horse tone.

"Lady Maine never offers an invitation twice," the messenger said, allowing the envelope to dangle in the air.

"Please tell Mrs. Maine that Rosa Lejeune has denied her request," she said with finality. The man offered an incredulous nod before accepting the preferred envelope. He balled the jewel in his fist and lifted it back to her.

"*Doctor* Maine says the jewel is not a gift from her, but from the late Dr. Ferguson. He intended it for you, and she says she is now ready to let go of the spite and deliver it."

Rosa looked to the man's eyes, her heart suddenly thudding. *Spite?* Why would Lady Maine have felt spite? Dr. Ferguson had never shown any interest in Rosa beyond mentorship, certainly no feelings over which his ex-marital contract should feel spite.

"I only relay what I'm told," the man said, reacting to Rosa's wrinkled brow. Rosa allowed him to drop the jewel into her palm. She stared blankly at it until the man shifted his weight. "I'm going to ask you once more before leaving," he started.

"I don't do parties," Rosa declared.

"Very well then." The man tucked the envelope away and took a step back. After a moment of contemplation, he said, "Friendly advice?" Rosa was not eager to hear why she should seriously reconsider Maine's offer. Still, she nodded. "You're hung up on an admirer no longer alive to admire you. You should be more concerned with the admirers currently watching your pin's every move."

Rosa watched as the man's eyes flitted up beyond her. He then turned around and shimmied his way through rows of cyclists. Although glad to see the back of him, she knew any chance for reviving her path to stardom left right along with him. She sighed, just now realizing how hard she'd been working to appear unruffled by the encounter. She followed where his eyes had trailed, turning in her seat. And there he was, standing by the Smartifice print machine, sipping at a BurstMyte bottle. He wore blue jeans and a deep stare so intently fixated on her, she could hardly breathe.

Johnny Angelo.

5

THE HACKER

SUNDAY NOV 10, 186 PCE

As soon as he lifted his VerteBrain, exiting the wake, Kris Johnson's lap was greeted roughly by his business partner, Aztec, who proceeded to stick out his tongue and pant.

"Well?" sounded Aztec between eager huffs. "Regale us. I require a reenactment of every off-color interaction to the finest detail and the resulting befuddled facial expressions."

Kris ruffled Aztec's mane as the feelings in his limbs returned, then engaged in a long yawn-infused stretch. "Jesus, Az, how long was I in?"

"Tell us how it went!" Aztec exclaimed, the 'us' being two other currently-mersed roommates.

"Az, you know you're too big to be jumping on my lap and yelling in my face," Kris rebuked. Crestfallen, the sable-spotted Jack Russell hopped to the floor to squat on his haunches and present a pair of first-rate puppy-eyes. Kris dropped a begrudging hand to Aztec. "All right, come back. Jesus, how'd you get so sensitive?" With unabashed enthusiasm, Aztec leapt back onto his owner's lap, lifting his ears.

"The deets," Aztec demanded. Kris couldn't recall a time

his terrier left a question unanswered. A trait they shared. Kris, a short, skinny, brown-skinned black kid from the Broonx, complete with thick accent and beard, gained the impressive resume expected of any Fame Academy graduate by way of professional cyber-sabotage for high-class clientele.

"Nothin' wild happened at the service," Kris started. "Your average cast and crew: Academy notables, research colleagues. Pebble Whittaker came out the woodworks. Oh, and Michelle Brier showed face, Becks." He peered over to his roommate, Becky, who remained motionlessly immersed.

Kris's roommates were both former Testing Farm subjects sporting a myriad of resultant disabilities. Having also begun his career as a test subject, Kris wove together his band of misfit TFs into a tight-knit family, turning down prestigious job offers in order to help his poorly equipped friends transition into post-school society. He wanted a simple cramped-Harlem-apartment life shared with old friends...and a tricked-out, super-smart, award-winning dog-bot, Aztec.

"Kris, what was Michelle Brier wearing? I'll dispense the details to Becky later." Aztec's tail wagged at the prospect of Becky's future positive feedback.

"Actually, I'll do you one better, Az. Ross was there." At this, Aztec leapt from Kris's lap to dart around in a frantic circle.

"Ross?" Aztec yapped. "Oz Corp's Torian Ross?"

"The very same," Kris assured. Kris had done his home-work on Torian Ross. The TerraGuard-trained, highly advanced transhuman and private eye for Oz Corp had become the stuff of legends. Ross was not the type you just bumped into in MetaLife. With Ferguson's recent death, a sit-down with the high-profile fixer was paramount. Oz Corp, however, proved impervious to even the most advanced security inter-ference.

Impervious until Patrice Fan.

"Did he appear to have noticed the infiltration of his account?" Aztec asked.

"Nah, I don't think so," Kris puzzled, tugging at his beard. "He was in the back muttering to himself. Actually, I'm not sure *what* he was doing."

"Seven hours and fifty-six minutes, Kris," Aztec announced.

"Huh?"

"Earlier you asked how long you'd been immersed. It has been seven hours and fifty-six minutes since you immersed at twelve thirty." Aztec grinned, hoping for a reward.

"Shit! It's that late?" Kris jumped in his seat. Aztec recoiled to the far corner. Had Kris really been milling about in a merse for eight hours? He had to trigger the hack this instant. It expired ten hours after activation, which gave him less than forty-five minutes to finagle his way into Ross's account and get him talking.

Kris pulled up a terminal window on his wallscreen, his fingers gliding across his keyboard holo and swiping through displays with frantic precision. He retrieved the necessary schematics of Patrice Fan's Ncluded, and Aztec sprung to attention awaiting instructions.

Kris uploaded the schematics to a temp folder on a dark-verse directory then got to work applying his signature Search and Seizure scripts to locate Patrice's login access points. Though heat signatures were the most popular authentication practices, every account had an alphanumeric entry code. Kris located the access point to which Ms. Fan's alphanumeric code could be applied then said, "Az" without raising his glance.

"Whisky tango zero niner ampersand bravo one eight..." Aztec spewed on like a high-powered text-to-speech drone. Kris plucked ferociously, knowing the quick keystroke timing to be of importance.

"Passcode, Az. Come on." Aztec proceeded to list off another series of curated digits. "Authentication key. Stat!" Again, the dog spouted robotic verbiage. And then the enter key.

Sitting on the edge of his seat, Kris stared down the barrel of a loading ETA bar. "Come on, you sexy son-of-a-bitch. Work!"

"Assuming you've entered everything correctly, your access should certainly be granted," Aztec chirped.

"Don't scare me, Az. You know I hate when you do that." At this Aztec pouted and curled into a ball, but his grief was short-lived. A bell chimed. Kris leapt from his chair with a fist pump, scooped up Aztec, and said, "We're in! Good dog."

Developing the undetectable wormhole in two nights had proven the most arduous of tasks. But no amount of midnight oil could surmount the payoff of bypassing Oz Corp security.

Kris scrambled back to his seat to sift through Patrice Fan's Ncluded profile and quickly located the code to his Plus Sign virus. In line with his reconnaissance, Kris inferred Patrice would take the sexpionage straight to Ross on the soonest empty slot in both their schedules—today. And she did. And the virus slithered right on into Ross's profile.

High on the rush of his illicit success, Kris hardly noticed Becky and his other roommate DZ simultaneously arise from their immersions. They'd been at a birthday social. As they pulled up their chairs to huddle around him, Kris greeted them with a slightly menacing, "I'm in. We're either 'bout to be superheroes or locked up for a very long time."

* * *

The four sat in determined silence as they watched the black box at the corner of Kris's wallscreen, waiting for the user on the other end to notice and touch-activate the live virus. The hack assumed Ross would touch a cartoon plus sign floating in the virtual ether without first calling up security protocols. Another big assumption, but Torian Ross wasn't the type to let others fight his battles.

"What the hell..." A distant English lilt sounded from Kris's speakers accompanied by a floating live caption. Kris's heart pumped through his temples as he watched the black box peel down to reveal the furrowed face of a very curious Ross. Kris held his breath.

Ross, seated at a dimly lit desk and sporting an array of intricate body art under a sleeveless tee, wore an Ncluded Glass over one eye and chewed on the backend of a tactical knife. "This some sort of sick joke?" were Ross's first measured words after a thorough study of Kris's countenance. That was Ross. No nonsense.

"Had to reach you, T, by any means necessary," Kris blurted. "So much to say, I don't even know where to start. Can I call you T?"

"Absolutely not. And you can start by telling me how you managed to infiltrate Oz Corp security."

"Well," Kris started with a nervous chuckle. "I hacked it. I'm a hacker." He paused. Ross did not acknowledge the levity.

"Now," Ross said.

"Woah, buy a girl a drink first, bro." Kris's nerves pumped through his chest, still processing his situation. "Look, truth is," Kris stumbled on, "you need to check into your girl, Patrice. She's got piss-poor judgment when it comes to her profile."

Ross bunched his lips to one side, doubtful, then asked, "How'd you get access to her profile?"

Kris hesitated. His answer could either sow seeds for trust

or guaranteed arrest. He opted to go with honesty.

"Finding someone smart enough to work at Oz Corp but desperate enough to get social-engineered was the hard part. Bumping into her at a bar in MetaLife and getting her to invite me to her place IRL was the easy part. I got that baby face." Kris felt a rush of diabolical giddiness, the supercilious glee of a villain divulging his masterminded plans.

"You slept with her for her authentication codes?" Ross noted with dry accusation.

"No, I didn't *sleep* with her," Kris retorted with umbrage. "Just stole her identity a little. Jesus, what kind of person you think I am?"

"A person scrolling through personals adverts from an incarceration unit. Excuse me." Ross shifted his weight to survey another portion of his screen while rapidly plucking a keyboard holo.

"Hey, no! Wait!" Kris rose to his feet, scrambling to get in one last line before Ross disappeared forever. Aztec bounced in fright but knew better than to speak in the presence of outsiders. "Just be sure to put me in the same cell as the *murderer* who *murdered* Dr. Ferguson."

Kris got the response he'd hoped for. Torian Ross's typing came to an abrupt halt.

"What did you just say?"

"I said I'm willing to risk my life and the lives of my friends to request your services." Kris gestured toward the friends seated behind him as he returned to his chair. Now that he had Ross's attention, Kris could waste no time playing beta. Ross wrinkled his brow, took a long introspective breath, then turned to face them.

"Is this a secure line?" Ross asked.

"Yes, but it'll expire in half an hour."

A brief moment elapsed before Ross said, "So that was you

at the service?"

"Yeah, I was there. Surprised you were. Don't take you for the tears and flowers type."

Ross arched an eyebrow. "Who was on the other end of that fancy earpiece?"

"Fancy earpiece? What earpiece?"

"Demetrius Marshall."

Kris offered a blank stare and halfhearted shrug. He took a mental note of the name and watched Ross betray a look of perplexity.

"I don't dance," Ross said. "If you're crying murder, back it up."

"Okay," Kris started. "After tracking Ferg's signals for years, you know, just for kicks, I noticed a text he sent to his top guy, Pelleher, saying, 'They know. Don't come in.' Couple hours later he's literally toast. Everyone's talking accidents, and no one's doing a deep dive." Ross appeared to be taking notes. Kris remained uneasy, uncertain where he stood with Ross.

"That all you got?"

"Well, that and million-year-old Ferg's not the type to accidentally die. Also, he never used an unencrypted line before. He knew something was going down and was trying to warn anyone."

"So, let me get this right. You breached Oz Corp security to tell me Dr. Ferguson was murdered, yet are basing your allegations on a five-word text and a hunch?"

"No. I'm basing it on a five-word text, a hunch, and the fact that you haven't hung up yet." At this, Ross studied Kris's face.

"Why come to me? Why not go to Nforce?" A fair question. Kris looked down for a beat. He knew why Ross asked the question, knew the answer Ross wanted and gave it earnestly.

"Torian Ross, you're the only person I can trust with this. Period. Ferg had a lot of enemies just waitin' for the postmortem loot to rain down. I mean, this is Ferg. I'm sure it goes way up. Like Deep-State level shit. Places Nforce red-tape can't reach but maybe you can." Ross did not readily respond. Kris could hardly take it. He followed up with, "I know you're all about the truth, proper justice. And the credit-hoarding, power-hungry assholes behind this bullshit need to be brought to justice."

Kris and his cohorts watched Ross key a few more notes. Ross finally let out a sigh and said, "We do this in person." And that was it. Ross was in.

Kris stifled a jump. Ross had access to everything and everyone. Where Kris had an authentication barrier, Ross had an open door. Where Kris had a firewall, Ross had a dinner invite. "Fly me the text message and its envelope data, and give me a second to assess my schedule," Ross said.

DZ, a tall but squat Guatemalan, gave Kris's shoulder a rough congratulatory squeeze. Aztec stood on his hind legs, applauding awkwardly with tiny paws. Becky, a portly Louisiana mop-top, mouthed a histrionic "Thank God" then turned to her wallscreen to upload the attachment to Ross through the hack's secured line.

Kris exhaled as the anvil in his chest fell to the ground. He wasn't being carted off to prison...yet, and he'd finally be able to start paying off his self-prescribed debt to Dr. Ferguson.

Growing up in a poor Ascete neighborhood, Kris knew the street-urchin struggle. He never attained Ferg Pet status but felt an unspoken bond with Ferg for seeing something in him, and accepting him into a world of promise. Most significantly though, Kris was grateful Ferguson hadn't expelled him after he'd been falsely accused of harassment by Davia Valenti.

The Valentis owned the Smartifice and Pharma Farm brands. And though the allegations were baseless, Davia's word held power. All but his tight nucleus ostracized Kris as he obsessed bitterly over exonerating himself. To Kris's surprise, Dr. Ferguson publicly denied the Valentis' request for expulsion. Kris would stop at nothing to do right by Ferg's final text message.

"Dang it," came Becky's southern drawl from her desk. She continued at a whisper so as not to alarm Ross. "I hit send, but now the screen's frozen." Everyone looked to her screen.

"What's the matter, Becky?" DZ signed, the caption of his sign language floating beneath his hands.

"Some random chatbox popped up that says, 'CONTACT ME,' Becky said. "But it has no username, and it's all wiggly-like, like it's superimposed. Look." She steered her floating captions off to where Ross couldn't see them. Kris squinted up for a moment then dropped his chin to his chest and rubbed at his temples. He'd felt a pounding at the base of his skull where he'd once had a BrainDrive implant. Becky turned to him. "You okay, Kris?" He raised his eyes to his own screen and noticed a slightly throbbing chatbox coalesce on his screen as well.

"I got one too," DZ signed. "Is something wrong with the network connection?" Kris swirled a lazy finger in the air to activate his menu icons to no avail. He breathed through the pounding headache and rising panic. Now was not the time for a freeze. Aztec ran to the bedroom to conceal muted howls of malfunction-induced pain. The others did not demonstrate any adverse symptoms, so Kris figured an electromagnetic interference must have futzed up his biohack and Aztec's hardware.

"All right," Ross announced from his corner window. As soon as Ross spoke, the chatbox vanished, breaking the freeze. "The text checks out. I've sent you coordinates. We meet Tuesday at half past eighteen. No trails, no pins. Come with everything. There won't be a second meeting."

"Got it," Kris hailed, fighting to appear relaxed.

"You all right?" Ross asked sincerely.

"Tuesday; half past eighteen; no GPS. Got it."

"We'll discuss the matter of your blatant violation of Ms. Fan's privacy another time. If you've any inclination toward self-preservation, you will disconnect from her and my profiles immediately." Kris affirmed with a salute then exed out of the window.

"What in the hell was that?" asked Becky as she reached for a desk drawer. She pulled out several pairs of anaglyphic 3D glasses. "Thought I'd never have a reason to put these on. But the boxes were moving all weird. I'm gonna use these to see if I see anything else weird-like on the screen."

"Want me to print some pain relief pills?" DZ signed to Kris as he headed over to the unbranded printer they'd rigged together. They'd never purchase a Valenti-owned Smartifice dispenser with its Soma-infused muck.

"Nah, I just need to sleep it off. I wore out my brain the last couple days." He'd have to look into the strange interference tomorrow after a good night's rest.

"Uhm...guys?" Becky blurted nervously, utterly petrified. 3D glasses perched on her nose, Becky pointed a trembling finger at the far wall. DZ snatched the two remaining pairs from her desk and placed one over his eyes. Instantly, he too stiffened in shock.

"What? What the hell are you guys looking at?" Kris exclaimed. Without moving his eyes, DZ slowly lifted a pair of the glasses to Kris.

It was like nothing Kris had ever witnessed. Scrawled over every inch of the walls and ceiling in every direction, he saw dozens upon dozens of instances of the words CONTACT ME in a glowing, slightly stirring font, smattered in all different sizes.

It was there. It was definitely there.

And they all saw it.

6

BIONIC SHOWDOWN

MONDAY NOV 11, 186 PCE

"An unending network of illusions."

— *DIARY OF THE MAD GLEE*

Fearing another panic attack at the sight of Johnny Angelo, Rosa hastened back to her dorm, locked herself in a BedBooth and lay awake all night on a beach by a Caribbean shore.

Nature called at seven the next morning. Rosa scurried to the public lavatory making sure not to glance at the mirrors lest she trigger a barrage of ads. She instead focused on the mounted hand-dryer just past the countertop, desperately trying to clear her mind.

"You look good," he called with his syrupy Latin baritone from behind her. How hadn't she noticed him come in? She froze in place before turning to face him. Jonathan Angelo Boulevardo Marino: the brawny mix of Columbian and Sicilian muscle that single handedly shattered her stardom before it could start. A neck-length mane surrounded his charcoal eyes—

one of which was bionic, deep and inset like the business end of a gun barrel. He had trouble holding a direct gaze due to a slight jolt of the head every few seconds. He had no trouble staring her up and down, however.

Working to remain cool despite bubbling anxiety, Rosa managed an, "As do you." Johnny Angelo took one long stride toward her, taking a quick glance at the mirror and activating an ad for Alabaster Spring cologne. Rosa used the brief distraction to swipe blindly at her Ncluded in a doubtful attempt at a service-call then crossed her arms over her chest.

Johnny let out a sigh. "Don't be like that, *cariño*, not after all this time." His words came soft, apologetic. She'd heard that tone before, been made a fool by that tone.

"You're close enough," Rosa said, Johnny's broad shoulders a thick cage around her. With apparent disregard, he took another step. "I swear. Come any closer and I will scream."

"You always did have a lovely voice," Johnny chuckled, an unsettling intimacy in his words. Though he'd yet to broadcast any destructive energies, she sensed them looming. "Okay, okay," he assured, taking two small steps back. "Look, I'm here to make amends, *cariño*."

"I got your weird message," Rosa blurted, working to keep shivers from cracking her façade.

"What message?" he asked, his lack of reaction verifying his ignorance. Perhaps it had been Tommy Frank after all. God, how she missed her little sanctuary.

"What exactly do you want?"

"What do I *want*?" Johnny laughed. "Oh, maybe just what I'm owed." His harassment against Rosa lay in his claim that she terminated their courtship contract without fulfilling mandatory assurances in the copulation clause. "Think you can make a promise then jump ship?"

No rearrangement of deck chairs could keep your ship from

sinking, she wanted to say, or perhaps the more poignant *You're a piece of ship!* She couldn't quite gather the nerve. At the academy she'd taken pride in defending underdogs, parrying with witticisms and wisecracks. But now, five years cloistered, such vigor would be impossible to resurrect.

"Cams everywhere. You should leave," Rosa managed. "Now."

Johnny smirked with an inadvertent jerk of the shoulder. "Or what? The restraining order's up." That Rosa owned no possessions, no credits, and was holed up in a cycling dorm was all public information. "Listen, I know you lost everything, *cariño.* But I can get you back up in high places where you belong, *pan comido.*" Rosa tensed as Johnny ran thick hands through his hair. "You know I'm in with the Maines now. I'm the one who got Lady to drop her grudge and consider sponsoring you."

The only thing you two could offer me is the stamp of betrayal against Ferguson you so openly bear on your foreheads, Rosa spat in her mind, longing to defend Ferguson's honor. "I'll pass. But so long, and thanks for all the fish," she snarked instantly regretting it. Johnny's human eye flashed like a penny in a fountain, contrasting the abyss of its cobalt partner.

"That pretty little prissy mouth," he said. "Lady ate a lot of ego 'cause of you. *I* ate a lot of ego 'cause of you," his tone lower, darker. Rosa felt those old familiar energies of silent anger and aggression coalescing around him. She swallowed another flash of stress attack. She knew better than to bait him. Johnny let out a calming breath and crooned, "Oh, *mi cariño.* I really missed you." He took a step closer. "Come as my plus-one to the Maine Event." Rosa immediately shook her head no.

"I got plans," she blurted.

"Oh really? What?"

"Uh...watering my—"

"Do you remember the last words you said to me before Nforce slapped me with the restraint?" Johnny narrowed his eyes, his rapid-fire emotions seeping into her skin. "You said to never come anywhere near you again. Like I was a filthy animal!" He suddenly punched hard at the wall inches from her head, burrowing deep into lavatory tile. Rosa jerked backwards, heartbeats bursting against her chest.

Johnny stepped in close, suffocating her with the inhuman movements of his cobalt eye. He whispered, barely audible above the now hissing hand-dryer, "If you ever need a place to crash, I still have that slice of skin I took off your middle finger that one time. I programmed it into the fingerprint recognition at my spot in Midtown." Rosa fought off a shudder.

Johnny Angelo was the worst kind of indignant powder keg. With him so close, she could feel the physical menace radiating from his being, a deep, amorous hunger.

"Is everything all right, Ms. *Lejeune*?" came the voice of Ray Marx from behind Johnny Angelo. Johnny abruptly stepped back, allowing Rosa a deep sigh of relief. The hiss of the hand-dryer came to a halt. "I received your service call. Please let me know how I can be of assistance."

"Everything's all right, Sir," smiled Johnny, aware the android would auto-report any suspected foul-play. Marx remained still, cheerily assessing the room.

"Unless you're aware of something the world isn't," came yet another voice from behind Marx. "He'll only respond to the owner of the service call." The voice bore an accent with which Rosa was vaguely familiar. In strode a well-built, pale-skinned man, wearing blue jeans and an Ncluded Glass over steely gray eyes. Upon examining his complex web of invisible radar signals, Rosa knew him to be Torian Ross, the transhuman she'd seen in many-a-trending biohack videos.

Ray Marx stepped aside, allowing the four of them to

create an inter-being quadrilateral: a transhuman, an android, an empath and a jackass. A moment of awkward standoff ensued.

"Ms. *Lejeune,* please let me know how I can be of assistance," Ray Marx reiterated. Rosa opted to remain silent, knowing the bot would not leave until her dismissal. Torian Ross folded his arms across his chest demonstrating he too would not be leaving. Johnny broke the standstill.

"All right, all right," he surrendered and lazily meandered toward the door. He turned back to Rosa and whispered in a guarded tone, "*Nunca te voy a perder otra vez. Y esa oferta para salir conmigo al Evento Maine aún sigue abierto.*" And as he waddled out without so much as a glance in Torian Ross's direction, he closed with, "You hear me? The offer still stands, and I'm your only in."

She'd have to find a way to conceal her location pin again to avoid public ambush. Johnny Angelo's willingness to stand down was not a good sign. He was in it for the long game.

Well aware of Rosa and Johnny Angelo's history, Tory held his ready stance as Johnny left the room. Though no match to the giant's physical stature, Tory literally had a few tricks up his sleeve he'd been itching to deploy on a deserving prick. His Ncluded Glass instantly presented him with swaths of information. He saved the latest audio scans of the conversation, while noting Rosa's panic indicated by her vitals. She'd been terrified. She nervously dismissed Marx, leaving herself and Tory alone in the lavatory.

As a chief fixer for Oz Corp, Tory enjoyed the rare privilege of meeting people IRL. In most cases the in-person presences of those he'd met paled in comparison to their souped-up photoshopped thumbnails. Such was not the case with Ms. Lejeune. Although her past images and videos were a paragon of beauty, the allure of her actual physical being far outdid her virtual persona. It wasn't the photo-ready, honey-glazed skin, the tight athletic body, the devilishly dark eyes or loose red waves that spurred Tory's imagination. It was the aura about her, a warmth, that drew within him an instant attraction to her so primal, he had to keep his Eyesearch calculator running summations to keep him slightly distracted. The absence of a bra only exacerbated his efforts.

"I'm here to talk," he greeted, maintaining a fair distance.

"Okay." She spoke timidly but with a familiarity Tory appreciated, her voice a mellifluous mezzo. Her vitals calmed slightly as she looked to the mirror and exed away a resultant ad.

Feeling the light buzz of each hidden surveillance camera in his magnetized fingers, Tory said, "I'm here IRL to avoid scans. I know a more private place we can converse in the—"

"I prefer here in public, if you don't mind," Rosa said, a hint of arrogance.

"Of course," he said. "I'm taking a few steps closer so we can speak discretely. If I get too close or my signals start to bother you, let me know. I'll back off." Having survived abuse himself, Tory believed it a categorical imperative to foster caution when dealing with fellow survivors. Rosa stiffened once Tory got to arm's length, so he stopped there.

Tory's reconnaissance on Rosa revealed that she spent her childhood as a Ferguson and Maine test subject, was admitted to the Ferguson and Maine School of Excellence, spent a year in high-fashion entertainment then disappeared from the chatverse after a public restraining battle against Johnny Angelo.

Tory leaned against the countertop. "Let me start by

offering my deepest condolences for your loss." Rosa wrinkled her forehead.

"What's your MO here? I figure a hybrid like yourself would hack away the need to pee."

"I'm not quite a hybrid. I'm in fact mostly human," Tory pointed out. Rosa's lips twitched at this. A delicate shift of her waist immediately drew Tory's attention to her pink shorts. "You know who I work for," he continued.

"I do."

"Then you know I'm here as a friend."

"Really," Rosa said squarely. "That's funny, according to FaceGram I have no friends."

"I don't use FaceGram. When I'm ready to drain my self-worth for a few shoddy likes, I'll let you know." Unaware of how long his gaze had drifted, Tory lifted his eyes to find Rosa watching him. He hadn't known himself to be such a letch, but the woman had magnetism. If he were made a woman in his next life, he prayed to be unattractive. "You've got friends at Oz Corp," he continued. "It's only a matter of time before the chat-verse storms your profile with tags, messages, requests. As a former Fame SOI you're a commodity, and—"

"What does Oz Corp want?"

"He's throwing an exclusive gala tonight and would like you to perform. You'd play the piano and sing live for thirty minutes."

"IRL?" she asked, the slightest hint of excitement. Tory nodded. Only the elite were awarded the rare opportunity to play a live physical instrument. A major ego boost to an academy-trained pianist, such as herself.

"A skystretch would call for you at quarter to nineteen. You'd be styled, press coverage, ushered to the hall by security, full buffet, the works. And a hundred thousand credits on completion."

"Is Oz Corp planning on courting me for sponsorship?"

"Perhaps," Tory said. If not the authentic food and hefty payout, Tory was sure the guaranteed press to reboot her public face would rattle this otherwise stoic girl. Rosa instead looked down at her hands.

"Why me? He couldn't get Current Generic Pop Diva on such short notice? I'm obviously a day-old croissant."

"Not to Oz Corp," Tory said. "Frankly, I'm not told any more than I need to know. I do know any deserving SOI should always be celebrated. Always." He noticed Rosa's heart rate spike in response. She whipped her face toward him, looked into his eyes, dissecting his every wrinkle. Though never one to back down from a stare-off, especially not with such a stunning opponent, Tory averted his gaze.

"They say transhumans never lie," she started.

"They would be correct to assess that transhumans have a general aversion to taking on the physical burden of deception for long periods of time among other idiosyncrasies, yes."

Rosa introspected for a beat, took a breath then simply said, "Okay, I'm in." Tory valued this. Her trust. She didn't seem the type to trust easily.

"The skystretch will collect you here."

"Why send you, his big fish, for such a small ask?"

"Not small to him," Tory said. Rosa's cheeks reddened around a slight, nervous smile.

"Will anyone else of note be there?"

"I'm not privy to the guest list."

"You'll be there?"

"Not a big enough fish," Tory shrugged.

Rosa hummed as if she should have known. Tory looked to the ground then back to her measuring eyes, mulling over whether to broach his next line of questioning.

59

"There's more?" she asked as if able to hear his internal quandary.

"Yes, actually," he exhaled. He dropped to a near whisper. "I know you've just resurfaced, but have you noticed any strange activity within your circles?"

"Well, you're looking at my circles," Rosa admitted with a quick gesture around the lavatory. "An old woman had a heart-attack in the exercycle beside mine yesterday. People keel over all the time, but this one was pretty...cinematic."

"Cinematic how?"

"Well, for one, her eyes were blood red. She kicked pretty instantly." Rosa made no comment as she watched Tory subvo-calize the info into his BrainDrive.

"Listen," Tory pressed on, "I've been tipped off about foul-play surrounding Ferguson's passing. I need to know if you know anything." Rosa looked back to the mirror, allowing a thick moment of silence.

"I wouldn't know. I deserted him. Now he's dead." She closed her eyes and let out a subtle shudder.

"I didn't mean to upset you. I just—"

"No, I'm just...sorry I can't help you," she said. "I only know that Ferguson was into pretty dark, God-bending alchemy, most of which he kept to himself." This was not news to Tory. The quintessential Mad Scientist was infamous in the darkverse for his wild alchemical experiments. "Is this an offi-cial Oz Corp investigation?" Rosa asked.

"No," Tory stated abruptly. "Right now, I'm keeping this close to the chest. Very close." Especially since his employer had just as much motive as anyone to off the professor.

Rosa nodded. "I'm no Nancy Drew, but I'm here if needed."

Tory took her offer to heart. Considering her anxiety level remained fairly high throughout their conversation, he appreciated her will to remain poised. He again gave his sincere condolences, and this time she genuinely accepted. He bid her adieu and made off to his next appointment, eagerly anticipating tomorrow night's nightcap with the either estimably ingenious, or clinically bonkers, hacker.

7
MAKING WAVES

MONDAY NOV 11, 186 PCE

"Tip of the pen with which I write
Of microcosmic link
Step out to the vastness beyond your sight
To see you are mere ink"

— *THE DIARY OF THE MAD GLEE*

At twenty to nineteen Rosa waited outside of the facility in flip-flops and shades. The indomitable array of flashing ad colors painted their consummate emblem of consumerism beneath the night sky. She strained to keep a rising vertigo at bay. Being so exposed was definite fodder for a panic attack.

Several onlookers gawked at Rosa, attempting to recall her identity to varying degrees of success. Rosa had come across several #RosaSpotted tags in the chatverse, though luckily nothing viral yet. But as she hid from the recognition, a deeper flame within burned for a second chance in the limelight.

Like clockwork a sleek, double-decker skystretch, the

length of a city block, pulled up to the skypole before her. In all her years Rosa had never seen such a massive vehicle. Up slid a tinted door panel, and out stepped a tall chauffeur. "Good evening, Ms. Lejeune. Right this way." He ushered her down most of the block to get to the passenger door. Reminiscent of a first-class jetliner, the coach comprised an array of plush couches, a full bar and a two-room suite: all gold-rimmed surfaces.

"Good evening, Ms. Lejeune," called a squat, fast-talking suit as Rosa entered the vehicle. "I'm Dex, they/them. I'll be coordinating your prep. Please excuse the second-rate accommodations. We couldn't arrange for the priority skystretch on such short notice." Still taking in the marvel, Rosa could hardly respond.

Dex presented two garment bags. "We've got you a backless mesh from Chantel's Little Black line and a sleeveless pencil from Brier's Body Language line. There's a changing room straight back. Unsatisfied with either selection? We've got plenty more. We also have a wide selection of Tiffany LeRue heels." Rosa nodded, acquiring the bags, and allowed herself to be ushered to the changing room like a lost child, hardly noticing the skystretch take flight.

She quickly undressed and studied her nude figure in the wall-to-wall mirrors, complimenting herself on her upkeep. She imagined him, the great and powerful Oz, admiring her, needing her, and steeled herself to dismiss such girlish thoughts. She settled on the sleeveless pencil, a dress too scintillating for a simple piano set.

Once Rosa stepped out, Dex escorted her to a stylist who also greeted her politely. Though the whole staff was human— not an android in sight—everyone behaved so robotically pristine, emitting a perfect halo of positivity. A little *too* perfect.

Strange perfect. While she admired the old-school, human touch, a tingle of fear never left her side.

As the stylist worked a high chignon, Dex assembled themself beside Rosa with a tablet. The screen projected a cheerful woman with a light brown frizzy mane, dimpled cheeks and a skin tone not quite as dark as Rosa's but certainly ethnic.

"Good evening, Ms. Lejeune," hailed the woman with a bubbly rasp. "I'm Sherri Weiler, Oz Corp's Chief of Staff and Arcology. I'll be shuffling you through tonight's curated press." Sherri spoke with an easy confidence Rosa envied. Was Rosa such a V.I.P. that the Chief of Staff would shuffle her around?

"Not to be too forward," Rosa finally gained the wherewithal to speak, "but will Oz Corp be discussing sponsorship with me tonight?"

"Tonight is for you to have fun and be amazing," Sherri said. "Dex will get back in touch with you soon after to talk officialdom."

After the completion of hair and makeup, Rosa began her virtual press tour. One by one, Sherri prepped her for each upcoming outlet, and with a prim and proper smile for the webcam, Rosa gave her pageant-ready non-answers. Though all questions appeared handpicked to her benefit, never discussing Johnny Angelo or even her hiatus, Rosa prided herself for carrying on like a Normal. *So far so good*, she told herself. *Don't screw this up.*

The skystretch slowed at its destination in Historic Central Park.

Oz Corp.

The campus, an array of towering cylindrical buildings amid fountains and foliage, boasted an eight-hundred-and-forty-acre private park for its backyard. An embroidered fence encircled the main structure, and a marble spiral staircase led to its large glass doors. *Definitely not in Kansas anymore,* Rosa thought.

Sherri Weiler, complete with headset and tablet, bustled over to greet Rosa. Though a bit shorter than Rosa, Sherri carried herself as if she alone ran Manhattan. Rosa sensed an energy of pure and thick self-confidence from Sherri. The Chief of Staff raised a hand to signal a pair of aides, and the group of them hurried Rosa through the glass doors. They scurried along so fast Rosa hardly had time enough to admire the impressive interior. She likened it more to a lavish hotel than an office building, especially considering all the ornate vegetation. Rosa watched as crème de la crème employees draped themselves atop plush chairs, lifting their noses from laptops to politely greet her.

After pleasant small talk down a few halls, Sherri dropped Rosa off in a fancy, private greenroom. The buffet table festooned with genuine gourmet hors d'oeuvres was a marvel in itself. Rosa picked out a piece of dark chocolate and allowed the sweet, gooey morsel to fill her being with a juicy bliss she hadn't tasted since the academy. Everything she'd consumed under Tommy Frank had been reconstituted Smartifice puree. She fought to resist the urge, but decided she was not above shoving fistfuls of chocolates, wrapped cheeses and whole fruits into her newly acquired handbag.

Pouring herself a glass of wine, she sat down at the beauty station, pleased to view her reflection without the bombardment of an ad. She embraced the quietude, and in that stillness, reality struck her like a steel-toed boot to the gut.

Dr. Ferguson was dead; she hadn't taken her panic meds in over twenty-four hours, had just openly rejected the infamous Lady Maine, and been threatened by her ex-courtship. And now she was planning to sing some songs at a party? She suddenly felt very alone. The tiny room seemed to expand to unfathomable widths around her, her forehead perspiring, her vision blurring, her shoulders trembling. *No. Not now. Please, not now.* Yet her efforts only exacerbated her growing panic fit. That eerie ethereal feeling returned, slithering around her ears. A low external breathing, asymmetrical like faulty pipework, enveloped the room.

"Maaahhh...k," hissed lightly through the walls, a living magnetic force.

"Wh... who's there?" she called through a tightened throat, trying her best to feel silly. Suddenly she felt an ice-cold whisper of wind flutter ever-so slightly past her cheeks, setting the tiny hairs at the back of her neck to stand at attention. And then—

"Ms. Lejeune?" called Dex from the hall, breaking the unnerving spell. "Did you drop something?" Rosa found she'd been kneeling on the carpet staring at her hands. She had no recollection of getting to the floor, but there she was. These panic attacks were growing more and more peculiar.

Rosa shook her head and smiled as Dex helped her to her feet. "Curtain call," they said. Scarcely able to hold onto consciousness, Rosa allowed Dex to escort her down the short hall to the backstage area. "Nothing to fear, Ms. Lejeune. You look great, by the way." Dex left Rosa alone behind the thick, red curtain. And as the doors slid to a close behind her, the curtains spread.

* * *

Rosa stepped forward to meet her audience. The spacious auditorium held dozens of rows of posh red chairs fixed with little black dinner tables. The elevated stage held only a spot-lighted grand piano and boom microphone. There was no announcement, no applause. In fact, the room was deathly silent save for the echo of her heels. There sat only one audience member.

It was him.

Paul Oscar Ryland Perry, founder and CEO of Oz Corp, and owner of over forty percent of the free world.

He sat in the third row in a snug sweater and tailored pants, a glass of red wine in hand. The smell of the well-seasoned steak atop his plate filled the theater. Apart from the broader build and lightly peppered stubble, he was still the curiously charming boy she'd secretly admired back at Fame Academy. His dark, perfectly manicured hair matched a set of dark calculating eyes that could only be described as singularly beautiful. Having grown into quite the Adonis, he certainly lived up to the ballyhoo. Planet Magazine voted him 'Sexiest Being on the Planet' four years in a row, though he seldom stepped foot outside his kingdom.

Rosa wondered if this was some sort of audition. No doubt a creepy atmosphere.

Paul was, in a word, intense. He leaned back comfortably in his chair, owning the situation. His wholly penetrating gaze pierced through the space between them, inspecting her so mercilessly, Rosa could hardly hold herself erect.

She had to focus on something other than his eyes or she'd simply melt away in embarrassment. As she fought to ground herself, she felt a flush of warmth cloak the room, an empathic residue far stronger than she'd ever felt before. As clear as day, she knew no harm would come to her. Had she generated the sensation of her own accord? Regardless, it straightened her stance.

"All right," she whispered. "Showtime."

Rosa made her way to the beastly piano, the black and white keys staring up at her, challenging her to remember them, to understand them. She could feel Paul watching her, waiting for her to impress him. She swallowed a lump then started with Vernon Duke's Common Era jazz classic 'Autumn in New York,' concentrating exclusively on technique to keep from a nervous breakdown. But as she journeyed through the piece, she found her body coalescing with the harmonious waves created by the wood rim and steel strings of the living instrument. Fully engrossed in melodic swirls, Rosa felt soothing slivers of joy lightly massage her being, a feeling she hadn't felt in years.

Without allowing for an awkward pause, Rosa followed up with her second piece, one she'd secretly caught Paul playing back at the academy—Gershwin's Rhapsody in Blue. She'd fallen in love with it that moment, those many years ago. As she performed, an overwhelming flood of appreciation resonated throughout the theatre walls, weaving through the complex story of the tune and peaking at Gershwin's infamous 'Love Theme.'

Once completed, she stepped around the piano and looked to her audience. The steak was gone. Paul held her gaze. After a long, agonizing stillness between them, Paul took a sip from his wine glass, then spoke. "Your selections have been exceptional." His voice held a more self-assured tone than she'd remembered, though still very calm and quiet, and with that slight vulnerable rasp that drove her mad.

"Thank you," she beamed nervously.

"I'd like to hear an original piece. Your latest."

"Oh, no," she blurted then paused to pace herself. "You wouldn't enjoy my originals. They're too, you know. They're sort of uhm..." her words tapered into a muffle. Her original works were intimate, a foray through her anxieties. Certainly not suitable for this already awkward situation. Paul waited, unstirred.

"I'm sure I'll love it," he graciously insisted. A sharp tingle slinked up her spine like a stealthy spider. Afraid she'd go beet red on the spot, she returned to the piano bench, took a deep breath and began to sing her latest piece, a jazzy waltz she'd composed on one of her lonelier nights.

"*Where are all the roses?*" she sang in a honeyed alto. "*They'd once shone brightly red. Or were they posing? Had I just been misled? Or are they frozen? For all the roses are now blue. Where is the springtime? I once could feel its warmth. Or were they green lies, that had been pouring forth? For everything dies. And all the roses are now blue.*" Rosa felt a rapidly swelling compassion envelop her, envelop the room, and her eyes instantly filled with cathartic tears. She pressed on.

"*How could the sun have gone away from here? Now a darkness where all had once been clear. To go it all alone is far too much to bear. So, won't someone please tell me where...are all the roses? For all the roses are now blue.*" She reiterated the verse then finished the piece with a tri-octave glissando to end things on a relatively positive note.

Rosa remained at the bench for a moment to calm her nerves and wipe her tears. Again, she stepped out to address her audience. Paul now stood in front of the first row, following her hands intently as she wiped them on her dress. The way his eyes measured her every movement, sent a chill through her. Rosa felt a dense wave of gratitude emanate from his being. "Thank you for sharing that with me," he said earnestly, "I truly appreciate it."

"The piano does most of the work," she stammered. "I am merely its dance partner." She attempted a smile, but was having trouble handling his proximity, his full and complete attention.

"Dex will get you back to your skystretch and process your fee. Have the driver take you to whichever hotel you'd prefer for tonight. On us of course."

"Thank you," she said, holding back childish excitement. "The pleasure was all mine." Again, his words came low, stern. "Goodnight, Ms. Lejeune." He pronounced her surname flawlessly. Stifling a shiver at the sound of her name against his lips, she watched as he turned and walked up the staircase to the back exit, taking the feeling of welcoming warmth along with him. It wasn't until the doors slid shut behind him that she realized her right hand had been outstretched toward him, reaching for him.

* * *

That night Rosa whirled around on a real, open bed in her high-class luxury hotel suite, her mouth full of scrumptious chocolate and well-aged wine. She could think of nothing but his dark eyes on her, observing her, appreciating her. Over-analyzations could wait. The chatverse could wait. The world could wait. She hadn't felt this good in a long time, if ever, and planned to savor every last minute.

She felt beautiful.

She ran her fingers up her middle and massaged her breasts, casting her hands as his. She wanted nothing more in that moment than for Paul Oscar Ryland Perry to explore and appreciate every fold of her. She closed her eyes and allowed her vivid imagination and her fingers to roam freely.

Feeling a buzz at her wrist, Rosa found she'd been awarded a payment of 100,000 credits entitled 'Live Performance' and a second payment of 900,000 credits entitled 'Tip.' She sat up abruptly. Could the tip have been in error? She'd have to send a message to Dex to straighten that out. She clicked on the transaction to investigate further, and...*That can't be right.* The from-field for 'Live Performance' read Oz Corporation, but the from-field for 'Tip' read 6561fefa9i.

8
USUAL SUSPECTS

"Lose the pet," Tory demanded. He'd taken excessive measure to mask his location pin, particularly from his employer, while Kris arrived with the massive footprint of two companions and a Jack Russell bot. Tory had picked the vacant, unsurveilled lot beneath Queens Plaza since the smorgasbord of moving pins above would muffle any activity below.

"Nah, he's cool," came Kris's cavalier defense. "Killed his trace like I killed mine." Tory firmed his grip on a duffel bag at his shoulder.

"The dog. The band. They walk or I walk." Tory's reconnaissance on Kris had alerted him to Kris's 'Impressive Things' award for his advanced canine-droid. Regardless, Tory had no interest in risking the bot's potential log-trail.

"Okay, okay. Jeez." Kris turned and handed the bot to cohort, Dean Zapata. "DZ and Az will keep watch at the far end, but Becky stays." Tory frowned. "She's my sidekick, bro." Tory, aware Rebecca Thompson aided Kris on a handful of microjobs, nodded after a moment's contemplation. As a

71

former soldier, Tory could respect the loyalty Kris inspired with his team of eccentrics.

"Familiar with all the exits?" Tory asked DZ.

DZ waited a beat, gently placed the bot onto the ground, then maneuvered his hands in sign language along with expressive mouth movements. The words "May you please enable your speech to caption setting when speaking even if not addressing me directly?" appeared just beneath his hands in the air-display field. At that moment Tory realized small text had been appearing at chest-height in front of Kris while Kris had been speaking.

Tory turned to Kris with an abrupt, "Not gonna work."

"Errrt," Kris sounded, simulating a game-show buzzer. He pointed to DZ. "He addressed you. Not me."

Tory took a second to swallow the affront. Any other day he'd appreciate the stark correction. His Glass and fancy gadgets were deactivated, so everyone patiently waited as he sifted through his wristband's settings. "Okay," Tory said, as the same words appeared before him. "For security, everyone including you will have to power off their Ncludeds. Can't move forward if we can't agree to that."

Kris and DZ exchanged glances. "Okay, sounds fair," DZ signed. "I'll have Aztec bark once if we suspect someone's coming." Everyone nodded and shut off their wristbands. DZ picked up the dog and waived as he turned on his heel. Tory prayed the brief air-display conversation was hidden enough.

"Lost his hearing pretty young. Botched human experiment," Kris said. "TF life. So, how's your boy, Paul Oz?" The three assembled around a concrete slab. Tory steadily regarded the hacker's small frame.

"Who are you?" Tory asked.

Kris looked around. "I'm guessing, 'Kris Johnson' ain't the answer you're going for."

"A wrong move from you could end me. Now, there's a disconnect in your story. You studied signal theory at Fame. No Nforce demerits. Yet you make a living in black-hat cyber thievery."

"Oh right, that. Look, I'm just a mercenary. I mostly only take gigs that robinhood off rich assholes." Kris inhaled, tugged at his beard. "I started off-the-books, programming neurologic code for Psy Institute. Something 'bout creating procedurally generated humanoids. Living NPCs. Didn't keep my attention though. Programming for a corporate's like working a penciled-in maze."

"Right, so you ditch the prestigious trajectory and pen the sign 'will hack for rent?'"

Kris palmed out toward his roommate. "Tough decision. Don't regret it. Wanted to stay close to my people. These days it's impossible to have people, real IRL people, you know?" Yes, Tory knew. Live human interaction was precious and rare. His own father made good money hosting IRL conversations.

"So darkverse hacking then?" Tory pressed on. "Punish the wrong doings of rich assholes by...doing wrong?"

"Look, I'm not the frickin Pope, aight?" Kris shrugged. "Jeez, you really are an investigator." Tory smirked. He decided the hacker was all right. Not exactly an immoral deviant, but not exactly not an immoral deviant.

"Dang it, y'all!" Becky interrupted waving an arm. "As much as I love watching y'all make out, I really think we should get on figuring out who killed Dr. Ferguson, seeing that's why we're here." Both men straightened up.

Both Becky and Tory pulled out physical writing pads to piece together Ferguson's general narrative. Handwriting was a handy arcane talent for avoiding trails.

* * *

After receiving his Nobel Prize at age twelve, Ferguson became a high-profile name in innovation. In the 50's PCE, he discovered a microbe that greatly enhanced human energy, which soon birthed the BurstMyte energy drink. The resulting international attention drove him to open the Ferguson Testing Facility where he conducted self-regulated human tests, patenting numerous innovations. In 99 PCE he partnered with business tycoon, Titan Maine, to create the Ferguson and Maine School of Excellence, and their SOI quickly soared to number one.

Ferguson died during an alleged chemical explosion in his private lab in Howard Beach Queens on Thursday, November 7, 186 at 19:48 hours. Nforce removed two bodies from the scene: one identified as Dr. Ferguson, the other his assistant professor, Philip Pelleher. According to Ncluded logs, they'd been the only two on the premises. With a growing pool of envious contenders burning to sully his name, Ferguson's final text *"They know. Don't come in"* encouraged a firm possibility of foul-play.

* * *

"I hate to be Mr. Obvious, but it was the Maine's," Kris started. "I already got the Wikipedia entry ready." Tory frowned.

"I'm risking my job meeting you here," Tory said. "Give me something or don't waste my time."

"Okay, okay," Kris conceded. "Look, after the EMP blackout of 162, right? Ferg found some new biochemical element we weren't allowed to talk about." Tory raised an eyebrow. "I only know he called it Indigo. From the little I overheard, it's not an earthly element. Its atoms are like our atoms but with weird, unnatural quirks or something."

Tory jotted at his notepad. "Do you mean quirks or quarks?"

"Woah," Kris mused looking to the ceiling. "Bro, that just blew my mind."

Tory recalled the well-dressed ReBuild and his anxious repetition of the word 'Dingo.' Was he referring to this strange element, Indigo? Tory waited as Kris mulled over a thought.

"Anyway, Ferg shut Titan Maine out from his findings, and Maine and Ferg split after an eighty-year partnership. Maine managed to steal Ferg's wife though. People say Ferg and Maine split 'cause of his harlot wife, but it was definitely 'cause of the secrets around Indigo."

Tory didn't appreciate the pejorative but moved forward. "So, Lady Maine," he said, scaling his list. "She starts as Ferguson's marital contract and goes by Madame Ferguson. She beds Maine, and now she's Lady Maine."

"She's hot, you know, in a classical sense," chimed Becky. "She's like ninety, and looks thirty-five. I'm hoping her lady parts also look sixty years younger, am-I-right?"

"Ferg shut her out too: which is like, duh, you fucked my business partner," Kris said. "Right before graduation, she and Maine came down hard on Ferg trying to break him. Lady's one crazy Ice Queen, dude."

"I'd prefer we avoid the name calling," Tory said.

"Oh, would you prefer *murderer* then?" Kris chuckled. "Pharma Farm also had motive though. They're a real slimy bunch. Done some freelance hackery for them too."

"Quite the working-girl then."

"I get around. Look, anyone with a wallet and something to lose needs a contractor with low scruples. Pharma Farm's the keep-the-masses-addicted-to-what's-killing-em type. And the CEO, Leland Fart, is a major asshole. So yeah, I've wiped a few trails for 'em."

"That's Leland Shark," Tory corrected, licking his fore-finger to slide to the next page in his notepad. He felt like a Common Era neanderthal. "Jonathan Angelo Boulevardo Marino," Tory spouted. "Did he have..." Tory tapered off as he watched Kris's countenance sag. Kris exchanged a subtle glance with Becky, sucked his teeth, then looked to his hands.

"Jarhead Johnny? He...all the testing...it fucked him up."

"He courtshipped your friend," Tory stated, referring to Rosa Lejeune.

"She's my...she *was* my ace, my ride-or-die. But while Ferg messed him up, he messed her up." Kris closed his eyes and balled his fists, then straightened up through a long sigh. "He was a couple years older than us. Ferg kept him a TF, denying him any SOI access after he started a few fights. Some people called him a Ferg Pet, but he was really just a tool, a guinea pig. Ferg eventually kicks him out for all the bullshit with Rosa. Johnny begs to be readmitted and flips a bigger shit each time Ferg rejects him. Now Ferg's dead and Rosa's pin's back on the street, so..."

"Now he's a Maine Academy grad with deep loyalties to the Maines," Tory added. Kris took to hand shuffling sans response. "Michelle Brier was another student of Ferguson's with an axe to grind," Tory continued, hoping to move things along.

Becky bounced in her seat.

"Becky's gaga for Brier," Kris apologized. "She's a murder suspect, Becks. Simmer down."

"The thing is," Becky started, "I didn't know her back when she was Michell, but she took some classes at Fame while we were there. Now she's an ultra-famous celeb. I keep telling Kris there's only three people I'd go straight for. Tell him, Kris."

With a harried eye-roll, Kris recited, "For me, Paul Oz and for Michelle Brier if she ever reverted to identifying as male."

"Damn right!" Becky beamed.

"Brier bailed as Ferguson's press secretary," Tory went on. "Why?"

"Uhm, hello?" Becky snuffed. "She got an Oz Corp sponsorship. You know better than anyone; you drop everything when you get an Oz Corp deal."

Tory frowned up at her, biting back a betrayal of incredulity. Measuring his patience, he said, "Her Oz Corp deal came years later. Check your claims."

"Well, not to throw shade at Brier in front of Becks here," Kris said. "But she spread some pretty nasty rumors about Ferg being transphobic in the chatverse. Then she covered it up. I know the guy she hired to wipe it."

"That ain't nearly enough to suspect her of murder," Becky defended.

"Money, motive, purged evidence," Tory said to Becky, his words dripping with strain. "These all brand her a candidate. She also—"

"Ugh," Becky dutifully interjected. "Transhumans always hatin' on transgenders."

"Excuse me?" Tory said.

"Oh, y'all know what I mean. Prance around here with your fancy British accents. When really you—"

"English. It's an English accent. Not British. Britain includes England, Wales and Scotland." The pair stared at Tory stunned. He'd bit back harsher than intended, but anti-transhuman ad hominems skirted his limits. Becky offered a half-hearted harrumph then slinked back to her notepad.

"So..." Kris began. "We at Paul Oscar yet? I mean, everyone talks about how perfect he is, but the kid's a fricken bastard. I know it."

"Firstly," Tory said, "he was actually born out of wedlock, so careful how nonchalantly you toss around that term."

"My bad!" Kris threw up his hands. "Didn't mean to blaspheme."

"Don't be a prick," Tory snarked. Preserving mental fortitude with one's main biohacks disabled would be difficult for any transhuman. Tory exhaled. "But, yes, he's a suspect. He and Ferguson were close."

"Close? More like *clones*," Kris said. "Paul was weird and quiet, so no one asked him about the secret shit he did with Ferg. He drops out two years before graduating, I assume to kickstart his Nforce App project. Maine Academy offers him an iron throne and he openly rejects it." Lines creased Kris's forehead as he considered his next words. "And we both know Paul Oz was promised a ton of stuff in Ferg's will. Ferg's estate leaked as much. And if Paul knew he was getting loot in advance, he'd have every reason to, you know, speed things up."

"I don't trust leaks. I trust facts."

"Okay, here's a fact: Ferg's dead and Paul's fucking psycho," Kris snapped. Tory said nothing, letting the hacker's emotional appeal pass.

"Pelleher," Tory said. "He died beside Dr. Ferguson, making him a possible vehicle—"

"Pelleher has been Ferg's right hand since the dark ages," Kris said. "I mean he got the warning text, and people that tight with Ferg would die with Ferg," This earned a nod from Becky.

"We've exhausted my list then," Tory said, rescanning his notes. "Next steps. Gain intel. Chase leads."

"We can help with research," Kris said, "but it'll be tough to hack higher-ups. I'm waiting on access to Secure's Delta mainframe for some high-level background checking, but even that may not be enough."

"Right," said Tory. "No interest in involving you further."

"Oh. Well, you forgot to say, 'no offense.'"

As Tory began packing up, he felt a light buzz at the electromagnetic sensors in his fingertips. He assumed it was a response to random atmospheric residue.

"Quick question," Kris said, squaring his shoulders. "So, this is gonna sound kooky, but Sunday night, my biohacks went haywire. Then a weird message appeared in the air-display that read, 'CONTACT ME' and nothing else. Crazy right?"

"Hm." Tory recalled the similarly eerie experience he'd dismissed as a headache. "I got a similar invasion on my wallscreen. It read 'I NEED YOU, NOW'."

"Woah!" Kris exclaimed.

"Now I'm even more freaked out," Becky added.

Tory rubbed at his temple. Someone able to hack the air-display knew both Tory and Kris would eventually be working the case. This meant Tory would have to bring Kris all the way in. "An untraceable ReBuild hacked into the Conservation Garden and tipped me off to look into the possibility of murder," Tory said. "You know anything about that?"

"An untraceable ReBuild?" Kris cried. "Okay, we're definitely in the middle of some crazy shit. Getting rights to a ReBuild is a heavily documented procedure."

"It is," Tory ceded, "but this Demetrius Marshall lived and died before documentation on ReBuild acquisition was a thing. Either someone obtained the ReBuild from a third party who'd owned it before proper ReBuild log trails, or—"

"Or someone boss enough to hack 'CONTACT ME' into the frickin air is also boss enough to snag a ReBuild untraced."

"Woof!" came from the far end of the lot. DZ and the bot dog sprinted over as the buzzing feeling in Tory's fingertips grew from light to portentous. He stifled a shiver. The lot had no surveillance. They were safe. Right?

"Everything all right, Deez?" Kris called, raising an eyebrow. Though no text appeared in the air-display, DZ responded with a quick gesture.

"Huh?" Kris puzzled.

"What did he say?" Tory asked.

"He says there's an ad somewhere, but—" Before Kris could finished his sentence, everyone's Ncludeds simultaneously powered on, flashing bright red error icons. Becky, Tory and Kris leapt to their feet. "Close your eyes to avoid the ad," Tory commanded. Everyone obeyed. Ads had a nasty habit of recognizing iris signatures. DZ and the bot dog could have triggered a hidden panel and already be compromised. But this backlot had no panels, no surveillance. Tory was certain of it.

"Oh God! We're gonna get Nforced," Becky squealed.

"No," Tory assured. "Not if it's just an ad. Some faulty ads trigger errors." With his eyes shut, Tory knelt to his duffel bag, picked out a pair of ad-shield goggles then looked up to find Kris already donning a pair.

"Okay," Kris said with a slight tremor as he pointed to a spot directly behind Tory. "Nobody move or open their eyes. But Ross, you should definitely look at that ad right now."

Tory slowly rose to his feet and turned where he stood. Red letters over a large white window floated leisurely toward him, parking right before his nose. A very short and very simple message. "Torian Ross. My office. Tomorrow morning at eight hundred hours. –Oz."

9

CLOSE ENCOUNTER

TUESDAY NOV 12, 186 PCE

"To exist is to transfer energy."

— *DIARY OF THE MAD GLEE*

A short text to Dex landed Rosa in a skystretch back to Oz Corp the following evening. The exchange had been brief: Rosa insisting she return the tip to Paul and Dex fiercely resisting, maintaining there'd been no mistake and that Paul was impossibly busy. But after a brief hold, Dex assured Paul would receive her that evening to discuss her concerns.

Rosa was ushered back onto the superstructure by Sherri Weiler and given star-quality treatment. The pair ambled leisurely through the halls, allowing Rosa to appreciate the eerily impeccable Oz Corp culture.

"...and the renewable energy complex on the roof of *this* building is powered by a photovoltaic surface coating," Sherri had been saying as they ascended to the top floor in a mirrored elevator. Rosa felt she must have appeared anxious when Sherri said, "Mr. Perry's still finishing up a call in his apartment. Gustav's put together a few plates for you while you wait."

"Oh," Rosa started as saliva pooled in her mouth. "I hate to be *that guy*, but I don't eat—"

"Red and white meat. You do eat seafood and have been known to sneak duck on occasion. You don't eat enough vegetables but do like orange zest in your red wine. Though peppered sangria is your actual weakness. You aren't big on sweets, but since you've been on Smartifice the last five years, this may have changed. We've got you, Ms. Lejeune. This is Oz Corp." Sherri's words came with a toothy-grinned pride. Rosa studied herself, in her short backless dress, against Sherri's power suit. God, what she wouldn't do to borrow Sherri's confidence for but a moment. The Chief of Staff escorted Rosa off the elevator and into a vacant, candlelit dining hall. "Enjoy your jumbo shrimp, Ms. Lejeune." she said, handing Rosa off to a white-vested waiter.

The waiter seated Rosa and presented her with a glass of peppered sangria and a long-stemmed rose.

A portly chef Gustav soon replaced the waiter, cordially introducing himself and explaining the evening's menu. Rosa appreciated the attention. And after an appetizer of gooey spinach dip and two more glasses of sangria, Gustav delivered the main entrée—one large, honey-glazed jumbo shrimp half the size of Rosa's face over a bed of ghost peppers and lettuce. Honey had been declared extinct for nearly a century, yet here it sat in its true form. All so devilishly decadent.

"I'll never finish this," Rosa joked, but the second the chef disappeared, she woodpecked at her plate with predatory efficiency, hardly allowing her pallet the true experience. The very thought of consuming natural food, harvesting energy from a being that once lived. For the first time in years, she felt... human. *God, Smartifice goop was a cruel, cruel thing.*

"Gustav is a best kept secret." His lax voice sailed in from behind her. The world paused. The air went out of the room. It was him. Paul. *Damn it.* Paralyzed, Rosa remained hovering over her plate with a mouth full of shrimp. *Don't look up right now; you look like a chipmunk.* She felt him walk around her and casually seat himself across from her. Rosa's knees buckled at his proximity. Without having to listen for it, she felt a thick welcoming wave of emotion emanate from his being. A frequency so warm, so strong, she could almost hear it. She could forever bask in that warmth. It allowed her to relax. She swallowed her mouthful as diplomatically as possible.

"Hi Paul," she heard herself say, attempting to meet his formidable gaze. His black shirt, the top two buttons frivolously undone, rested so taut against him, Rosa could detect the brawny hard-lined body underneath. She blushed. "Thanks for agreeing to meet."

"Of course, Rosa." The waiter brought Paul a glass of the same peppered sangria. Paul thanked him, calling him by name and asking briefly of his mother. Had Rosa seemed rude to the waiter if even Paul Oscar would grant him such attention? As the waiter retreated, Paul raised his glass. And though on her third drink, Rosa responded in kind. "To your talent," Paul said firmly. They waved their glasses and sipped.

"Again, I'm honored," Rosa smiled. "You've really done well for yourself." Rosa felt Paul's energies evolve from warm welcome to deep compassion. The sudden change in pressure physically shook her, diffusing deep into her skin.

"That last piece you performed, the original. So powerful. So raw. It plagued me all last night."

All night? Rosa fought desperately not to react. A hot tingle teased her spine at the thought of him considering her in his bed. Betraying a nervous chuckle, Rosa looked down to her plate, then to her wine glass. Paul studied her movements intently, waiting patiently for her eyes to finally find his before he continued.

He propped his elbows on the table, folding his hands under his chin. "You're also a dancer. Perhaps next time I'll have you dance for me." His words low and measured, his stern eyes cutting straight through her. Rosa sensed an impish menace in his air.

"Well, I'm not so sure you could afford that," she ventured, coy, girlish. Before she could regret the statement, Paul let out a dry puff of amusement. Were they flirting? She couldn't tell. The atmosphere was far too intense. *He* was far too intense. His eyes so keenly fixed on her. Could she engage in a witty dalliance with the likes of Paul Oscar, Sexiest Being on The Planet?

Say something science-y; he'll like that, said her years of escort experience. "It's funny," she started, stirring her Sangria with the ornamental umbrella. "This drink is super thick, but it and everything in it is just vacuum." She closed with a coy smile, taking pride in her little gem of knowledge.

"Actually, quantum fields and associated fluctuations permeate what most would consider true vacuum," Paul corrected. *Oh, right; he's a genius.* Mortified, Rosa felt a burning flush flood her torso as she attempted to implode into her seat. She could feel no belittling judgments in his aura, and again her muscles unbuckled. He followed up with a light, "Take another sip. Let's test the theory."

"For research of course," she smiled before shooting back an overtly generous swig. The wine encouraged her to change gears. "So..." she said, "tell me what Paul Oscar likes to do for fun?"

"I like fire." His answer came sharp and matter-of-fact as if he'd anticipated the question. "I like to play with it, feel the pain of it against my skin." Sensing a profound sincerity in his words, Rosa quickly realized she wasn't ready for casual conversation at his level.

"Me, I'm into books, banned books especially," she blurted nervously. "Worn, lived-in books made of pulp paper. But physical books are impossible to come by."

"Hm," Paul mused. "Finish your wine. I'd like to show you my library. I've got a few books I think you'll appreciate." *An entire library?* In over five years of intensive searching, Rosa had gotten her hands on only two physical books, neither of which were banned. With physical books being practically extinct for everyone but Mandala monks and SOI students, Rosa bounced in her chair at the prospect. The burnt pages, dog-eared creases, chewed-on dust jackets. Paul got to his feet. "I'll let you finish."

No, don't leave, she howled in her mind, not yet ready to part with his perfectly warm energies. She dabbed at her face with a napkin, rose from her seat and said, "I think I've had enough for now."

"Right then," Paul said as the waiter rushed to pull away her chair. "This way."

Rosa followed as Paul thanked his dining staff and strolled out. Each stride came long, confident, and resolute. He kept a level distance from her, almost as if she hadn't been accompanying him. Eerie indeed. As they sauntered through the corridors, Paul exchanged a personal greeting with each passing employee, an act Rosa appreciated. She noticed each employee kept a decisive distance from Paul as well and detected the reverent fear he inspired in them, painted broadly across both their faces and their mental energies.

Paul brought Rosa to the round, steel door of his apartment.

"I don't welcome many guests into my home," he informed. "But it offers a shortcut to the library."

A sea of royal blue carpet flowed throughout the luxury

apartment. Clear solar paneled windows landscaped the walls, all furniture rimmed in a mix of gold and foliage.

Paul left Rosa to explore as he attended to an urgent video-conference in his study. Rosa took in the scent of fragrant salts, ran her thumbs against the leather couches, peered behind the wet bar and into the sauna. Never before had she seen an active indoor fountain, an inset sanded fire pit or original carvings and paintings. Everything was so absolutely perfect and so absolutely real. Painfully, beautifully real.

Anyone could buy virtual things: a virtual plant, pet, window, and virtual skins to place over those virtual things. The elite could buy real things: real plants, real pets and real homes with real windows. But there was one thing credits couldn't buy: heart. And Paul Oscar's apartment...it had heart.

* * *

As she admired the exotic fish of an aquarium inlaid into a living room wall, Rosa sensed Paul's warm presence emerge from his study, settling into the room several feet behind her. Never had she felt such a strong empathic connection, stronger now than it had been in the dining hall. She sensed him scaling her body with his eyes, admiring the curves of her back through her backless mesh.

Unable to remain poised under such scrutiny, Rosa turned to find him watching her, studying her. The color of his frequency shifted ever so slightly from admiration to curiosity. A drum thumped in her chest as he took several leisurely strides toward her. *Do not reveal your empathic ability,* she cautioned herself, *it's your only semblance of control.* Paul stepped up close to her, so close she could feel the warmth of his breath against her forehead.

Rosa focused on the two undone buttons of his taught, silk

shirt, not yet ready for a close-range tango with his intoxicating stare. She sensed him analyzing the curves of her breasts, his growing curiosity so full now, so intense, she could feel his active restraint. She steeled herself in anticipation then dared to match his gaze, a mistake so bittersweet she could hardly maintain her composure. His eyes were deep, onyx pools of indomitable thirst, validating every vibration echoing from his being.

Paul brought his eyes to her lips, his searing curiosity suddenly exploding into a deep hunger for her mouth. Rosa reflexively pouted her lower lip, and like a hawk snatching prey, Paul grabbed at her mouth with his.

A million tiny needles of pleasure tickled her lips as Paul bit down. Though he emitted no trace of transhuman modification, Rosa was certain she could feel a buzzing electromagnetic current against his lips. He kissed her with such full and complete focus, as if his sole purpose of existence had been to kiss her in that moment. Though bolted in place by the overwhelming weight of his energies, Rosa managed to run her fingers to his head and press him closer.

As he explored her mouth with ease, Paul rested a finger on the bare skin of her thigh and traced upward. A charged whirr from his traveling finger—lightly vibrating like a motorized toothbrush—left a streak of pure, agonizing stimulation in its wake. Rosa appreciated the contrast of her golden skin against his. She hadn't been touched in years, and he felt so good. *Too good.*

"God," he breathed into her neck once his finger crept passed the rim of her dress. Her body tensed at the sudden sound of his voice and light stubble against her. Every particle in her body cavity buzzed against his charged skin, drowning in the maddening ocean of his arousal.

He pressed her against the inlaid aquarium and cupped her

breasts decisively before running his hands meticulously down her belly, drawing sharp shockwaves through her torso. He slid his fingers between her inner-thighs and applied a light pressure. Rosa shuddered as she resisted him. Her body knew what it wanted. Her head uncertain. Her heart pointedly silent. Paul placed his lips close to her ear and dropped all manner of pretense.

"Please." The word came quiet yet undeniably commanding. This vulnerability, this desperate untamable desire for her, seized Rosa. She knew he could feel her body melt before him, but could he hear her inner voice screaming 'Yes! Oh God, Yes! Please let me satisfy you!'

Paul emanated a wave of stark determination as one hand gripped her bottom to hold her steady while the other made its way up her inner thigh to settle on her soft, wet, lacy sex. At the touch of his buzzing fingers, Rosa arched her back, betraying a shivered whimper. And though Paul made no change in outward demeanor, Rosa felt a mixed rush of excitement and gratification surge out of him like wildfire.

His eyes fixed on her, Paul used two buzzing fingers to press at her two times, sending two charged pulses up her spine, through her chest and down her arms and legs. Rosa moaned bitterly as her muscles convulsed through painful bliss. Could a mere poke cause such immense pleasure? Paul pressed again, and again, and each time Rosa wailed in relentless climactic ecstasy. He held complete control over her entire body, and he enjoyed that control.

Rosa's muscles eventually petered out, riven with bliss. Paul placed a hand on her chin and brought her eyes to his. He then placed his other hand, with its dampened fingers, into his mouth and let out a deep moan as he relished her taste. He wanted her to watch him taste her. Rosa could do nothing but titter in embarrassment, drunk on his aura. He smiled back at her, all boyish dimples, like it was their little secret. The pure, aching splendor of his smile was so severe, so infinitely profound, Rosa was absolutely convinced she sensed divinity.

Then the mood changed.

The air thickened. Paul burrowed his face into her neck as he worked at his belt buckle. The sheer force of his raw emotions somehow spooled Rosa in closer to their origin point within him. Her empathic curiosities tumbled into the depths of him like moth to flame.

She first came upon a frequency of perfect tranquility within him: a stillness held in place by immovable self-assurance. Yet as she ventured deeper into his psyche, she felt that frequency evolve into something dark. Cascading further, she passed through a maelstrom of assumed privilege encircling vast waves of loneliness, and finally settled upon the nucleus of his being. She'd found it. She'd found *him*, a deep, impenetrable force of visceral rage, a miasmic Gordian knot of bitterness so thick it crushed Rosa's breath. Her perceptions could not penetrate further, as if his thick ball of internal bedlam was solid matter. A writhing soup of anger, entitlement and sexual gratification pumped through to the skin of his buzzing tip as he nudged insistently against her upper thighs.

"Wait," Rosa whispered, with a gentle push. Paul, apparently unaware of her internal foray, only pressed against her more firmly. The raw, billowing ire she'd found in him now surrounded her, consumed her, choking her insides like an opaque cloud of black smoke. "Stop," she breathed. Suddenly she was suffocating, drowning under the weight of him. Panic crept its way to her fingers. Paul's surging desire to anchor himself inside of her peaked as he tugged a hand assertively at her lace shorts. At this Rosa quickly jumped to attention.

"No!" she resounded definitively. Seething with righteous shivers, she pushed up against the wall, using the momentum to tear him away from her, freeing herself from his billowing darkness. "No. I said no. N. O. Do you understand?"

Paul backed away in two long strides, the stillness of his gaze lightly stirred by his cavernous breaths. His thick erection remained exposed before her, daring her to acknowledge it. "Understood." His words low, stern.

Rosa stared back at him, struggling to suppress the army in her chest so she could decipher his energies. With no change in his unyielding composure, Paul first projected a hot, bitter wave of shock followed immediately by a forced calm. For the briefest instant she thought he would rush her. But he only watched her, calculating. And just as Rosa considered forgoing any ill feelings, Paul emitted an emotion that irked her so fiercely she wanted nothing more than to kick at his exposed manhood. He emitted disappointment, not in himself, not in the circumstance, but in her.

Disappointment in *her*? She knew him now. She felt him. His entitlement. How dare he subject her to the billowing blackhole that was himself, then have the gall to be disappointed in her?

Paul turned his back to her to readjust himself, allowing her an unforeseen courage to speak up with her own bout of reciprocated disappointment. "Not used to not getting what you want?" she said, her words cross. Paul immediately stiffened. He raised his head to the ceiling, pensive. Rosa figured he'd hurl a snarky retort or hurtful defense, but he didn't. What he did instead was far worse.

A piercing zap of writhing, hot pain stabbed against Rosa's ear canals, a crushing high-pitched ring so severe she braced forward in an eye-watering cringe. She let out a slow exhale as she fought for her bearings, allowing her ears to acclimate to the growing agony. But as the poignant ringing abated, Rosa realized she hadn't been hearing a ringing at all. She'd in fact been experiencing the complete opposite. An instant and complete silence. A cold, cosmic emptiness. Paul had shut her out of his emotions, cut her off from receiving his frequency, and he'd done it on purpose.

Immediate regret coursed through her. Suddenly Rosa wanted desperately to apologize, to plead, anything to bring back the warmth of his aura. In a day he'd given her everything she ever wanted, everything she needed, and in return she teased him and meddled in his psyche, where she certainly should not have been.

His back still turned, Paul said, "I'll have Dex escort you to the library," without a trace of indignation. Her nerves completely shot, Rosa couldn't bring herself to respond. She could only watch as he keyed at a device he'd pulled from his pocket. All she wanted in that moment was to find a quiet corner, curl into a ball and die.

* * *

The three-story open-center library gave off the slightest hum of living breath. Towering shelves and glass-fitted bookcases lined wooden walls; everything Rosa imagined of the pristine libraries of old. The faint smell of aging glue and wood paper calmed her frayed nerves.

Though instructed by Dex to touch nothing, well...Dex was out in the hall. Rosa slid her fingers across the book spines, feeling each book's tiny whispers of life, of will—the deeper the meaning of its contents, the stronger the resonance.

Though the Classics and Memoirs sections exuded hefty magnetism, Rosa was drawn to the case marked "Religion." Its top shelf books—The Holy Bible, The Bhagavad Gita, The Book of Shadows and The Maths of the Mandala—oozed such a powerful force of living energy, Rosa had to place her hand on its glass door to keep from falling. These were books she'd only dreamed of experiencing IRL.

Had religion called to her because she'd run out of options? She'd obviously shattered her one opportunity at the perfect alliance. Did Paul really intend on forming an alliance with her when attempting to procure her from Tommy Frank? Or was she just another million-credit whore?

One thing was certain, Paul was definitely not normal. She shuddered at the memory of his impenetrable miasma of fury, by far the worst of her empathic encounters. And then there was his ability to thwart her empathic perception. What *was* he? The spots where he'd touched her, kissed her, still embered hot against her skin. Suddenly she felt exposed, unarmed in unfamiliar territory. Each of the holy texts tugged at her, begging her to turn to them. She raised a trembling hand to open the glass door, and—

"The Quran is out on loan."

Rosa whirled around in honest fright to find Paul watching her from a second-floor balcony with a porcelain mug and a different pair of pants. How long had he been there? She hadn't felt him enter the room, could not feel his frequencies at all. He walked down a spiral staircase to meet her, keeping deliberate distance.

"This library is amazing," Rosa offered, waving toward the book-lined walls.

"It is," Paul said, indecipherably polite. Rosa cursed her heavy dependence on empathy to read even basic emotions. She felt nothing of the darkness pumping through him and could only suspect his resentment of her.

"Listen, Paul, I actually came here because I think your tip was in error."

"It wasn't."

"Well, I can't accept it."

"You're certainly free to give it away," Paul shrugged.

"I mean, I can't accept it...from you. Not after—" she stopped, cut short by a slight shiver.

Paul studied her for a long minute then said, "I can have a skyjet out front for you in two minutes if that's what you want." He keyed a button on his device.

"I don't want that."

"Then what *do* you want?" She didn't need an empathic connection to detect the accusation in his voice.

"I'd like to...I want you to—" She stopped herself. She wanted him to respect her. To value her as an intelligent woman. To understand how deeply he'd hurt her. To forgive her. But who deserves a respect for which they had to ask? At the very least, she wanted to understand his manner of body-hack. "I'll go ahead and take that skyjet," she said. Paul regarded her a while longer before pointing his mug toward the top of the Religion display. He indicated a small, worn journal with yellowed pages Rosa hadn't noticed.

"He gave that to me," Paul said, implying with a glance that she pick it up. "And now it's yours." On its cover, in Dr. Ferguson's signature scribble, read, *Diary of the Mad Glee*. Her guard faltered as a pair of tears escaped her. Rosa was holding a physical book from Ferg himself. She felt no living will among the pages and skimmed through to find them all blank. "Reading it requires a special light," Paul said.

Rosa looked to Paul wanting to ask about Ferguson, about the special light, about anything, but could only say, "Thanks for this." Paul nodded then turned to face a magazine rack. "God, was he not mad as a hatter?" Rosa whispered, hoping to ease the tension through commiserate grief. Paul gave no response. She continued awkwardly. "When Torian Ross mentioned possible murder I—" she stopped short, fearing she may press a wrong button, but Paul remained a still pond. He allowed a long moment before answering.

"Apart from his research into asteroid-mined materials, he was working on a new collection of next-gen technologies." Rosa perked up. The string of words had been one of Paul's longest. Proof that he too missed Ferguson. "He was working on super-crystals, hyper-dimensional nanotubes, was exploring the gut flora of Alaskan wood frogs and deep-sea micro—" Paul paused to look over at her. "And Indigo."

"Of course. Indigo." Rosa vaguely recalled the term whispered around the academy.

"He couldn't effectively parse out Indigo with Plank's constant since the photonics of its particles released a visible color undefined by our naturally visible spectrum," Paul said, returning his attention to the magazines. Rosa knew he'd soon lose her with techno-babble but allowed him to prattle on. "He'd mentioned tachyonic meta particles, which would go against basic theories of causality. To account for observation biases, he'd begun working on obtaining a perfect-vacuum lab system for perfect microscopy."

He'd gone too far for Rosa. At the risk of sounding rudimentary, she ventured, "So, how would one define Indigo exactly?" At this Paul turned his full body toward her, unabashedly inspecting her from head to toe. Rosa stiffened, wholly unsure of the nature of such a stark reaction. A double beep chimed from Paul's device.

"Your skyjet's ready."

* * *

He accompanied her to a pair of glass doors. A paved roof landing stretched above an Historic Central Park down below, one of the few places devoid of ad-pollution.

A single skypole lit the landing, and a long black skyjet hovered at the ready. A flight attendant approached and helped Rosa board before heading to the front. Relief rushed over Rosa as she settled into her seat, proud she'd made it through the night sans panic attacks. She peered down from her window to address Paul.

"Paul, I apologize for..." Rosa started. "You know. I mean, I just—"

"Never apologize for a decision you stand behind," he interjected decisively. Rosa blinked at this. She simply wanted to feel his energies again, but in no way could she ask. Paul took a sip from his mug, walked backwards a few paces and said, "Goodnight, Ms. Lejeune," then turned away to disappear into his library.

10

DELTA

K ris Johnson hopped out of his BedBooth at dawn. With everyone still asleep, checking for the results of his job application to Secure—the most advanced cyber security firm— would be far less nerve-wracking. He'd applied immediately following Ferg's death, knowing he'd need access to highly secured information, like the To-Do histories of Pharma Farm CEOs.

Now that he could be following Ross to Oz-Corp-style corporal punishment, Kris prayed for the off chance he'd received an acceptance letter overnight. He'd use Secure access to gather intel against their line of suspects: namely their biggest current threat, Paul Oz himself.

An unopened message from Secure sat at the center of Kris's wallscreen. "Come on, you sexy son-of-a-bitch," he murmured. Bracing himself, he read the first word of the message, '*Unfortunately,*' then stopped. He took a deep breath then pounded his fist. "Screw this," he resolved. A mere rejection letter wouldn't keep him from accessing Secure.

Kris pulled up his terminal window and called his Leroy

script, a script he'd used to send innocuous spiders to thousands of accounts at a time. The script caused an audio file yelling "Leroy Jenkins!" to pop up on the victim's screen then disappear, leaving no residue. It wouldn't be enough to infiltrate Secure, but someone on the team would have to bite back, starting a conversation.

Kris hit the last stroke on his keyboard to implement the hack, then got up to print some breakfast. He hadn't taken two steps before an error buzzed in his earpiece. A chatbox usurped his wallscreen bearing a message from Sam Fishman, the founder of Secure. It read, "I was watching to see how you'd react. Yes, the decision still stands." Kris pulled up his keyboard before his butt hit the chair, trying to crunch out a response before Fishman disappeared forever.

"It's an entry-level micro-position for which I'm overqualified," Kris typed. "I murdered your hour-long exam in eighteen minutes."

"True statements," Fishman message back.

"Okay?" Kris said aloud as he shuffled anxiously.

"Sexual harassment much?" Fishman responded. Kris stared blankly at the words in the chatbox. His heartbeat jumped to a sprint against his ears. His fists grew damp. Though Kris hadn't even been on the premises at the time, Davia Valenti claimed he groped her breasts back at Fame Academy. The incident continued to plague Kris regardless of his efforts to bury it. Having never been officially exonerated, Kris occasionally fell into deep, dark places. An aching pit in his belly longed to confront her, to ask her the simple question: *why?*

"No, I have not," Kris typed back.

"I should believe you over documented evidence?"

Kris's shoulders wilted. He'd done all he could to rid the chatverse of the incident, well enough for Ross not to catch wind, yet apparently the Streisand Effect had other plans when it came to Secure. Kris decided against being defensive. The antisocial Fishman-types preferred the humble smartass. Kris resigned to typing, "I'm a black kid from the Bronx. If I had groped a rich white girl, I mean really done it, I'd be Strange Fruit right now."

After five minutes sans response, Kris swallowed an assortment of expletives and printed up some generic breakfast puree. The Valenti-owned Smartifice muck sped up aging: Kris was certain of it, so he stuck with open source, off brand recipes. After fifteen minutes, Kris woke Aztec to accompany him in his agonizing and likely vain anticipation.

"Talk to me, Az," Kris said, slumping back in his chair.

"What would you like me to talk about?"

"Anything, I don't care."

"Well," Aztec began, a bit too chipper for dawn, "I recently read that, prior to the Great Pandemics of the 2020s CE, humans used to gather in masses of tens to hundreds of thousands of people to watch sports, concerts, speeches."

"Uh duh," Kris chuckled, "that's *why* the Great Pandemics happened."

"Back before the overthrow of the federal governing system, there had been a mandate to...mandate to.... mandate to—"

"You okay, Az?"

Aztec huddled close to a wall and plugged his tail into an outlet. "There. All better." Aztec prattled on without being prompted. "But the EMP blackout of 162 PCE—which is now believed to be an extraterrestrial event—took out power in North America for three days, and society reacted with the same level of unpreparedness."

"Technology. Solves everything but dumbass," Kris said. He looked to his screen. No new activity. He sighed, biting back an urge to barrage Fishman with messages. "We somehow ran on fossil fuels and exchanged paper currency. I can't even fathom life without maintenance bots. Like, how did they catch crime without everyone surveilling through the Nforce App? It had to have been like, 'You stole my girl!' Stab. 'You're in my way!' Stab."

Aztec gave Kris a blank stare then buried his head into his bowl of mixed updates. Kris steeled himself for another glance at his screen, and there it sat.

A chatbox from Fishman. "Fine. You're hired."

"Holy shit!" Kris exclaimed. Aztec lifted his head and wagged his tail, unsure the cause for celebration.

Kris received a video call from Secure two minutes later. A pale red-head appeared on the screen. "Hello," called a haughty voice mid-yawn. "I'm Aim. My pronoun is Aim. White, freckles, shoulder-length red hair. I'll be testing you. You pass, you're in. You fail, you never interact with me again." Kris didn't know if he should feel affronted nor what to do with the pronoun Aim.

"Okay, Aim, shoot!" Kris said. Aim frowned unimpressed.

"I'll need you to dim your wristband. I'll also need your... dog, Aztec is it? I'll need Aztec to exit the room." As Kris prepared to protest, Aztec shot to his feet and ran out as if he'd been held against his little, dogbot will. "Now, you have forty-five minutes to complete two assignments in the Secure interface, Delta."

Three folders appeared on Kris's screen. "The first folder contains temporary passcodes and procedural info," Aim continued. *Wow*, Kris thought, *complete access to Delta?* With no further instructions Aim said, "Your time starts now." Kris stared blankly at

Aim, fully aware that asking for more information would cut into his solution time. And before Kris could process the thought, Aim's window vanished, granting an eerily trusting lack of supervision.

Kris dove in. Having already researched Delta ad nauseum, it took him under ten minutes to get the workstation running. Many prospectives undoubtedly wasted precious time on this step.

"Hey, Kris," Becky's voice croaked from the bedroom door, breaking thick layers of precious concentration.

"Becky. Out," Kris snapped without looking up. "I need the room." Didn't she know their lives were at stake, that he had no space for distractions?

"But I think the—"

"Becky, I swear to God. Out. Now!" Kris felt himself shaking as he spoke. The door squeaked shut behind him. Apologies would come later. Right now, he required all his wits. His mission: complete the two assignments in record time and use any remaining time to snoop into the personal account activities of the Maines, Leland Shark and Paul Oz.

Kris's first task was to catalog any suspicious activity in a jury teleconference. The trial in question was of Chuck Burgen —an older man who'd been caught butchering Nforce bots the previous Saturday. Anyone not among the crowdsourced Nforce App users who helped convict him could be called into the digital jury to determine his verdict. Kris noted the scenario was not a mock-up but an active case. He seamlessly identified tons of well-masked unauthorized activity that he'd never have been able to detect without Delta. Hack attempts, break-in attempts. His second task required him to quickly yet thoroughly report his findings, which Kris completed effortlessly.

Eleven minutes to spare.

Kris first performed a lookup on himself to test Delta's

accuracy on the activities of a person who hid well. Delta pulled up over seventy percent of Kris's clicks, searches, locations, purchases, and messages. He swallowed through the embarrassment. It hadn't picked up any of his darkverse movements, at least; but still.

Kris would have to tread lightly; his activity in Delta was certainly being monitored. He executed a general search of the Maine Academy, and to his chagrin, found the profile thumbnails of Titan Maine, Claudia Maine, Johnny Angelo, and a host of other search results to be unclickable. A hot burst of panic consumed him, but he made neither a sound nor a click. Not even Secure, the world's leading security firm, had tabs on the Maines. Gathering evidence on them would be near impossible.

He performed a quick look-up on Oz Corp, now knowing what to expect. No direct Oz Corp employees were clickable, including Torian Ross. Paul Oz protected his people. *Damn it.* Kris then conducted a search on Pharma Farm, but in the next instant his sharp focus escaped him. His heart raced against his chest as his mind fell blank, crowded with an immeasurable fog of dejection. He could do nothing but stare vacantly at his screen for several seconds, knowing he had to reactivate, rethink, reassess, and fast.

"Kris," called Aztec beside him. He hadn't noticed Aztec pop back in.

"Yeah, Az," Kris responded, a hint of defeat to his voice.

"You're doing it again." Kris snapped to attention and realized he'd been staring at Davia Valenti's unclickable thumbnail. Small and slightly pixelated, the thumbnail had emerged among the columns of Pharma Farm results, as Davia had recently endorsed a Pharma Farm supplement. She was beautiful: thick, dark Italian hair, dark Italian eyes. How long had he been paralyzed by her? It had been nine minutes. He propped himself up in his seat. *Nine minutes?*

He'd done it before, gawked absentmindedly at anything Davia for long lapses in time. What he felt toward her was neither hatred nor anger, but a rage so deep he'd not yet assembled an emotion for it, let alone a word.

Kris exhaled. "Az, let's pray ol White Freckles Redhead didn't notice anything weird."

The Delta window disappeared a minute later, replaced by a video call from Aim. "Congratulations," Aim said, dry as desert. "You start today at eleven. You'll be given personal passcodes and full access at that time." Kris let out a long breath and thanked Aim for what normally would have been extraordinary news. "As a welcoming gift, here's a Hampshire presence-capture cam from us to you." Kris immediately dragged the attachment pop-up onto his home screen. Any other day he'd have been ecstatic. Presence-capture cams were virtual cameras able to take snapshots IRL and reopen those shots as VR-dimensional inter-mersive stills. An app found only in the arsenals of elite cyber-wizards. Kris again thanked Aim.

"By the way," Aim concluded, "I'm your supervisor now, so I'll be keeping your last little search and stare under wraps until I need it for leverage. I'm certain I've made myself clear."

11

COUNTING CROWS

WEDNESDAY NOV 13, 186 PCE

The problem? Tory owed Paul Oz his loyalty. Though the chatverse teemed with accounts of his public philanthropy, Paul's unyielding generosity towards his staff remained private. Such was the case with Torian Ross. Two days after hiring Tory, Sherri casually asked him what he'd want if he could have anything. He'd said he'd want his two sisters and mother in America with him, away from his drug-peddling stepfather, and that he'd been trying to bring them over for years.

Within a month, Paul himself, accompanied by Tory and a small extraction team, jetted to England to retrieve Tory's mother and sisters. Each of them, once victims of domestic maltreatment, were now thriving in academics. Though evergrateful, Tory gave his best effort not to resent the debt. And now he'd betrayed Paul's trust by purposefully concealing his location pin.

To keep from envisioning the plate of crow awaiting him at his upcoming meeting with the boss, Tory spent the night researching an intriguing lead. A connection between Chuck

Burgen—a man convicted for attacking Nforce bots, and Loretta James—the woman who'd mysteriously croaked at the Bay Ridge cycling dorm. They'd both shown signs of nascent madness and had both been subjects in a neurological study conducted by Dr. Pelleher under Ferguson's supervision.

If Ferguson and Pelleher had been conducting behavioral manipulation research, an assortment of claws would certainly take interest in seizing the raw data, including Paul Oz. Tory also noted that Oz Corp—primary owner of Ncluded—would be the most capable in forcing chatboxes onto projection fields.

At 7:30, Tory placed another voicecall to his sister, again to no avail. Though it had been two years since the extraction, his siblings and mum maintained sour feelings for his supposed abandonment of them. Their snubbing of his outreach cut deep. Fortunately, his biohacks helped protect against bouts of dejection on the matter.

An unencrypted voicecall from Kris came in. A dangerous move. Kris informed Tory that, while his new job gave him access to highly sensitive information, good-old-fashioned hacking wouldn't work. Approaching the suspects would require major clout. Tory took in the news, taking care not to instinctively log the conversation into his BrainDrive. And when Kris signed off with "Seriously wishing you good luck at work today," Tory prayed he would not need it.

* * *

At eight sharp, Chief of Staff, Sherri Weiler, hustled out from Paul's office with her signature frizzy hair, tight pantsuit and active tablet. Tory admired her. She demanded respect and looked good doing it: juggling an impractical schedule while remaining a paragon of congeniality. Paul Oz had personally groomed her for perfection. As his right hand, Sherri had full access to his affairs and was allowed a healthy level of authority as his signatory-in-fact. The chatverse dubbed her #ScarySherri for her lengthy list of accolades.

"Just finished the morning briefing. He's ready for you," Sherri said, handing Tory a quick smile.

"Should I be afraid?' Tory asked.

"Only if it motivates," Sherri grinned. Tory nodded, took a deep breath and sauntered into the office. The few times he'd encountered Paul Oz IRL had been nothing short of intense.

"Torian Ross. Good morning," came Paul's polite salutation from behind a glossy desk. The meticulously organized space held a bold IRL authenticity: from the foliage, to the fish tank, to the face clock. No Smartifice dispenser, no augmented skins. Just refreshing, natural life—a hefty flex.

Paul rose from his seat, studied a glass bottle marked Dalmore Scotch on a shelf behind him, then poured liberal portions into two glasses. He offered one to Tory and gestured toward a chair opposite his desk. As they sat, Tory noticed that Paul's tailored, white Drexel and Crawford shirt put his scruffy T-shirt, jeans and arm tattoos at a startling disadvantage.

The meeting began with a long silence. Tory wasn't certain how long, considering his Glass wasn't permitted in the office to superimpose its deluge of information. Perhaps half a minute passed, during which Paul took a slow swig from his glass, folded his hands under his nose and stared into Tory. Though the seconds ticked by like hours, Tory made a point not to cow beneath the inspection. *He's just a twenty-four-year-old kid,* Tory reminded himself.

"Forty degrees, four minutes and twenty-nine seconds north." Paul coolly broke the silence, his voice a precise instrument. "Seventy-three degrees, fifty-seven minutes and thirty seconds west." Tory's ears burned at the mention of what were obviously the coordinates of his location pin the previous night.

Paul took another sip, allowed another brief silence, then said, "Entertain me."

Tory took in a mouthful of whiskey. A lifetime Smartifice subscriber, he hadn't had honest-to-God liquor in eons. His throat was ill prepared for the citrusy burn. Paul's eyes followed Tory's hands as he attempted to cover a cough. Tory cursed himself. He loathed showcasing any form of weakness in front of Paul Oz. He noted to program a tolerance for rough liquor into his person.

Paul had a low tolerance for useless chatter, so Tory put forth his best effort at succinct confidence. "I need to be allowed the freedom to do my job," he said, matching his employer's quiet resolve.

"This freedom, it should include going dark against Oz Corp?"

"If I have reason to believe Oz Corp's withholding information that I need to do my job effectively, I do what's necessary to find the info for myself." At this Paul leaned back in his chair.

"If you have a question, ask," Paul said with flippant authority. Tory subdued a smirk. Paul Oz wasn't the answer-questions type. If he didn't want you to know a thing, you simply didn't know it. Tory had a mountain of questions he needed answered, not the least of which was whether or not Paul had slept with his younger sister, Cindy. While Cindy denied it, Tory held a nagging suspicion that Paul felt claim to her for extracting her and the rest of the lot from England. Tory sucked in air to calm a simmering nerve, and once again dismissed the thought.

"I got tipped off at Dr. Ferguson's wake that he may have been murdered," Tory started. "The source was an untraceable ReBuild for which I've not been able to locate the claimant, so naturally I took the allegation seriously. The quick death, the ensuing silence, the brief news cycle...and a text—" Tory stopped. He was rambling.

"What's your question for me, Torian?" Tory suspected Paul Oz already knew and was simply baiting him.

Tory took a breath and went for it. "Were you involved in the murder of Dr. George Q. Ferguson?" He braced himself for a reaction, but Paul merely stared back at him pokerfaced.

"And if I was?" Paul asked a bit too casually.

"Then I ask you why. Then I ask myself if I'm willing to realign my values to match yours." Paul considered the response, scrutinizing Tory's face for a heartbeat too long, the slight delay his strongest display of emotion. Paul finally accepted Tory's answer with a modest nod.

"I was not," Paul said; his words now measured. "Now, you can choose to accept that, or you can choose not to. Either way you keep nothing from me." The consequent stare-down lasted an eternity. Tory used the time to reflect on how he could have been so careless in masking his location, why he'd masked his pin at all. If he hadn't, no suspicion would have been raised. Had he been out of the Guard so long to have lost his keen discipline? "Expect my request will be honored," Paul said.

"Understood," Tory ceded. To Oz Corp staff, Paul's indecipherable stare-downs were legendary, as they implied a blanket forgiveness that clearly kept tabs. Such cognitive dissonance made it difficult for Oz Corp coworkers to forge any real-life aspirations outside of striving to match Paul's unattainable perfection.

Paul spoke up. "Your other suspects?"

Appreciating the move forward, Tory withdrew his notepad, and placed it on Paul's desk, as physical contact with Paul Oz was strictly prohibited. "Maines, Pharma, Brier, trusted assistants..." Tory spouted as Paul skimmed along. "I'm sure you've others to add."

"I have my theories. With whom are you working, apart from Kris Johnson and the ReBuild?"

"No one else. Just Kris's team. They aren't exactly the A Team, but Kris isn't sold separately. We've kept it need-to-know." Tory considered for a second then added, "I also mentioned it to Rosa Lejeune."

"I'm aware of that," Paul said, displaying the tiniest, almost imperceptible hint of irritation, evidenced only in the speed of his response. Tory eagerly took note. He didn't have much on the ever-stoic Oz, but now, at the very least, Tory gathered the lovely Ms. Lejeune might be a soft spot. He chided himself for assuming Rosa would keep her mouth shut. Paul probably managed to open many things Lejeune last night. Tory again dismissed the sour thought. "Where are you right now with this?" Paul asked.

"Kris has an in at Secure. But we're looking at an uphill battle gathering field intel on the more elite prospects. I also discovered a woman who recently died on an exercycle. She and the man who'd gone berserk on bot cops were both Pelleher patients. New York has less than ten murders over the past ten years, then a swarm of fatal assaults in this one week? I'm betting there are more correlations to uncover."

"So, you'll need Oz Corp's clout and resources for your elite prospects," Paul deduced. Tory averted his gaze. "You've an interesting way of asking for my help, Torian." Now it was Tory who initiated the silence. He fidgeted with his glass, aching to indulge in more Scotch, yet fearing another rough swallow. "Other than Sherri, Dex and myself, no one else on staff is to be involved unless I involve them. I'll provide you with whatever you need, but this is not an official Oz Corp investigation and will not affect your other assignments."

"Clear," Tory affirmed. The slightest outside suspicion that Oz Corp was probing the matter could destroy years of diplomatic relations. Tory only needed Sherri to facilitate a few meetings: he could handle the rest himself. Having Oz Corp at his disposal would make things infinitely easier for Tory. Still, Paul's willingness to lend resources did not demonstrate proof of innocence.

"Kris Johnson?" Paul asked.

"He's crass, but he's smart. Fast enough to land a gig at Secure. I'd put my word on the line for him."

"Then I'd like to meet with him. Right now." Paul plucked at his keyboard.

Tory could only imagine Kris's horror upon receiving a meeting request from Oz Corp. "Perhaps, I should inform him you'll be calling."

"No need," Paul dismissed. A moment later Dex's face emerged at the top corner of the slimscreen. "Dex, proctor the direct immersion of Kris Johnson into this office. A private line. No logs. Push back my sit-down with the Ambassador."

"Of course, Paul," Dex confirmed before disappearing.

Paul looked back to Tory. "While we wait, educate me on the matter of Patrice Fan."

* * *

"Sorry I snapped, Becks. Uncool." Kris sat at his desk, keeping busy by dragging files from his wallscreen to Aztec's directory. Both DZ and Becky sat at their workstations eating printed doughnuts.

"It's all good," Becky said. "Just imagined you were talking dirty." The group let out a dry laugh.

"Guys, I gotta be honest," Kris started. "This is bad. Real bad. I'm pretty fucked if Oz Corp finds out Ross went dark 'cause of me. I'll do my best to keep y'all out the Klieg lights. Just keep your head down when shit hits the fan."

"Uhm, I don't think so," Becky said alongside a nod from DZ.

"We're all in this together," DZ signed. "We will always stand with you, Kris. Always."

"I'm in too!" Aztec added from the corner. "I'll number-crunch and smart-search and data-store until the cows come home. Unless you program me otherwise."

"Means a lot," Kris said, though he would still never implicate them. He alone had been the architect.

Like clockwork a videocall came into Kris's wallscreen.

"Speaking of Oz Corp," Aztec sang.

"Oh crap," came from Becky. "You need us to leave?"

"Nah stay," Kris breathed through a muted quaver. "Group therapy." He opened the call. Oz Corp's top bulldog, Sherri Weiler, surfaced on the screen. *That can't be good.*

"Good morning, Mr. Kris Johnson. I'm Sherri Weiler calling from Oz Corporation. How are you today?" She had a dimpled smile, spunky frizzes and an affable voice. *Definitely pure evil.*

"Friend or Foe?" Kris asked.

"Well, I personally am certainly not your foe, Mr. Johnson."

"Uh huh," Kris sighed, wishing they'd met in more auspicious circumstances. Any other day he'd enjoy pretending he was worth flirting with her. "Just tell me what your dark overlords want."

"Mr. Perry would like to meet with you in his office. Are you available for a quick direct merse?" *How could she ask that so cheerfully knowing I'm mersing to my doom?* Kris thought.

"Kris," Aztec whispered. "It's just a merse. That means they want to parlay." Kris found a modicum of comfort in this. "Although there have been cases of people trapping victims in direct merses and holding them hostage until their IRL bodies decayed." *Jesus, Az.* Kris wanted to toss the terrier across the room.

"I'm sorry, Mr. Johnson, I'll need an immediate answer."

"Can I ask you something, Sherri?"

"Shoot."

"Are you a bot?" Sherri let out an open-mouthed laugh. "That I am not. Just a regular, fleshy human. But thanks, I think."

"I ask because you're way too cheery for knowing I'm about to die."

Sherri looked off screen and nodded to someone then said, "Kris, I'm not privy to why Mr. Perry would like to meet with you, but I do know it's urgent," her smile gone. "It will be a private direct merse. I'll need your verbal consent before I can proceed."

"Sure. Fine. Like I have a choice," Kris muttered while grabbing at his VerteBrain visor. This private direct immersion would certainly be untraceable, leaving no proof it was Oz Corp who'd held Kris's avatar hostage until his IRL body decayed. He clicked the merse icon Sherri sent to his display, and he was off to see his old Fame Academy classmate.

Kris felt the temple nodes gyrate as his muscles relaxed. A direct merse, as opposed to a merse into LifeConnect, entailed the projection of a merser's avatar hologram onto another location IRL. In most cases the avatar could interact with AR skins, but passed through most IRL objects within the bounds of the projection.

Darkness around Kris materialized into a pristine office, full of prestigious awards and high-class art. The plants, the fish, the light smell of rosemary—all flawless. But not near as impeccable as the chiseled, expertly dressed gentleman behind the desk. Paul had definitely grown up since his two-year stint at the academy. He was buff. He looked like a guy to whom women would gladly toss their panties. To see him here, in his element, Kris couldn't help but respect what the once lanky, awkward kid had made of himself. There wasn't going to be a parlay. Paul Oz had already won.

"Good morning, Kris Johnson. Have a seat." *Where's Ross?* Kris thought, as he plopped onto the proffered AR chair. *Already at the guillotine?*

Paul folded his hands on his desk and fully examined Kris. A sudden ocean of panic flustered Kris, being a defenseless hologram in sweatpants. Was he being sized up for slaughter? He waited. He fidgeted. The silent psychoanalytic scrutiny seemed to last entirely too long. *Screw this,* Kris thought, recalling why he reviled Paul Oz. Paul was just another arrogant high-and-mighty. Like the Valentis. Kris was not going to succumb to this asshole. If he was going to go down, he would go down fighting.

Paul finally spoke with comfortable command. "Tell me why I should trust you."

"Fuck you, Paul," Kris spat. He tended to react to visceral fear with headstrong antagonism, a trait he'd contracted from his father. Unfazed, Paul Oz filled a glass with a fancy Scotch, took a slow introspective sip, then continued.

"Because Torian Ross put his word on the line for you, I'll offer you a second chance at that. Tell me why I should trust you." Kris didn't need anyone bestowing second chances onto him. He tried to relax and respect Ross's integrity, but Paul Oz's smugly perfect face kept him amped.

"People trust the good guy," Kris said, his words spoken more defensively than intended. "I'm good to my people. I protect my people."

"Protect them? From what?"

"From smug, rich assholes that take take take and make everyone else feel like garbage."

"And these smug, rich assholes you speak of, how is it they make your people feel inadequate?"

Kris could smell a trap but stepped in anyway. "By treating them like they're part of some second-rate species that don't also have goals and aspirations. It's my job to give 'em a place, let 'em know they're worth something, and that they deserve respect." Kris stared directly into Paul's eyes now. He would not yield to Paul's staring contest.

Paul let a lengthy silence swim by then asked, "I'm curious as to the nature of your animosity toward me, Kris Johnson."

Without missing a beat, Kris said, "'Cause you're a textbook villain. Obviously." At this Paul let out a muted snort, and Kris found himself pleased to have gotten any kind of rise out of him. "Anyone who thinks it's okay to own forty percent of the global market share is a villain. Oh, and you're so loving and giving. Jesus incarnate. The Second Coming. It's all self-righteous bullshit. Yeah, I'll say it. You ain't fooling me. I know you."

"You know me."

"Bruh. You're a privileged, born into money, white, entitled brat who gets everything handed to 'em like the rest of these one-percenter assholes. Have been since Fame. Facts are facts."

Paul took another sip at his Scotch, interlacing his fingers. "I'd like to share a personal story with you, Kris," he said. "Back when I attended Ferguson and Maine, Dr. Ferguson noticed I'd been struggling socially and advised me that a particular student on campus took in outcasts and gave them a place. So, against my better nature, I approached this student...and his people. Not only did he openly reject my appeal, he proceeded to address me with names like freak, psycho, asshole, up to about, say thirty seconds ago. So again, I'll ask you to elucidate this longstanding animosity."

Kris took in the anecdote, his mouth slightly parted, for once at a loss for words. There was no denying Paul's account. But Kris's rejection of the weirdo Norman Bates-esque wall-flower seemed so perfectly rational back then, until he heard it retold by this well-built celebrity zillionaire before him.

"Jesus, Paul," Kris began deflated. "That was like a decade ago. Your life is boss now. Why are you still holding onto that?"

"My precise question to you, Kris Johnson," That Paul Oz had even felt emotions at all was unreal to Kris, let alone the sting of rejection. Kris knew his errors, the false dichotomy. He'd rejected a freak from his band of rejected freaks. *He* was that asshole who'd made an outcast feel inadequate. *So cliché*, he thought. Underneath it all he was just bitter that Paul had overcome the snickering torment of Kris's crew to become the most accomplished and envied man on the planet. No protection necessary.

Paul waited patiently for a response, seeming to have absolutely nowhere else to be. "A bunch of rich kids screwed me over at Fame. You were an easy target to outlet," Kris started. Paul continued to wait, unmoved. "Look Paul, what do you want? I'm not one of the good guys. That what you wanna hear? I did and do bad shit and surround myself with people who aren't as privileged as me. I couldn't accept you because obviously you were better." Kris waived an arm indicating the lavish office, just then noticing he'd been shaking. "And that was self-righteous and shitty. There."

They both allowed Kris's words to hang in the balance. Paul kept his eyes hard on Kris until Kris's gaze faltered. Paul leaned back in his chair. "Thank you for sharing that with me, Kris." Kris tensed. The matter-of-factness with which Paul spoke should have upset Kris. He wasn't the type to surrender, but just couldn't bring himself to reignite. "Now that we under-stand each other," Paul continued, "I can communicate with you effectively. I can trust you to investigate Dr. Ferguson's death on my terms?"

"I owe my life to Ferg," Kris said, nerves abating. "I'm down to do whatever it takes to bring Ferg justice." Again, Paul waited. "So...yes," Kris said.

"Good. First thing's first. Clear your BitCredit account, all two hundred thousand credits, along with your hidden accounts holding roughly four hundred thousand. You'll need to award these credits to Patrice Fan. You will also issue her a written apology for violating her privacy. If she still decides to press charges, you will serve out any subsequent sentence."

"Jesus Harold Christ!" Kris exclaimed. "She's loaded. She doesn't need my credits."

"This is correct; she does not. It will accompany her severance package."

Kris flinched. *Severance?* Losing an Oz Corp position was akin to flushing a winning lotto ticket down the drain. "Fine. I mean, that's only fair."

Paul sat up straight and keyed a device on his desk. "Torian Ross will reach out to you. Enjoy the rest of your afternoon, Kris Johnson."

* * *

Kris felt his surroundings fade to black as he regained feeling in his limbs. He removed his VR headgear to find his roommates huddled around him.

"Are you all right, Kris?" blurted Aztec. "Please tell us everything, so I can begin to compile our defense."

"Guys, Paul Oscar Ryland Perry is one intense fucking dude," Kris said thoughtfully.

"What happened?" Becky asked.

Kris let out a slow sigh. "We're in."

PART II
SEEKING

1 2

ELEVATION

THURSDAY NOV 14, 186 PCE

"As we nurture, so we are destroyed."

— *DIARY OF THE MAD GLEE*

I t was her first time in an android church. The Re Church, where bots came to pray and recharge, was your average Common Era chapel save for the charger-fitted pews. After her moving experience by the Religion bookcase, Rosa longed to attend church while avoiding human contact, hence the Re Church. With Johnny Angelo on the prowl it was best to remain in public anyway.

Among a handful of androids, Rosa listened as a pastor bot prayed for anything tagged #PrayFor in the chatverse. A harsh flu breakout, causing high fever and spouts of delirium, was trending, so the pastor prayed for humanity not to have another Great Pandemic. Though she again felt hissing spectral whispers refract among the church walls, Rosa felt safe amid the bot-congregation.

Since her Oz Corp performance, Rosa's name had been

LACHI

popping up throughout the chatverse. She'd soon need an agent app to sift through it all. For now, she muted all forms of Ncluded notifications, not yet ready to face the public. Ferguson had specifically instructed her to contact Paul if she ever needed someone, and for a brief moment she thought she'd found that someone.

Oz Corp did not contact Rosa about sponsorship. She spent the better part of Wednesday coaching herself against texting Dex a barrage of maudlin messages. She'd eventually settled on a 'Hi' emoji to both Dex and Torian Ross, to which neither responded. To allay her restlessness, Rosa had busied herself with fastening Lady Maine's jewel into a necklace. She'd also taken to deciphering the blank pages of the *Diary of the Mad Glee*, attempting to read it under all manners of lighting to no avail.

It wasn't Oz Corp's apparent disinterest in sponsorship that stung. It was how their perfectly upstanding demeanor was so easily shattered by her audacity to defend her womanhood. 'Not used to not getting what you want?' The phrase rang mercilessly in her head, sparking recurrent fits of anxiety. She'd hurt him. *But did he not deserve it? No,* she thought, *he didn't.* She had no business penetrating into his deepest, darkest emotions without *his* consent.

Plagued by the memory of his whispers against her neck, Rosa couldn't shake his perfectly obsidian eyes and boyish dimples from her mind. What *was* he? His electrically charged skin. His ability to raise an empathic wall. His seething ball of dark rage. So many questions to which she would now never receive answers. She'd been put out of his mind, and she would have to accept that.

"Lejeune," came a harsh whisper to her right. Rosa clutched the necklace she'd fashioned with Lady Maine's charm, and turned to find a tall, shapely dark-skinned woman.

The woman, wearing scrubs over tight jeans, hadn't been present a moment ago. Even in the dim church lighting, Rosa detected the woman's slight translucence: a direct merse.

"Friend? Foe?" Rosa asked.

"Friend. Aliyah Davis, forensic pathologist contracted by Torian Ross."

"Okay," Rosa replied, curbing her excitement at the mention of an Oz Corp employee.

"This stays low key. My team's trucking out to the Bay Ridge morgue to get acquainted with Loretta James."

"Loretta James?"

"The old woman who cashed in at the cycling dorm. We're doing an autopsy."

"Huh? Wait. You're stealing the body?"

"No time for legit protocol. Can't go far with the corpse without triggering surveillance, so we'll need a controlled location. Seems you're staying at a hotel near the morgue, and—"

"Woah, you want to use *my* place?" A bot in the pew ahead turned to shush her. Aliyah slid to the empty side of the pew. Rosa followed.

"Need a confirm asap, Lejeune."

"Are you serious? Is she serious?" Rosa whispered to the room. She pictured the old woman's carcass rotting on her kitchen table. "I wasn't planning on entertaining guests," Rosa said.

"You mean, yes?"

"I mean, I watched her die. That does something to your gut flora."

"This may take days, Lejeune. Jump on. Be sure." Rosa didn't appreciate being rushed with something so invasive and frankly ludicrous. There would be strangers in her private space carving up cadavers, and she would be responsible for any damages, staines, hauntings.

"Is this through Oz Corp?" Rosa asked.

"Ross says he's acting independently."

"So, it's not through Oz Corp," Rosa concluded demur. Aliyah shook her head impatiently.

"Look, Paul Oz's obviously involved. He's involved in everything. If he wasn't, I wouldn't be entertaining the risk."

Rosa took a sharp breath at the mention of his name and scolded herself for being so dotty over him. She suppressed the thought of Paul alone with this bright, elegant woman, who probably already knew vacuums were actually full of quantum fields. Rosa looked down to her vibrating wristband. Aliyah had forwarded a nondisclosure agreement. Rosa sucked in a deep breath. *Here goes nothing.* "Okay then," Rosa said. "Yes."

"Sheesh," Aliyah sighed. "Groupies." Aliyah's avatar vanished before Rosa could object.

* * *

Rosa bustled through the lobby of the Bay Ridge hotel she'd been calling home determined to spruce up her suite before her guests arrived. Yes, one of them was a dead body, but she'd be damned if she was going to be judged on her pre-autopsy cleanliness. As she tapped the button for the elevator, she again felt an eerie wisp buzz past her ears. She looked over-shoulder to find nothing out of the ordinary. *I'm frickin losing it*, she thought, as she stepped into the elevator.

Rosa very pointedly did not look up as a fellow patron entered alongside her. *Ugh, other lifeforms.* She began to scroll through the chatverse on her wristband looking for #OzCorp tags, but as the elevator doors slid shut, an onslaught of dread poured over her like a thick bleak storm. No sooner did she hear a word that stopped her heart cold.

"*Cariño.*" The word sailed through the enclosed space, soft and assured. Rosa sucked in, hoping against hope that it was someone else, anyone else, as she hadn't sensed his customary energies. But it was him. Rosa looked up to find Johnny Angelo grinning back at her from the other end of the elevator. "So, where were we?" His cobalt eye stared deep into her being as his natural eye scaled her body. "Oh right, I was talking about the Maine Event, and you were busy not listening." He turned to approach her. "You never listen."

Rosa tried for a retort as she stepped back, but her shoulders slammed against the wall behind her, snatching her breath. "Loved that little number you wore at Oz Corp," Johnny sighed. "Fit you right in all the right places." Rosa simply needed to reach her arm just past arm's length so she could run her fingers down all the buttons and escape on the nearest floor. But paralysis took hold, followed by dense waves of debilitating tremors. It was claustrophobia. The four walls sliding in closer. Closer. Closer. "Think you're better than me? You dirty little Oz Corp slut." Johnny's words came sharp, filling the chamber with a mix of bitterness and Alabaster Spring cologne.

Rosa did not respond. She couldn't. She could hardly breathe. Johnny pounded hard at the door. "Think you can dump me without my required fuck? Answer me!" The entire chamber bounced and came to a jagged, flickering halt. The walls slid in closer. Closer. Johnny stepped up to Rosa, inches from her face. She tried to wrench her buckled legs, jerk her stiff arms, but the panic attack was in full swing now. Johnny placed a hand at her neck, and with his touch came a rush of that ethereal hissing.

"Mahhhh...k," came the syrupy whisper, whirling through every crevice of her bones. Was this it? Was she going to die here, drowning in a thick pool of Johnny Angelo's vindication? Squished into a paste by these encroaching walls?

Johnny leaned in close to Rosa's ear, just as Paul had done, and breathed the word "Please." But it wasn't his voice. It was Paul's voice.

That did it.

A hot fuse sparked through Rosa. She lifted her hands to her ears, shut her eyes tight and let out a gut-wrenching scream so intense, she lost her voice by the end of it.

The spell now broken, Rosa opened her eyes, prepping herself for a righteous sprint past her hulking ex. But...there was no hulking ex. Johnny Angelo was not there in front of her, his Alabaster scent gone as well. In fact, the elevator walls were as normally spaced as they'd been when she entered. Rosa's jaw dropped, her shivers still violent as ever.

"You okay, lady?" asked an unassuming teenager in the far corner. "You just started freaking out over there." As he spoke, Rosa noted a whiff of ozone. The elevator chimed, the doors opened, and Rosa shuffled out confused. *What the hell is happening,* she thought. She whirled around in adrenaline-fueled paranoia. And when she noticed the teenager stepping out and heading toward her, she bolted.

She headed for the nearest fire exit and proceeded to run down the staircase from what was apparently the seventh floor. She skipped steps and flew around the banister curves, determined to escape the choking walls of the hotel. She sped ahead with such fervent aggression, she hardly noticed herself crash headfirst into a woman carrying a pot of soup up the stairs. The woman screamed in agony as Rosa flew by. "Holy crap! This is boiling hot! Are you not in pain?"

Get outside. Get outside! All Rosa could hear was, *Get outside!*

When she finally made it to the lobby, she rushed through the front entrance. Aliyah and a small crew stood at the bottom of the front steps, fumbling with what was obviously a body bag. She looked up at Rosa genuinely perplexed.

"Woah, Lejeune. The hell happened to you?" Rosa wiped the sweat and tears from her brow, peering down at her clothes. She stood head to toe bedecked in steamed spinach and chunky meat broth.

"Soup," Rosa managed to say through short gasps.

"Here. Come hang in the van." Rosa allowed Aliyah to usher her down the block to a parked blue skyvan and settle her in. "Need anything?"

"Medication," Rosa said. "I need my medication."

"Ah," Aliyah smiled. "Oz groupies. Always a little nutty." Rosa raised an eyebrow. "Relax. I'll have someone grab your prescription." Her nerves still shot, Rosa leaned back in her seat and checked the Nforce App for Johnny Angelo's location pin. He was at the Maine Academy in New Jersey and had been there all morning.

13
TAKE THE LEAD

THURSDAY NOV 14, 186 PCE

An Oz Corp skycar hovered along the ad-lined airways of Forest Hills, Queens, approaching the massive Pharma Farm national headquarters. Dex had swiftly contrived an official Oz Corp walk-through for Torian Ross. As soon as he touched down in his signature suit jacket, jeans and Glass, a uniformed woman greeted him and his associates. She escorted them to a padlocked door, where she performed all manner of security protocol to let them in.

Once inside, two suits led them to the lobby, where an endless line of prospective visitors extended along the wall. Thankfully, the security staff allowed the Oz Corp party to forego any bioscans, as Tory's vast array of internal gadgetry would certainly set off a symphony of alarms. Tory's personal tour guide, a pale, female bowtie, eagerly approached them.

"Not a bad rack for a mousy," Kris intoned from a bud in Tory's ear. The hacker had piped in remotely, linking his workstation to Tory's Glass for schematics and security tracking, and to apparently eye-bang Pharma Farm employees. Tory had already decided he'd mute Kris if the backseat chatter began to interfere.

On the ground floor the guide pointed out the Genetic Sequencing arm where researchers streamlined personalized medicines based on individual genotypes. They next visited the Nanotechnology department and the Stem Cell halls. The staff heads at each tour stop gave Tory their full attention. Such hospitality would be true of any company fortunate enough to receive an Oz Corp visit.

By the time they'd gotten to the third floor, Tory had witnessed some mind-blowing innovations all while listening to Kris recite the heinous hacks, he'd committed for each division head. As the tour group left the Printed Cures arm, Kris said, "Shark attack, nine o'clock."

The Glass confirmed his identity before Tory recognized him. CEO Leland Shark, a slick, gray beard with dark hair and a black overcoat, hurried into a distant elevator tube. Tory immediately requested the tour guide arrange a sit down with Shark. After a quick voicecall on her wristband, the guide said, "Leland Shark will not be available for the rest of the week, but if you'd like, Ted Husk may be free after the tour."

"She's bluffing," Kris snorted, but her vitals revealed the contrary. Tory knew it wouldn't do to make a pompous fuss during an otherwise discreet visit. Opting for risk aversion, Tory settled for Husk, the press secretary for Pharma Farm and vocal Confederacy Rebirth advocate.

"I'd prefer to meet with Husk straightaway," Tory said with assumed authority.

Frazzled, the guide poked at her wrist again. After another brief voicecall she said, "Could you settle for a videochat in an hour?"

"If it's no trouble, Oz Corp would feel more welcome promptly sitting with Husk face to face."

"Of course," the guide said.

"Yeah! You tell 'em!" Kris cheered.

After another quick Ncluded swipe, the guide led them to an elevator tube, and pressed for the fourteenth floor. As the guide babbled about Pharma breakthroughs, Tory felt a buzz at his wrist. He peaked to find a 'Hi' emoji from Rosa Lejeune. Unencrypted messages could be tracked by the simplest of software. She knew that. She either had new intel or decided she wanted a higher degree of involvement. Either way, he'd deal with it later. It was Ted Husk time.

Tory's associates remained in the hall as an aide led him into Husk's office. It was rather austere. Aside from a desk, chair and large bay window leading to a patio, the office only featured three file cabinets: one by the door, one behind his desk, and one by a printed plant in the corner. A Smartifice dispenser and a rubbish bin full of printed cups stood beside a sealed door leading to either a restroom or a closet. Tory's Glass flooded with updates, reporting that Husk had been in that smaller room for almost an hour prior to the current meet.

"Well, if it ain't Torian Ross in the flesh," said the big forty-something man from behind the desk. He wore a brown leather jacket and matching Stetson. The echo of his affected drawl bounced against the empty walls as he rose to offer a firm, old-fashioned handshake. "So, what can I do ya for?" he asked, gesturing toward a chair. "Can I print ya a drink?"

"Quite all right, Mr. Husk. Not planning to impose for long." Husk nodded with an attentive smile, the kind of big smile required of an international brand ambassador. They sat. "I have a private matter to discuss unaffiliated with this Oz Corp visit."

"Go on."

"I'm sure you're aware of Dr. Ferguson's passing."

"Who ain't?" Husk's voice grew low, his vitals painting him wary.

"I noticed Pharma has yet to issue an official statement. I recognize you had your differences, but Pharma and Ferguson once had a pretty tight relationship, no? You can understand my curiosity regarding your public diplomacy."

"Mr. Ross, the good folks here at Pharma Farm have nothing but the utmost respect for Dr. Ferguson. As soon as a statement is drafted, you and the rest of the nation'll be hearing from us."

"Right." Tory scratched at his chin. "My concern is, it's been a full week since Ferguson's passing. The optics don't look good."

"Well listen, sometimes things take a li'l longer 'round here than expected, what with all the press and attention. Y'all know somethin' 'bout that over at ol' Ozzy's, right?"

"I'm sorry, Mr. Husk, I can't say that we do. Things get done on time at Oz Corp." Husk's good-natured countenance vanished. "Those opting to make statements made them." Tory said. "Those opting to pointedly remain silent made their points."

"And what point ya reckon that is exactly?"

"Well, it'll be hard to tell now that Ferguson's been removed from the equation."

"Mr. Ross, I'm not entirely sure what you're suggesting," Husk said in a threatening whisper, "but, I am sorry, I do have a client I should be attending to now."

"Really?" Tory asked.

"He doesn't. I'm in his calendar," Kris chirped.

Husk brought back a bright smile. "I wanted to squeeze ya in for a sec, Ross. Make Ozzy happy. But you can see how things get 'round here." Tory rose to his feet without argument.

"Well, I'll let you get back to it then," Tory said, offering Husk another firm handshake. "We're all good?"

"All good," both Husk and Kris managed to say simultaneously.

"Hey, next time y'all come 'round," Husk called to Tory's back as he walked out, "bring ol' Ozzy. I hear he's a riot!"

* * *

A row of large glitzy silver doors lined the dim pink hallway of the Manhattan ChatTV broadcast center. Kris and Becky sat on a bench at the end of the hall, watching as crewmembers and bot-tographers bustled about.

Sherri had worked her magic to get Becky's name drawn, ostensibly at random, for the 'Meet Brier' pick of the week. As expected, Becky was a nervous wreck, but Kris himself could hardly keep from jittering over the morning's successful infiltration of the oh-so-distinguished Pharma Farm. This was no game. And the hefty Oz Corp NDAs they'd poured over that morning only amplified the fearful excitement.

A maintenance bot came to escort the two to Michelle Briar's dressing room. They followed the android past an open filming area swarming with drone cams, roving screens, stunt bots, and holographic controllers.

"Here we are," said the android as they came to another silver door, this one with a crystal-studded *Michelle Brier* sprawled across the top. The bot knocked lightly. "Ms. Brier, your weekly fan's here for the photo."

"Becks, you're literally shaking," Kris whispered as bustles sounded from behind the dressing room door.

"I just can't believe I'm about to meet Michelle frickin' Brier!" she wailed. The door slid open, and Becky jumped as a makeup bot squeezed out holding a cup of brushes. But before the door slid shut, a tall, striking woman stepped out with long, wavy black hair, a perfectly sculpted face and plump red lips. She wore long satin finger gloves, ridiculous heels, and a black dress so tight-fitting, Kris prayed her colossal breasts would flop out at a moment's notice.

Michelle Brier, the fashion kitsch of ChatTV, hosted a gossip column that soared in popularity once she scored her Oz Corp sponsorship and consequent celebrity status. She looked down at her guests. "Which one's Rebecca?" Michelle's voice sailed over to them, maintaining that high, prissy air the chatverse had grown to both love and hate. Becky remained shook as a statue, lips a-putter. "I don't have all day, ladies."

"She is." Kris nudged at Becky. Michelle prepared to head for the Meta TV backdrop, but took a double take toward Kris.

"I know you," she said. Kris's heart lurched, and not simply because the top of her dress faltered at her sudden movement. Could she have remembered him from Fame? She'd hardly been there a full year. "Okay, let's hurry up and take this photo, people." Kris stayed behind and watched as Michelle placed an arm over Becky's shoulder and posed for the cam. Becky, proverbially soiling herself, looked like such a Herb beside the life-sized Barbie doll.

After Michelle commandeered the camera to approve and yassify certain snapshots, she and Becky returned to Kris. "Okay, come on in, ladies," she offered in a far less presumptuous tone.

Her dressing room was all decorative mirrors and velvet couches. She gestured for her guests to sit and pulled up an ottoman for herself. Kris steeled himself not to gawk at her fishnet thighs as she crossed her legs.

"So, I'm your b-b-biggest fan ever in the entire world!" Becky blurted clumsily.

"Okay. She goes. You stay." Michelle demanded snootily to Kris while applying a second coat of lip-gloss.

"She stays," Kris said as Aztec snuck out of Becky's tote bag and onto Kris's lap.

"So, commanding. I like," Michelle crooned. "Do you remember me, Kris?" She leaned forward, placing a fist under her chin. Kris winced at her mention of his name.

"Well, you were in Lady Maine's etiquette class same time as me: back when you were Mitchel and she was Madame Ferguson."

"That's all public record. He doesn't remember," Michelle pouted. "I had the hugest crush on you. And that beard! And you always had me dying. You were such a smartass to Madame Ferguson."

"I was, wasn't I?"

"And you were so sweet."

"Me? Sweet?" Kris snorted. "Now *you're* the one not remembering right."

"Hm. Guess I need refreshing on how sweet you really are then. How 'bout you give us a taste." She flashed a pearly smile.

"No, thanks. I—" The words fell out more aggressively than Kris intended. Michelle glared and sat upright and stared him square in the face. "You're seriously hot," Kris stumbled on "and obviously super smart. I'm just not—" He wised up and stopped himself.

"Aww, you're ignorant and still learning. I love that for you," Michelle simpered, her smile fading.

"My bad," Kris resigned. "Uncool, I know."

"Meh," she shrugged, flipping a stray curl from her cheek. "The age-old Cis-het bluster. As if underneath these bags of meat, we're any different. I'm over it, though."

Kris conceded. "I'm sure you get a lot o' bullshit."

"Oh please, it's as old as any -ism." Michelle switched the

cross of her legs, and again both Kris and Becky fought respective gasps. "Here's a fun one I get a lot. Some goofies believe I receded intellectually post-operation on a phrenological level, like transitioning from male to female makes you lose brain mass because women are simply dumber than men. Like that makes any post hoc sense. So, I've been compiling a whitepaper on gender identification and perceived intellect."

"Don't you already have an honorary doctorate?" Kris recalled from his reconnaissance.

"From Fame Academy," Michelle nodded.

"So, you're doing a post-op post-doc?"

"I'm doing a post hoc ergo propter hoc post-op post-doc," she snipped. Aztec howled in amusement. "Oh my God, I absolutely own this dog now." Michelle opened her arms, allowing Aztec to jump gleefully onto her lap. "Can I keep him? Can I?" she begged as she scooped him up.

"Well, he's got a chip in him. I use him for...unorthodox cyber-security work."

"You mean hacking?"

"Tomato, To-mah-to."

"More like Tomato, To-Bullshit." She puckered her lips and crooned to Aztec as one would a newborn. "Right? Isn't it more like Tomato, To-Bullshit, little guy? He exploiting you for illegal passwords, little guy?"

"It's either him or a bunch of chimpanzees with typewriters," Kris interjected.

"Ugh." Michelle rolled her eyes. "Even though I hate you, you're still so funny." Kris beamed. If Michelle hadn't been superbly out of his league and Becky hadn't been so obsessed, Kris would consider asking her out, assuming she wasn't a murderer. He hadn't had an enjoyable conversation with a woman in eons, and she was that. A woman. "Why are you really here, Kris? Oz's people set this up, so obviously it wasn't just to accompany Silent Bob over here."

"You're right," Kris said. "I'm here to talk about Ferg." Michelle bent her chin to her chest, loosening her grip on Aztec. "I know you and Ferg had differences back when you were doing press work for him. Told the chatverse he was transphobic. Now that he's passed, I'm just tying up loose ends."

"Uhm, you think I had something to do with his death? Is that why you're here?" She thought for a second then shot to her feet, freeing Aztec.

"I mean, he was your boss, then you randomly turn around and call for his head on a spike. Now he's dead." Kris was impressed with how well he held his composure.

"So, you seriously come into my private dressing room," she said with growing irritation, "utter my dead-name, accuse me of what...murder?" Michelle flitted her eyes toward the door, "And I'm supposed to let you keep breathing my air?"

"Hey now," Kris said with a placating palm. "No accusations. No bad juju. We're just talking." Kris considered for a beat. "And the dead-name? Won't happen again."

Michelle tilted her head in thought then asked, "Oz sent you, huh?" She returned to her ottoman and let out a long sigh. "Look, he had Pelleher build me a bot-double to help with video ads while I toured. Ferg caught me misbehaving with it en flagrante. I mean, come on. You said yourself, I'm smoking hot; even I can't resist myself! Michelle Brier dopple-bang? Would you not pay to see that? Anyway, I couldn't live it down, so I quit and played an -ism card. Sue me. That's the full tea. I had nothing to do with his death. Period."

"Okay, okay," Kris said. He noticed Michelle's emotions begin to flare up again. "Look, I'm just tryna find anything on who or what took out my guy, you know?"

"I know," she said, her tone thoughtful. "Ferg was like a

really good guy, Kris. I was privileged to know such a legend IRL. And I seriously regret not fixing things before he passed away. Let me know how I can help."

"Well, first off, no one can know I'm snooping around. Second, point me somewhere to snoop that I haven't already been."

"Hm...well, I'm sure you're already all up in the Maine camp," she thought aloud. "How 'bout the creepy guy, Whittaker? Pebble Whitaker. He stayed Ferg's friend despite heading up the rival SOI, Pioneer School of Innovation. By the time Ferg hired me for press, they were fighting constantly."

"Right," Kris realized. "They were old research buddies. But the Psy School's no rival. It's more for freaky Tesla types. My friend DZ applied there for his trippy 4-D paintings."

Michelle laughed. "Whittaker's obsessed with weird. Cringe weird though, like the weird secret goulash Ferg was cooking up."

"Notice anything screwy between them while you were there?"

"Girl, please," Michelle sang. "Screwy, all through. Whittaker originally wanted Ferg's help with uploading human consciousnesses into bots, but eventually the two fell out over Ferg's secrets. They went through a dudevorce after that. Stopped communicating. Definitely coulda been jealousy there."

"Well, that and Whittaker seems like the type to just pick up a machete and go to bat on a small town for no reason," Kris added. They both nodded. A knock came at the door warning Michelle she was due on set in sixty seconds. Michelle drew out a drawer from under her ottoman and pulled out a foot-long black box.

"A gift," she said, handing the box to Becky. "Okay, as you know, I starred in award-winning space porn. Yes, award-winning. So, I'm starting a new line of these." She pointed to the box expecting Becky to open it, but Becky remained petrified. "Ugh, well it's a motorized back-massager that emits a red space beam when prompted."

"Oh," said Kris. "A vibrator laser? Pretty sweet."

"We're going to call them Blazers. That's an autographed pre-release."

"Th-Th-Thank you!" Becky managed to say through tearing eyes.

"You're welcome. Enjoy it, Rebecca."

* * *

Later that night Tory rounded up Kris and his cohorts for an emergency merse. And though Tory insisted she enjoy her evening off, Sherri Weiler volunteered her presence as well. Everyone was to merse in and scavenge the precise 3-D virtual mockup of Ted Husk's office that Kris had taken with the Hampshire presence-capture camera he'd linked to Tory's Glass. Ted Husk was obviously hiding something, so a direct mockup of his office was a good first place to go fishing.

14

FARMER'S MARKET

THURSDAY NOV 14, 186 PCE

While DZ and Becky took to the file cabinets, Ross and Sherri Weiler rummaged through the desk drawers of the dim office mock-up. Too exhausted to deliver his A-game, Kris retreated to silently riffling alongside DZ.

Kris marveled at the powers of the inter-mersive presence capture. The capture didn't allow for opening the patio door, but it did capture the entire room with micrometer-accuracy, even catching the differentiations of ink on a page buried in a filing cabinet. The office doors could slide open to reveal the adjacent hall, but the capture blurred anything further. While Kris hadn't noticed a baseball bat by the doorway earlier, the presence capture did. The capture did not, however, pick up organic forms such as Ted Husk's being. And though thoroughly secure, Kris still felt an eerie sense that they were being monitored.

Ross, who'd busied himself with decoding the calligraphy of a worn notepad, tasked Kris to go investigate the lock-screen area, as someone appeared to be having trouble mersing in. Ross had given the capture's entry code to Paul Oz, so Kris figured it was another Oz Corp nobleman. He tapped at his wrist and exited into the capture's lock-screen region, an electric blue VR vastness featuring only a two-dimensional number pad that seemed to always face its observer.

Once established in the unwieldy realm, Kris looked up and stopped short as his eyes settled on the avatar of his old acquaintance, his ride-or-die. Wearing a jasmine-colored charm over an outdoorsy tank, Rosa was still a vision. The toffee skin, the long legs. But her eyes were less defined, puffy from recent tears. He wanted to feel for her, to have missed her. But a bitter rush of resentment came first. "Fancy meeting you here," he spat, his voice echoless in the lock-screen chamber.

"Let's not, Kris."

"Oh no, of course not."

"Look, Saint Peter, if you're gonna gatekeep, I'll just merse back out." She tugged at her Ncluded.

"So, you gave Paul what he needed, and he gave you an Oz Corp sponsorship?" He waited for a response. Received none. "Which dropped first his dime or your skirt? Hell, did he even ask, or was he your first stop after getting kicked out the escort industry?"

Rosa winced. "I'll carve off some flesh. That what you want?"

"You know what? Even though I was a whole giving tree to you, I never asked for anything from you. But with the way you toss yourself around, I really, seriously should have."

Rosa let the statement hang. She took a breath and asked, "Friend or Foe?"

Kris finally let his shoulders relax. He could see she'd been through a lot and didn't need his disapproval of her life choices piled on top. "It's good to see you, Roe."

"Good to see you too, Shorts."

"I actually just go by Asshole now."

138

"Finally took the plunge?"

"Heh. Shitty pun." Kris began punching in the code to the office capture. "Hey listen. Next time you wanna piss off for five years without saying bye, do me a favor; send a text." Before Rosa could protest, their surroundings metamorphosed into Husk's office. "Ladies, Gentlemen, TGNC and whatever Tory is...I present Ms. Rosa Lejeune," Kris announced. Rosa looked around, surprised at the array of characters before her.

Sherri Weiler sounded off a warm welcome, her frizzy halo bobbing at her cheeks. DZ greeted Rosa with a long wave while Becky simply stared. Rosa had once been part of their crew, but had left the circle when Ferg took an interest in her.

"Hi," Rosa said, managing to avoid all eye contact. She'd once been an uplifting spirit, a force of positive energy, but Johnny Angelo had torn it all out of her. Kris regretted greeting her with such harsh rebuke and handed her a few folders to sift through.

"Lejeune. News," hailed Ross, now squatting over sheets of crumpled paper on the floor.

Rosa rummaged through her Ncluded to enable her speech to caption before she spoke. "The news is, there are two women having tea in my kitchen; only, one's carving up the other one."

"Brilliant," Ross said. "What's the latest?"

"Before I left, Aliyah mentioned something going haywire in Loretta James's brain. So, they'll be doing some neuroimaging."

"In her brain?" Kris asked, recalling the recent bizarre flu outbreak. Those infected complained of massive headaches.

"They kept saying, 'She's filled with it. She's filled with it,'" Rosa continued. "I wanted to stick around and ask what 'it' was, but... the smell. So..."

"Hey Ross," Weiler called, now seated behind the large desk. "Any reason why Husk's got two VerteBrains in a bottom drawer?" Kris caught an eye-roll from Rosa at Weiler's interjection before she stowed away silently in an empty corner. Ross shuffled over to appraise the visors.

"He'd need two headsets for hosting IRL collusion sessions post-merse," Ross inferred. "Husk values the privacy offered IRL, the lack of cyber-trails, evident in his paper filing system." He positioned two pieces of scrap paper onto the desk before Sherri, shined a penlight and said, "Case in point."

Sherri squinted to read the first sheet aloud. "Something something 'stop at nothing to' something something 'age defying sap...Don't know why he won't hand it...' I think it says... 'over'?" Everyone stopped shuffling to listen. Ross shined his penlight over the second sheet.

"You like that; you'll love this."

Sherri struggled through the second sheet's scribbles. "'Have Husk turn BV on Ferg like M&Ms.' Hm."

"M&Ms: Titan, Lady," Ross concluded. "BV: Bianca Valenti." Kris stiffened, breathing through the mention of the Valentis. "Even the smell of Husk's jacket was sniveling," Ross spat, his English lilt coming to the forefront. "After Pharma denigrates Ferguson in the 'verse to no avail, they strategize to sick the Valenti empire on him. All for this age defying sap."

"Ferguson and Lady Maine have always looked very young," Sherri remarked. "They said Lady is eighty, but she looks well under forty. I'm fairly certain she's actually a hundred and twenty."

"The Valentis stay young-looking as well," Ross added. "And with Bianca and Lady trapped in a forever-war veiled in endless treaties and trade-secret exchanges, having them unite against Ferguson only allows for one outcome."

"A lab accident," Sherri hummed, reevaluating the scraps.

"This won't open," Becky informed, rattling the lever handle of the closet.

"The capture won't allow for opening the closed door to a separate vicinity," Kris said. "Must be a newly added bathroom or something though 'cause it's not in the schematics."

"Hm," Ross puzzled, examining the door. "An old-fashioned key-lock is overkill for a personal restroom and underkill for a private safe. There's nothing precious behind that door, but certainly something worth keeping from Nforce scans."

Rosa crawled over to Kris, handed him a folder and whispered, "Check this out." Kris turned to her and on a stray impulse trailed his eyes down her smooth legs. She shoved the folder at his chest and frowned so hard, he could hear it. The folder's handwritten label, which read 'On Leland,' instantly piqued his interest. The document was the printout of a YouSpace page that must have been a century old.

"Uhm...got some real crazy shite here, folks," Kris said. He headed over to the desk and planted the printout under Ross's penlight. Both Ross and Weiler stared at the sheet wide-eyed. On the page sat a profile thumbnail of a young man, definitely Pharma Farm CEO Leland Shark. But beneath his picture read the words: Leland Ferguson (Deceased).

"So...Leland is Dr. Ferguson's son," Weiler stated for the record. "I spent a summer working a project under his supervision and marveled at his intellect. I see now where he got it."

"YouSpace folded decades ago," Becky chimed as she hunched toward the desk.

"Explains the life-long personal vendetta between Pharma and Ferguson," Ross noted.

"Why delete his past self?" Rosa puzzled, disinterested in taking credit for the find.

"Perhaps that past version of himself was getting old, losing clout, tired of living in daddy's shadow," Ross said with a finger tracing down the page. "Everyone felt entitled to Ferguson's secrets. The secret is a longevity cure and this man, his son, was willing to stop at nothing to get it."

Weiler placed a finger on the printout as well. "I've worked with Leland. I don't see him murdering his own father."

"People are fucked up," Kris blurted, reacting to the proximity of Ross and Weiler.

"Okay." Ross straightened up. "Regroup. The Valentis have their tentacles in everything but are so private we have no way in. The Maines have close ties with them and are more accessible." Ross turned toward Rosa.

"Lady Maine hasn't consorted with Oz Corp since we rejected her partnership offer," Weiler offered.

"We'll have to tread carefully with the Maines, and—" Ross stopped for a moment and seemed to listen for something. He tapped at his wrist, quickly sifted through a control panel of icons, then continued. "Kris Johnson, I'm sending you back to Pharma. You've got the schematics. This VR evidence is no good to us, we need hard copies."

"You want me to break into Pharma Farm, walk right up to Ted Husk's office, and dig through his unmentionables?"

"Get yourself in and out undetected. You've got his calendar and office layout."

"On it," Kris saluted. The proposal was hands-down impossible, but if Ross trusted Kris could do it, so much so that it was a simple command, then Kris had no excuse not to trust in himself.

"We've also got to chase the Pebble Whittaker lead," Ross said. "Wouldn't put murder past someone Planet Magazine described as a 'certifiable headcase.' Problem is, Whittaker doesn't talk to strangers. Not sure how we'll get close to him."

"Everything's political with Whittaker," said Weiler. "If we can devise a reason for Oz Corp to meet with Psy Institute, I can get you a sit-down. Paul hasn't spoken to Whittaker since leaving Fame, specifically to respect Ferguson's advice on keeping a healthy distance."

A beep sounded from DZ's wrist to get everyone's attention. "I recently applied," he signed. All eyes flew to the letters dangling before him. "I recently applied to Whittaker's Pioneer School of Innovation arts program. I aced the application but still got a rejection letter."

"Psy's a tough school to get into," Ross assured.

"Bro, you haven't seen this kid paint," Kris said. "It's some 4-D, high-precision, augmented reality meets physical colors shit. He didn't get rejected 'cause it's a tough school. It's all about connections with these hoity-toities."

"My family has no name," DZ added.

"Perfect then," Weiler said. "People love diamond-in-the-rough stories. Get me your transcripts and portfolio. I'll set up an Oz Corp sponsorship and get Ross a sit-down as soon as tomorrow if Whittaker's free."

"Would..." DZ hesitated, the folder shoved under his elbow revealing a quiver. "Would Paul really sponsor me?" Kris understood DZ's trepidation. He too had been among those who'd rejected Paul back at the academy.

"Upon my advisement, yes," Weiler said. While no trace of braggadocio touched her words, Kris saw it in her eyes. Ross and Weiler were intimidating paragons of Oz Corp excellence, and Kris was proud of his quiet friend for speaking up to them. Though just a tiny chess move in this hefty game, DZ would get into one of the best schools in the nation and sponsored by the top firm in the world.

Rosa sat up abruptly. "Congratulations on your Oz Corp sponsorship DZ." Her words came sharp and awkward and just a bit too forced. Everyone looked to her. Kris wasn't sure if others could tell, but he knew what it looked like when she was wholly embarrassed. She slinked back to her corner.

"Paul Oscar may have to be involved in this play," Weiler said to Ross. "Whittaker may require his presence."

"Right," Ross agreed. He paused for a moment, again listening for a distant sound. Was an outsider tampering with the merse? Ross went on. "I'll need someone to hit the streets, go into the cycling towns and scope out the Ascetes. I want more on this brain flu outbreak, and how it relates back to Rosa's houseguest. According to my intel the cases are centered around these areas."

"Only someone accepted by Ascetic communities can speak with them," Weiler followed up.

"Me and Deez can talk to the Ascetes," Becky said. The difference in confidence-level between Kris's gang and the Oz Corp monoliths was painful.

"Yeah, my mom's house is in an Ascete town," DZ added. "I'm still kind of accepted there. I can ask around about the—"

Suddenly there was a strange visual shift within the capture, a ripple in the field, as if someone had thrown a rock into a sea of the merse's particles. Everyone stiffened. Ross prepared to speak, but the ripple recurred, this time lingering a bit longer. Kris looked at his hands as the wave passed through and watched his fingers flail side to side like cilia. Kris knew this low-level hack. It was a hard merse-rip most likely set by a malicious spider. Errors buzzed throughout the ceiling.

"All right people," Ross announced. "Time to shut it down. Sherri Weiler will set up the sponsorship. If all goes well, I'll be off to Whittaker's. Kris Johnson, make plans to visit Pharma; Lejeune, you've got the autopsy at your place. DZ and Becky, you're hitting the streets. Everyone clear?" Everyone nodded. "Okay. Merse out."

* * *

Rosa sat knees to chest on an old couch in the backroom of Sandy's Coffee Shop in MetaLife, not particularly anxious to return to her coroner suite IRL. As she awaited Kris's immersion, Rosa opted against reliving the elevator episode, and instead introspected on her once-formidable friendship with Kris. They'd known each other since childhood, having both grown up in the same South Bronx Ascete town. When mom blamed her for dad's abandonment, Rosa took to spending most of her childhood at Kris's.

Rosa eventually returned the favor by recommending him to Ferguson for admittance to Fame. She'd also advised Ferg against Kris's expulsion following the Davia incident. The pair grew infamous for their legendary banter and their proclivity to championing underdogs. But eventually, inevitably, Kris professed love; Rosa awkwardly declined. And her later involvement with resident jock, Johnny Angelo, introduced an unforgivable wedge between them.

"You awake?" Kris said, two coffee cups in hand. He offered her a cup and plopped down, allowing a comfortable distance between their avatars. "Careful. It's hot."

"I thought you might not show," she said as she straightened up.

"You're the one who left, Roe."

"Let's not talk about that yet." Rosa removed the coffee cup's lid and gulped down the piping hot brew in two swigs. Merses allowed for the perception of all senses. Yet though her tongue felt the heat, her brain receptors didn't register pain. Kris curled a brow at her.

"Maybe try enjoying it," he said.

"It's just ones and zeros."

"And the occasional ternary gray code," Kris needled. Rosa shrugged. Hot beverages never seemed to register properly for her. Kris went on. "You keep up with avoiding logical fallacies like Ferg taught us?"

Rosa harrumphed. "So, because I worked for an escort service, you assume ipso facto, I don't keep up with what I learned?"

"Right, so that's what we call a straw man argument," Kris patronized.

"Quit being an ass, Shorts."

"And that's what we call ad hominem," Kris said. Rosa prepared to toss her empty cup in his direction. "Ferg said if we don't keep watch on our fallacies, we'll become victims to our own arguments."

"Yeah? Well, that's an appeal to authority."

"Touché," Kris said. "Tou-fucking-ché." Kris smirked and gave a nod of approval as he sipped at his cup. Rosa smiled back. It felt good to smile. "Missed you, Roe."

"I missed you too, Kris. I really did."

"Talk to me, Roe. I mean...why'd you disappear on me?" Rosa leaned back. She knew Kris well. He never let anything go without understanding the why.

"I just needed to Schrodinger's cat it for a while, you know? Be there and not there."

"You mean be assumed dead and not dead. Ever consider how that might affect me?"

"It's not your moral obligation to account for every human being on the planet, Kris."

"Oh, don't give me that bullshit, Roe. We were best friends."

Rosa turned away and fiddled with her charm, reacting to the word *were*. "You saw my life," she said. "Everyone in the 'verse saw my life. I was standing there like Buridan's ass at a Morton's fork: either disappear and leave everyone behind, or keep descending into the crippling abyss of Johnny Angelo." It felt cathartic to finally speak the words. It felt necessary. "Making a choice at all was a huge achievement. If I'd stayed out there in the public eye, I'm not sure I'd have survived it."

"Of course, I get that, Roe. But why didn't you come to *me*? You know I'd be there for you."

"I..." Rosa looked to her knees. "I couldn't face you." They allowed the words to dangle midair. He'd warned her against Johnny Angelo, and naturally she'd dismissed it as frivolous jealousy.

Kris took another sip before moving the conversation along. "Guess I can't blame you. I'm an asshole. I live off 'I told you so's." They both let out a needed chuckle. "I'm sorry you didn't think you could come to me, Roe."

"I was just scared and irrational. I should have reached out."

"Why'd you leave Ferg's protection in the first place? He kept Johnny from you."

"I know. But Ferg kept Heisenberging me."

"What the hell is Heisenberging?"

"You know. He kept trying to force me to settle in one spot while I was trying to hustle, then kept trying to push me to hustle whenever I settled down. I can't move and stay still at the same time."

"Wow, that's a really complicated word."

"Yeah well, Ferg was really complicated. So, I had to leave."

"And now, tada! Look where it got you. Starting over. You're like a hummingbird: you can't walk forward, but you can fly backwards."

"Hey!" Rosa snapped. "Well, you're like a cockroach: you can survive without a head somehow."

"Woah. Now that's below the belt. You know I'm short. How 'bout this: you're too tall. Take that."

"Well, elephants may not be able to jump, but when we die, we die standing."

"Nice!" Kris clapped over his cup. "Pretty good for out-of-practice."

Rosa's good nature faltered. "I can't help but feel like a big idiot though. I definitely made a fool of myself at Oz Corp."

"Oh. Well, Paul Oz ain't no cakewalk."

"Nope," she whispered. She felt her body tense at the thought of him. His buzzing fingers against her skin, those eyes after she'd rejected him. His deep-seated ball of whirling darkness.

"You know you can talk to me, Roe," Kris said. And waited for her to breathe through a sudden fit of chills.

"He brought me to his apartment and he..." she started quietly, making sure no one else in the empty backroom could hear. "You know, he tried to..."

Kris sat at attention, placed down his cup and faced her. "What did he do to you, Rosa? Did he hurt you?"

"No. In fact he was weirdly polite about the whole thing. It's just, he wanted more than I was willing to give, and I'm fairly certain the term 'no' doesn't directly translate in his lexicon. Needless to say, I didn't come out feeling the victor." She let out a nervous laugh, neglecting to mention her nonconsensual foray into Paul's inner being and her subsequent attack at his pride.

But she did have undeniable, paranormal empathic abilities. Constantly battling and tempering those abilities kept her from ever truly relating to anyone. The only being with whom she'd ever felt a glimpse of genuine, substantial, albeit inexplicable, connection was Paul Oscar.

"What I tell you 'bout these white boys, Roe?" Kris said in earnest. Rosa wrinkled her face exasperated. "I'm just sayin', you sure know how to pick 'em."

"Is this some kind of advice?"

"Okay, okay. Look, if Paul or anyone ever makes you feel small, you stand up. Microaggressions are the stuff of micro-ass people, and you, Rosa, are an elephant. Be the elephant in the room." Rosa nodded as Krises words struck a tiny but resonant chord in her. "'Member how we used to rip on that kid so hard back at Fame?" Kris chuckled.

"I never did," Rosa sputtered, cutting short any sardonic nostalgia.

They both said nothing for a moment before Kris finally let out a pensive sigh. "Jesus, Roe, you had such a fire in you before Johnny. You were frickin' unstoppable. Nobody slept on Rosa. Even Mount Venom couldn't take you out."

"You're right. I'm not who I was." Another brief silence. Rosa was once a headstrong powerhouse of social justice, fraternizing with the popular and underprivileged alike. But she was young and untested then. Now she seemed to be drowning under the weight of her empathic curse. "My freakouts are getting worse," she said, just above a whisper.

"You still on the horse pills?"

"Yeah. TBH, I might up the dose. I could handle it in hiding, but now that I'm out it's...it's just a lot."

"You think about talking to someone?" Kris asked. Rosa thought she was talking to that someone right now. "You know, you now also have access to the topmost transhuman GOAT in the country who also happened to have served in the Terra-Guard. You should talk to Torian Ross 'bout those PTSD micro-dose inserts people been raving about."

Rosa considered this for a moment, but she could never open up to another human being about her empathic condition. The little she'd shared with Kris was already the toughest thing in the world. "How's Becky and DZ?" she asked suddenly, eager to change the subject.

"They're good. Come back and join the fam, Roe. We *got* each other."

Rosa smiled a sad smile. As much as she enjoyed belonging to something, she'd outgrown the down-at-heel collective. "That really does sound nice, Kris. But I don't know. I'm still out here chasing the dream."

"I hear that. But you may wanna work on that foot in mouth disease you got first." Now Rosa did toss her cup at him. "Hey! All I'm saying is stop eating Smartifice dribble. Scientifically proven to cause depression and erotic behavior."

"I actually have been cutting down," Rosa smiled. "Hey, thanks for this, Shorts. When this is all over, I want to hang IRL."

"'Course, Roe," he said. "Just promise me you'll get that fire back, you know?"

"Yeah," Rosa exhaled. "I promise." She watched as he carefully sipped more steaming coffee. It felt nice reviving such a close friendship. Though he was a different being than her, was not an empath like her and could never truly fill that void in her —no one could. Still, it felt nice.

15

TO SURVIVING WHITTAKER

FRIDAY NOV 15, 186 PCE

The flight attendant filled Tory and Paul Oz's champagne flutes with a Pernod Ricard Perrier-Jouët. The pair of them reclined on leather seats at the rear compartment of a skyjet while two armored guards played Nforce App up front. Paul leaned in to clink glasses with Tory as the attendant shut the divider behind him.

"To surviving Whittaker," Paul toasted before taking a sip. Tory followed suit. It had been over a year since he'd relished the fizz of true carbonation. He could almost hear many tiny particles popping on his tongue before jumping merrily down his throat.

"Hear he's quite the interesting card," Tory said. An understatement. His reconnaissance painted Whittaker as such a paranoid recluse that Tory cautioned against wearing his Glass.

"I advise you not to partake in any refreshments he offers," was Paul's solemn response. He tapped a button, causing a wide slimscreen to descend before them, comfortably alerting Tory to his disinterest in small talk. Tory looked out his window to watch the bustling skycars swirling along skypaths surrounded by colorful Oxytrees and floating ads.

A particularly bright yellow ad flashed fiercely at almost every street corner. Tory assumed them PSAs advising jackets. It was November, so the weather would finally start dropping below ninety. However; on closer inspection, Tory noticed the ads warned, 'Stay Indoors.'

"What the hell?" Tory muttered. The flu outbreak had harsh symptoms, but had it gone so wild as to require such cautionary notice?

"...And here with us live is Christen Monar," pronounced a voice from the slimscreen, "chief correspondent for the CDC. Christen?" Tory found the screen split between a location map and a dark-haired woman standing before the CDC headquarters. Beneath her broadcast flowed the infinite scroll of chatverse commentary.

"Thanks, Leslie. It appears a small influenza outbreak has taken hold of parts of New York City. Because there hasn't been a case of the flu in decades, the CDC is taking it quite seriously. We encourage everyone to wear masks when outdoors and advise anyone experiencing any symptoms to put in a ticket to their Doctor Kiosk. We can't yet confirm the number of cases, but the CDC is already taking control of the situation. There are no plans for quarantine at this time. Leslie?"

"Thanks, Christen. The chatverse has taken to calling it the 'brain-ache,' with those exhibiting symptoms being referred to as 'Infecteds,' and boy are people—" Paul Oz switched the station. A black screen bearing a single white treble clef beneath the text "Common Era Jazz Music, A Gershwin Medley."

"You don't mind, do you?" Paul asked. Tory shrugged and returned to his window. But he did mind. An infectious disease threatened to fubar the city. Had Paul Oz no interest in whether this 'brain-ache' correlated to Pelleher's clinical trials? Tory could easily watch the remainder of the broadcast on his Eyesearch, but that was hardly the point.

Tory's relationship with Paul had been so expertly strained. But apart from Paul's de facto authority over him, Tory maintained healthy trepidation for a more personal reason.

In a memory often suppressed, Tory had witnessed an aspect of Paul Oz he wasn't meant to see. It was when they'd extracted Tory's family from their drug-lord stepfather in England. Paul had Tory lead the rescue team as they freed his mum and older sister from a desomorphine cookhouse. His stepdad had been out on business at the time, but Paul allowed for the team to savagely beat the minions they found. Hours later the team uncovered a closet in a hidden cellar. Within the closet they found a malnourished Cindy Ross. And though the ghastly sight of his baby sister brought Tory to near heaves, what Tory witnessed next forever chilled him.

What Paul Oz had done next.

"We're here," called the attendant. The bodyguards escorted Tory and Paul to the front gates of Pebble Whittaker's East Side mansion where an array of androids ushered them straight to his office. The mansion, with its rickety wooden banisters and lacquered floors, smelled antiseptic yet dungy, like a nineteenth century haunted house.

"Ooh, is it them?" a high yodel roared from behind the office door. "Oh, do let them in! Do let them in!" An android opened the door to the dim, cluttered living space. Neatly arranged scientific knacks adorned the walls while disorganized papers and gadgetry peppered the desk.

Pebble Whittaker sat upright in a wooden rocking chair, wearing black knee breeches, a vest and jacket, and a jabot lace cravat, as if he'd been transported straight from the Mayflower.

He simply needed a felt hat over his sleek black hair and to shape his mustache puff, and he'd be well on his way to typical Common Era slave owner.

With one hand petting a black poodle on his lap, Whittaker gestured for his guests to perch at a couch opposite him. As they sat, a flamboyant outburst of high-pitched giggles escaped him.

"Pardon our manners," Whittaker began in a slithering somewhat minacious tenor. "We'd shake your hands, but Shotzie and I've just taken breakfast and are prepping for brunch." The words came with the illusive superiority one would expect from an out-of-touch, cloistered highbrow. He took up his dog's paw and waved it.

"Thank you for receiving us on such short notice, Mr. Whittaker," Paul responded. "No need for apologies." Paul gestured to Tory. "My associate, Torian Ross." Tory gladly accepted the backseat. The whole thing was just *creepy*. A barely contained madness.

"Well, Mr. Paul Oscar Ryland Perry. I hear you're doing well, what with BitCredit further solidifying itself and with the spread of Ncluded to the Turk states. Bravo, young grasshopper. Bravo."

"I am doing exceptionally well. Thank you. I hear the Institute has recently acquired several patents."

"Yes," Whittaker said thoughtfully. "Indeed, we have." He brought his lips to his poodle's mouth and kissed the dog more intimately than Tory felt appropriate. "We've finally gotten a patent for my physical consciousness prototypes," Whittaker prattled in a fit of excitement. "I want to dive in like a junkyard tornado and build men, replace all parts with undying materials like Theseus's ship, so the only thing left to distinguish one's identity is one's own life signature!" Both Tory and Paul nodded politely. "Oh, Paul," Whittaker crooned. "I remember when you were just an itty-bitty boy. Now you're a very beautiful man. One could categorize you as...appetizing? I should have you over for dinner sometime." Whittaker exploded into a deafening guffaw that lasted all of two seconds and ended abruptly with a harsh sniff.

"I'm well aware of the type of cuisine you fancy, Mr. Whittaker. I'm here to talk."

"You? Talk?" Whittaker torpedoed through a terse paroxysm of glee. "Well then...to what do I owe the pleasure? You don't honestly expect me to believe you emerged from the Land of Oz, your sanctum sanctorum, just to bore me with talks of sponsorships."

"It's my understanding you only accept business calls."

"Everything in life is business, Sir Oz."

"I want Dean Zapata in Psy."

"We have absolutely no space for new applicants at the moment," Whittaker hissed indignantly. Paul immediately prepared to rise.

"It appears I've taken up too much of your time, Mr. Whittaker."

"Now wait just one minute, my boy," Whittaker laughed. "You've come all this way. Do stay for cream corn truffle and pompous banter. I'm enjoying you." Paul remained at his seat's edge, his eyes intent on Whittaker. He would walk. Paul wasn't the type to oscillate. "I love how hard you drive your...bargains, but you didn't let me finish. The Pioneer School of Innovation is a Hilbert's Hotel of sorts. We have absolutely no room at the inn. But for those I deem favorable, spots have been known to miraculously manifest."

"Manifest a spot for Dean Zapata," Paul coolly demanded.

"And what do I receive in return?"

"This afternoon of riveting conversation."

Whittaker bounced in his seat with a chirp. "Properly vetted I assume?" he asked.

"To my standard."

"Fine then. Done. Getting in bed with you, Sir Oz, is an opportunity I could never let slip. But I will not speak to him until he impresses me," Whittaker scoffed.

"Reasonable," Paul said, relaxing his stance. Tory smirked at the absurdity. Rich-old-boy's-club-speak. How easily they bought and sold people they hardly knew. "I'm here to discuss other matters," Paul continued.

Whittaker rocked in his chair with the excited eyes of a child. "Oh! Will Shotzie and I be getting to know you and your scrumptious friend a little better?"

"Not in the way I presume you'd prefer, Mr. Whittaker."

Whittaker let slip a hedonistic purr. "Hmm. Oh, how I wish you appreciated my magniloquent humor, keeping things a trifle, you know, Kafkaesque atop my mind's theater. But you? Alas. You're so charmingly tame." Again, he kissed at his poodle's mouth. "Very well then, talk away."

"I expect this discussion to remain within these walls."

"Naturally."

Paul wasted no time with circumlocution. "Your thoughts on Dr. Ferguson's death."

"Oh, that stupid old fool," Whittaker spat. He patted his dog who'd reacted poorly to the outburst. "Did *you* murder him? Everyone seemed to have been trying."

"We're operating under the assumption that I did not, Mr. Whittaker."

"Ha! Well, Shotzie and I strongly advised George not to tinker with that Indigo. We told him it would cost him his ever-so-precious life. The Doubting Thomas dismissed us as armchair critics, but as per usual, Shotzie and I were right." He let out a maniacal cackle, his pointy nose dancing between epicanthic folds. "When he mentioned Indigo interacted with the TPJ, I wanted in. It sounded like mind control, and nothing propels me more than being entertained at another's expense. But as was his way, he got protective, ignored my warnings, and now the worms are having quite the banquet."

Tory sat upright. There was that word again, Indigo. He hadn't been able to find anything online defining the term in a chemical context. After a furtive waltz of the eyeball, Tory subvocalized TPJ into his Eyesearch.

It stood for the 'temporoparietal junction' part of the brain, which is attributed to self-versus-other distinction, religious beliefs, and out-of-body experiences. It was also dubbed the 'God Module' by popular media.

As Tory downloaded the wiki to his BrainDrive, a comely young blond in a short blue dress entered the office. She presented a small breakfast table and ceramic bowl filled with odorless food. "My wife," Whittaker said with a hint of contempt as she set the table between them.

Tory hid his disgust at the age difference, but the contents of the bowl proved far more revolting. Despite his programming, Tory swallowed a heave of regurgitation, fairly certain the bowl was brimming with tiny, warm *finger segments*.

Whittaker snapped and the woman quickly stood at attention. "Have Miranda bring cream corn truffle and Brandy," he barked, and the woman scurried off. *Goodness, he had her hypnotized.* Tory suddenly felt on edge in the man's presence. How he managed to maintain such high social rank remained a mystery to Tory. Whittaker grinned at Paul. "Finger food?"

"We're not here to indulge," Paul said courteously. "But thank you, Mr. Whittaker, for the offer."

"Perhaps when you're in a more experimental mood," Whittaker chortled. Tory curbed another gag as Whittaker placed a few finger bits into his mouth, only to feed some to his poodle. "Beef tartare," Whittaker announced through his mouthful. He looked to Tory then said to Paul, "Why the arm candy?" Tory didn't appreciate being addressed in third person.

"Torian Ross is my Chief Crisis Officer. I respect his analytical and investigative skills." Tory bit back a surge of pride.

"Does it speak?" Whittaker sang. "I want to hear it speak. Say something." The command came somewhat puerile in manner, but Tory played along.

"Your pin history puts you here the night of Ferguson's death," Tory said.

"Oh, I like the directness. And it comes with an accent?" Whittaker said to Paul. "Do get me one for my next dinner party." He turned to Tory. "Yes. I was here playing Yahtzee with Shotzie."

"You and Dr. Ferguson were close," Tory went on. "But you cut communication with him once you took issue with his Indigo research."

"Ha! Everyone took issue."

"And why's that?"

"Hmm." Whittaker lifted his poodle to cross one leg over the other. "Tell me, young Sherlocks, how much do you know?"

Paul sat upright. "We've come to you to be enlightened," he said.

"Oh my," Whittaker chuckled. "Enlighten you I shall. But you, Sir Oz, must promise Shotzie and I claim to your beautiful corpse once the subsequent odyssey kills you like it killed old George."

"If I decide to have an open casket, you may attend and salivate," Paul joked. Whittaker shattered with mirth.

"For shame!" he bellowed with a sudden jerk at the shoulder. Tory couldn't begin to wrap his head around the depravity of the joke, let alone find the humor. "It all began with that

pesky EMP attack back in 162. Lousy Kremlin or whoever."
Whittaker slammed down a fist to his poodle's disliking. "Twas
the year you were born if I'm not mistaken, Sir Oz?"

"Correct."

"Everyone knows the details: three-day power outage;
commoners go missing. Some return; others don't. Pelleher
went skulking around the EMP's origin site in downtown
Manhattan and discovered traces of Indigo residue in Battery
Park. While the particles hardly obeyed any age-old laws in the
lab, he was able to concoct a detector, and detect it he did,
mounds of it soaking all of lower Manhattan." Another hiccup
of glib amusement.

"Pelleher's tests," Paul added. "They tested Indigo against
different isotopes and were planning to test with the collider."

"Like the insurmountable parliament of fools they were,"
Whittaker snarled. "The collider, the vacuum chamber. Hell,
I'd be surprised if Pelleher hadn't added it to his morning tea."

"Had they done any human testing with Indigo?" Tory
asked.

"Oh, George was testing all sorts of things on those poor
TF fools. His rejuvenation serum, his perfect recall pills, his
ludicrous energy drinks. With Indigo, I do believe he had
voiced concern over a test subject, Loretta... Jones? James? If
I'm not mistaken." Tory tried not to jump at the mention of the
woman Aliyah Davis was currently dissecting on a kitchen
table somewhere. Paul too perched forward ever so slightly
with interest.

"But alas," Whittaker said to Paul. "I should be asking *you*
about its effects on humans, shouldn't I? You and your fellow
Ferg Pets *radiate* the stuff." Whittaker narrowed his eyes and
grew solemn, his voice dropping several registers. "I would love
to sink a blade deep into that firm belly of yours and see what
comes oozing out. Oh, how that would please me." He paused,

allowing for the disturbing suggestion to fill the dim room. Tory slid his eyes to Paul Oz assessing his reaction. Paul remained perfectly poised, utterly unfazed by Whittaker's blatant menace. Tory did find it peculiar that Paul's birthdate fell right around the date of the EMP—this apparently Indigo-bearing EMP. And now it turns out Paul Oz radiates the stuff?

"Aren't we having fun?" Whittaker cheerily pressed on. "Such is the case with all the Ferg Pets, is it not? Let's see, there's the delicious you, the even more delicious Rosa Lejeune —my, was George ever so fond of her. He collected you like rare Pokémon. And of course, there's the Mandala Mother who nearly got George killed several times herself."

"You mean Karla," Paul said.

"She'd asked George to address her as Windy, I believe. Though her name is actually Khalidah Nejem. A quaint little Arabic delight." Tory looked up Khalidah Nejem with his Eyesearch. She, also born July 162 *like Paul, like Rosa,* belonged to the flagship Mandala monastery in the Bronx. She'd tested into the Mandala order as an archivist by age nine, but there wasn't much else on her or her family, which was to be expected of an Ascete.

"I've yet to witness her legendizing Mothering myself," Paul said. The Mandala generally held a reverent acceptance of Paul Oz, allowing him unprecedented access to their otherwise exclusive monasteries. However, Tory could find no record of Paul having visited the Bronx chapter in over eight years.

"Were you not aware of his obsession with Khalidah Nejem?" Whittaker asked Paul.

"He visited her on occasion."

"Oh, Sir Oz," Whittaker chirped. "Not just on occasion. He climbed into bed with her entire monastery. How George managed to live so long after bedding the Mandala is beyond me. They wield a force within their walls that modern man cannot withstand. It's those infinity stamps they bear on their foreheads. They are the Forever Men. Once they got wind that George harbored banished monks like that Pelleher fellow, they put the death curse on him, and it's only now delivering."

If Ferguson was secretly squabbling with the Mandala, it meant he was tinkering with darker forces than the current technometry trade would sanction. "Pardon me," Tory spoke up, realizing he'd get more concrete information from Whittaker than Paul. Whittaker and Shotzie both looked to him. "Is there a deeper connection between the Mandala monks and Indigo other than Ms. Nejem?"

"Well, aren't you an original Watson?" Whittaker snickered. Tory instantly regretted the attention. "George worked with powerful materials. What better place to begin asking questions than the monasteries where men live their entire lives solving for X. Besides, Nejem and Pelleher were in some sort of cahoots, and George played their Hermes of sorts, the old fool."

Curious as to why Ferguson would be a go-between for his assistant, Tory asked, "What were Nejem and Pelleher plotting?"

"Who can ever tell? The Mandala and their riddles."

Tory scratched at his chin. "Apart from tampering with the TPJ, what other conclusions did Ferguson's human trials involving Indigo unfold?"

Whittaker flashed his teeth. "Well, aside from tickling the pineal gland and causing a massive eruption of dimethyltryptamine, I'm afraid I don't have much more. However, I am certain someone else in this room has a-plenty."

"I am aware of what I am." Paul's voice came low. "As well as my fellow brothers." Tory wondered to whom Paul was referring, as Paul had no male siblings on record.

"Aliens!" Whittaker yelled through a fit of hysterics. Both

Tory and Paul waited it out. "Indigo plus Mandala makes for a dead George," Whittaker crooned. "Before you young Sherlocks go sniffing around Khalidah Nejem, do heed that the only people who've managed to get close to her are now decomposing. She's rumored to have upended lives by speaking to men in clear Aramaic in the voice of King David without quivering a lip."

Paul prepared to rise, deciding the meeting's end. "Thank you for your time and your help, Mr. Whittaker. Truly."

"Help? No, I was no help. We only spoke of Dane Zapata's upcoming reign at the Institute. I love my dear friend George but will not jeopardize my place on the game board. There are heavy names and heavy forces plucking heavy strings, Sir Oz. My lab will not be the next to succumb to an *accident*." He again kissed his dog.

"I can't fault you for taking that position, Mr. Whittaker."

"Look outside, Sir Oz. Whatever mad concoction George brewed up has apparently boiled over, and its tendrils are spreading through the unaware even as we speak." Whittaker's eyes again flashed with childlike glee. "The plague is rising, Sir Oz! And I must admit it is ever so fun to watch the world as it tips into the fire to burn. Every enemy I've endured, every foe, every tyrant, they will all be consumed, gobbled up by this cancer on humanity. This cancer *of* humanity! And I will be here with my Shotzie and my bowl of beef tartare, watching. Fascinated."

* * *

Paul Oz kept silent on the return flight. *What was he?* Tory thought. Anyone would easily kill for research concerning an alien element capable of affecting the brain's God Module. And if Paul Oz had this element coursing through his veins and his doctor kept him from understanding why, then he'd have just as much motive as the rest to kill Ferguson. Paul had been estranged from his family for nearly a decade. *Did they too possess Indigo?*

Tory broke the silence. "How do people trust that man with their children's futures?" Paul, who'd been flipping through slimscreen options, let a full minute go by before responding.

"Dean will be fine," came his curt response. Tory wondered if he was still outside of Paul's good graces: the GPS masking and all. Or perhaps the curtness was a symptom of Paul's increasingly sharp focus. They'd both taken in a lot at Whittaker's mansion. Either way, Tory found no interest in stewing in thoughts of inadequacy and instead looked over his notes. Not a minute later he felt a buzz at his wrist. A videocall from Aliyah Davis.

"What you got for me, Davis?"

"Well, some curious results from the autopsy."

"Shoot."

"Loretta's body was filled with clumps of molecules we'll have to take back to the lab. The top of her temporal area had been severely damaged and her epithalamus rung dry. The creepy part? She'd been dead since Monday, and her Ncluded verifies the ETD. But we found her pineal gland still active while her brain muscles actively liquefied before our eyes."

"Actively liquified?" Tory puzzled. "What's her current status?"

"Okay, so that's the thing, Ross. I can't tell you."

The dread came fast and hard. "Why not?"

"Around noon, we locked up for lunch. When we came back, the corpse was gone."

16

ALPHABET CITY

To save on a few credits, Kris and his troop piled onto a subway train headed for Alphabet City, one of Manhattan's most congested cycling towns. The metro stations trumpeted a cavalcade of flashing advertisements, while zip-lined train cars scrolled PSAs. Most hustlers and bustlers kept to themselves behind their emergency face masks. As the team squeezed into a cramped car at the Washington Heights station, Aztec peaked out from Becky's purse to assess the scene.

He messaged Kris's Ncluded. "I have detected seven sick human adults, one sick child and a sick transhuman on this train car. I cannot determine if they have the brain-ache but they have alarming fevers."

Kris nodded at Aztec, and spoke through his muffling mask, "Everyone stay close. Don't touch the poles 'til your gloves are fully secure." The doors slid shut behind them and off sped the train. The riders were mostly average-class people silently headed to an IRL workplace. Kids climbed onto ceiling beams like jungle-gyms while teens splayed Ncluded spreads across the air-display field, sifting through menus or commenting in the chatverse.

After the first stop in Harlem, the doors opened to a flood of bombastic commuters who spoke over the ads. Aztec messaged Kris to report a higher number of sick passengers boarding. Kris messaged back, "Can you tell what state they're in?"

"Currently all appear to be at the preliminary onslaught stage, with several not yet aware they are sick." Kris took some comfort in this. People did still get colds in November, right between Indigenous People's Day and Native American Heritage Day.

The train came to the Times Square station. In crushed a multiracial array of the transgender and the transhuman, holographic avatars and bots, townies and tourists, everyone yelling over ads, arguing for space, swiping at airborne menus and sucking down Smartifice muck.

As the train raced along, Aztec sent Kris a series of messages marked urgent. The first was a recent thumbnail of a smiling Eastern European brunette named Delilah Ivanov. The second was a snapshot time-stamped for the previous day of a haggard woman with skin like burnt flesh, red circles rimming her eyes, and a fist at her mouth guarding a cough. It was the third message that sent wriggling snakes down Kris's spine. Two simple words. "Six o'clock."

Kris froze in place, his limbs encased in stone. The last thing he needed was for this Delilah Ivanov to be standing directly behind him, dripping with brain-ache. He took an inconspicuous peak over his shoulder and found her seated comfortably behind him, her wrinkled blood-shot eyes fixed on him. He exhaled to loosen the quickening in his chest then turned back to his circle. "I'll have the team move trains," he messaged Aztec.

"That is not an optimal solution," Aztec sent back. "We cannot say with certainty that the neighboring car will be better. I'm monitoring Delilah Ivanov's heart rate against yours and as yours increases, hers follows. I suggest you first calm down before making any decisions." Kris stiffened, uncertain how to react. How could this stranger know his current heart rate, and furthermore mimic it at will?

Kris did what he could to calm down. Repositioning himself around the pole to face the woman, he looked to Becky and gabbed with her about their wild experience with Michelle Brier. Becky, eager to oblige, engaged in her overtly fabricated version of how the events played out.

The woman continued to stare into Kris's face, apparently waiting for him to drop his guard. Once the train passed the Lower East Side station, the woman abruptly got to her feet and approached Kris with slow, serpentine grace. Kris held his position, fearing his heart rate would rise exponentially with any sudden movement. But keeping calm seemed nearly impossible as the woman stopped to stand directly beside him. The team, engrossed in conversation, hardly noticed her. But the dog, Kris's ridiculous dog, sent constant buzzes to his Ncluded.

Suddenly the woman turned toward Kris, revealing a close-up look into her furrowed, blood-rimmed eyes. And then Kris heard it. Though barely audible above the surrounding chatter, there was absolutely no mistaking it, not at such close range. The woman resonated a deep inhuman growl that spiked every blade of hair on Kris's neck. The woman was deliberately trying to rouse him, sizing him up. He closed his eyes to calm himself through her snarls and through Aztec's incessant messaging, then looked back to her with a polite nod and smile.

As the train stopped at the next station, the woman snapped to attention and walked purposefully out of the open doors. Kris watched as the doors slid shut behind her before allowing his pent-up fright to pour forth like a geyser. As the train resumed movement, commuters watched in alarm as the woman spun around to bang furiously against the train car to claim her prey.

"Jesus H. Christ, Az," Kris barked through his mask. Aztec disappeared into Becky's purse.

"What is it?" asked DZ.

"Nothing. Screw it. We get out at the next stop no matter where it is."

* * *

Clouds painted blue and white forests over a sunny Avenue A. The outdoors were entirely rare for micro-transactional workers like him, so Kris appreciated the light breeze. Cycling towns consisted primarily of cycling dorms and Ascetic projects, housing poor, often under-privileged, estranged or generally unskilled laborers.

The sidewalks here were just a tad more unkempt, the buildings more rundown. Very few grass pads, ad panels and sky poles decorated Alphabet City. And though the streets were twice as populated than their more privileged counterparts, the neighborhood seemed deathly silent in comparison. Becky made a disgusted face at several unsightly globs of sludge on the ground.

"This is the reality our technology covers up," Kris whispered. "There's no cow in the field. The cake is a lie. Stay close." Becky huddled close to Kris, locking her arm with his.

As the team ambled down the avenues to DZ's mother's Avenue D apartment, they stood out sorely, with their modern clothing and upright postures. Scores of children sitting on porches and staircases stopped whatever little they'd been doing to stare.

With such eerily perfect stillness, Kris could easily spot outlying behavior among the onlookers. Apart from the rather inbred appearance of cycling class folk, every once in a while, Kris noticed someone acting erratic, like pounding his or herself on the head, rolling around on the hard concrete, or chanting howled obscenities. By Avenue C, Kris spotted another pair of blood-rimmed eyes.

"Don't look at the ones with bloodshot eyes," he whispered. "I think they can sense fear."

"How's that possible?" Becky asked.

"I dunno, Becks. It hasn't hit the 'verse yet, but there's something real screwy 'bout this brain-ache."

As they approached Avenue D, ramshackle project complexes replaced the cycling buildings. The group had now reached DZ's Ascete stomping grounds. If they'd felt out of place passing the cycling dorms, they were in for a rude awakening with the Ascetes.

Because Ascetes valued the complete rejection of technology, none wore or even understood the basic principles of an Ncluded. As a result, such areas never submitted maintenance requests. Basically, a massive hovel. In any case, modern droids were not equipped to handle century-old plumbing and sewers systems.

Kris grew up in an Ascetic town. So, though the surroundings were quite foreign to Becky, Kris almost felt at home. Along with being self-proclaimed luddites, Ascetes wore full-length, loose-fitting gowns stained from overuse and spent most of their waking hours paying ritualistic homage to Gaia. Their communities farmed or scavenged for food, sent messages by foot, and followed an arcane code of law unrecognized by Nforce. Childhood was spent studying analytical math and natural sciences so as to fulfill their ultimate purpose, to become a monk of the Mandala order. An Ascete either became a Mandala monk or raised a future one.

The group approached an apartment complex and was first greeted by a circle of willowy children seated on the building's porch. They'd been engaged in drawing a strange pattern in chalk on the porch ground but took to ogling the outsiders. From what Kris could see, the drawing was a quite skilled attempt at a multicolored hexagonal mandala symbol.

DZ stepped ahead, leading his group past the gawking children and through the unhinged doorway. The interior was as rundown as the exterior. No carpeting, no working lights. They padded across a dim hall of colorless rubberneckers, some peering out from doorless doorways, others standing slouched in corners.

"¿*Quién es?*" asked a quiet voice an inch behind door 702 after DZ knocked six times.

"Hi Ms. Zapata. It's Kris. I'm with your son, Dean."

"I don't know no Kris," the woman said.

"Mamá, it's me," DZ called, his words gruff and labored with a heavy pinch to the nose. Kris hadn't heard DZ speak out loud in years. There was no response.

"We brought food," Kris added.

The voice behind the door waited a beat then said, "You infected?"

"We're not sick now, but if you don't let us in, we might be," Kris said. A bolt slid from behind the door, and everyone filed in.

The dark, bare room harbored only an old couch and a plastic cooler on the tattered linoleum. A bedroom door protected three or four sets of hungry eyes peeking from behind it. DZ's mother, a short, older Guatemalan woman, appeared as if she'd lived several lives and lost each time, her thin, graying hair matching her stained graying tunic.

A worn poster of Paul Oz's first Planet Magazine photograph hung on the far wall, the one luxury in the apartment. Being the only philanthropist willing to respect and engage the arcane Ascetic charity customs, Paul received near deific acceptance for his patronage. The ultimate irony: the luddite apotheosis of the world's most celebrated technocrat.

Becky hadn't closed the door behind her before the woman barked, "Where's the food? *Y esto no es un refugio.* Who are all these people?"

"We won't be long, Ms. Zapata," Kris started as he nodded at Becky to retrieve the bag of oranges from her purse. DZ had felt it wise to offer organic food, as opposed to ersatz prints. "I just have a few questions before we move on to our next stop." Ms. Zapata stared eagerly at the oranges but made no moves. Unsmiling, she waited for Becky to hand the bag to her. She thanklessly accepted the fruit, headed over to the bedroom door and allowed the bag to disappear into the grabbing hands behind it.

"May we sit?" Kris asked, but the woman simply stared at him as if she hadn't understood. DZ made no effort to facilitate. It in fact appeared as if DZ and his mother hardly knew each other.

"Don't want those things near the couch." Ms. Zapata pointed to her wrist, indicating the Ncludeds. "You say you're connecting together with those things. We're the ones finding true connection to this earth while you destroy it with your voodoo." She leaned against a wall, her lips a firm line.

"We're tryna get some info on this flu," Kris started. "We're here 'cause it's spreading rapidly in Ascete towns, and we wanna help contain it. Through DZ you were our best lead."

"*No sé nada,*" was her terse response. Kris knew this game. He decided he didn't have time for it and gestured for Becky to flip over her hefty purse. Out poured Aztec along with a mountain of wrapped muffins, bananas and a double liter bottle of water. The snacks had cost a tiny fortune, money Kris didn't have after his settlement with Patrice Fan.

As soon as the dog and the food hit the ground, five boys, ranging from toddler to teen, tumbled out from the bedroom. They dove for the snack mountain, all of them eerily identical to DZ. Each grabbed a snack before assembling themselves into a circle for a briefly whispered prayer, then chowed down. The two youngest took to cavorting with Aztec who accepted the role of a normal dog quite elegantly.

"It started like a week ago," Ms. Zapata began after a generous bite into a muffin. "First, they get really tired and sick, like bad headaches and a fever. Sometimes they start vomiting and can't sleep. Next, they get kind of confused and angry, start kicking things and yelling at people that ain't there. Then they start looking really old, like gray old, and their eyes get all red, like bloody. Then..." She paused to take another bite. "Then they change."

"What do you mean by change?" Kris asked, afraid to confirm his suspicions.

"They get quiet, like real quiet. Then they go loco and break stuff or hurt people. Then they get really quiet again. They don't talk. They not themself no more. Don't know what they are." Kris wanted to press the issue, wanted to know about the growling.

"How does the flu spread?" Becky asked.

"It ain't no flu," Ms. Zapata snapped, betraying a snicker. "They can cough in your face and you won't get it. They get you with biting and scratching." Kris removed his mask. A shiver crept down his spine at how easily the woman on the train could have reached over and scratched him.

"How long does it take before they change?" Becky prodded as Aztec and the toddler tumbled over her feet.

"At first it was longer, but now it's shorter. Now it's like two days from when you catch it to when you go loco." All in the room but the two youngest and the dog stood in stunned silence. Kris fought a burning urge to snap on his Ncluded and do some searching.

"How many outbreaks do you know of?" Becky kept on.

"Don't go outside no more," the woman shrugged.

Kris exchanged glances with the others. "Thanks, Ms. Zapata," he said. "You been a huge help. And hey, I got some good news for you. DZ just got accepted to Psy for his art. It's one of the best schools in the nation."

The woman did not look up. "First, they took his ears away. Now they wanna make him do art." Then she sat at the couch to watch her children quietly consume their snacks. "*No te acompaño hasta la salida,*" she said to DZ.

"I'm no Charo, but I think that's our cue," Becky said. Kris collected Aztec, and the group shuffled off to their date with Ted Husk's IRL office.

17

AN EMPTY HUSK

FRIDAY NOV 16, 186 PCE

Once outside Alphabet City, the crew opted for a skycab to the Pharma Farm headquarters. As they traversed the skypath, Kris updated Ross through their encrypted line on the broad strokes of what he'd learned from the Ascetes. In turn Ross informed Kris that whoever murdered Ferguson had not only sought the longevity serum but the Indigo research as well, and that Indigo may be causing the flu.

"Whatever this Indigo is, the human body is not liking it," Kris messaged back. The skycab landed at Pharma Farm to a distressed multitude at the front gate. Aztec assessed the crowd and reported that a good many demonstrated signs of early onset brain-flu, and a handful had bloodshot eyes. They were all calling for medicines, but were being denied access to the facility.

Kris led his team to an undisclosed trapdoor from an adjoining parking lot as indicated by his schematics. The trapdoor stood unmanned, as most security staff were maintaining the front gate. Wasting no time, Kris tore off the cover to the door's lock pad. The word Secure in silver block letters lined the pad's interior. "You sexy son-of-a-bitch," he whispered. He'd save his fancy B&E skills for another day.

Kris logged in his work passcodes, praying his string of apophenic luck would keep this blatant misuse of company trust from haunting him forever. He deactivated the lock and with DZ's help lifted the heavy metal door from the ground.

The group sprinted down a dark staircase and subsequent basement tunnels, lit only by the shimmering blue schematics hologram floating alongside Kris. Aztec yipped helpful directions at a harsh whisper from Becky's bag.

A security android guarded an approaching stairwell. "Nighty night, Az," Kris warned as he called up a script that put all bots in close range to sleep-mode. The security bot's shoulders slumped, and the group embarked on their thirteen-flight climb to Ted Husk's office.

By the eighth floor, DZ was forced to lock arms with Becky and hoist her up. Husk's schedule placed him in a meeting in New Jersey until a quarter to sixteen. If they hurried, they'd have roughly thirty minutes to locate the files. They reached the fourteenth floor, jetted along the vacant halls, located Husk's IRL office and burst in.

Before his eyes could readjust to the well-lit room, Kris's heart leapt like a popped cork. Ted Husk sat there upright behind his desk, glaring directly into the eyes of his intruders as they jerked to a halt. Before Kris could assemble a reckless, witty one-liner, Aztec, now back in full swing, shouted, "It's a bot!" His caption floating into the air-display. And within seconds DZ swooped up the baseball bat by the entrance and slammed down mercilessly on Husk's head, no holds barred.

"What the hell, DZ!" Kris yelled. "Az, you sure?"

"Yes." The four of them watched as the bot toppled over with a heavy thud onto a growing puddle of bottery fluid. Becky let out a low whistle.

"I didn't want it to log and report anything," DZ defended. *Good point.* "Guys, we know where the files are," Kris started. "The desk. The file cabinets. Let's go." Becky hurtled to the cabinets to retrieve the YouSpace printout while DZ lugged bot Husk away to search his desk for the scrap sheets. Kris took the time to message Ross their current status.

Ross simply replied with, "Check the closet." Kris let out a puff, feeling a tinge of resentment. Ross never seemed impressed. Perhaps that *was* the compliment. He placed his hand to the closet's doorknob and rotated. Unlocked. He opened it just a crack, and...

"Kris," Becky called. Startled Kris breathed through racing heartbeats. "There's only one VerteBrain here. In the capture there were two." The missing headgear. The bot decoy. Husk was immersed somewhere nearby.

"Thanks, Becks. Keep rifling. DZ, guard the office door." Kris turned back to the closet and turned the knob. He found a small room faintly lit by a desk-lamp atop a conference table. Seated at the table were Ted Husk and Leland Shark, both reclining in their chairs immersed.

Kris backed out of the room, shut the door and faced his team. "Guys, I'm 'bout to do something real fucked up," he announced in a sobered hush. Everyone stopped to listen. "They're in there mersed out." Both Becky and DZ gawked like a pair of grouper fish. "Keep it quiet out here. Becks, give me the VerteBrain. Az, you're with me." Aztec hopped out from Becky's bag as Becky tossed over the visor. Kris spun on his heel, slipping back into the conference room with Aztec. "Pull up the proximity mersing access key we generated," Kris whispered as he got to his knees and rerouted his Ncluded to the new headgear.

After a moment of silence Aztec replied, "I've got it pulled up, Kris. But may I first remind you of the ethical misgivings of—"

"Oh, don't pretend this ain't what we do, Az. Now shut up and start talking."

"Kris, breaking into an immersion is a violation of personal privacy even black hats tend to avoid."

"I know, Az. You gave me this speech with Patrice Fan, and alas. I'm broke as hell, but it got us here. Now give me the code. Once I'm in, stuff your ass back in Becky's bag, and don't come out 'til we're safe."

"And if we're never safe?"

"The code, Az!" Kris placed the VerteBrain over his head, input the access key Aztec provided, then he leaned back against the wall as his muscles relaxed.

Kris's avatar reemerged in a simulacrum of Husk's office, bathing in soft moonlight. He stood alone in the main office and could hear arguing voices from the dimly lit conference room. He peered in through the open door slit, remaining out of reach of the room's lamp.

In the room, Kris found Husk, Leland Shark and two others, a man and a woman. He froze at the sight of the woman. Though somewhat older and a bit rounder, she was the spitting image of Davia Valenti. Perfect hair, perfect skin. Transfixed, Kris could do nothing but watch and listen as Husk admonished the others.

"...And now that little hybrid, half-bot bio boy is coming 'round asking questions. Asking me to my face 'bout foul play."

"I can't imagine Paul Oscar would be so reckless as to get involved," came the stern voice of Leland Shark. "The transhuman may indeed be acting on his own accord."

"You frickin' kidding me, Lee? Nobody at Ozzie Corp takes a piss without ol' Ozzie's consent. And if he's fixing to gear up an official investigation, we're all done. We're all frickin' done."

"You've told him nothing, Ted. They've got nothing on us."

"All's I'm saying is I reckon Ozzie don't play nice."

"Let's not be hasty," Leland said. "We have control over what Torian Ross knows, and...What is it, Bianca?" Leland looked over to the woman. She'd wrinkled her brow and raised her head. She turned and looked at the doorway, directly where Kris had been hiding, then shot to her feet.

"We've been compromised," Bianca hissed. "Someone else has mersed in. Everyone out. Now!" Kris snapped to attention.

"Shit, shit, shit!" he whispered then mersed out, thankful to be the first one fully conscious IRL. Kris pulled at his legs to no avail as he scooted out of the room on his butt.

"Find the notes and the printout?" Kris howled to the team as he messaged Ross their situation. "Tell me you found the notes and the printout!" He'd been distracted by the Valenti woman and was now ill-prepared for the impending confrontation. And all his friends were there with him, ripe for the slaughter.

Becky and DZ held up the evidence in question. DZ held out the bat. Kris jumped to his feet, dove to Becky's bag and found a safely stowed Aztec. He rifled through the back pouch to grab the black, autographed Blazer Michelle Brier had gifted Becky. Everyone assembled into formation to greet the perpetrators. About twenty seconds elapsed before Leland Shark and Ted Husk came bumbling out from behind the door still woozy from the merse.

"Awe hell," Husk said. "Bunch o' Ozzie's henchmen."

"Where's your firearm?" Leland whispered.

"Dang it!" Husk spat.

"We're not with Oz Corp," Kris said, as calm and collected as a browsing deer. He pointed the Blazer at the two men, clearing his throat for his rehearsed one-liner. "I'm freelance, and I'm here to take you down for the murder of

Dr. George Quintus Ferguson." Both men reached for the sky.

"What'na hell is that thing?" Husk woofed.

"Something that'll make you regret calling my transhuman friend a half-bot bio boy; that's for damn sure."

"He's bluffing," Shark said, making no moves to substantiate his claim.

"You've just come out of a merse," Kris said. "Your brain muscle is currently reacclimating. This here? This stagnates that readjustment so it never quite fully recovers. But you're old, so you won't mind. Becky?"

"Why'd you kill your dad, Leland?" Becky sang holding up the YouSpace printout. "Cause he was gonna stay young forever right under your aging nose? At this point you look way older than he ever did." The men remained silent.

"Nice suit jacket, Leland," Kris chimed. "Think it'll pair well with brain damage?" Kris pressed a button on the Blazer and its laser tip lit a bright red speck against Leland Shark's forehead.

"All right!" Shark exclaimed. "I'll admit to resenting the man who was supposed to be my grandfather. To being sour he'd keep secrets from his own blood. But all I'm guilty of is snooping at his will. It's his investors who feel entitled to his research. They're the ones you want."

"Watch yourself, Lee," Husk warned.

"That's all you're getting out of me," Shark said and tightened his lips. Ferguson had to have a heap of investors. Kris prepared to continue hounding, but just then a blonde staff member barged into the office, then locked the door behind her. She spun anxiously and backed against the door to hold it shut.

"Dr. Shark, Sir, I'm not sure what's going on out there," she began, frantic and shivering, "but people are biting and punching each other and running through the halls, tearing the place apart!" Becky moved quickly to open the patio door and peered over the banister. DZ followed suit while Kris slowly backed toward the patio, holding Shark and Husk at bay with the Blazer.

"I want names, Leland," Kris said.

"What are you gonna do? Jump?" Husk laughed, and upon his last chuckle a strong set of knocks pounded against the office door, so hard the staff woman flopped forward. Everyone froze. The banging came again accompanied by pleadings for entry.

"Should I let them in?" the woman cried. "They sound desperate, and it's really scary out there."

"Are you crazy?" Kris asked. "Those people are infected, and they're feeding off your fear. So, calm down and let's think this through."

"Uh," Husk mused. "That ain't the strongest door. If those guys really want in, they're gettin' in."

"Hey y'all?" Becky called warily. "'Member how somebody suggested we jump?" Kris stepped onto the patio and looked over the banister. The surrounding mob had escalated the frenzy to a riot. There was no way to detect who was infected from such heights. When Kris turned back from his swift lean over the rail, he met with Husk's broad form suddenly in his face. Husk grabbed hard at Kris's neck, whirled Kris around to face outward against him, holding a cold, metal common-grade pistol to Kris's temple.

"Ye ain't such a big, bad wolf now, are ye boy?" Husk crooned as he turned his back to the banister to face his calcified audience. Firearms, once common among civilians, were now a mere storytelling device to scare children. To be up close to such an arcane killing instrument, to be threatened by one, was the stuff of nightmares.

A clear visceral dread washed over Kris as the weapon

rested against him, rendering him helpless. But while he very keenly feared for his life, a rush of several thoughts obscured those fears. Foremost, Kris loathed knowing this would be the last moment he'd ever share with his friends, though he was pleased to have patched things up with Rosa and even Paul Oz. Nonetheless, a deep bitterness of never knowing the 'why,' concerning Davia Valenti coursed through him like a molten liquid fury. "Now," Husk continued. "Here's what's gon' happen. The weird Spanish kid and the girlie gon' hand over the evidence to Leland all nice like. Then—"

A hard kick resounded against the office door, denting it. The staff woman jumped. "The screams for help are getting worse," she called. "I can't take letting them just suffer out there!"

"Don't you open that frickin' door!" Husk roared, swinging his gun arm toward the woman. In that instant DZ back-handed the gun from Husk's hand, and it soared off into the afternoon sky. "You idiot! That was the only gun up here!" Kris took the opportunity to spin around and knee Husk twice in the scrotum with startling force. DZ matched the attack with a hard strike of the bat against Husk's shoulder. Husk toppled over as his bot had done and wailed in bitter agony.

"Fuck you, your fat fuck," Kris spat, shaking off the immediate post-traumatic jitters.

As another thud pounded against the wilting door, Becky pointed to a distant form amid the clouds. "Look y'all!" In from the west flew an Oz Corp Skyjet.

"Well, I'll be," wheezed Husk through gritted teeth. "The Wizard of frickin' Oz."

"Everybody line-up, and get ready to mount," Kris instructed. "It won't be able to land, so we'll have to jump in. DZ help Becky on first then you follow. You're the only one that can help lift Cartoon Cowboy and Dr. Evil."

"Screw that," DZ protested. "I'm not helping that guy. He literally just tried to kill you."

"We ain't saints either, DZ. But we don't let people die. Get 'em on." Kris headed back into the office to find the staff worker sobbing on the floor, her left eye bruised. Leland Shark had likely struck her to keep her from opening the door. "Damn it, Shark!" Kris cried and rushed over to help the woman. "All right, up! Come on! Let's Go!" But the woman, riven with tears, proved impossible to help assemble to her feet.

"Kris!" Ross's voice sounded with concerned anger from the sky jet at the patio. "Get your ass out here! Now!" Kris turned to find Husk and Shark bickering over which of them should be lifted into the jet next. He looked back to find the woman had slipped back down to a slouch, had raised an arm to the door handle, and was currently unlocking it.

"Christ!" Kris yelled in manifest horror. An Olympic-grade sprint brought him to the patio in seconds. DZ and Ross began plotting how to lift Leland Shark, but when Ross spotted Kris approaching, he ordered, "Kris first!"

"Fuck that!" shrieked a wild-eyed Husk.

"I've got info on Ferguson! You need me!" added Leland.

"No time to explain basic physics," Ross barked from behind his Glass. "Move aside. Kris, hands!" Things grew very loud and muffled behind Kris as the office door swung open. He allowed DZ and Ross to hoist him into the jet and chuck him like cargo behind them. Kris turned back to find DZ and Ross hastily lifting Shark's torso while the plump sobbing face of Ted Husk contorted in tow. It wasn't long before Kris realized why the grown man had succumbed to sopping tears. What he saw behind Husk gnarled up his insides with an unalloyed horror more real than the back of his own hand. Behind Husk, the blond staff woman who'd let in the banging horde was now a heap of bloody mass actively being torn to shreds by her guests.

There were only three. Kris could not determine their genders. They had withered gray skin, gray tufts on their head, blood-rimmed eyes, their fingers and lips dripping with fresh scarlet blood. They did not appear slow or impaired, just viscerally enraged with no purpose but to assuage their implacable hatred by tearing at the flesh of their prey. One had gouged out the staff woman's eyes and was blotting at her empty viscid sockets while another gnawed at the woman's thigh through her skirt. Their low, rumbling, inhuman growls would forever haunt Kris. The roaring physically shook the walls, a gyrating snow-globe of blood.

These things, these monsters; were they not people?

Kris, shocked at the site, was pushed to the backseat to sit beside a stunned Becky.

"They're frickin' coming!" Kris heard Husk cry out. "They're frickin' here! Please! Hurry up!" Kris watched through blurred eyes as Ross and DZ pulled Shark into the vehicle. Through the haze Kris heard Ross yell that Shark had gotten nicked at the ankle. He followed up with a muffled command to retreat, unwilling to risk the safety of everyone else.

And as the jet headed back for Manhattan without Husk, Kris shut his eyes tight, *I can't watch Cartoon Cowboy get torn to pieces. Not even he deserves that.*

18

THE GREAT AND POWERFUL OZ

SUNDAY NOV 17, 186 PCE

"There is no Good, Evil, Strength, Weakness.
There is only Will."

— DIARY OF THE MAD GLEE

H is eyelids cover his eyes, still he sees and appreciates the foliage draped loosely over each corner of his bedroom walls. It is early dawn. He is lying awake. The smell of jasmine overpowers the usual mix of earthy wood, calming his nerves as he focuses on the minutiae of circulatory regulation. In tune with his kinesthetic rhythm, he accounts for as many blood vessels as he can readily distinguish and gradually increases blood flow to his muscles at a rate he sees fit. Once certain his energy levels are spread accordingly throughout his body, he concentrates on releasing the precise number of essential hormones.

Paul eases his brain deep into theta state, opening his mind to listen as the dark leaves of the foliage communicate with each other, with the walls and with him. They express elation, an affirmation of a full living experience as they await their forthcoming share of the sun.

His eyes still shut, Paul examines his crystal-lined ceiling fan, listening for the contentedness among its perfect diamonds. They disseminate blissful lines of energy for fulfilling their combined purpose—being a decorative fan. Paul basks in this ecstatic contentedness. He needs it.

Paul slowly disengages from conscious reality and engages his reticular activating system, permitting his brain to sift through short vignettes of arbitrary memories. It is a routine of reliving he practices in place of dreaming, as he has yet to experience true sleep. Like the dolphin, his trance leaves open one proverbial eye of consciousness, allowing an indistinct current of music to permeate the back of his subconscious.

His first memory comprises a six-year-old Paul playing a game he dubs "crash" with the broken fire truck and headless superhero doll his father's wife has scavenged for him. He is in a studio apartment in the Ascetic town of Essex, New Jersey. It is a Tuesday.

"If you don't answer me right now, I'll take those toys away from you, Oscar," his father's wife warns from behind. Her threat is idle. She knows better than to ever again physically disturb him. He does not need to face her to know she is weeping. "Please, Oscar, talk to me." He ignores her. She is crying because he is a Bad. He considers the Euclidean geometry of the shapes formed using his two toys and a pencil, while creating the sounds necessary for a train to crash into a headless hero. He must ignore her to remain calm.

"I don't know what to tell you, Julie," his father announces, pacing behind his wife.

"Tell me what the hell is wrong with your son?" At this time Paul does not fully understand that he is not also the son of Julie Ryland. "We're going to have to uproot our lives again. I can't keep picking up and leaving because of this...this...child!"

A second memory soon charges to the forefront of Paul's mind. It is the Sunday evening prior to Julie Ryland's confrontation. While roaming the streets of a nearby cycling town, Paul spots a blond prostitute trip over a short metal pipe on the ground. He watches as she gets to her feet and replaces her heel. To him she is just a woman like Julie Ryland is a woman.

"The hell you looking at, kid?" she snarls. Paul continues to survey her. She walks over and bends low to his face. "It's rude to stare. Most people out here would kick your ass." Still Paul watches as she scurries off into a nearby alley. Intrigued, he follows. As he turns into the alleyway, he notices two large men grab the woman. He watches as they wrestle her to her knees, attempting to rip a purse from her grip. She screams for help. She is crying like Julie Ryland cries when a Bad makes her angry or sad.

Paul retrieves the metal pipe from the ground and returns to the scene. A mild earthquake rattles the sidewalk beneath his feet. Through the quaking and the woman's screams, the men do not notice Paul's approach. With the force of a much stronger being, Paul strikes one of the men at the base of the skull. A fatal blow. The prostitute wriggles out from beneath her dying assailant. She and the second man watch agape as the six-year-old pummels the corpse to gory pieces in silent rage. Upon complete decimation, Paul kneels beside the corpse, digs a hand into one of its open wounds and fishes out gooey bits to examine.

Though the man and prostitute stare, they do not see the full spectrum of emotion that breaks over Paul. They do not see that he is now aware of his victim's name, Thomas Leach, and that all Thomas wanted was acceptance from his mother, an acceptance for which Paul also longs. The onlookers cannot see the swirling silver fractals flashing over Paul's eyes as he feels a consummate wave of intense euphoria wash over his body. It is Paul's first experience of the Death High, an intimate, spiritual Schadenfreude that he does not yet comprehend.

A new memory comes to pass as the muffled music in his subconscious amplifies. It is two years ago. A young, whipcord thin brunette straddles him naked on this very bed. Cindy Ross. He holds her in place at the hips, studying her brittle neck as she uses him to pleasure herself. Though he did deny her prior advances, he appreciates his current role in her journey to take control of her sexuality.

His mind jumps to relive a strange communication he receives seven days ago while reclining in the bath. The phrase 'Know me' rings through his mind telepathically like a million siren screams. 'Know me. Know me.' He does not understand how to communicate a response and recalls his frustrations at the lack of control. 'Know me.' He has not received another such message since.

His mind's eye quickly offers another memory to assuage resurging frustrations. It is nine years prior. He is a teenager. He stands alone in a classroom at the Ferguson and Maine School of Excellence where he has just accidentally knocked down and completely destroyed an intricate replica of the asteroid belt assembled over months by a team of esteemed students. He works strenuously to force calm over a brewing chaotic storm of unfocused fury. He did a Bad. He is a Bad. He knows he will not be able to control his subsequent actions if confronted. He will destroy everything standing.

But then *she* arrives. He feels it, the instant connection. Never has he been so close to her. He longs to touch her. She is warmth. Everyone loves her. Though she is not so familiar with Paul, she is keenly aware he is a social pariah.

"Oh crap, did you do this?" she asks in muted shock from the doorway. Paul is not yet equipped with the capability to respond. "They're gonna slaughter you when they see this." Before she can utter another word, they who'd built the replica return. She steps in front of Paul and graciously takes the blame for Paul's mishap. He watches as she allows them to berate her. She later helps them rebuild the replica. She seldom crosses paths with Paul again and moves on oblivious that he has never thanked her. Oblivious that she has completely transformed his life. Acts of selfless championing come so naturally to her; she likely does not remember the deed. It is the first and only time anyone gives Paul anything unobliged and with no ulterior motive.

Paul's declarative memories fade into the depths of his psyche as a vivid reverie usurps his headspace. He imagines her, his champion, in the present. She is draped over his lap. They are engaged in a deep kiss. Paul attempts to free himself from the impetuous imagery to no avail. He imagines his bed. He imagines himself stretched across the length of her body, deep inside of her, oozing his energies into her. Pressing intently against the heliocentric warmth at her center. It is a bright writhing flame. She is more than mere flesh. She is a greatness. But he cannot help himself. A moth to her flame, he must have her. Her warmth. Her light. The music in his subconscious has now taken root at the forefront of his mind. It is her song, "...for everything dies, and all the roses are now blue."

Paul realizes he has been massaging himself to the thought of her, her skin, her mouth. Her poetic declaration of loneliness. The strength she did not yet know. He searches for the bitterness at her rejection but is ripped from reverie by his plants' flamboyant reaction to his radiating affection. They dance in his aura with unmoving climactic delight.

Paul sits up to mentally prepare for the day's trip, and as if in prophetic confirmation, Dex buzzes his messaging device with a note. "Good Morning, Paul! Rosa Lejeune is here, and she is demanding to see you."

Paul responds, "Send Ms. Lejeune up to my apartment. Thank you, Dex."

19

FIRED

SUNDAY NOV 17, 186 PCE

"One thought infinitely expressed."

— *DIARY OF THE MAD GLEE*

Rosa was surprised her name alone got her through the gates at Historic Central Park. With the city in disarray over the outbreak, she had no plans to return to her undoubtedly infected hotel. She needed safety. She needed a haven in which to stow away, and neither Kris nor Torian were responding to her texts. So, she turned to Oz Corp. She ached to resolve things with Paul and fought hard not to resent Dex for ghosting her. Dex was just doing his job: building up then tossing aside any woman Paul fancied.

Rosa pulled her hair into a ponytail, wearing a long-sleeved tee and jeans to keep any funny business at bay. She took umbrage as she rode the elevator with a mannerly attendant. Did she no longer qualify for star treatment?

Rosa rang the doorbell to Paul's apartment and was again surprised to hear the door click open. She made her way through the elegant space, and before long she came upon the inlaid aquarium, the spot where she'd rejected him. She trembled at the memory. At his gnarling knot of dark rage. Knowing she wouldn't be able to detect his approach empathically, she swiftly looked over her shoulder, the sudden bout of paranoia suggesting she leave, or at least wait out in the dining hall.

Rosa turned to exit, but as her tremors abated, she noticed clanking sounds behind a stray mote of light from a partially opened side-room doorway. Then came the destinesia: it was as if the time between hearing the clanks and standing directly before the side-room door hadn't existed. She placed a hand at its hinge and lightly pressed to open.

She found a bright pristine bedroom bathed in striking green and blue foliage. The low hanging chandelier gave the room sublime shadow vines, and the plush open bed was like something out of a magazine. Though Rosa could have spent hours analyzing the majesty of the bedroom, its splendor paled in comparison to something far more majestic.

Paul Oscar. He stood at the center of the room barechested, wiping a pair of steel tongs, studying her meticulously. She gaped at the excruciating perfection of his physique. His statuesque arms. His expertly sculpted abs.

Rosa took two cautious steps forward and heard the door shut behind her. Then lock. Paul watched her, his eyes pinning her to the door. And there they stood, in an everlasting staredown, each passing second adding mountains of gravity to the confrontation.

Paul broke the stillness. He discarded the tongs and took a few leisurely paces toward her, his dark Gordian Knot likely roiling just beneath the surface. He stepped up close. Rosa sucked in with a fierce shiver as Paul lifted a hand and cupped the jewel against her clavicle. Rosa felt her fists unclench, allowing herself to exhale through his light touch. She hadn't realized until that moment how desperately she'd been aching to feel his charged fingertips against her skin. He studied the jewel for a second then brought his eyes to hers. Again she found herself falling prey, drowning, wanting only to entangle her mouth with his. Her lips quivered, and at this she felt him tense in answer. Instantly he pulled back as if she were a live wire.

"We learn from our mistakes," he said evenly. His first words to her. *So, she was a mistake?* Rosa never did like the royal 'We,' and Kris was right; no longer would she let herself feel small.

"Wow," she whispered, catching her breath, holding back a volatile outburst of repressed emotion. "You are the worst thing that's ever happened to me, Paul Oscar."

"I get that a lot." His nonchalance gnawed at her insides.

"You also get me fired from my job."

"According to your credit balance, you've no longer a need for it."

Rosa winced. "So, you dress me up in a skimpy little outfit to sing for you?" she began, her voice steadily amplifying. "You throw credits in my face; you try to force yourself on me; then you toss me—"

"I try to force myself on you?" Paul stepped back a few more paces.

"Then you have your people ghost me. We both know what happened." Shivering fiercely, she took a righteous step toward him.

Paul raised a palm. "Do not come any closer, Lejeune."

"Oh, so I dare to speak up, and suddenly I'm textbook crazy?"

"I advise you calm down, Lejeune," Paul warned. The words 'calm' and 'down' in that order were the tipping point.

"Right, I need to calm down. *I* need to calm down. *I'm* the wretch here, and you're so frickin' perfect!"

"Lejeune, if you're unable to dial it back, I will have you escorted off of my property."

"Are you frickin' *kidding* me?" Rosa shrieked. "How the hell can you be so...so...Ugh!" Tears streamed down her cheeks as she watched him pull his call device from his pocket. She stared in stunned silence, waiting for him to key in the garbage-chute code. But when he did not, when he simply stared back at her, she realized it.

Of course. He was also an empath, and she was suffocating him with negative energies. She knew that feeling. She took a deep breath to calm her nerves. If she wanted to communicate with him, it would have to be on his level.

"I saw you," she said, her tremors abating. "The real you."

"I know." He put the device away and pointed to an ottoman behind her. "Have a seat; I'm making eggs," he suggested, restoring the polite tone to which she'd been accustomed. *He knew?*

Unsure of how to respond to such a rapid shift in timbre, Rosa sat and wiped her face. She allowed herself another long inhale, observing Paul as he turned to a countertop bearing an inset electric range. *Woah*, she thought. *He not only ate natural foods but prepared them too?* Culinary prowess was wholly rare in Smartifice America.

Rosa split her attentions between surveying Paul as he tinkered with a skillet and marveling at his idyllic bedroom. She didn't want to be impressed yet couldn't help but silently awe at the zen with which Paul doted over a concoction of eggs, cheese and peppers. It felt as if he was directly communicating with the food. And he was just so damn comfortable in his skin.

"So..." Rosa started, hoping to assuage the tension. "You have a lovely room."

"It's where I sleep." He didn't look up. She wondered if

coming off exceptionally polite yet undeniably curt was a skill he had worked hard to master.

After another brief silence he turned and pointed the tongs to her. They held a ball of piping hot, droopy eggs swathed in stripes of molten cheese and peppers. As he approached her and brought the bite to her lips, she noticed the cheese was actively boiling. Why would he offer her actively boiling food? Would she burn her tongue simply to avoid rejecting him again? She sat face to face with his toned torso and loosened pant lace, rational thought hardly an option. She took the bite. She'd always been good with hot food.

Paul smirked, his eyes ruthlessly scrutinizing her as she chewed, prompting her to raise a hand to her mouth. "Uhm," she began nervously, "I'm feeling a little watched."

"Because I can't help but stare at you?" he asked sweetly, without missing a beat. Heat rushed Rosa's neck and blossomed in her cheeks. She curled her toes to keep her knees from buckling.

"These eggs are amazing, Paul. Thank you."

"I'll fix you a plate," he proposed. "First excuse me while I grab a shirt." Rosa wanted to suggest he not bother with the shirt but thought better of it. As Paul headed for a hall to an adjoining room, Rosa noticed something so peculiar she wasn't entirely certain it happened. As Paul approached the corner, he happened by a pot of sagging tulips. While passing directly before them, their drooping bulbs lifted slightly as if coming up for air, then depressed again once he'd gone. It had been undoubtedly bizarre. Had he some sort of ability to disseminate preternatural force? Rosa began to seriously reconsider her safety alone with this...this being.

Paul returned in a snug gray polo holding two gold breakfast plates. Rosa regarded him as he again passed the flowerpot and noticed he very casually touched a hand to their soil in afterthought. She watched as the flowers rose to attention, remaining upright behind him. She drew in a quick breath and repeated to herself not to jump in fright.

Paul offered her a healthy portioning of the eggs along with a shiny fork. Rosa stood to accept the plate, but she purposefully botched the receiving balance and watched as the plate, eggs and fork raced toward the spotless carpeting.

And then it happened.

Rosa guessed it would. And it did. The plate, the fork, the eggs all remained completely intact, comfortably suspended, hovering an inch from the ground as if remotely controlled, traces of silver slivers warping around them.

Their eyes met.

Rosa whirled around and took several hurried paces toward the exit, almost stumbling over the ottoman. "What the hell are you?" she yelled. Paul reached out and grabbed her arm. She tried to yank free, but he gripped her firmly at the middle, while grabbing for something behind him with his other hand. "Listen, I don't even know what I saw," Rosa said as she continued to pull away. But before long, she felt a dampness at the skin of her bare forearm. In seconds, Paul had somehow attained a small fuel canister, lifted her sleeve and was applying a coat of accelerant to her arm. Her eyes went wide with terror. "What the hell are you doing?"

She didn't know where it came from, the blue, butane lighter. Every bone in her body went rigid when she saw it. When she felt him back away as he lit it against her forearm.

Then whoosh.

Fire.

All she saw was fire. She screamed so hard she felt it in her spine. Her full forearm, from the base of her elbow to the tips of her fingers, was completely engulfed in crackling yellow flames.

Riven with hysterics, Rosa swooped her burning arm before

her eyes, howling as hard as her lungs would allow. She cried and cried and...then she stopped crying. She felt no pain. She felt the white-hot burn; she felt the millions of tiny excited particles bouncing on her arm, but no pain. In fact, she felt a hint of pleasure. In most genuine astonishment, Rosa stared at the dancing flames agape. "What the...?"

"You play my hand, I play yours," Paul said coolly from behind the flame. "Sit." Rosa plopped onto the ottoman with unthinking obedience. She studied her fire-gloved fingers so intently she hardly noticed the plate of eggs float freely to the countertop. "The fire should subside as you absorb it since you're not yet aware of how to manipulate it." He was right. The height of the flames had indeed dwindled.

Rosa could scarcely form her words. "Wh-what is this? What am I?"

"I've been using the term fire elemental for you, though it's actually more complicated than simple pyrokinesis." *Fire elemental?* Rosa didn't know where to begin with the questions.

"But...how? Why?"

"Your ability to feel others' emotions, their motives," Paul said. Rosa nodded eagerly. "It's because you can communicate."

"Communicate? As in subliminally? Can you? Are you like whatever I am, whatever this is?"

"I am similar to you, but I am not like you." Paul paced to the countertop and stared down at the eggs, his back to Rosa. "We were created with an element not of this plane: an element that defies quantum order. Dr. Ferguson named it Indigo after the color of the Ajna."

"I don't understand." All her sheltered life she'd been conditioned to avoid fire. Yet there she sat watching the flames at her skin subside, leaving behind a whisper of smoke. Paul let a long minute go by before responding.

"We're different," he said. "We have the ability to see things, hear things, interact with things at the subatomic level. I can consciously communicate with my inner system to activate my Observer, press my right parietal lobe and pineal gland to release melatonin." Rosa raised a brow behind him, and he responded as if he'd noticed.

"Some call it the Sight," he said. "I prefer the borrowed term *deepsight*. Deepsight is an awakening of another group of senses, allowing me to see without eyes, to see through objects, to see the many individual compartments of anything including myself. It allows me to perceive the many colors of time as a radial spectrum, to smell fear like a sour odor, to hear anger like screeching nails, to taste pleasure like..." Paul paused and turned to her. "Exponential perception. I communicate with the ether to catch a plate just as easily as one communicates with a bat to hit a ball."

Rosa heard the words but couldn't fit them to reality. She'd been living with her body for twenty-four years; never could she actively communicate with her insides. "So, when you activate deepsight," she puzzled, "what do you see exactly?" Paul leaned against the countertop and regarded her.

"Everything." The answer came with casual finality. "Physical sight itself is insignificant."

"So, Ferguson kept us around to study this phenomenon," Rosa mused as she came to her feet, running her fingers down her forearm. Then she shook her head. "No. This...this can't be true. You must have put something on my arm to keep it from burning."

Paul shrugged. "You saw what I can do, Rosa. And you reacted accordingly."

"Yeah..." Rosa said with uneasy resignation. She certainly could not deny her very eyes. "So, I can communicate with fire..."

"You have a strong affinity for fire, but you could essentially work with anything, since everything is everything else." *A strong affinity for fire?* That explained why she'd never burned her tongue.

"Wait a second," she said. "But isn't it a Catch 22? In order to activate deepsight, you need to be keenly aware of your inner system, but to be so keenly aware, you'd need your deepsight activated."

Paul responded with a slightly upturned nod, like Ferguson would do when pleased by an intelligent question. "It's as much a paradox as communication and understanding in itself. Once you're able to communicate with something, you can understand it, but you must understand it before you can communicate."

"And what if you have no way of communicating with something? Say if there's no medium: for instance, no lighter fluid?"

"The only way to no longer communicate is to be in perfect vacuum. And even the vacuum between subatomic particles is imperfect." Paul tilted his head in ponder. "Recently they've assembled a perfect-vacuum system, but its only use has been in controlled laboratory environments."

As she watched him, another question beset her. "Paul," she said, drawing his eyes back to hers.

"Yes, Rosa."

"If you can see and know everything, how is that any different from God? From complete perfection?"

"My imperfection is that I am human," he said matter of fact. "Stifled by physical and emotional limitations."

Rosa considered the darkness she'd found in him. Had that been stifled power? She thought for a moment more then asked, "Will you teach me?"

"I can certainly show you the mechanics, but anything more you'll have to figure out on your own."

"On my own?" Rosa balked, averting her eyes. Deflated, she sat back down and continued. "You see I'm not the strongest wrestler on Team Confidence. You tell me I'm some sort of fire priestess, that I can manipulate nature. Then say, 'now go forth and figure the rest out?'"

"Yes," was Paul's simple response. He would never understand how much she feared him, feared herself, feared how little she knew. She was genuinely surprised she'd held herself together this long. Paul looked hard at her for a long moment then said, "You are very strong, Rosa."

She'd have never expected those words, not from him. They come with a chilling, disarming finality. "You must not know a lot about me," she said. "I get anxious, panicky. Not exactly the constitution of a fire god."

"You may essentially be having developmental issues coming into your *godhood*, as you call it."

"Wait, so I'm a disabled god?"

"I prefer god-first language, myself," Paul said.

Rosa fixed her eyes to his. "How long have you known this about me?"

"I've suspected it since the Academy. And I reaffirmed it when you allowed me to taste you."

A hot quiver flushed Rosa's body at the memory of that moment, of those boyish dimples as he licked his fingers clean of her. She didn't notice herself rise and step up close to him, inches from him. "You could have just told me, you know. Instead of setting me on fire."

Paul straightened up and lowered his forehead to hers. "Where's the fun in that? I finally have someone to play with."

"You play rough."

"You can take it." Paul said. And like the painful yet necessary rush of hot water over frozen hands, Paul reopened his deep well of vibrant emotions to her. His energy signals flooded into her, through her, around her like a heavy, rippling volcano. It was pure bliss. She staggered backward, hardly able to handle the full consumption of his energies. Paul placed a hand lightly at her hip to steady her, and her body raced with pleasure at his electric touch. She could feel her desire reflected in his frequency. And her eyes rimmed with tears, as she felt his most resonant emotion in that moment was affection toward her.

"So, are you saying I'm your friend?" she asked, sliding her fingers onto his shoulders.

"More like worthy adversary." He brushed at a tear that managed to escape her eyes.

Rosa appreciated the weight of the title and took it as a profound complement. *Finally, someone who could possibly understand me,* she thought. She looked into his eyes; he responded in kind. She looked to his mouth. *Here we are again,* she mused, eager to minimize the space between them. She suddenly became very aware of the very inviting open bed beside them. She felt his energies swiftly react with excitement to her consideration. She gasped. *He can hear me, my private thoughts.* She felt his amusement at her befuddlement.

"Woah," she marveled. They were essentially communicating telepathically. As dizziness threatened her, Rosa sat back down at the ottoman. She swiped a knuckle at her runny nose and found a speckle of blood. "So, this was passed down from my parents?"

"No," Paul said. "But the combination of your parents' genes created a superior haven that attracted Indigo to infuse with it."

"Superior haven? But my dad was a—"

"Failed architect."

"And my mom was a—"

"Town drunk."

"Is there anything you don't know about me?" Rosa asked.

"There are a number of things I'd like to explore," Paul said, impish droplets from his energies.

"Then tell me something about you, something no one else on Earth knows."

Paul considered this for a second. "My biological mother was originally from Egypt, outside of Cairo. She's since passed."

Rosa sat stunned, thoroughly shocked by Paul's heritage. Was he an immigrant? Adopted? Had he been raised Ascetic? *Don't psychoanalyze him. He can hear you.* "I'm sorry for your loss," she said.

Just then a bell chimed from his device. He gave it a quick glance before keying a response. Rosa attempted to listen for nuances in his resonance to see if she could decipher his thought strands and piece together his message. She felt him think of Dex, of a daytrip, of a dark temple. He looked up to her and smirked.

"You're handing me those, aren't you?" she asked.

"It's good you're already so receptive," he said. Rosa let out a nervous chuckle at having been caught...doing what? Reading his mind? A layer of ethics she was not yet ready to infuse into her already complicated life. "I've got something for you that will help demonstrate the physical process of activating your deepsight. As for your origin questions, I know of someone who can explain it far better than me." He turned toward his counter-top and began arranging things. "I'll be heading out to meet her shortly. *We'll* be heading out."

"Where?"

"The Bronx." He faced her. "The Mandala monasteries. We're going to see another like us. We're going to see Karla."

20

THE MANDALA

SUNDAY NOV 17, 186 PCE

"Seek to escape ignorance.
Freedom from the box
Now shackled to the knowledge.
A Seeker's Paradox."

— *DIARY OF THE MAD GLEE*

As they traveled the skypath sipping martinis and enjoying a Miles Davis channel, Paul inquired about the jewel on Rosa's necklace. Rosa revealed it was a gift from Ferguson by way of Lady Maine. But when Paul advised she attend the Maine Event for clarification on the jewel's significance, Rosa kept quiet her intentions never to attend the event. Quiet even from the forefront of her mind.

Paul spent the voyage attending to three separate conferences, keying one-line responses on two tablets while telekinetically interacting with a slimscreen. He emitted an energy field of high-level flow-state and managerial command. Rosa watched him, captivated by his ethic. Certain Paul had no interest in discussing his business affairs, Rosa busied herself with tracing a lighter's flame against her skin while gazing out at the skypath. She wasn't sure she'd have been able to survive the havoc starting to form out there. But she didn't have to, thanks entirely to the privilege afforded by this chilling, curious man beside her.

Rosa pulled up a Mandala Wiki. The order of secular monks committed to preserving natural intelligence through the exploration of complex scientific and mathematical theories. Monks in the order devoted their lives to two things: responding to theoretical inquiries submitted by outside researchers and assembling the infinite pieces of the Cosmic Equation.

A hypothetical offered by Pierre Laplace held that if a demon knew the exact location and momentum of every particle, it could translate the universe into a single formula, a wave that would include all past and future. So as a pastime, Mandala monks puzzled out this equation.

Mandala Mothers would compile thousands of the Equation's puzzle pieces submitted by the monks, and attempt to find their connections. These Mothering ceremonies were extended affairs of deep meditational chants and prayers. Rumors maintained that ritualistic human sacrifice occurred at these ceremonies, and a stint of laymen heart attacks eventually closed Mothering ceremonies to the public. Rosa wondered how Paul managed to get himself invited. Well, he was Paul Oz. His name held high merit among the Ascetic.

Rosa jumped in her seat at his touch. He'd taken hold of her hand to place a small container in it, sending a sweet jolt of static through her. "Take this."

"What is it?" It looked like a tiny shampoo bottle filled with thick white swirls.

"Something that'll help your brain simulate the mechanics

needed to awaken your deepsight. It's not something I could ever explain in words. You'll simply have to experience it."

"Right. What's in it?"

"A combination of substances, most of which naturally occur in the human body. It may cause some hallucinations, but it only lasts a few minutes."

"Where'd you get it?"

"Given my position, I have access to many things."

"Oh, right. How do I consume it?" Rosa asked as the sky jet touched down.

"You poke a hole in the top here, and inhale as much of the vapor as possible. Then you hold it in for as long as you can before exhaling."

The contents in the bottle appeared solid or possibly a hard liquid, certainly not vapor, but still she said, "Okay," and stabbed a fingernail at the aluminum seal. Paul grabbed her hand before she pierced the foil.

"No. Not now. When we come face to face with Karla."

* * *

They landed a block away from the aptly named Fibonacci Abbey, the monastic headquarters of Edenwald, Bronx. Rosa, Paul and two Oz Corp attendants approached the front gate of the tall Gothic structure. A black-robed man bearing an infinity tattoo on his forehead assessed them, granting entry to Rosa and Paul alone. As the two were escorted along a pristine pebbled path, Rosa felt a rising anxiousness. The building radiated an eerily impending threat somehow spiritual in nature. She felt as if she'd been banished to Hell by Saint Peter and was walking the pristine pebbled path to its front gates.

Within the long desolate halls of the dim abbey, Rosa sensed the tall ominous walls staring back at her. Each intermittent crescent lamp offered an air of menacing benevolence, as if to say, 'Welcome' and 'Be sure to signal when you can breathe no longer.' The three came to a dressing room brimming with rows of brown robes. Upon shutting the door behind him, the Black-Cloak finally addressed them.

"It is my honor to greet you and your guest, Sir Ryland Perry. I am Brother Stephen," he began in lightly accented English. Paul nodded in acknowledgement. "You are here because a Mother has approved your witness. Remove your shoes, deactivate all devices, and cover yourself with a robe." The monk's tone came brash. Rosa half-expected Paul to bite back, but he soundlessly obeyed, exuding energies of veneration. Rosa followed suit, powering down her Ncluded for the first time in years and placing a billowy brown robe over her clothes. Paul waited for her to finish then stuffed her bag and shoes into a duffle bag he placed in a corner.

"We are ready, Brother Stephen," Paul announced. The Black-Cloak ushered them down another long corridor, eventually leading them to an open rotunda. Dozens of male and female brethren in red robes stood waiting, engaged in warm quiet greetings.

"Our chapter has three Mothers in Intellect," Brother Stephen whispered, "Mother Annabel, Mother Thomas and Mother Khalidah. Today we will witness the Mothering of Mother Khalidah." He lifted a hand to the high-rising chapel entrance into which the brethren shuffled. "The mass will be held in the main chapel."

"I'd like to consult with Mother Khalidah after her Mothering," Paul said.

"Impossible. After Mothering, Mothers must stand completely still until nightfall as the spark of Intellect recedes from the body. Guests will have been asked to leave long before then." Paul simply nodded and allowed Brother Stephen to usher them into the chapel's wide nave. Could Paul Oscar be so easily denied a thing?

Once in the chapel, a vibrant energy rushed Rosa from every corner, a consummate living energy far greater than that of Paul's library. The waves came in piercing whisps. Rosa could feel the room itself humming a soft haunting tune. There was dampness in its melody, a subtly hissed warning, a lachrymose arrogance. Rosa sensed its memories. More than one life had been taken in this chapel.

She knew not what to expect. Noticing all other robes in the chapel were red, Rosa realized she and Paul were the only guests. Paul found an empty spot on the floor within the horseshoe-like arrangement of the brethren and motioned for her to sit cross-legged beside him. It took quite some time, but eventually upwards of a thousand, soundless Brothers joined the horseshoe. An elder Brother then stepped forth and sat at its center.

"Oh. Oh. Oh," the elder sang in long, rotund notes, filling the room with deep resonant acoustics.

"Oh. Oh. Oh," responded the mass in a unison so complete even Georg Ohm would find difficulty parsing deviations. A deep rumble shook the heavy walls as the group sang. The elder's call came again and again came the response. Each call and response emanated more purely in tune than the previous, with brighter overtones and brassier echoes approaching a limit of tonal perfection. Several of the men bellowed notes at an octave so low, Rosa could feel their resonances rattling her bones. She noticed Paul participating, so she closed her eyes and followed suit.

The elder then switched to an 'Ooh,' singing the first note of the scale then the major third note of the scale. The mass responded in kind. A second elder joined singing at a minor interval above the original tones. The chilling harmonics produced by the response's reverberating echoes was too much for Rosa to bear. They, along with an overwhelming sense of otherworldly presence among the walls, kneaded tiny fingers into the crannies of her brain. This euphony of beautifully swirling frequencies from such devout concentration rocked her soul near mad.

She was uncertain how long it had been, seconds, minutes, days, but somewhere in the middle of the chordal chant, Rosa felt the physical barriers of her skull loosen ever-so slightly. The gooey writhings of her brain muscle opened, readjusting to the extra space in her head-cavity: the rest of her body a tree stump holding up the light of her opened mind. As part of this magical ensemble, she was helping create this beautiful pathway to her own transcendence. *Speak to me, God,* she thought. *If I could never hear you before, I can hear you now.*

After infinite rounds of this majestic vocal symphony, the chanting came to an abrupt halt. Rosa basked in the ever-mollifying stillness for an eternity. Not until she felt a slight change in pressure did she open her eyes. How long had there been a young, blue-robed girl, possibly a teenager, at the center of the horseshoe surrounded by mounds of paper? The girl, hunched over in prayer, knelt as deathly still as her audience. Rosa could not bring herself to glance over at Paul; her body was simply too heavy.

Suddenly the girl raised her hands to the ceiling and drumming commenced. Roaring ethnic drums resounded an atypical five-four rhythm. Rosa felt the thudding in the valleys of her chest. A group of Brothers broke into an indistinct chant, followed by a separate group with a completely different chant, and yet a third. Though none of the chants appeared to match, they blended seamlessly over the pounding drums.

Rosa watched as the young girl sifted gracefully through the pages, rearranging them almost without touch, assembling the puzzle pieces of the great Cosmic Equation. Rosa could hardly keep her eyes open to witness the Mothering through the intense chanting. She'd been forever changed. Forever opened. She fell back into the wondrous bliss of what she now knew was true prayer.

21

KNOCKERS

SUNDAY NOV 17, 186 PCE

"I saw some things, Dad," Tory said. He maneuvered a white bishop across the chess table in the backroom of their Nottingham pub. "Things I'll never unsee." Abel Ross rubbed at his chin as he studied the board.

"Couple of sick blokes trying to get some meds. Can you blame them?"

"These weren't just sick blokes, Dad. I'm honestly not sure I could categorize them as people. They were...I don't know... Wolf like. Even my Glass couldn't parse them."

"Wolf like?" Abel smirked and used a pawn to take out Tory's last rook. "Well, it hasn't hit our side of the 'verse. You know what I think? I think you're just overwhelmed. I can't even get a good game out of you."

"If you were there, Dad, if you saw what I saw. There's sick, and then there's...changed." Tory reclined in his chair reliving the scene. Three bloody-eyed patients, their skin rife with accelerated decomposition, ripped through Husk's torso like knives through cheese, tossing him aside like a dead rat. Tory shivered.

"Tory, if you're in real danger, you should leave the city. See your mum in Boston." Tory frowned. Abel knew better than anyone that Tory's mum didn't forgive easily. While Tory longed for her to cease painting him a family deserter, he'd long since given up begging for it.

"Can't leave the city, Dad. I'm too deep."

"No, you're just stubborn, aren't you?" Tory remained silent, too shaken to argue. "At the very least, get sorted. Focus on turning this outbreak into an opportunity."

"Right now, I need to focus on what's turning New York City into a Thriller revival party. People are changing. Literally changing."

"Well, if you ask me, *you've* changed." Abel looked into his son's eyes. "Ever since you started working for that sweatshop, you've slowly been losing it, haven't you? It's an amazing post, yes, but it's not healthy, Torian. You need to focus on your own legacy, instead of putting yourself in harm's way for someone else's."

Abel hadn't been in the line of fire, hadn't witnessed those predators tear through anyone and anything in their path. It was no flu. Tory and his father said nothing for a long while as Tory worked to clear the gore from his mind.

"How's mum and your sisters?" Abel asked cautiously.

"They're fine, Dad."

"Where are we in convincing your sisters to merse in for a game?"

"Still working on them, Dad." Tory ran a restless hand through his hair. He considered how open he'd always been with his biological father. His weekly chess chats with the great Converser of Manchester had been Tory's safe haven for banter and advice in an otherwise solitary world. A heavy question coalesced. "Dad."

"Yeah, Torian."

"From what you know of Paul Oscar, do you think he..." Tory paused. Abel whirled a wrist impatiently. "You think he's had relations with Cindy?"

With no hesitation or even slight dismay Abel said, "Oh, I'm sure of it. The bloke feels entitled to her."

Tory grimaced, irked by Abel's cavalier tone. "But he's not entitled to her, Dad. The hell. She's your daughter for Christ's sake."

"She's there with you in America, IRL, as you wished. Any feelings of his entitlement toward her lies on you, son, doesn't it?" Abel's words came more as hard facts than accusations.

"Well, he's not entitled to her. And I'm done talking about it." Tory leaned toward the chessboard to feign a few mental calculations over the game.

"Hate to say this, Torian, but I'm certain he believes you accept his right to her." Tory said nothing and kept his eyes on the board. "His feelings of entitlement come from the way you bend at the knee to his every whim."

Tory slapped the chess game to the floor. "I said I'm done fucking talking about him!"

"Woah," Abel placated. "Because you haven't access to your fancy trancy gadgets, you can't contain those anger issues of yours in a merse?"

"Ef that!" Tory spat.

"Oh, look at you. You're a perfectly healthy male. Why you chose to be a half-bot, a second-class citizen, is beyond me."

"I'm out of here." Tory rose to his feet and turned on his heel.

Abel rose as well. "Oh, yes," Abel sang, sarcasm seething from his lips. "Walk out on your father. Put me in my place."

"My father, right?" Tory whirled around, indignant. Abel was correct in that Tory's inability to access his biohacks in a merse made composing himself untenable. "Where were you,

Father, when Stepdad was bashing us about? Where were you, *Father*, when Vi and I spent two weeks looking for Cindy only to find she'd been—" Tory paused. "Where were you when we needed you?"

"You know exactly where I was, Torian."

"Yes. Gone. And now mum, Vi, Cindy, they say *I* abandoned them. I went off to set up a better life for them. But they blame *me* for Stepdad. Shun *me*. But who else would they blame? You?"

"Watch it, Torian."

"Right. Watch it. If you hadn't left there'd be no Stepdad." Abel gave a defiant look but did not respond. "I've got more pressing matters to deal with than this bullshit."

Tory mersed out.

* * *

Tory found himself still seated on a foldout chair in a small Oz Corp suite. An open bed held a snoring Leland Shark, who'd lost consciousness soon after they'd hoisted him onto the skyjet and who'd now been out for almost sixteen hours.

"He's still asleep," Kris informed. He and DZ sat cross-legged on the floor, staring up intently at the Pharma Farm CEO. Having volunteered to keep watch over Leland, Tory hadn't the chance to rest, wash up and more importantly reboot his biohacks. He was running on low. "Cool tats," Kris blurted. He and DZ were ogling the blanket of tattoos on Tory's arms.

"Cindy an ex-courtship or something?" DZ asked, pointing to expertly calligraphed ink bearing the name.

"My sister. I've got my other sister, Viola, on my other arm and my mother, Alice, across my back." The two gawked at him in admiration as if he'd just revealed the true meaning of existence. Disinterested in the attention, Tory got to his feet. "I'm done waiting. Force the wakeup."

Kris grew excited at the prospect. "I can zap him," he said. "I'm hooked into his Ncluded, so I can send a shockwave through him. He ain't gonna like it though."

"Will it hurt him?"

"Hope so. According to his vitals he's sick as hell, Ross." Unable to use his Glass on Oz Corp property, Tory was forced to rely on Kris's assessment. He mulled it over a moment then affirmed the zap, hoping to grab Leland before he lost coherence. If DZ's mother was right, Tory feared the brain-ache was actively evolving to reduce its incubation period.

Kris swiped at a few buttons, and Leland Shark sat up like a sharpshooting target. Leland coughed, gasped, flailed about in discomfort, looked to his current company, then laid back against his pillow unimpressed. His face was a pale, withered balloon, and his once slick black hair a fuzzy gray mat. Dark pink circles framed his puffy eyelids.

Taking care to remain out of arm's reach, Tory pulled a chair beside the bed. "You said you had info. Sing."

Leland spoke with a slow, wheezing bark. "I speak to no one until I get my counsel at my side, a mouth on my cock, a beer in my hand and a steak. And not that Smartifice piss milk. A real steak. A man's steak."

"I saw what you saw, Shark," Tory said. "Please know I'll do whatever I've gotta do to get an explanation."

"You think I'm afraid of you, Ross? You think I'm afraid of Oz Corp?" Leland lifted his right leg. A deep red stain at his ankle shone through a bandage around his foot. "This is what I'm afraid of. God is what I'm afraid of. Now either get me what I want or—" He broke into an abrupt violent fit of coughs.

Tory turned to DZ. "A cup of water and a soaked face towel." DZ hopped to his feet.

"I don't want your cold compress," Leland slurred. "I want what I asked for."

Kris sent a message to Tory's wrist. "Vitals were better off while asleep. May not last thru night." Tory nodded at Kris, sliding his chair away from Leland's bed.

"Okay," Tory yielded. "No one's giving you oral, and you'll be dead before your counsel can get here. We can get you the beer and the steak." Tory messaged the request to Sherri.

"At least let me see Sherri Weiler's knockers. Damn, if she's not a piece of ass."

"The steak. The beer. That's it." Tory said. Sherri messaged him back with '15 mins' which Tory displayed to Leland.

"Oh, thank God," Leland exhaled. "Will she be the one to serve me?" He let out a rasped cackle inviting another outburst of coughs. With no other staff privy to the situation, Sherri could very well be the one to deliver the meal. DZ returned with the cup of water and a cold compress. Tory cautiously stepped forward to hand the items to Leland then stepped back to his chair. Leland took a long sip from the cup.

"Shark, you see your meal's on its way. Show your hand," Tory bargained.

"I don't trust you, Ross," Leland purred.

"I just risked my life to give you a cup of water," Tory defended. Leland examined Tory with the face of a bulldog chewing on a wasp then grunted a slight nod.

"The Maines," Leland whispered. "Lady Maine."

"What about them?"

"They've got a video file. Their thug swiped it from a security cam right after Ferg's death...murder...whatever. The thug's got it on a hard drive in his apartment."

"So, Occam's damn Razor all along?" Kris exclaimed. Tory stifled a wince at the interruption, his patience bone thin.

"No, no. You're not listening," Leland huffed, struggling to keep his compress in place. "They have the video, but they're holding it for—" he broke, appearing to choke on his own saliva. Tory and Kris both hopped to their feet uncertain how to proceed. However, the choking was short-lived. "They're holding it for Bianca, or over Bianca's head. Who knows with them."

"The Valentis?" Tory asked. He looked to Kris who did not appear the least bit surprised. Kris knew something about the Valentis' role in this that he didn't. Tory didn't like that. "What's in the video?" Tory pressed. "Why'd the Valentis want Ferguson dead? Did they steal the components needed to manufacture this brain-ache from his lab? What are they planning? What is this experiment? I need answers *now*, Shark."

The CEO's eyelids fell to an unblinking droop. "They're coming to take me, Ross," Leland whispered. "I hear them. I feel them. Don't let them take me."

"What are you playing at?" Tory asked.

"Woah," Kris said, edging toward the doorway. "His vitals are off the chain. He's gonna tap out real soon."

"It's going to say I'm dead," Leland snickered. "But I won't be dead. You will, though, if you don't kill me first." His voice had dropped several octaves during the course of the sentence. Tory touched a finger to the TerraGuard-grade gauss pistol tucked at his back. Though he hadn't fired a round since his days in combat training, Tory had his pistol's magazine fully loaded.

Tory turned to Kris. "Assemble your people in a suite. Lock the door." Kris nodded. He and DZ shuffled out without a word of protest. Tory pulled out the pistol and sat back down.

"You have no idea what it's like, Ross, being the offspring of a great man. Him not caring you exist."

"We've all got daddy issues, Shark."

"I built the largest pharmaceutical complex in the world. Still, it pales in comparison to the great Dr. George Quintus Ferguson." Leland croaked out another cackle. "And now watch me as I die at the feet of another one of his mad creations."

Tory leaned back in his chair, spinning the pistol in his hands to test its weight. "And what exactly is this mad creation, Leland?"

Leland opened his eyes in a fit of sudden terror and roared at a tearful yell. "He put millions of his tiny minions in my head! They're going to take me and make me do bad things!" Leland tried to rise but plopped back with hard finality. The cup of water and cold compress fell to the ground. "He's punishing us for our sins," he whispered before closing his eyes.

Tory watched as the motionless CEO withered before him. Leland Shark was indeed a great man, despite his recent decisions. His Pharma empire generated scores of game-changing technological advancements, some of which Tory publicly endorsed. He'd respected Leland Shark for embracing the transhuman movement. And now he was going to end Leland Shark's life.

While Paul Oz was off gallivanting with Rosa Lejeune, here Tory stood at the precipice of their investigation, a pistol and a man's life in his hands. He tried to convince himself it will have been the disease that killed Leland; but the disease wasn't sitting on the business end of a high-powered coil gun. Killing a man changed a person forever, a change Tory never wanted to know. Once capable, always capable.

Uncertain how long he'd been trapped in thought, Tory grew keenly alert upon hearing a short rumbling growl emanate from Leland's throat. He almost dismissed it as some sort of auditory hallucination, but it came again, this time louder, more feral. It seemed to come from beneath the man rather than within him.

As Tory strained to listen, both he and Leland winced as the door creaked open. Tory got to his feet to find Sherri Weiler with a tray bearing barbecue steak and a pint of beer. He cursed himself for neglecting to call her off.

"Weiler. Out. Now," Tory mouthed as he tilted his head toward the door. He did what he could to keep the pistol out of view. He didn't want her to ever know this of him, that he was a killer, or was to become one shortly. Too goal-oriented to heed Tory's caution, Sherri set the tray at Leland's bedside table then returned to stand beside her colleague. Tory's muscles calcified at the sight of her brief proximity to Leland. He tried to whisper to her while stepping in front to shield her, but Leland boorishly overpowered him.

"Sherri Weiler!"

"Dr. Shark. How are you feeling?" she asked, peering over Tory's shoulder.

"Sherri, give us the room," Tory said now that everyone was talking.

"Sherri, I'm dying," Leland croaked, his eyes now wholly bloodshot. "You remember when you worked with us on those supplements for prolonged merses?"

"I do," she said gravely. He'd been a substantial mentor to her and had attempted to steal her from Oz Corp on numerous occasions. But whatever bond the two may have shared meant very little right now.

"Not going to ask you again, Weiler," Tory said, his eyes hard on Leland. He wanted to turn and simply shove her out but opted against sudden movement.

"Ross, I'll thank you to let me see my friend through his final moments," Sherri snipped. Her sternness triggered a contented sigh from her mentor.

"Sherri, can a man have a dying wish?" Leland's words came choked and pained.

"Oh, Dr. Shark," Sherri exhaled. "I don't know what to say." She didn't know what Tory knew. She hadn't seen what Tory had seen. "Of course. Anything."

"Show me those knockers." The request came low, serious. Tory got into stance, placing the gauss pistol's muzzle to the floor. He pulled back the slide to chamber a round, and the sound of the slide-back stiffened Sherri abruptly. "Come on, Sherri. You see me dying right in front of you." Sherri did not, could not respond. "Don't be shy, babe. Ross won't mind." Leland let out a throaty snarl. "I'm sure I'm not the only man in here *dying* to get between those legs." Save for a slight tremble, Sherri upheld her perfect stillness.

Tory superimposed a virtual bull's-eye over Leland's chest. "Don't try to be a hero, Ross," Leland rasped. "You're just a pawn. You're just the shadow of a greater man." Leland lifted his head. His voice grew preternaturally grisly as it doubled with the accompaniment of a growling undertone. "You think you can stop me? You think you have power? You have no power! You are nothing before me! Now get out of my way! Let Daddy get to those knockers!" Leland leapt from the bed at full force toward them, all weakness gone.

In that instant, Torian Ross trained his weapon on the charging target and pulled the trigger. Bursts of deep blue energies poured forth from the gun and pumped into the man's body, perforating him with a half-dozen perfect holes as if he were construction paper.

Tory watched as Leland Shark shuddered with the push back of each blow. Tory felt the depressions of each slug's impact against the man's body, felt the profound release within him as he steeled himself against recoil. He tasted it: that force of having completely dominated the living will of another being. He felt the power; the control. And somewhere beneath the many layers of his decency, he enjoyed it.

Sherri remained silent as she and Tory jumped back, allowing Leland's body to fall face first to the floor. Tory stepped around the corpse, looked up to Sherri's contorted face. "You don't want to see this part." And after she backed out of the room, Tory pumped two more rounds into Leland's skull.

22
GONE WITH THE WIND
SUNDAY NOV 17, 186 PCE

"All patterns observable by man are limited to man's acuity."

— *DIARY OF THE MAD GLEE*

Paul helped Rosa to her feet. "How long was I out?" she asked, surveying the room to find most monks, including the young girl, had left the chapel. Paul held a finger to his lips and briskly ushered her out of the chapel. Rosa struggled to keep up with his determined strides. While a few Black-Cloaks gave them sidelong glances, none of the Red-Cloaks even noticed them.

Paul led Rosa to a room marked 'Archives.' The cramped mega-library smelled of spice and pine. Several Black-Cloaks perched on ladders or knelt underfoot, arranging books. This library exuded a perfunctory whisper, a busied hum, like a cat occupied with yarn.

Paul turned a few shelved corners before stopping beside a short, bald black man in a black robe and glasses. Rosa couldn't remember the last time she'd seen real glasses. The young man, who'd been attempting to replace a book on a shelf just beyond his reach, looked over to them and gave Paul a wide smile.

"Well, if it isn't Paul Oscar in the flesh," the man said. Rosa detected an African accent.

"Brother Ori," Paul greeted. Each bent at the waist in a slight bow.

"You look good, man," Brother Ori said.

"Thank you. You look smart." Both men looked to Rosa. "Rosa Lejeune," Paul introduced. Rosa said hello and offered her hand, but Brother Ori made no moves to receive her.

"Pleased to meet you, Ms. Lejeune. I am Brother Ori Eze, Master Archivist of the Fibonacci Abbey. Do not take offense. I cannot shake your hand due to a personal vow." Rosa nodded and stepped back. "I've known this man since before that oh-so-tumultuous boarding school." This intrigued Rosa. She wanted him to regale her with tales. Ori addressed Paul. "Remember when we engaged in that dilemma argument? Aye! It was a spar of the ages! Determinism versus indiscriminate chance versus freewill versus divine command. Man, what an epic battle. While the other folks fought with sticks, we fought with quips."

"Thank you, Brother Ori, for arranging this visit with such short notice," Paul said, uninterested in trekking down memory lane.

"How dare you thank me? Anything for the great Paul Oz." Ori turned to Rosa. "This man saved my life, not once, but twice." Rosa wondered at this. Everyone, including herself, seemed indebted to Paul Oscar.

"Get me in with Karla," Paul said, again with the quiet command.

"Getting in to speak with Mother Khalidah will be very difficult. She's on a strict vow of silence until sundown."

"I don't necessarily need to speak with her. I just need her audience."

Brother Ori considered this for a brief moment. "Hm. Okay. These books here need to go up there in descending alphabetical order." Ori first pointed to several dozen books in a cart beside him then back to the shelf he couldn't reach. With no further prompting Paul set to the task of arranging the books on the shelf. Ori again turned to Rosa. "Ah! This is the life."

Rosa smiled back at him. "Brother Ori," she started. "What I've read about the Order pales in comparison to the mass I just experienced. I'd like to know the purpose of a Mandala monk from a true monk."

"Well, I'm hardly a true monk, Ms. Rosa," Ori chuckled. "Black-Cloaks are auxiliary; Red-Cloaks are practicing; Blue-Cloaks are Sparked. Most Reds and Blacks are male, holding a higher penchant for rote solution, while the Sparked tend to be female, having a greater propensity to find connections. Me—I archive external inquiries." Rosa hummed with interest as Ori spoke. "Though Schools of Intelligence spit out innovative advancements, they first bring any problems requiring divine computation to us. Comfort corrodes the mind. We Mandala embrace the hardships necessary for superior innovation."

"The monotony of a quiet life stimulates the creative mind," Rosa quoted.

"Albert Einstein," Ori nodded. "Ms. Rosa, the brain can carry two petabytes of information and is capable of ten to the sixteenth processes per second. Imagine sculpting yourself to maximize that power. Through our denial of luxuries, we live a rich life of the mind."

Rosa sensed the pride broadcasting from his being. "Why the Cosmic Equation?" she prodded.

"So, we can figure out how to observe the universe," Ori

shrugged. "The only difference between classical and quantum observation is our limited understanding of observation."

"But you're devoting your entire life to adding small bits to an infinite equation you'll literally never be able to solve." To this Brother Ori's wide grin returned.

"The same reason I wake up every morning to archive books; the same reason you followed Paul Oscar here to visit the monastery. Ms. Rosa, we don't take this vow of monastic intellect simply to solve an impossible equation or to contribute research to SOIs. Using a pencil and paper to harness principles of unobservable reality is true magic. We do it for the pure fascination."

Paul looked back to Ori. "Done."

Rosa hadn't realized Brother Ori was blind until he grabbed his white cane. He did nothing more than walk Rosa and Paul back to the main chapel, informing them that Mother Khalidah had returned to the chapel to observe her vow of silence. "If you simply want her audience, there she is."

"Well played," Paul commended.

"As a Black-Cloak, I cannot follow you into the chapel. My friend, it was an honor." Again, Ori and Paul exchanged bows.

Paul and Rosa entered the chapel to find several monks scattered in silent prayer. Rosa tensed at the handful of Black-Cloaks supervising them from the entrance. Karla stood motionless in front of the altar with her arms outstretched, her forehead's infinity symbol as blue as her robes. She was remarkably beautiful. Dark hair complimented the silver studs above and below her lips and at the inner circles of her eyes. Rosa tried following Paul to greet her, but he palmed for her to remain by the entrance. He brought his lips an inch from her ear and sent an undeniable thought-wave into her mind. 'Now.'

As Paul approached the altar to kneel before Karla, Rosa dug into her collar, recovering the tiny bottle held taught by her necklace. She looked to the silent praying brethren around her, and thought, *Here goes.* She poked the bottle's aluminum seal and sucked in the thick white vapor. *This smoke tastes of old mothballs* were her final thought as a being on the conscious plane.

* * *

Rosa is immediately aware of every crevice in her brain. She feels the shift, the gelatinous writhing of her brain's hemispheres as they unfold into an open plane. She senses the lift of a proverbial flap at her brain's center, letting previously unseen light pour in. The living forces in the chapel echo so stridently, Rosa can almost understand the words to their distinct song, not quite, but almost. A deep, calming euphoria pervades her body as the room begins a steady rowboat sway. Her physical body leans against the wall behind her and is no longer important.

She is coasting on an astral plane of sentient wavelengths. She experiences visual perception from beyond her eyes, the screen of her mind now encompassing her full head. The chapel shines cartoon-bright caked in a menagerie of undulating fractals. The face of each structure doubles and triples into whirling waves of interactive color.

Before long, everyone and everything around her fades to black, everyone but a klieg-lighted Paul and Karla. A quivering ice-blue haze envelopes a kneeling Paul Oscar who wears the full armor of a regal knight, complete with hilted sword and open helm. His face and hands are drenched in crimson blood. A dark ball of insurmountable rage sits where his heart should sit, trapped within a steel cage of forced calm.

A column of gray haze surrounds Karla, who appears floating several meters from the ground. She is wearing an elegant black gown and loose-fitting headscarf over a black gossamer of silken curls, all flowing vigorously as if wafting in a formidable storm.

"Wind," Paul addresses Karla without moving his lips.

"Healer," she responds in kind. "The Fire does not burn bright." Rosa feels a sharp tug at her consciousness. She has been addressed. She cannot yet participate and can only Observe.

"She is still learning," Paul says.

"The Healer is too kind to The Fire."

"I am." Paul's voice breaks with a hint of vulnerability.

"The Wind has not witnessed the Healer for many Earth cycles."

"We've chosen different paths."

"Indeed. The Healer has chosen to indulge in games," Karla nods. "And now the Healer visits."

"I seek information."

Karla regards him. "Must The Wind trust the inquiries of a white knight with a dark heart?"

"As much as I must trust an uncovered Muslimah."

Karla exhibits a strong force of defense that shakes the chapel. "The Healer is aware that this body in which The Wind presides is covered in mind and heart. The captors of this body fear the one true God. That fear has thoroughly corrupted this Brotherhood. But The All-Forgiving and All-Mighty God allows this body the right to Mother, so the captors still worship the one true God, however unwittingly."

"I mean you no insult," Paul says.

"The Wind is not insulted by The Healer's brazen ignorance. The Wind will grant The Healer one free inquiry for The Healer's gracious visit. A second will cost The Healer an open favor of any scope."

"I accept your terms. Offer me any knowledge you have of a plot to eliminate Dr. Ferguson."

"Yes," Karla begins. "The Doctor sought answers from The Wind regarding Indigo. The Wind disclosed certain answers in exchange for promises the Doctor's corpse cannot fulfill. A fortnight preceding The Doctor's expiration, Valenti asked this body in which The Wind presides if it sought freedom from its captors. Valenti offered this body a chance to be reunited with its true love."

"Pelleher," Paul notes.

"If this body's true love completed a favor for Valenti, Valenti would reunite the lovers. Unfortunately, this body's true love perished alongside The Doctor prior to the exchange."

"And you accepted the trade to be reunited with Pelleher?" Paul asks.

"This body did accept."

"My second inquiry—"

"The Healer has already asked The Wind two questions." Karla says. Paul remains silent for a moment, lowers his head in thought, then returns his gaze.

"Grant me another question."

"This third inquiry will again cost The Healer."

"I understand, and I accept."

"The Healer is kind to The Fire and impulsive with The Wind," Karla muses. "Perhaps The Healer is foolish." Rosa finds Paul's fallibility reassuring.

"He is no fool who gives what he cannot keep to gain what he cannot lose," Paul says. A Jim Elliot quote, Rosa notes. Karla responds with a radiant smile, permeating the chapel with a bright golden warmth. Paul carefully considers his next communication. "Before I present my third inquiry, will you not grant Fire a question?" Rosa appreciates the consideration.

"If The Fire grants The Healer voice on The Fire's behalf,

The Wind will permit The Fire one free inquiry for the gracious visit."

"She wishes to be enlightened on the origins of the Mayik."

Mayik? A sharp jolt ripples through Rosa's consciousness at the beautiful, onerous word. *Mahhh...k.* It has been swimming in the soup of her subconscious for an eternity.

"The Wind will gladly oblige," Karla breathes. "Mayik, from Sanskrit *Māyika*, shadow, was coined by a Mayik: a host body conceived of the element Indigo. Though Indigo is not mere element. It is a conceptual fundament—the physical thought particles of The All-Being. These fundaments concocted this universe, but could not exist within it, as a balloon blower cannot exist within the balloon the blower is blowing." As Rosa struggles to understand, she feels herself slowly corporating back to the conscious plane. She holds fast to this whimsical plane, as she's been waiting all her life to hear these very words.

Karla continues. "This Mayik, Khalidah Nejem, houses the fundament of ignited matter, or Wind. While the more primary concept of super ignited matter, or Fire, is housed in Rosa Lejeune. Paul Oscar Ryland Perry houses the primary concept of creation and restoration. There are others: liquid matter, solid matter, destruction, light..."

The contours of Rosa's being firm up along the wall behind her. She strains to listen to Karla's words as they fade. "As the ever-expanding balloon of this universe increased," Karla says, "so thinned the constitution of its bubble, so much so that a breach emerged, a tunnel, a Gateway. This Gateway allowed for these conceptual fundaments to diffuse into this universe. Each concept suffused a proper, most evolved host to create its Mayik, So, the Fire chose Rosa Lejeune as its Mayik. All but the concept of superdense matter, which manifests itself as The Invader—found a proper host. But the physical limitations of this universe do not allow superdensity to exist comfortably, so The Invader splattered among the asphalt after diffusing through the Gateway."

"So, the Indigo in Pelleher's tests solely comprise The Invader," Paul says, his thought-wave now a distant murmur.

"Ironic Invader would invade improperly."

"If this is The Healer's third question, The Wind will answer," Karla says.

After a moment's contemplation, Paul says, "My third question is, who killed Dr. Ferguson?"

"Paul?" Rosa called, having fully reverted to a normal state of consciousness. Apart from Paul, all in the chapel were unabashedly ogling her, including Karla, who again stood on solid ground. With one outstretched hand, Karla pointed a finger at Rosa's face, then down to the necklace. Rosa looked down to find the jewel casting an oddly quivering green glow against her brown robe. Quick and short motor-like bursts spurted through the jewel as its temperature rapidly increased. A Red-Cloak approached Rosa from the far end of the chapel and stood directly before her. He stared intently at her clavicle. Before she could utter words of protest, he reached out and grabbed at the charm, thoroughly examining it.

Rosa stepped back, meeting the hard wall behind her. In the next instant she found herself encircled by Red-Cloaks and infinity symbols above awe-struck grins. Icy-green light flailed from the gem as monks stumbled over themselves to close in around her. They began reciting a rumbling, scarcely discernible chant. Rosa cupped the jewel to her chest and shoved forward, but did not get far. Though the monks appeared nonviolent, panic-ridden tremors started up her spine.

A deep dreary menace permeated the chapel walls complete with that oh too familiar ethereal wisp. As the tumultuous chanting amplified, some Brothers grabbed hold of Rosa's arms, tugging her body in either direction, while others continued to touch at the glowing charm at her breasts. The initial Red-Cloak who'd come to inspect the jewel placed his hands on her neck, feeling for the clasp. It was when she saw that he had one cobalt eye—that they *all* had one bionic eye— that she realized she was having a full-blown panic attack.

Dozens of Johnny Angelo's tugged and snatched at her body. Her arms buckled. Her legs buckled. And as the Red-Cloak fumbled with the clasp, his breath against her cheek, she could do nothing but stare up unblinking at the candle-lit chandelier. As she battled to break the spell, the ethereal whispers usurped her senses. The candles in the chandelier danced with her fear. The harder she strained to free herself, the brighter they shined.

Rosa gathered her full wit and screamed to within an inch of her breath. The candles screamed with her. As if on cue, their flames flared outward, clapping against the rope holding the heavy light fixture, and the chandelier came crashing to the chapel floor. Wails and shouts of terror ensued as hands of smoke engulfed the room.

Suddenly a pair of arms gripped firmly around Rosa's waist, yanking her backward. She kicked back hard but could do nothing to break the fierce grasp. The sheer force of the yank ripped her arms free from the tugging Brethren, causing the assailant behind her to stumble backward.

She whirled around to find a panting Paul Oscar. He wasted no time in bending forward, grabbing her at the hips and hoisting her over his shoulder. He then spun on his heel and charged through the raucous, resonating a thick shield of determination. Rosa cringed through the electric pulse of his arm and shoulder.

"Arms out. Flap your wings," Paul called to Rosa. Red-Cloaks persisted in grabbing toward her, but faltered back in pained recoil as she flailed her arms about. As Rosa kept the monks at bay, Paul plowed through their nonviolent pursuit.

The monks followed them to the front lawn. Paul stormed across the pebbled path and through the gate to where the Oz Corp jet hovered. The Brothers did not follow past the gate yet continued chanting, hands outstretched.

"We only want to harness the glowing power of that charm," the Brothers pleaded. Paul ignored them, practically tossing Rosa into the jet. Attendants helped her settle in as Paul remained outside, dispensing an air of managed control.

"Disrobe," he ordered Rosa as he did so himself. Rosa conformed but bit her lip at the brusqueness in his tone. "Anything important in your bag?"

Though she would have liked her shoes, she shook her head and tossed over the robe. Paul walked over to the chanting Brothers and kindly draped the robes over one of the outstretched hands.

"Thank you for having us."

* * *

The skyjet sailed in silence. Once her nerves calmed enough for rational thought, Rosa tried to question Paul about what the hell just happened. But he simply powered on a tablet and began working, radiating a wall of forced calm. A thought shield. "A minute," he rebuffed. But minutes came and minutes went. She wasn't asking for a full Jungian analysis; she simply needed to know what she was, to understand the composition fallacy that was her very self. Had she caused the candles to blow? Had she truly danced with fire?

She certainly *felt* human, yet evidently, she was extra-dimensional, made from God's thought particles that...flowed in from a rip in the cosmos? And there were others of these... personified thought concepts. Other...Mayiks? How did Karla even know all this? And what the hell was up with this gem? Rosa felt she deserved answers.

She tried a new line of questioning to Paul, asking why Karla had pointed at her or why the Red-Cloaks freaked out. Paul still did not react. Rosa made the bold mistake of placing a hand on his arm. She felt his body stiffen at her touch. He emitted a wave of labored restraint so thick she could almost see its hefty barricade. She backed away from him, her heart suddenly racing. She wanted to be grateful to him for freeing her from the frenzied Brethren, but was it not he who'd put her in harm's way in the first place? He opened this outlandish world to her, threw her in headfirst, and gave her nothing by way of explanation.

"You know," Rosa sighed as she looked to the window. "Now that I know what I am, I don't think I'm interested in the damsel in distress role." Her statement hung there for a minute as a few beeps chimed from Paul's tablet.

"I can respect that," he finally said without raising his eyes. She wracked her brain wondering if forced calm was his stasis or if he was annoyed with her. One thing was certain: Paul Oscar was thoroughly exhausting. She looked to her Ncluded and busied herself with searching out all possible spellings of the term Mayik as her frayed nerves cooled.

A minute later, the flight attendant peeked in. "Paul, I've received word they've just called an official quarantine on New York City."

23
SHOTS FIRED

SUNDAY NOV 17, 186 PCE

K ris heard a yell, then the crack of six fired gauss slugs, a brief silence, then two more shots. "Oh hell," he said in awe. He and the team were sitting quietly at the breakfast table of their Oz Corp suite sifting through chatverse tags for brainache posts. There hadn't been many reported cases, perhaps a baker's dozen, yet the chatverse teamed with sightings of people dubbed #Infecteds.

"So that's how we deal with them?" Becky asked. "You know...the zombies. We just shoot 'em?"

"They're not technically zombies," Aztec corrected. "They don't crave brains for sustenance. Their symptoms appear more similar to rabies, albeit an outlandish variant."

"Couldn't we put poison in a syringe or zap their Ncludeds instead of shooting 'em?"

"We'd be hard-pressed to find bio-weaponry as civilians," Aztec said. "Besides, approaching an Infected to insert a syringe would be very dangerous."

As the group conversed, Kris kept his head clear. He was on Oz Corp property working on level with Ross, Weiler and

Paul Oz. They trusted him to keep alert despite coming perilously close to more than one Infected, despite having been threatened at gunpoint. Kris was determined to remain valuable.

Everyone knew Johnny Angelo to be Lady Maine's thug-apparent, so it was he who possessed this telltale video file. Kris nearly gagged at the thought of him. Johnny Angelo had ruined Rosa, then went off to live the good life while Rosa receded into reclusion? Why she settled on jarhead Johnny remained a mystery to Kris. He swallowed, pulled up Johnny's current apartment, assessed the security protocols, and verified that Johnny did have an active external hard drive on the premises.

All conversations at the table ceased as Torian Ross stormed the suite. He'd always projected an air of badassery, but that air was now tinged with an '*Oh, and I just killed a motherfucker.*' And everyone in the room felt it. He ignored the stares, advanced to Kris, and stared down at the hacker with an austerity that could melt ice. "First," Ross said, his voice low and terse, "what do you know about the Valentis that I don't?"

Kris fought against reacting at Ross's hard tone. "I saw Bianca Valenti in a private merse with Husk, and Shark and a man named Charles Tyler, who is working to decrypt Ferguson's will." Kris paused then said, "I committed a first-degree immersion assault."

Ross kept a hard face as he mulled this over. "You don't keep that kind of intel to yourself no matter how many planes you hijacked to get it. We clear?" Kris's quick nod of affirmation softened Ross's ire a bit. "Ferg shuts out the Valentis, his principal sponsors. So, they team up not only with Pharma, but also with the guys decrypting the will."

"Looks like it. All to get their hands on Ferg's postmortem grab-bag."

"Right." Ross scratched at his chin. "And the research."

"Is this Indigo some kind of age accelerator?" Kris asked. "The Infecteds seem to get old really quick."

"No," Ross said evenly. "Mind control." Kris flinched. It did make sense, considering the woman on the subway's ability to detect Kris's fear. Yet she hadn't acted in response to his change in heart rate, but in conjunction with it. "What've you got on Johnny Angelo?" Ross asked.

"He's got an apartment over on Forty-First and Eighth," Kris said, projecting a screenshot hologram of the area. "He's got a running external on site, but I can't determine an exact location, what it looks like or what's on it from here. Bad news is there's an army of front desk bots. Worse news, you need a fingerprint to get into his unit."

"It's fine," Ross said. "I know a way into his apartment. Just find out if there are any other drives on location. We need to get the video file. Now."

"On it."

* * *

Rosa and Paul sat alone in the parked skyjet beneath a setting sun. Rosa had spent the bulk of the journey grappling with thoughts, questions, theories. Was she to believe she sprung up like Athena from a particle in outer space, or more precisely outer space's outer space? She'd witnessed her skin very clearly absorb fire. She'd witnessed Paul revitalize flowers and levitate eggs. And there was the chandelier. One thing was certain, she was definitely more than just an empath.

"You'll need to attend the Maine Event and consult Lady Maine," were Paul's first words since she'd given up questioning him earlier. He continued keying dutifully at his tablet.

"So that's how this works? Your wish is my command?" She kept her voice calm, tempered.

"That would be convenient."

"Do you speak to everyone like you own them?"

"I speak with authority where I have authority."

"You don't have authority over me," Rosa said. She felt Paul's eyes on her, studying her.

"I believe you've made that very clear," Paul said. "However, your charm—which perhaps cost me future visits to the monastery—demonstrated a convincing reaction to the forces wielded throughout our conversation with Karla. And it was given to you by Lady Maine." Sensing no frustration in his energies, Rosa leaned back in her seat.

"Can't we figure it out on our own? Don't you have labs for this sort of thing?"

"To clarify, you're suggesting I jeopardize my research teams to said forces, in lieu of a two-minute conversation with Lady Maine."

"That's not at all what I'm suggesting," Rosa lied. "Look, I've already turned down Lady Maine, and she doesn't reissue invites."

"I'm assuming the offer to accompany Johnny Angelo still stands?"

Rosa fought to stifle an outburst. How could he have known about Johnny Angelo's offer to escort her to the Event? Had he been spying on her back at the cycling dorm? Torian Ross must have caught the tidbit and reported it back to Paul Oscar like a good little minion.

"But he...there's got to be another way," she said. She could hardly express the gravity of her very real PTSD to anyone, let alone Paul Oscar.

"Of course," Paul said lightly. "We could forgo a comprehensive understanding of Indigo and of how and why Dr. Ferguson lost his life." She sat up and spun toward him. He looked back at her expressionless. How dare he put that all on her? Could he be so apathetic to her very public history with Johnny Angelo? Did he have no human emotion? Rosa breathed through looming tremors. "Call him," Paul suggested so coolly she could hardly bear it. "Man up. Play to win."

"I can't play at your level."

"Can't?" Paul shrugged with a flippant gesture toward her Ncluded. "We're gods, Rosa." Rosa blinked through it. It killed her that he was right. A sit down with the otherwise unattainable Lady Maine was the ultimate play. Lady was a main puzzle-piece in the convoluted tomfoolery surrounding Ferguson's death.

Against every fiber in her being, Rosa sucked in and messaged "Got a minute?" to Johnny. Five seconds later she received his videocall. Not yet ready for a face-to-face with her ex-courtship, Rosa let it ring out. Johnny put in two more video-calls then a voicecall, which she answered.

"So good to hear that sexy voice, *cariño*. I knew you been thinking about me." His mellifluous accent filled the jet from her Ncluded speaker.

"Listen, Johnny." Simply uttering his name sharpened her innards. "I'll go with you to the Maine Event."

"*Realmente?* Oz Corp not treating you well?" he snickered. She glanced over to Paul whose attention had returned to his tablet. She breathed through the silence. "I'll be at the Maine manor from now 'til the event," Johnny went on, "but I'll have you picked up Tuesday at nineteen hundred from your hotel."

"Okay, then."

"I can't wait to see you, *cariño*. I can't wait to hold your—" Seething, Rosa continued to pound at the disconnect button long after the call disengaged. She swallowed back an honest gag.

Paul completed a message on his tablet then turned to her. "Good. Now all we have to—"

"No," she interrupted. "There is no *we*." Paul raised an eyebrow at her. She pressed the exit button at her door handle. "Something happened between me and those candles in the Chapel. So, I'm going to figure out what I am on my own." She climbed out of the jet.

"Received," Paul matched. He turned back to his tablet. "Best of luck to you, then."

Wow. She spun to face him, irked by his flippancy, and now awfully glad she hadn't given herself to him. Paul twitched a finger yet remained otherwise still.

"You know what, Paul?" Rosa said. "It's really just...hard with you." Paul did not react. "I've seen the real you. The angry, lonely, dark and shitty side of you. And the reason you're so angry and alone," she lowered her voice further, mimicking his cool composure, "is because you're on a self-entitled, inconsiderate and completely self-absorbed, high high throne. And the weather up there sucks."

She watched him. Still Paul's eyes remained on his tablet, his energies maintaining forced calm. For a moment Rosa wondered if he'd heard her, if he'd even noticed her exit the jet. But his next action proved his keen awareness. With a bit less force than he'd projected previously, Paul snatched away her ability to receive his mental frequency.

Again, the fissure physically pained her like a cold, hard blow to the gut, and the resultant cosmic silence was unbearable. She stumbled but caught herself. Her first instinct was to beg him to bring back his presence, his warmth. But she fought against it, opting not to apologize for a decision she stood behind.

"Right, of course," she whispered. "Jerk me around then shut me out. At least you're consistent." She stammered off through Historic Central Park toward the nearest egress. She'd rather wander the frenzied flu-infested streets barefoot than owe Paul a night in an Oz Corp suite.

As Rosa marched through the grass her wrist buzzed.

"It's Asshole. You all right?" came from an encrypted sender.

"I'm good, Shorts. Safe," she messaged back. "Going to the Maine Event with Johnny Angelo."

"Is there another Johnny Angelo? Cause you damn sure don't mean jarhead Johnny."

"Paul says it's Lady or bust."

"Paul's a ducking lunatic," Kris messaged along with a gif of a duck in a grocery store. Rosa breathed through the levity. My, how she needed that. "Well, you're a better man than me," Kris sent. "Do you know what Jarhead'll be up to prior?"

"Working at Maine manor up until the event."

"Seriously? That's Perfect."

"Why?"

"'Cause Ross says we'll need your middle finger to break into Johnny's apartment."

PART III
STANCE

24

PARANOID ANDROID

MONDAY NOV 18, 186 PCE

With all six New York City boroughs under strict quarantine, very few pedestrians roamed the streets, leaving even Manhattan a ghost town. And though the chat-verse buzzed with brain-ache concerns, just as much buzz circled the glitz and glamor of the upcoming Maine Event.

Rosa Lejeune toppled out of the unmarked jet once they touched down at Eighth Avenue. She fell with all the grace of a ballerina in her sharp heels and racy tights. Tory, posing as her bodyguard, watched as a few passersby snapshotted her mishap. He spotted a pair of bloodshot eyes turn a corner opposite their direction, but he kept calm, remembering Kris's assessment of their thirst for fear.

Tory had burned the midnight oil replaying the fateful moment in his mind. The moment he'd taken Leland Shark's life. A highly contagious, delusional beast had accosted Tory and his colleague. *He had no choice, right?* Paul Oz had left their briefing disappointed. Perhaps because Tory had fired his sidearm on premises. But Tory dismissed Paul's discontent as a new normal.

"Ms. Lee Jone," called the front-desk droid of the luxury high-rise. "Nice to see you again."

"Thanks Winston," Rosa responded, squinting at his name tag. Tory caught a strange feeling. He was certain Rosa had never been here before. The bot asked Rosa the identity of her companion while prepping a recognition-scanner. But Tory had equipped himself with an identity scrambler, one of the many reasons the public distrusted transhumans.

"He's just Oz Corp staff escorting me through the mayhem," Rosa smiled. The bot nodded and allowed them through to a crowded elevator bank sans bioscan. Rosa hesitated at the prospect of entering an elevator. A handful of erudite residents recognized her, offering sidelong glances and ogles of admiration.

Tory and Rosa headed to room 2307. The mission: get in; acquire the external hard drive; get out. Rosa's finger did indeed grant them passage through Johnny Angelo's security system. Tory decided it was none of his business how Johnny set up this openly depraved security measure.

He lingered by the entrance as Rosa demagnetized a surveillance cam with a small magnet. Kris had ensured that deactivation of the offline cam would trigger no alarms. The apartment: like new, moderately Spartan. Johnny spent very little time here. Signs of an external hard drive were not readily apparent.

The two searched in silence, which Tory preferred. On the way over, Rosa had mentioned Karla's confession: the Valentis had offered Karla freedom from the monastery to pursue love with Pelleher in exchange for Pelleher's loyalty to the Valentis. Would Pelleher make an attempt on his boss's life for the pursuit of love? The stolen video file would answer this.

Rosa and Tory checked inside drawers, behind fixtures and

under furniture, taking care to restore everything to its proper place.

"I'm guessing I'll be the one to check the bedroom," Tory said.

Rosa raised a brow at him. "You really *are* as smart as they say," she snipped.

Tory smirked and headed for the bedroom. The room appeared newly furnished. The apartment must have been a safehouse for paraphernalia Johnny couldn't keep onsite at Maine manor. A walk-in-closet behind a heavy-duty Secure lock let slip a sliver of light at its base. Tory pried open a secret compartment within a desk drawer to discover a heap of items Rosa would loathe to ever know existed. Revealing photos, news clippings, mismatched jewelry pieces, half used lipsticks and perfumes, undergarments. All Rosa. All lurid implications of Johnny's perverse obsession.

Tory's Eyesearch matched some of the photos to Rosa's past shoots and performances fresh out of Fame Academy. But he stumbled on a snapshot taken as recently as her walk to Oz Corp in a black shirt and jeans the previous morning. Tory was surprised Johnny didn't have a full shrine dedicated to her. That Rosa agreed to this mission at all was entirely ubermensch.

As Tory considered whether he should be wearing gloves, he found a key card beneath the pile of photos. On it read Secure in block letters. Tory spun to the walk-in closet. As he stood before its doors, he felt a slight tug at the magnetic implants in his fingers. He thought for a second he could hear light clanking behind the door and placed an ear to it. He detected the thin whirr of what could have been a generator. He also sensed changes in pressure behind the door, ever-so-slight movements. He hadn't brought his gauss pistol, fearing

Nforce would demerit him for concealing a TerraGuard-grade weapon in a civilian residence. He now regretted this decision. Whoever or whatever was behind the door knew Tory and Rosa were in the apartment. A pet perhaps? Johnny Angelo seemed the guinea pig type. Tory slid the Secure card against the security reader and pulled open the closet door.

What Tory saw in the walk-in closet lay beyond his brain's ability to accept. Apart from the psycho-obsessive shrine to Rosa Lejeune, complete with wall-to-wall clippings and digital frames, Tory found something else standing straight at its center. And what he saw chilled his bones so deep, he had to take several steps back to keep his knees from faltering.

* * *

Rosa was some kind of alien. No. Host body for primordial alien intelligence fit better. Mayik. The Mayik of ignited matter, of fire. So, the Indigo flowing inside her was the physical manifestation of that alien intelligence, of that fundamental concept. She could hardly grapple with the proper terminology. She'd spent the better part of last night attempting to set everything in her hotel room on fire through sheer force of will. But no manner of concentration, frustration or verbal mantra was successful. Though she had no difficulty setting ready-made fire to her arms, legs and even her hair, she did learn that such resilience did not apply to her clothing or the carpeting.

Rosa could hardly manage to clear her mind, so accessing deepsight without stimulants proved near impossible. It wasn't the dread of the Maine Event that preoccupied her, nor was it the over-analysis of her encounter at the monastery. It was Paul Oscar.

She couldn't shake him from her mind for even a second.

He'd again spent the entire day giving to her—from perfectly manicured eggs to profound insight into her very existence. And she again thanked him by striking hard at his pride. She prayed he hadn't caught her unfounded thought that she'd been glad she hadn't slept with him, but she couldn't help recalling the twitch of his finger as soon as she'd thought it.

Nonetheless, those thoughts didn't deter Rosa from trying to set fire to every surface in Johnny Angelo's infuriatingly beautiful apartment. The time for fear and reclusion had passed. Paul was right. He was a smartass about it, but he was right. It was time for her to man up, to face the ugliness and float above it unassailable. She was what Paul was. If he could do it, she could do it.

Rosa heard Torian Ross murmur an expletive from Johnny's bedroom. She turned into the hall and spotted him standing in the dark room facing a backlit closet of some sort. He turned to her, immediately palming for her to halt. Rosa would never forget the look of pure terror on his face at that moment. Torian wasn't the type to scare easily. Before she could ask him the matter, she stopped short as she saw a dim shadow hover over his face.

Someone was approaching him.

The person emerged from the closet and stood before Torian. Exact build, exact posture and exact hair color down to the highlights—a wholly perfect robotic replica of Rosa Lejeune, wearing only threadbare tank and frayed underpants. Along with a tattered face, the android's arms and legs exposed inner metallic joints and loose artificial sinew as if it had walked out of an unfinished autopsy. Its many bruises proved the bot had been regularly abused. This week Rosa had faced some of the most bizarre things she'd ever known, but this? This was by far the eeriest.

"Hello," the android pertly intoned to a stunned Torian

Ross. "I am Rosa Thirteen, and you are not my master." Though slightly mechanized, the vocal timbre and pronunciations matched Rosa's precisely. "I have your iris match programmed in my archive as Oz Corp Piece of Shit. Hello, Oz Corp Piece of Shit."

"Holy Jesus," Rosa whispered as the depravity of this abomination's existence sunk in. A brisk inhuman twist of the neck brought Rosa Thirteen to feast its eyes on Rosa. With a front view of the android's face, Rosa noticed one of the bot's eyes was missing. Just an empty socket, like that of its master.

"You are Rosa Lejeune," Rosa Thirteen declared. For an instant, Rosa felt a surreal break in reality as the thing, the Her, addressed her. Then came a full body flush of terror as the android's shoulders also snapped toward Rosa. "You cause my master pain. You cause my master to mistreat my hardware."

"I..." Rosa could hardly do more than open her mouth in petrified awe.

The bot furrowed its brow and with a deep, mechanical growl bellowed, "You must be destroyed!"

The bot charged for Rosa with a hasty limp. Torian rushed to grab its arm, but it yanked free and jabbed him full force in the chest with an iron punch that sent him flying backwards. This was no woman. Underneath the simulated skin was cold, hard metal.

Rosa sprinted back toward the living room, but even with the limp, Rosa Thirteen revved up formidable speed. As it rushed forward, the android bumped against a wall-panel, and Vivaldi's Common Era concerto, *Andante*, blasted stridently through every wall in the apartment. The first song to which Rosa and Johnny had ever danced.

Rosa grabbed at an end table and raised it to thwart the coming bash. But Rosa Thirteen grabbed the table's legs and flung it across the room to crash against a mirrored wall. Rosa staggered backwards into a coat closet. She snatched a heavy coat from the rack as Thirteen rushed her and chucked it at the bot's face, causing the bot to halt and flail its arms, temporarily confused at the sudden darkness. Rosa grabbed the sleeves of the coat at its hilt, twisted and pulled with adrenaline-laden force. She felt gears snap at the base of the bot's neck.

Rosa ducked around Thirteen and dove for the kitchen, accompanied by a swell in Vivaldi's blissful strings. She seized a carving knife and cleaver from a cutlery set on the counter. The bot snatched off the coat and charged for the kitchen, its head permanently lopped to one side. Rosa swung the clever at the bot's head to finish the job. Thirteen knocked the cleaver aside effortlessly, but Rosa did manage to sink the carving knife deep into the bot's abdomen.

This impact caused minimal damage, so Rosa retreated back to the living room, this time headed for the exit. However, the bot reached out and gripped Rosa's arm just under the shoulder. The android lifted Rosa into the air and slammed her onto the living room floor with such velocity Rosa could hardly process it until she lay face up on the ground, her shoulder throbbing.

Thirteen stomped hard onto Rosa's belly. Rosa's breath escaped her along with bits of lunch. The bot then lifted its leg to stomp down on Rosa's face, Rosa searched for a final prayer, but her mind blanked under the terror. Before the foot could slam down, the android faltered and leaned off to one side, the bubbly concerto filling the brief physical stillness. Rosa squinted through watering eyes to find Torian Ross had taken a long-handle cross hammer to the bot's skull. Thirteen spun to face its assailant, and the two engaged in a raucous furniture-shattering battle.

As Rosa scrambled to her haunches, she noted Torian's unexpected prowess wielding a hammer. He used it to block the bot's blows and strike strategically at the bot's face and torso, tearing at its skin to reveal more artificial innards. But, Thirteen landed its devastating blows as well, and Torian's blood was very real.

Rosa attempted once again to open her mind. Thirteen was fighting to kill. If there was a time Rosa needed to generate fire, it was now. She concentrated on deep breathing, on communicating with her body to locate her parietal lobe and pineal gland. But she simply couldn't. It had only been a day since her deepsight had been in full swing at the monastery; why couldn't she harken back to that moment? She cursed herself. Clearing her mind would be near impossible, what with the deathly fight before her and the blaring concerto.

That's it, she thought. *I need to induce a panic attack.*

Rosa sprung to her feet to face the robot head on. She noticed Torian slouching on a couch with a useless arm and bruised chin, beads of sweat decorating his face. Thirteen towered over him, now holding the hammer at a slow rise. Rosa sprinted behind the bot. "Hey! Wannabe!" She gripped the hammer bell and yanked back hard. Thirteen spun on its heel and swiftly rounded on Rosa, slapping her full on in the face. Rosa spun in a full circle before dropping to the ground. The bot kicked Rosa onto her back then dropped to its knees to straddle her. Thirteen hunched forward, firmly grabbed hold of Rosa's neck and squeezed.

I hear the strings of Vivaldi like distant echoes. I gaze up at the gnarled grimace of my clone, with its empty eye socket and exposed hardware under broken skin. Its face, my face, with teeth bared in programmed anger, presses closer to mine. Its breath reeks of ozone. I see my own hands, the decorative rings on my fingers. I latch onto the android's grip in panic, attempting to tear its metal hands from my neck. I push up against its chest and dig my nails into its synthetic flesh. But through my diminishing gasps, I cannot gain leverage.

Then comes the drowning: a deep burn in my chest. A simmering pain arises behind my eyes as my legs turn to rubber. My entire body heaves for oxygen, demands it of me, but I cannot provide.

"Die." The android snarls. I sense an unrelenting Torian Ross behind the bot, hammering away at its back, but even that does not remedy the blackening around my eyes. My frantic clawing wanes to mere waving as my muscles relax.

My final vision is of Rosa Thirteen's face, my face.

Darkness.

My sight powers down like a screen monitor. The sounds of the room, the music, of Torian's struggle, they dwindle to nothing but the resounding thumps of my slowing heart. My body, now cold as winter and heavy as lead. A pervasive almost unbearable cloak of euphoria envelops me. I feel the physical folds of my brain peter into a flat infinite plane. I feel my pineal gland aggressively secreting chemical signals and realize I am dead.

My deepsight activates.

Cogito ergo sum. I am Avicenna's Floating Man.

I am an infinite particle in the space my body once lay, a blissful kernel of being wafting in a starless universe. Among the darkness, I spot a flame. Then a pattern of flames dancing around my full perimeter. Faces, places, memories and the experiences of my ancestor's zip past in a stark instant. This history includes that of the primates, water-dwellers and rippling plasmatic explosions that came before me, all of whom share this one infinitesimal particle that I now am. This one wave. This one thought. I experience infinite pain, infinite love, infinite knowledge. Then, blackness.

In the next instant, I am peering down from the ceiling of Johnny Angelo's living room. Everything from the walls to the furniture is awash with a golden overcoat of quantum reality. I witness my corpse lying flat on the rug among the soft rippling music. The jewel below my clavicle glows an active green. Torian Ross appears to have vanquished the now upturned android by bashing its head to the gears. He now kneels beside my unmoving body. Torian is afraid; he is in pain. His pain is beautiful. He is beautiful. Complex. He touches at both wrists of my body then touches at my neck.

"You can't effing die on me right now!" he bitterly commands. He has started a desperate attempt at cardiopulmonary resuscitation. Waves of his frustration resound through the walls far louder than his expletives. He sits in a shivered silence beside the corpse for a long moment first exuding shock, then denial, then a long cathartic flow of grief. "Damn it, Lejeune." His eyes mist with unshed tears. He is exhausted. I understand him. He loves. He truths. He takes acute responsibility. There is a deep suppressed anxiety, a shadow beneath his gadgetry. He fears the painstaking criticisms of his employer, of his family, of himself.

I feel a presence within my elevated plane. Another is watching with me.

"Who's there?" I project.

"We are," comes a response from all around me. But it also comes as "You are" and "I am" simultaneously. I myself have responded along with them.

"What are you? What am I?"

"We Observe. You Act."

"Where are we?"

"We are everywhere, but we are Observing here."

"Why?" I ask.

In that moment a ball of pink flame appears before me.

"Here, in this state of deep fullness, you will find me," the pink flame intones, still part of the 'Us' that surrounds me. I wonder if I am finally having that panic attack I'd ordered. "You cannot experience a physical thing in this state," the flame responds to my thought. "I... We are Fire. We are not conjured by fear. Fear is the great enemy of knowledge. Remember this place." The flame reaches out a proverbial hand and places a finger on my massless being.

And thus, it ends.

The journey back to consciousness is fast and bumpy. I feel my body corporate around me as its veins fill with the slowly warming blood of a slowly warming heart. The padded ground beneath me tickles my back as the rushing sound of atmosphere thrashes against my ears. I can still feel the pink finger on my being. It is touching at my pineal gland. I take great pains to remember that spot before opening my eyes to the under-whelming surroundings of Johnny Angelo's apartment. As I come down from the intense solipsistic euphoria, I feel searing physical pain at my throat, and immediately I miss the perfec-tion and bliss of the world beyond.

Rosa sat up abruptly, bitterly gasping for air and massaging at her bruised neck. Torian, who'd been hunched over the bot sifting through gadgets, jumped in a panic.

"Holy shit!" he exclaimed as he raced to attend to her. He maintained a slight distance, opting not to crowd her. "Breathe, breathe," he coached. Rosa obliged as her gasps waned to puffs. "Jesus, Lejeune. I swore you checked out. You all right?" Rosa nodded. "I'll fetch you some water." Rosa shook her head 'no,' though she could taste the remnants of his mouth on hers from his frantic attempt at resuscitation. Torian scurried off anyway, and a moment later, set a printed cup of water beside her. He knelt down and reached toward her. "Let me check your—" Rosa raised a hand to halt him. "I'll have to call off the Air Mule ambulance." Rosa nodded.

As her breathing normalized, Rosa noticed the music had stopped and that her jewel no longer shone. She watched Torian swipe hastily at his Ncluded. She studied his winsome eyes, eyes that nearly wept for her. Still awash in the afterglow of her deepsight, Rosa basked in the recollection of his beautiful anguish. Overwhelmed with compassion, she slid a hand lightly over his. She felt him freeze mid-swipe.

Touching him in that moment, Rosa could feel his resonance almost as sharply as she'd felt Paul's. She sensed his resignation to the repercussions of her death and his subsequent relief at her resurrection. She sensed his conflicted emotions toward her: his worry, his admiration, his fear. Torian suddenly disseminated a strong wave of caution over a surge of raw attraction and slowly removed his hand from beneath hers, taking with it her deep perception of his energies.

"Sure, you're alright?" he asked avoiding her eyes. "You were definitely toes up. I'll have to eat my hat on this one." Again, Rosa nodded. "Drink the water; you're burning up."

"I'm fine, Torian. What'd I miss?"

"Well, while you were busy being unconscious, I managed to locate the hard drive." He brought forth a small black case from a pocket. "It was tucked away in a chamber at the android's back. Somehow the circuits in its chest overheated and were literally melting when—" The mention of the bot ignited something vile in Rosa. She looked over to the bot lying lifelessly upturned behind Torian, its hands and feet reaching for the ceiling like a mannequin. Rosa was already on her feet headed for the kitchen before she could consider her actions.

"Lejeune, we really got to get the hell out of here before Nforce or building security decides to show."

Rosa could hardly hear Torian's warnings over her own fury.

Burn. Burn. Burn!

She rummaged frantically through the kitchen cupboards, telling herself with a singular focus she needed a can of aerosol while still in her elevated state. She had to burn the android abomination to ash. She ignored Torian's calls from behind her frenzied search, his words a distant haze.

Burn. Burn. Burn it all down!

Rosa spotted a slimscreen coating spray just above her reach and hopped to grab for it. *I am going to human-flamethrower this place to the ground!* As she jumped, she felt Torian place his hands on her shoulders to curb her frantic effort. Something deep and hot exploded in her. She promptly whirled around in reflex and backslapped him hard in the face. "Don't you *ever* touch me!" Torian's face whipped aside as he faltered back a step. Rosa stared in dazed silence, flabbergasted by her own action. She watched him touch a finger to his cheek and analyze the blood drawn by one of her rings.

Torian let out a long breath then made a point to look her in the eyes. "I have no moral authority over you," he said with muted strain. "If you want to burn the place to shit, be my guest. I certainly wouldn't blame you. But I advise we play it smart."

"Torian, I...I'm so sorry." She held her hand over her mouth, fighting back tears. She could scarcely comprehend the various raw emotions coursing through her.

"We'll sing Kumbaya later. Let's just get you out of here safely, Lejeune."

Through sheer impulse, she whispered, "I don't need you to protect me..."

"Rosa, I just witnessed your stalker's robot clone strangle you near to death. I'm going to make sure we get you out safely. Not for you. Not to protect you. But for me. It's purely selfish. Now, please, let's just bail."

This admission sobered her. He made no moves to approach or guide her. She appreciated that. Torian Ross was one of the good ones. He was smart, loyal, honest. A leader. *Paul Oscar was right to hire him*, Rosa thought. She sighed, straightened up her hair then headed for the exit. Torian followed in tow giving her adequate space.

As they passed wordlessly through the disheveled living room and the upturned bot, Rosa couldn't shake a crippling sense of fear. Not at Johnny Angelo nor the near-death experience, but at herself. She looked back at Torian's face as they stepped into the hall and wondered if he too could smell the whisper of smoke wafting from the livid burn mark she'd planted on his cheek.

25

CHAMPAGNE FOR CAESAR

TUESDAY NOV 19, 186 PCE

"You, okay?" Kris asked Sherri. They had holed up in a small Oz Corp conference room, sitting back-to-back, working through separate highly classified puzzles on respective wallscreens. Kris, with his dog perfectly still at his side, worked to crack the protected files on Johnny's hard drive, while Sherri sorted the massive virtual envelope of Ferguson's will sent to her by an insider with his estate. "If you need someone to talk to about, you know, whatever," Kris continued, "I'm here." She'd just witnessed a colleague murder one of her mentors, who just so happened to go mad with rabid dementia. Sherri made no effort to respond.

Kris focused on unlocking the hard drive's single empty folder. He'd have to whip out actual skill. He looked down to Aztec then to the back of Sherri's head. "So, Sherri," he began. "Uh...my dog talks. Just a heads up."

"Yes, I've been informed that your Jack Russell is an android you've rewired with human emulation." *Oh.* Kris wasn't aware the info had been spreading willy-nilly. "I apologize, Kris, but I really need to concentrate right now, so if

you and your dog could keep your conversing to a mini-
mum..." Kris hadn't planned on playing Name that Tune; he
simply needed Aztec to reel off command protocols. Kris
swallowed the notion that she viewed him as second tier. Yes,
he was no paragon of perfection. So what? He was good at
what he did.

He and Aztec conversed via text, implementing different
hacks. They were careful not to disturb Sherri with their
elations once they'd discovered a crack in the folder, allowing
them access to four hundred and sixty terabytes worth of
information.

Sifting through the countless documents would make for a
very tedious Tuesday, considering all filenames were a series of
digits. As they poured over files, Kris wondered if this drive
nonsense was simply a red herring Leland Shark concocted,
vowing to take his knowledge of mind-control fuckery to the
grave. After nearly twenty minutes of silent sifting, Kris felt
Sherri gasp behind him. She turned to face him.

"What's a champagne lock?" she asked.

"Just your standard file protection," Kris said without
looking back. "It's called a champagne lock when applied to a
file being passed down, usually in cases of inheritance." Kris
grew excited at the prospect of dispensing arcane knowledge.
"You'll see it with CEO's handing over corporate confidences
to replacements. Like cracking a champagne bottle against a
new ship."

"Do you know how to crack it? I've got a file here. The
read-me says it's champagne locked."

"Yeah, piece of cake. Most likely a standard lock." He
turned and watched as she rose from her chair and peered
down at him, implying he take her seat. "Uhm...those are Paul
Oz's private estate files, right?"

"Paul says he vetted you," she said impatiently. *Woah*, Kris thought. That level of trust from the Great Oz himself was the type that landed whole villages six feet under.

"Yeah, I'm not going anywhere near that."

"Due to the highly classified and threatening nature of this investigation, we've agreed it unwise to confide in anyone not already privy. That includes our on-staff security consultants."

"So, you're saying I'm the official security consultant on this? Paul Oz sees me as *Thee* hacker?" If so, Kris felt such a lofty title warranted at least a modicum of the respect they all tossed around to each other.

"We don't exactly have time for this. Can you hack it or not?"

"I can," he said, his words measured. "Not sure I have time to be spoken down to though." Sherri's face promptly rumpled. She apparently foraged through a rapid series of calculations in her head then softened.

"Kris," she said in earnest. "I'm under a lot of pressure to perform right now. It doesn't excuse any untoward behavior on my part. I'll do better to address you with proper respect going forward." It was immediately obvious to Kris he didn't deserve the apology and shouldn't have put her through saying it.

He plopped himself into her chair. "First, I'll need access to your profile." Sherri followed the instructions Kris gave, granting him temporary entry into the terminal of her Ncluded, one of the most private spaces one could allow another's imposition other than their own body. He clicked into her Oz Corp profile. In that moment, if he so desired, he could easily ruin Sherri's life. He could easily destroy Oz Corp with one click.

Kris located the archive entitled 'Paul Oscar Ryland Perry - Preliminary Ferguson Cryptology Results 19-11-0186.' The title sent chills up Kris's back. It was just so unnervingly private. He considered taking a stance against completing the hack. Yes, he'd broken into thousands of private files, often with malicious intent, but this? This was Paul Oz. Kris bit down, opened the archive, came upon the champagne locked file, and did his best not to memorize the other files present in the directory.

Kris asked Aztec to pull up their portfolio of protection scripts and waited. "Sorry for being an asshole," Kris said to Sherri without facing her. "I just...am one. Don't know what else to tell you." He couldn't believe he'd thought he had a chance at pretending he had a chance with her.

"Don't mention it," she offered.

"You ready, Kris?" Aztec chimed. It didn't take long before they cracked the document, a text file containing no more than a series of thirty-two alphanumeric digits. Sherri read them aloud to herself, but before she'd gotten half-way, the document vanished from the wallscreen, and the file disappeared from the archive.

"The hell? Where'd the file just go?" Kris swiped frantically through the air-display.

"Don't worry. He's got it now. May you log out of my system?" Kris rose from her chair as he logged out, presuming the 'he' in her scenario to be Paul Oz.

"Will I get to know what I just unlocked, or..." Kris trailed off expectantly, but Sherri simply stared at him expressionless. "You know, I'll be of better service to you guys if I'm kept in some sort of loop." Still no response, just a blank stare of composure Kris could only assume had been trained. He wondered how Paul did it: how he took perfectly intelligent people with vast leadership capabilities and made them bend the knee, as he'd done with Torian Ross and Sherri Weiler, and as he'd now done with Kris Johnson.

"You know what? Forget it," Kris murmured. He got back to parsing out Johnny Angelo's drive, having lost interest in constantly trying to prove himself.

"The number was a passkey," Sherri said from behind him. "He gave him everything. There will be meteoric fallout." Kris turned in his chair and raised a brow at her.

"Who gave who every what?"

"The estate is not yet releasing this information publicly. But Dr. Ferguson gave Paul Oscar everything: his research, his school, his fortune; everything. What you just unlocked was the pass code to enter his private research facility."

It was Aztec who stumbled upon a folder of interest in Johnny's drive. While the folder didn't host the video evidence they were looking for, it did have a handful of documents concerning the Maines' more gauche acquisitions. After examining a few receipts, Kris learned that apart from a doomsday-proof underground luxury building, the Maine's owned several private islands.

Aztec presented a similar folder on the Valentis. Kris found that they possessed even more unreasonably lavish assortments which included people, tons of people. They outright owned contracted rights to individuals' lives, names, estates, ReBuilds.

ReBuilds?

Kris found dozens of untraceable ReBuilds, many of whom had died by undisclosed means. This meant the Valentis were in the very shady business of black-market ReBuilds, and were likely involved in the ownership or exchange of Demetrius Marshal, the Rebuild Ross had encountered.

Kris couldn't help but frown down at Aztec every five seconds, unable to fathom the decadence of these highbrow snobs. Oz Corp was an equal player among the Maine and Valenti pompous regimes. But with Oz Corp acquiring Ferguson's legacy, Paul would soon become a giant among them.

Kris suddenly felt the onslaught of an approaching

migraine. He stared blankly at his wallscreen in silent intro-spection, not wanting to bother Sherri for painkillers. A light haze settled over his mind, and for a second, all the incessant clamoring in his head came to a serene halt. Uncertain how long he'd sat in reverie, Kris didn't snap out until his Ncluded buzzed. It was Aztec.

"You're doing it again," Aztec had messaged. Kris came to full alertness and noticed twenty minutes had slipped by. *Twenty whole minutes?* He'd been staring at a folder entitled 'Davia Valenti' and his brain had shut down, as it often did, unable to handle the thought of her. He mindlessly clicked on the folder, ignoring the ensuing bombardment of messages and howls from Aztec.

In the folder, Kris came upon documented conversations of Bianca Valenti trying to strong-arm Ferguson into handing over research for a concoction called Rejuve and for his Indigo find-ings. The Valentis had been planning to launch a product called 'Forever Young' which would regenerate subscribers to their most formidable state. Kris figured the Valentis planned to add Indigo to the formula to keep subscriber's subordinate. Bianca had then switched tactics and negotiated with Pelleher who played nicer. Unbeknownst to Ferguson, Pelleher occa-sionally passed them small nuggets of information in exchange for one favor or another. Kris always knew old Phil Pill to be sniveling but not to the extent of selling trade secrets.

Kris stumbled on their campaign image for Forever Young, a photo of a scantily clad Davia Valenti lying in a suggestive pose, holding a bottle of the product. Her tight, low-cut shirt revealed just enough of her bust to drive a heave of friction through him so violent, he shuddered in his chair. He must have fallen prey to another deep stare because Aztec pounced on his lap and barked in his face.

"She's a looker," came Sherri's voice overhead. Kris immediately straightened up and exed away the image. "You locate the file?"

"Yes, we have," Aztec said, speaking to Sherri for the first time. Had he? If so, Kris was thoroughly impressed. "Perhaps I should introduce myself. The name's Aztec, and I am here to assist Kris in any endeavors you wish him to accomplish." Aztec held up a paw and Sherri knelt beside Kris to accept the gesture.

"Well, hello, Aztec. I'm Sherri Weiler."

"Yes. Oz Corp Chief of Staff and Arcology, and Paul Oscar confidante."

Sherri blushed. "Well, I don't know about confidante." She looked up to Kris and placed a hand on his shoulder. "You, okay? Need some water?"

Kris wanted to explode with a mix of unfocussed anger and embarrassment but instead opted for, "No, I'm good. Thanks." As much as he had imagined having her hands on him, he seriously did not want her touching him at the current moment.

"You were shaking there for a second. I thought maybe you were suffering from either dehydration or..." she paused for a moment, removing her hand from his tensed arm, "or an acute stress reaction."

"I said I'm good," he repeated. Sherri took the hint and returned to her seat.

"Sherri's assessment of acute stress reaction may have been spot on," Aztec messaged.

"Hush. And show me the file."

Lo and behold, Aztec had actually located the video. Wasting no time, Kris pulled up the file to finally uncover the moments just before Ferguson's death. Moments the Maines and Valentis both went to great lengths to conceal.

26

THE MAINE EVENT

TUESDAY NOV 19, 186 PCE

"Evolution, an ever-admission of discontent"

— *DIARY OF THE MAD GLEE*

Rosa sat in a Maine skystretch wearing a scandalous red sequin number and heels that could cut teeth. She was determined to make her first public appearance in five years; one for the gossip columns. Despite the chatverse comments squabbling over whether she and Johnny Angelo would officially rekindle, she was not going to let him ruin her career again. It had been one day since her death tango with Rosa Thirteen, and she hadn't yet taken a moment to fully process the transcendental experience and subsequent burn mark on Torian. But there was hardly time for that now. Now she was to fly to New Jersey and accompany her hoodlum of an ex in visiting her mentor's sworn enemy.

Rosa stepped down from the skystretch to find Johnny Angelo waiting out front in a black suit and tie to collect her, shuffling his hands and shifting his cobalt eye. He was really physically there, no mirage, no hallucination. Rosa swallowed a strong urge to run back into the stretch. Behind Johnny stood the Maine mansion's monolithic exterior teeming with rows of bot-tographers at its front gates, snapshotting each incoming celebrity.

"Damn! *Voy a tener un gran problema, mi cariño pelirroja,*" Johnny called to her. "Maine wants me on behavior tonight, but that ain't gonna happen with you in that dress and those LeRue heels."

"Good evening, Jonathan." Rosa maintained her poise as she briskly sidestepped him and headed for the bot-parazzi-lined red-carpet. Johnny tried to grab at her elbow, but she placed a little red purse between them, spending the duration of their trek searching for an imaginary item. They'd once been a diehard handholding couple, but Rosa no longer knew this man.

Her attempts to keep his hands from her were short-lived. When the bot-parazzi halted them on the carpet for pictures and questions, Johnny Angelo took the opportunity to rest a light touch at the small of her back. She sensed the waves of lechery oozing through his fingers and bit back an instant need to regurgitate.

"We at Starz Warz would like to know," one of the bots called, "you two look amazing together. Are you an item again?"

"Well, she got all dolled up to see me, so you tell me," Johnny said, inciting a rumble of laughs and applause. Rosa opted for a simple grin and wave. Another bot shoved forward.

"Ms. Lejeune, you're here in a Michelle Brier dress. Brier is sponsored by Oz Corp. Tell our subscribers at Planet Magazine if you'll be switching your sights from Oz Corp to Maine."

"I'll do what a girl does," Rosa sang through a plastered smile, "get her feet wet." Another bout of cheers erupted. All

Rosa wanted was to escape the three salacious fingers lightly stroking her back. Other bloggers called out to the couple, but Rosa charged forward, making her way up the limestone stairs. She kept alert through the barrage of handshakes and hellos from faces she cared not to recognize along lavishly decorated halls she cared not to appreciate.

Rosa made it straight through to the Maine Hall without Johnny gaining leverage, but once they entered, an on-staff bot-tographer troubled them for an official step-and-repeat photo. Johnny nodded and wrapped an arm snuggly around her waist. She took in a long, steady sip of air, attempting to distract herself by admiring the ballroom with its plush carpeting, flowered candlelit tables, and countless service staff. The servers were human; that was a nice touch.

"God, you smell good, *cariño*," Johnny whispered against her ear, his bionic eye purring beside her temple. Again, Rosa breathed through the revulsion. When the bot-tographer beckoned for a second pose, Rosa lost her patience and scurried for the tables. Johnny grabbed her fiercely by the arm. "No," he snarled. "*Es mi casa.* We play my way here."

A sudden flash of Rosa Thirteen's fierce grip whizzed by her eyelids. A tremble trickled up her spine, but she held her composure. Rosa focused on his human eye and nodded in affirmation, allowing him his control. "You're right," she managed. "I was just wondering where Lady Maine was. I'm sure she'd like to see me."

"Anything you have to say to her goes through me," Johnny hissed. Rosa bit her lip. She'd have to play her cards at the right time if she was playing to win. Johnny escorted her through another maze of aggressive handshakes to settle at their table.

He pulled out her chair, but before either could sit, the Asian man who'd approached Rosa back at the cycling dorm approached, asking Johnny for a moment in the situation room.

Johnny nodded, whispering to Rosa, "I won't like it if you disappear." And off he went. Rosa surveyed the room of select Who's Whos. Their energies, a mix of conceit and insecurity, seeped in through her pores. She hadn't sat ten seconds before she spotted him, seated comfortably at the other end of the hall with someone else.

Paul Oscar Ryland Perry.

Her heart leapt. *Damn him.* Here she was at his behest gagging in her mouth at the touch of her personal boogieman, while he sat there in a fitted tux, sipping champagne with a high-cheekboned, taller, thinner size card. So, had he merely been playing with her? Yeeting her into impossible situations to measure his control over her? A hot spike of fury propelled her from her seat, and she was halfway across the hall before she realized it.

She paused to reevaluate, feeling everyone's eyes on her. She looked in Paul's direction to find him watching her stoically from behind his glass. Rosa stormed forward, but by the time she arrived at his table, her bout of fury had passed. Paul was just so insufferably beautiful with an aura so massive; it distinguished him even in this room of topmost elite. Besides, she wasn't going to make a fool of herself. Not today. Social strata: how true power keeps power.

She recognized the woman sitting across from him, a mid-mocha, stately beauty influencer draped in a perfectly white dress and a battlefield of hairpins: Lisa something.

"Oz, I thought I told you I didn't want to be bothered with your baggage tonight," Lisa scorned as she watched Rosa approaching.

"May I help you, Ms. Lejeune?" Paul asked lightly.

"I just wanted to stop by and say...whatup?" Rosa said nervously. Lisa's very apparent dismissal had obviously rattled Rosa. "Paul, the things I said the other evening, I—"

"Think nothing of it, Ms. Lejeune," Paul said.

And that was it. Rosa didn't quite know what to do next. She ran a hand through her hair in brief thought then opted to speak her mind. "I want you to know, you didn't deserve it. I was stressed by the situation and took it out on you. I want you to know I'm grateful for everything."

"Thank you, Ms. Lejeune," Paul said, his eyes steady on hers. She felt a sudden desperate need to feel his resonance, to know his silent frequency.

"Is *it* still here?" Lisa announced with decided distaste. Rosa couldn't fault Lisa. Rosa had no place at their table, and must have appeared quite the groupie.

The scent of Alabaster Spring cologne came suddenly and poignant. Rosa felt Johnny Angelo slide both hands down her back, allowing those same three wanton fingers to settle gingerly at the left cheek of her bottom. And then he gently squeezed. She felt the goose of a tickle race up her spine, and stifled the ensuing jump, hurl and wailing explosion.

"Lisa, lovely as always," Johnny greeted.

"You still manage to look like a hooligan no matter how many designer suits they try to stuff you into," Lisa responded with a wide grin.

Johnny looked to Paul. "Surprised they were able to fit your head through the door, Oz Corp."

"Mr. Boulevardo Marino," Paul nodded.

"I'd wipe that smug look off your face, Oz Corp," Johnny warned.

Lisa shooed a hand at Johnny. "Johnny, sweetie, you're all sizzle. Now go mingle. We're enjoying our champagne." Rosa initiated the retreat, scuttling back to their table, away from those three fingers.

The MC announced the night below a transparent caption screen, and Dr. Titan Maine—a short pale man in an oversized suit—followed with a bombastic speech regaling the Academy's past year of technological advancements. He acknowledged fellow board members, not least of which was his lovely wife, Dr. Lady Maine, who stood upon mention of her name. A tall, shapely woman with crystalline mauve hair stretching far below her waist, Lady was a daunting paragon of elegance, wearing a long diamond gown and ebony elbow gloves atop black pearlescent skin. She didn't appear a day over forty and in fact appeared far younger than she ever did as Madame Ferguson. Titan Maine handed the floor to her to unveil their big reveal of the year.

Lady stepped forward in her spiked heels and basked in the applause with flawless posture. She'd mastered her own signature halo effect, commanding every room so fortunate to have her. "Ladies, Gentle-Persons, Transhumans, Androids, The Non-Conforming and all other equally important self-identifications," she began with graceful charm. "For those preferring a visual description, I am a tall dark-skinned woman with looks to die for and expensive taste. I absolutely must thank my perfect husband for an entirely marvelous introduction; though no introduction could ever do me justice." Grandiose laughter and cheers followed. "I won't take up too much of your time. You're looking forward to dancing off your full serving of our Rare Shark Soufflé." Another rumble of applause.

Lady Maine waved a hand toward a curtain at a far corner of the hall. "Honored guests, I present to you..." an android pushed aside the curtain to reveal a tall, teenage blonde in a tight pink dress and pony-tale. Lilly Maine, Titan Maine's daughter, looked exactly as Rosa remembered her from the academy. But she was at least a few years older than Rosa, certainly no teenager. The girl stood holding a small golden spritzer in her hand. "Forever Young," Lady Maine announced.

The crowd wooed.

Lilly spoke her memorized lines with a post-pubescent voice. "To hit the markets mid spring, Forever Young is a simple mixture of healthful ingredients meant for daily consumption like so." She consumed two squirts for the audience. "It's rife with minerals and nutrients for a daily balanced diet."

"But what does it offer?" Lady continued. "Just ask the *turritopsis dohrnii* jellyfish. Endless youth. Vigor. Not just in looks, not just in strength of mind, but internal genetic makeup. Any and all skeptics, we understand it sounds impossible, miraculous, quite the astounding feat. However, I assure you, you are looking at, not one, but two living examples of its wonder." Again, the spectators wooed. Rosa felt a deep wrongness in her stomach, as if all the souls who'd perished from the brain-ache were somehow trapped in that bottle.

After the presentation, the center of the ballroom flooded as a live android band sailed through excerpts of popular ballroom jazz. Johnny Angelo gripped Rosa at the elbow and shuffled her to the dance floor.

"Actually, would you grab me a drink?" Rosa kindly requested as Johnny settled on a spot. She pouted her lips at him, following up with, "It's just so hot in here, Johnny." Relief washed over her as he acquiesced.

"*Hare cualquier cosa por ti, mi cariño,*" and he headed for the service table. She watched as an army of friends immediately accosted him. This was his turf. She'd have to tread lightly. Though she'd lost sight of Lady Maine in the crowd, her attentional bias naturally fell to Paul Oscar.

He was leaning against a wall engaged in conversation with a young man she didn't recognize. With Lisa nowhere in sight, Rosa wafted furtively in his direction. She again sensed all eyes on her and tried not to appear as awkward as she felt. *What am I doing?* She stood for a silent minute, her back several paces before him, again reevaluating her situation. She sucked in a stunned breath, paralyzed as the band switched from Van Moorison's Moondance to Gershwin's Love Theme. She felt a light touch at her upper arm that zapped goosebumps down the length of her.

"May I have this dance, Ms. Lejeune?" She was suddenly breathless. Every ripple in Rosa's body fell into perfect alignment at the sound of his voice behind her. She spun to face him. Paul Oscar. They watched each other for a moment. Paul offered his hands to her, a gesture so painfully open. Did she deserve such a tabula rasa? She took his hands in hers and allowed him to slide them to her waist. There they were, two gods dancing among men. Hardly able to keep composed against the buzz at his fingers, Rosa tried to focus on his eyes, only to fall prey to those too. *Healer indeed*, she thought.

"You've outdone yourself," Paul said, as his dark eyes—now undeniably Egyptian—swept a glance along her low-cut décolleté. Though the compliment felt obligatory, Rosa made no attempts to hide her blush.

"Lisa seems nice," she ventured.

"Maine will make no indications. You'll need to catch her at her private elevator," Paul said just above a whisper. Rosa's face wrinkled at this sudden shift to business. *Did he ever turn off?*

"Why are you here, Paul? Why hadn't I just come with *you*? Better yet, why don't you just confront Lady yourself?"

"She doesn't speak to me and would not speak with you if you'd come as my companion due to her principles on etiquette. However, these same principles require her to invite me."

"Quite the conundrum," Rosa mused. "Why didn't you just tell me this up front?"

"Now that you know what you are, you need no one telling

you anything." The comment came sharp, its polite delivery dripping with strain.

"Well, I'm obviously not a true Scotsman just yet," she chuckled. Paul's decisive lack in reaction spoke volumes. "Paul, again, what I said the other night—"

"Bygones."

"I said a lot of things."

"Nothing I haven't heard before," Paul said. *Oh right,* Rosa thought. *Empath.* Perhaps the dark orb within him was a collection of the negative thoughts constantly hurled toward him.

"I know it was difficult to arrange the meet at the monastery," she said. "You would've had more time with Karla if I hadn't mucked things up."

"I take full responsibility for letting you in," Paul said pointedly.

"There's no way you could have known the jewel would go berserk in the monastery."

"I don't mean letting you into the monastery, Rosa." His words came quiet, deliberate. Rosa lowered her gaze. It wasn't she who'd dug into his psyche to find his inner darkness, but he who allowed her in, allowing her that power over him. To know him. To hurt him.

Rosa parted her lips to speak, but Paul lifted his eyes beyond her, apparently disinterested in continuing the line of discussion. Showing vulnerability must have been entirely rare for Paul Oscar. *'The Healer is too kind to The Fire.' 'I am.'* He was physically healing her, literally restoring her body with his charged touch, and all she could do in return was burn him. "And thus it begins," Paul said, breaking the thick silence.

Just as Rosa raised a brow, Johnny Angelo advanced on them. "Get your fucking hands off my girl."

Paul tightened his grip at Rosa's waist, but despite her true desires, she backed away from him. "My sincerest," Paul simpered. "I wasn't aware your courtship contract had been renewed."

"You got something to say to me, Oz Corp?" Johnny snarled. Rosa attempted to pull at Johnny's arm as he stepped up close to Paul, but Johnny nudged her forcefully aside, anger lancing his face.

"I advise you calm down, Mr. Boulevardo Marino," Paul insisted coolly.

"Yeah? Well, I don't take advice from assholes."

"I'd never have guessed."

"Anyone ever tell you, you're a colossal dick?"

"Thank you for your feedback."

As several onlookers stopped to witness the faceoff, a waiter advanced the two men with a platter of shrimp cocktails and remained beside them until they backed down. Rosa noted that Johnny had taken the first step.

From the corner of her eye, she spotted an unaccompanied Lady Maine entering a golden elevator tube toward the back of the hall. Rosa weighed her options and chose a high-heeled mad dash for the elevator. As she sprinted tube-ward, she heard Johnny Angelo's distant voice call to her.

Ignoring all stares, Rosa stumbled her way into the elevator, her heart pounding. She whirled around to stand in lockstep with Lady Maine, and the two women watched as Johnny bustled up to the closing doors. As he reached the tube, Lady held a palm out to halt him.

"This elevator's full," Lady said with a plastered smile. And the doors closed.

27

LUCK BE A LADY

TUESDAY NOV 19, 186 PCE

"We, made of infinite waves, exist as one wave.
One answered question, one ever delivered message."

— *DIARY OF THE MAD GLEE*

osa watched their reflections as the mirrored elevator traveled horizontally along the mansion. She'd been marveling at the youthful skin of her former etiquette professor when suddenly Lady Maine vanished into thin air. Rosa practically jumped with a start. *Jesus, a hologram. Of course.* Rosa chastised herself for being too consumed with her own emotions to notice Lady's being hadn't been projecting any emotions.

The elevator doors opened to a private balustrade rooftop overlooking a moonlit Hudson River. Lady Maine sat upon a velvet throne at the roof's center, backlit by a circle of inlaid panel lighting. Two brawny men, wearing only tight jeans and dark skin, eagerly attended to Lady.

A bot approached Rosa, who stood stunned by the spectacle, and ushered her to a lowly bentwood chair at Lady's feet. A wholly manicured mood. Rosa felt like a feudal subject come to petition the Queen. She swallowed the indignity.

"Leave us," Lady snapped. All but a bot-tender scattered to the wind. Lady, the consummate monarch of etiquette, sat so positively upright on her regal perch, Rosa was forced to respond in kind. Lady swiped at her wrist to activate a surrounding soundproof grid. Though Rosa sensed no malevolence in Lady, she held her guard. A burgeoning tremble slid across her arms at the eerie stillness. *No.* Rosa said to herself. *Absolutely, not now.*

"Quite the dress," Lady began, peering down her nose as the bot-tender approached with readymade wine glasses. "I see the way my Johnny puts his hands on you. How does that make you feel?"

"I'm not here for me. I'm here for Ferguson," Rosa blurted. At this Lady relaxed her stringent stature.

"Ms. Lejeune, have I taught you nothing? A proper greeting must always encompass a genuine compliment."

Rosa searched for something nice to say. Certain any smarmy undertones would not be lost on Lady Maine, Rosa offered, "You have a lovely...terrace."

"Oh, Rosa," Lady chuckled. "So idealist. It aches my heart that George will never know the woman you've become. To George." Lady raised her glass.

Rosa followed.

"Ms. Rosa Lejeune," Lady continued. "The resolve you've employed to get here is commendable. To endure such advances from entitled men to get what you want. To come to my home, despite your misguided animosity. Only a true woman can harness our power as you have. I can speak with you openly, as one-woman wielding power to another."

Rosa blinked. How could Torian Ross, Paul Oscar and now

Lady Maine see something in her she had yet to see in herself? She caught the sneaking suspicion she was being played. "Wait, you knew I'd come to ask you about this jewel even though I rejected the invitation," Rosa noted, her mind racing, "Johnny Angelo was just some sort of sick test." Rosa massaged the charm at her neck, her nervousness morphing into indignation.

"And it seems you've passed," Lady said between sips.

"Do you know about the Android that that creep keeps in his apartment?"

"Ah yes, Rosa Seven."

Rosa blanched at Lady's blatant flippancy. "He's on Thirteen now."

"We both know Johnny can't have nice things," Lady smirked. "Anyway, I needed to be sure you were worthy of my audience."

"And your audience is worth serving me up on a platter to Ted Bundy over here?"

"Well, it must have been, dear. You're here." Lady tilted her head. Rosa fought against the rise Lady wanted. Besides, she was right. Despite all obstacles, despite her condition, Rosa had made it to where even Paul Oscar could not enter. "Rosa, I would be indebted if your investigation uncovered the mystery of George's death."

"Rich," Rosa snipped, a righteousness bubbling in her chest. "You left him for Titan when he needed you; you've shanghaied as many of his former graduates as possible; and you've evidently gained access to formulae he didn't want Titan to have."

Maine responded with a manicured smile before sipping again at her wine. "Just because an apple is green, it does not prove a raven is black," Lady said. "You've not known me since I've become a Maine, dear. Yet you are convinced your observations of my character are perfectly objective. A false continuum of sorts. And here I thought you a guru on eponymous razors and logical fallacies."

"Well, I do know that *your* Johnny is a classic case of Hanlon's Razor meets the Dunning-Kruger Effect. I'm also hoping Sturgeon's Law reveals your grandiose 'Forever Young' potion for the snake oil it really is. And as for your regime, I'm not sure I could classify it without invoking Godwin's Law."

"Well then," Lady grinned. "Perhaps if we minimized our Allen Curve, we could remain more familiar."

"I don't know that I could fraternize with a traitor," Rosa blurted.

"Oh, don't be puerile. You and I both know the one thing at which George prevailed was contingency planning."

Hm? Gears stirred in Rosa's mind. "Ferguson had you consort with Titan? To keep a hold on Titan while he continued digging into Indigo? No. That can't be right. He caught you cheating. You and Ferguson publicly arbitrated your divorce contract."

"The trick is to cease tying emotional reason to your contracts, Lejeune."

"I knew you never loved Ferguson," Rosa asserted. Lady Maine stiffened upon her throne at this.

"You will be wise never to allow such filth to fall from your mouth in my presence again, child," Lady hissed. She closed her eyes for a moment, visibly calming herself. "You with your late nights."

Rosa flinched. Lady was referring to Rosa's late-night tutoring sessions with Ferguson: he indulging in pontifications, she socratically consuming his essence. "I never did anything untoward with Dr. Ferguson. Not even remotely."

"Ms. Lejeune, let's not deny his unreserved attraction to you," Lady said. "Not for your beauty, he had me for that, and he was ever so uxorious. But for what you have inside you."

"Indigo."

"Its research has been the cause and destruction of all things," Lady sang. "Oh, does George toss in his grave."

"People are dying in the streets because someone's been tinkering with Ferguson's research. If you want us to crack this investigation? Give us something. Anything."

"Dr. Phillip Pelleher," Maine said before another sip. "He'd been the one to initially discover Indigo and disliked that George performed secret tests on his own. Naturally, Phillip leaked whatever he could to that powder keg, Bianca Valenti. So no longer needing George, Bianca opted to take him out."

"So, they promise Karla to Pelleher in exchange for offing Ferg? Jesus, you just buy and sell people."

"Smart girl. But you'd be smarter to recognize you'll be doing the very same if you continue your entanglement with the likes of Paul Oscar."

"What's the beef between you two?" Rosa asked.

"If you only knew what it meant to have *beef* with Paul Oscar. Without your wits about you, Ms. Lejeune; he will devour you whole. Lucky for you, he's on the more functional side of the spectrum these days." *Spectrum?* Paul oozed far too much confidence to have ever been on any kind of spectrum, Rosa thought. "Kudos for piercing through his sharp aversion to physical contact," Lady commended, "but be advised if a man ever attempts to harm you, my dear, it is only an imposition of his own weakness."

Rosa consumed the offered shards of wisdom. She felt a burning need to barrage Lady with questions on elite courtship and about Lady's private history with Paul, but more pressing questions coated her focus.

"So, the Valentis had Pelleher kill Ferguson," Rosa pieced aloud.

"A hasty conclusion," Maine said. "Pelleher's loyalty to

George once surpassed even that of my own. Me, who gave up my reputation of perfection in a fidelity scandal on George's order.

Such deep loyalty resurfaces upon pain of death." Lady appealed to Rosa's ensuing grimace. "With me married off to Titan, you missing in action, and Paul Oscar tucked away in his lair, well...all that was left was to rejoin Pelleher with his lady-monk bae and haul them off. He was distancing his loved ones, my dear, I believe from his laboratory." Lady placed a hefty emphasis on the second syllable of laBORatory as if in correction. She pointed to Rosa's jewel. "Do you know what that is?" she asked. Rosa had almost forgotten about it.

"Not exactly. I just know it glows when—" Rosa stopped short.

"When what, dear?" Rosa peered down at the jewel; certain she should not divulge information about the ways of the Mayik. When she didn't answer, Lady picked up a small purse at her throne's arm and pulled out an identical jewel. "There were three," she said. "One perilously active Indigo nucleus bound in these three jeweled encasements. He gave me two to take with me after our divorce. He'd informed me he'd take them back once he assessed how to manipulate the third, he'd kept for himself."

Lady offered the jewel to Rosa who stood up to receive it. Rosa felt its light buzz of presence, reminiscent of the echoing breaths that had been plaguing her all week. Like magnets, the jewels exhibited a gentle force of attraction toward each other. "George insisted I give one to you and the other to Paul Oscar if he died before drawing up proper findings, and to keep them from Bianca. You must get these to George's laboratory," Lady warned. "And you must take Paul Oscar with you."

Rosa looked up. "Why? Did Ferg tell you why?"

"Those jewels," Lady whispered. "They speak." She picked

up her glass for another sip, but when she moved to set it down, the overhead lights flickered out and the bot-tender powered down.

A split second of eerie stillness passed between the two women, each declining to be the first to react. A moment later, the brawny bodyguards scurried back into view as Lady swiped at her chair's arm, lowering it to ground level. The men hastily ushered Lady and Rosa to a door beside the now defunct elevator tube. Lady inserted a small key into the heavy metal door, and the group hustled up a flight of stairs. Rosa, trailing behind, turned back before the terrace door shut completely and wedged one of her heels beneath it to prop it open.

She caught up with Lady who sprinted along like a young athlete, certainly not like an infirm one-hundred-twenty-year-old. "What's happening?" Rosa asked as they scurried down a pitch-black hall.

"If even the bots are down, the grid has gone out," one of the bodyguards huffed. *The whole grid?* That meant the entire manner currently had no power. "Someone must have gotten into our fuse safe," the guard continued.

"Intruders attempt to sabotage Maine Events every year, dear," Lady added as they approached the Maine Hall. Rosa could hear the squawks and bawks of bewildered patrons. Before Lady could dash into the Hall, Rosa grabbed hold of Lady's elbow.

"What about these jewels? Tell me about these jewels?" Rosa sputtered.

"Ms. Lejeune, my manor could have been compromised. Get the jewels to George's laboratory. Reunite them with the third. Now, excuse me."

"But we don't have access to the lab—"

Lady vanished into the hall before Rosa could finish. Rosa poked her head through the hall entrance to find Ncluded-lit silhouettes bustling frantically. She recognized one face. Johnny Angelo. Someone shined a light on him as he knelt at the center of the ballroom collecting something off the floor. She watched him look up and face directly toward her, his eyes tumultuous and vivid. Unsure if he'd spotted her, Rosa backed away from the door, breathing through the racing thuds against her chest. Just as she tried to gather her thoughts to plan for escape, she felt a buzz at her wrist. An encrypted message from Torian Ross.

"At terrace," he'd messaged.

"Infected people are in the Manor!" guests clamored from the hall. Rosa grew alert, scurried her way back down the long hall and unwedged her heel from the terrace door.

Rosa spotted an unmarked skycar hovering by the ledge with its beetle-winged door lifted. She raced over ignoring all stumbles. Torian Ross hunched forward through the passenger's side to receive her. She paused to study his face. He wore a white tank revealing the muscled swirls of his body art and a hydrogel bandage around his left forearm. The light scorch mark at his cheek sent a hot flush through her body. She allowed him to grab hold of her and hoist her in.

"Anything good?" he asked as she settled.

"Ferguson's laboratory," Rosa said, keeping with Lady's proper pronunciation. "Whatever Bianca Valenti wanted, whatever research Ferguson died for, Lady believes it's still there."

Torian mulled over her words for a moment. "Well, dust off your goggles; we're off to chem lab," he said before setting the skycar in motion.

28

MOTORCYCLE

TUESDAY NOV 19, 186 PCE

The silent-film had been shot from a low frame-rate diary-cam fastened to the lab's hopper window. It began with Ferguson, his back to the cam. He was mixing chemicals frantically, poking at microscopes and scribbling notes. Pelleher, a lanky unassuming man, accompanied him. Pelleher was pleading to Ferguson, yet the doctor hardly noticed him. Ferguson poured the contents of a thumb-sized vial into a cup then scurried over to an off-screen apparatus. He returned a moment later, the cup still in hand. He hunched forward and swooped all contents from the lab table to the ground, including the cup.

With his back to a screaming Pelleher, Ferguson filled a plastic bottle with the cup's liquid and shook it violently. He searched frantically to find a small lighter and what looked like a pipe bomb. Pelleher spun and took two steps for the door before the explosion rattled the screen. Once the smoke cleared, both bodies lay dead atop the worktable, their skin visibly blistered and boiled. The bottle must have contained a deadly acidic solution. It wasn't the explosion that killed them.

They'd melted.

End film.

Kris sat in an Oz Corp briefing room; his crew huddled behind him in various states of silent shock. Sherri sat beside Kris; her eyes averted.

"Sent you the file," Kris managed to say. "You into classic splatter films?"

"It's been forwarded to Paul," Sherri said. "I have no intention of watching it myself." DZ and Becky plopped into empty chairs, and all five, Aztec included, sat wordless around the table. The clacks of Sherri's typing filled the thick air as she prepped to brief Paul Oz, who'd just returned from the Maine Event.

The Maine Event, the growing number of Infecteds, all of it paled in comparison to what Kris witnessed on that video file. The so-called accident. Kris had played through it twice, unable to parse it. *Suicide?* Though it exonerated all other suspects, it only raised more questions. Why would the Maines and Valentis cover up a suicide? To appropriate Ferg's research without raising eyebrows? And what could have driven this formidable man to take his own life?

As the shock settled, Kris mulled over a few other nuggets he'd unearthed in Johnny's hard drive about the king-making Valentis. Most importantly, he'd come upon exchanges proving that Davia Valenti had not only falsely accused him of groping her, but that she'd falsely pinned crimes on other young men, who eventually became untraceable Valenti ReBuilds. Kris also discovered that the incriminating documents were hidden in an underground bunker in Forest Park, Forest Hills. To get to and access the bunker undetected would be physically impossible. But if he could, he'd have enough evidence against the Valentis to have them publicly executed.

Kris jumped in his chair as a bell chirped from Sherri's

tablet. She clicked into the videocall, allowing for everyone at the table to watch. The head and shoulders of a young, attractive doctor appeared.

"Sherri, the first batch of support came through, but we'll need more supplies here at St. Isidore's. HAZMAT gear, SBCAs. We've quarantined dozens and are treating over a hundred injured, all showing signs of brain-ache."

"I'll have supplies deployed, Aliyah, but know that countless community centers are requesting our aid."

"Every little bit helps. With all the ambient grids down, bots are no help, and we've got a severe shortage of medically trained humans."

"The ambient grids went down?" Kris asked.

"Oz Corp has its own independent grid based entirely on concentrated photovoltaic energy," Sherri said. "The grid's been down for over twenty minutes now. But Oz Corp won't feel it." Kris found himself annoyed she hadn't informed everyone of this on the onset. "Stay safe, Aliyah." Sherri swiped out of the call to answer another at her Ncluded. "Torian. You got Lejeune?"

"Just touched down."

"We're in the south wing," Sherri said.

A few minutes after Sherri resumed her fretful typing, Torian Ross marched in with Rosa, who sported a sexy, little red number that would make any man question his morals. *That's who she is now,* Kris thought, *an unattainable class-A socialite.* Nostalgia washed over him as he watched her.

Sherri and DZ, rose at the arrival of the new company. Kris followed suit. Apart from a small periwinkle burn at Ross's cheek and a hydrogel bandage at his arm, both Rosa and Ross appeared unscathed.

"How's the weather out there?" Sherri asked.

"Infected," Ross said.

"The hell happened to your face, Ross?" Kris asked. "Should we be concerned?"

"No," was all Ross offered. "Where's Oz? Let's do this."

"Do what?" asked Becky from her seat.

"Well, we aren't finger painting," Ross said as a bell chimed at Sherri's Ncluded.

"He's here," she announced. "Clear the entrance." Both Ross and Rosa abided.

"Wait, why?" Becky blurted. "He infected?" No response. "Hello? Is no one going to answer me?"

"Drop it, Becks," Kris said. Though he'd warned his crew of Paul Oz's intensity, he hadn't quite prepared them or even himself for the culture to which Paul Oz forced others to adhere in his presence. The briefing room door slid open. Paul sauntered in in a dark blue flannel pushed back to the elbows and a pair of jeans. Was brooding lumberjack in season?

Sherri, Ross and Rosa all displayed reverence, allowing a healthy distance as Paul ambled past them. Dex scampered in tow. Paul made his way to the center of the room, settling an arm's length beside Kris, dropping a black duffel bag onto the table. Kris hadn't been in Paul's presence IRL since Fame, and couldn't help but feel something eerie about him. Paul emitted a physical aura of...of something.

All watched in silence as Paul rummaged through the duffel. Without facing her, Paul addressed Sherri. "You watched the video?"

"No, Paul," she said. "Kris gave me the summary. He's been super reliable and efficient."

Paul turned to Kris with a markedly stern gaze, and said, "Thank you." Kris gave an affirmative shrug fighting hard against feeling humbled. "Updates." Paul addressed the room, returning to his duffel.

Ross went first. "Grids are down, meaning the bots

programmed to maintain them are down. Botics is deploying solar powered androids. Problem is the Infecteds are starting to muck up the solar panels. So, we're good here at Oz Corp, but anyone or anything dependent on public grids in the greater New York City area are SOL."

"What exactly are the Infecteds doing?" Sherri asked. "They're sick. Aren't they frail?"

"If by frail you mean able to overturn vehicles on a whim, sure," Ross said. "From what I've seen, they go straight feral not too long after the change. They have a need, not just to destroy their prey, but to conquer them completely."

"To invade them?" Rosa spoke up from the corner.

"You could say that. And apparently intellect is not fully lost post-infection. Taking out the grids to disarm Nforce, that was a coordinated effort."

"Whatever Ferg was cooking," Kris added, "was either purposefully batshit or far beyond what he could have imagined."

"Those things out there, they're not human," Ross said. "They are apex predators." An apprehensive silence permeated the room.

"What was in the video file?" Rosa broke the stillness. Kris bit his lip. No one wanted to collapse her blissful ignorance of the fate of her beloved mentor. "Someone? Anyone?"

"He committed suicide," Paul stated as he uncovered a small circuit board from his duffel to examine its minutia. Rosa spun to face the wall and let out a pained wail. Then silence. There was a finality to Paul's words. He seemed the type to only speak when necessary. "What else?" he asked.

"The question is now why did Dr. Ferguson top himself off?" Ross said, "and who swooped in and copied his research to plague the city?" He turned to Kris. "Anything on the drive about the Valentis gaining access?"

"Well," Kris chirped, eager to share in the wealth of game-changing secrets, still high on Paul's gratitude. "Turns out the Valentis trade in untraceable ReBuilds."

Though several sets of eyes lit up, Ross simply nodded. "The Valentis cover up Ferguson's suicide," Ross uttered. "They plant an untraceable to send me on a goose chase to buy some sort of time. Next, the city gets eviscerated by an experiment that Lady Maine seems to think is still in Ferguson's lab."

"Still there?" Dex asked, apparently taking notes. Ross nodded.

"If I may," Sherri inserted. "Ferguson's will—which we've only recently gotten our hands on—holds certain stipulations dependent on his cause of death."

"Ah." Ross's eyes lit up. "And there it is. Leland Shark, Bianca Valenti and Charles Tyler, the man who worked to decrypt Dr. Ferguson's will, all turn up in a clandestine merse. Aware of the cause of death stipulation, they were just buying time to assemble their pillage-plan for his research and possibly his full estate."

"They're not murderers, just opportunists," Sherri deduced.

"They played a good hand," Ross said. "Only solves the intent of the cover up. Doesn't solve the intent of the plague." He looked to Kris. "Did the telltale drive reveal who hit our air-displays with force-window hacks last Sunday?"

"Jury's still out," Kris said.

"Force-window hacks?" Sherri asked.

"Someone hacked into the air displays of our apartment with the message 'CONTACT ME,'" Kris said. "They also froze our wallscreens, putting the same message on a forced-window."

"I received a similar message of 'I NEED YOU' and 'NOW,'" Ross added. "I'm also well-read on ReBuilds, namely that it's impossible to obtain one without a thick trail of documentation. I figure anyone clever enough to obtain an untraceable was clever enough to hack the air-displays. Clever enough to infect the unwitting populous without lifting the research from the lab. Keep their hands clean. Question is, if the Valentis sent the ReBuild, who did they partner with to perform the hack?"

"Or *what*," Rosa interjected just above a whisper. She turned to face the room. "I also got a message," she said.

"Woah, wait, are you serious?" Kris exclaimed. "What did it say?"

"It said, 'I KNOW ALL ABOUT YOU.'" The room silently absorbed the new information.

"So, 'I know all about you. I need you now. Contact me,'" Dex keyed into his tablet.

"But why send it to all of us?" Kris said. "Those hacks were beyond even the top guys at Secure. I mean, it even made Ross's biohacks go haywire."

"These messages affected your physical biome?" Paul asked as he studied a second tiny circuit board. The energy in the room thickened to miasmic soup on Paul's interest in the conversation.

"Slight malfunctions," Ross said. "Headaches."

Paul wrinkled his brow at this. "Any precedents?"

"Hacking the air-display shouldn't affect someone's physical being," Kris said. "It would be like hacking a slimscreen to have a live hand come out and slap a baby. Impossible."

"We talking supernatural or something?" Becky offered.

"Ferguson worked with and pissed off a lot of powerful people," Ross said. "A lot of powerful forces."

"Maybe that's why he offed himself," Becky said indelicately. "All the enemies, all the secrets?" The question riled something in Rosa.

"No!" Rosa roared, pushing out from her corner. Kris knew Rosa to have zero emotional filter. "Paul, you don't—" her words came with muted tremors. The way she looked at Paul and addressed him, it was as if no one else existed in the briefing room. "Ferguson would never, ever do that. Not on his own accord. You know that."

All eyes looked to Paul. He dropped the second circuit into the duffel bag, ran his fingers through his hair, then pressed his palms to the table. He lowered his head. "I'm going to the testing facility," he said. A few apprehensive sighs wafted about in response. No one but Nforce had been to the facility since Ferguson's death. "I plan to do a sweep. Only present company is invited to join me. If you so choose, you are responsible for your own life." A flurry of murmurs ensued. "You're welcome to remain here at Oz Corp," Paul continued, zipping shut his duffel, "but if you are going, you're going now."

"We'll need weapons," Ross said. "The city's crawling with Infecteds."

"Paul, our jets won't make it far without the grids," Sherri added. "We'll need to tap into the antique streetcar collection to get to Ferguson's lab out in Howard Beach." Kris marveled at Paul, Ross and Sherri's instinctive valor: ready to jump into hurricanes, though they could easily sit back safe in their cushy apartments. They were fighters like him, ready to risk every-thing for the cause. Kris looked to his team as they waited for him, their leader, to make the call.

"I'll need a change of shoes," Rosa announced. "I'm going, Paul." Rosa grabbed at her necklace as she spoke.

Sherri whipped her neck to Paul so fast, Kris thought her head would fling across the room. "Paul," Sherri protested. "I advise against—"

"Get her a change of shoes and a jacket," Paul ordered. Sherri nodded to Dex. "Then you and Torian head to the arsenal. Pick out whatever you need. Nothing automatic. I want minimal bloodshed."

"Oz, you haven't experienced these Infecteds firsthand," Ross said to Paul's back. "They aren't the type you want to parry with."

"We disarm. We injure. We keep the death count low."

"Again, Paul, I strongly—"

"Nothing automatic," Paul reiterated, a stern echo bouncing off the walls. Kris watched as Ross went beet red. No one wanted to die at the hands of a rabid Infected; however, if a cure did exist, well...they were still human. *Weren't they?*

Ross shook off the rebuff and took the floor. "Okay, people. Operation Facility. The mission priority is to locate and analyze Ferguson's latest research, interactions, anything cluing us in to the growing epidemic or the suicide."

"Aliyah Davis needs supplies at St. Isidore's," Sherri said to Ross, who agreed to take on the side quest. As the two continued to parse out the plan, Kris spoke up.

"I'm in," he said, and his partners assembled behind him. "We can help with the comb-through. We're TF's. He's experimented on us dozens of times there so we know the place."

"All right then," Ross said as he turned for the door. "Time to suit up."

Sherri, Ross, Dex and Rosa shuffled out while Kris's crew made their way from around the table. As Kris headed for the door, Paul breathed the word, "stay," to him under his breath. Kris winced through a combined feeling of resentment at the command and fear.

"Paul Oscar." The words wafted in the air-display and settled before Paul. DZ approached holding Aztec, making a point not to come too close. Paul did not look up. "I just wanted to thank you for sponsoring me," DZ signed, then gently tapped the caption toward Paul's eyeline. Paul made no attempts to respond. "I mean, if there's a world after all this...Uhm, basically no one ever gave my family anything. But uhm...you just gave us everything." DZ set Aztec on the table and lingered awkwardly.

Finally, the word "Acknowledged" appeared before Paul without him having typed anything. He gave DZ a nod to excuse himself and DZ conformed.

"Guess you get so many thank-yous, they all just run together, huh?" Kris said once the door slid shut. Paul turned to him, rising to his full height.

"I used him for personal gain," Paul said easily. "You, however, unlocked Ferguson's champagne lock, devoid of ulterior motive."

"Well, a hot girl asked me to, I guess. Sherri, I mean. By the way, what's her deal? She on the market?" Kris was babbling, hoping to lighten his discomfort at being appreciated by Paul Oz.

"No one touches Sherri," Paul said, again with the eerie finality. Kris wrinkled his face with no retort. He watched as Paul reached into his breast pocket to reveal a tiny envelope. Paul placed it on the table. "Take this to the front office. They'll give you access to an unmarked motorcycle. You familiar with how to operate one?"

"In theory."

"Good enough. Handle it as a bodily appendage. Trust your people will be safe with Weiler if and when you rejoin them." Kris liked that. *His people.* Paul was addressing him leader to leader.

"What are you asking me to do exactly?" Kris picked up the envelope, feeling a PVC card inside.

"I'm repaying my debt to you."

"Oh sweet, by giving me a motorcycle?" Kris asked.

Paul lowered his eyes for a moment then brought them

back. "By giving you a means to get over her." Paul fixed his eyes steadily on Kris who shivered at the inference, a battering ram suddenly pounding against his chest. How much did Paul Oz know about Kris's... obsession? "Universal surveillance is down," Paul said. "Whatever you need to gather or destroy, now's the time."

"So, Sherri told you about the photo she caught me staring at from the drive?"

"Your personal vendettas are none of my concern," Paul said as he turned to straighten his duffel bag. "I'd like to see the drive." Kris fished a hand into his pocket, brought out the small black hard drive and placed it on the table. "Have you saved a copy to your servers?"

"Not yet. Wanna wait 'til I can dark-cloud it securely."

Paul picked up the drive, dropped it in his duffel and said, "I keep the drive," with such sculpted diplomacy, Kris almost bit back his objection.

Still an obligatory "Hey, what the hell, bro?" tumbled out. Paul did nothing to acknowledge the protest. Though Kris wanted to yammer further, he knew he had no claim to the drive. Besides, a bigger part of his mind fixated on the motorcycle and its implications. Paul slung the duffel over his shoulder and headed for the door.

"So that's what you do?" Kris asked Paul's back. "You figure out the most fucked up thing someone wants, and you give it to 'em?"

"I figure out what someone wants, and I give it to them." Paul looked over his shoulder. "Whether or not it's above board is subject to your personal morality." And with that he left Kris and Aztec alone in the room.

"So, we're off to Forest Hills then?" Aztec asked. Kris tucked his Jack Russell under his arm and nodded. They were off to the Valenti bunker to gather the evidence they needed to discredit Davia Valenti for good.

* * *

The motorcycle, a classic black Coventry Eagle, came with matching jacket, gloves, and badass nightstick. A small, motorized hoverboard sat in a basket at the front. While Kris familiarized himself with the controls, Aztec, now running on his internal lithium battery, iterated the motorcycle's user guides. Before long Kris and his dog were soaring across the East Side toward the Queensboro Bridge. Though the bike was an unwieldy beast, Paul's advice to recognize it as an appendage proved more useful than anything in the manuals. Near death slim-turns aside, the true rush of the ride came from Kris's focus on his mission. On the long overdue unraveling.

29

TRAPPED

K ris kept a keen eye on the road, making a point not to give off signals of fear. Most Infecteds took to flipping grounded cars and pulverizing fearful citizens into rags of flesh. The curfew and dimmed ads kept the side streets relatively tranquil. Kris snaked through thick black Oxytrees, which without their green luminosity, gnarled like outstretched skeletal fingers under the dark sky.

Kris reached Forest Park in less than twenty minutes. The beginnings of a light drizzle decorated the unnervingly still park. Kris dismounted the bike, freed Aztec from his pouch and fastened the nightstick at his back. The pair quickly set on all fours, searching grass panels for signs of a trapdoor. Kris kept an ear out for the low growls of approaching Infecteds as they explored.

"Kris, over here!" called Aztec as the downpour amplified.

"What you got, Az?"

"There's something peculiar about this patch of grass." Aztec circled around an area as if he'd claimed it. "My canine senses detect adjacent depth and past activity in this specific spot." Kris knelt beside Aztec to examine the area, removing a glove to feel the grass blades.

"There's another one over here too, Kris!" Aztec called from several yards away. Kris continued to feel at the wet grass and eventually came to a small patch he could press down like a keyboard button. His heart skipped. He tore at the patch to find a tiny number pad beneath. Kris didn't need an eidetic memory to recall the access code he'd noted for the bunker; the numbers just came to him, stapled to his eyelids. A click sounded, and the pad lifted, revealing itself to be a grass-covered metal hatch.

"Oh, you sexy son-of-a-bitch," Kris whispered. He peered down into the blackness. "Az, how deep is this jump?" Aztec sidled up eagerly.

"Not too steep. About nine or so feet." Kris raised the hatch, gathered Aztec in one hand, and held onto the door's latch with the other. He jumped feet first into the hole, slamming the door above him.

Darkness.

"Rudolph it, Az." Aztec's nose emitted a small white light. The light revealed a bundled rope at the ceiling beside the trapdoor. "We'll have to get that rope down to exit," Kris noted. To his dismay, the room was nothing more than a small rickety den with a few bales of obsolete fiat money and gold bullion stacked in a corner. The Valentis were stockpiling for a tech downfall. Kris noticed a door at the end of the room. He stuffed a small gold bar into his pouch then headed for it. As he navigated a steady path, he felt a loose floorboard squeak underfoot. It felt for a second as if the floor would collapse beneath him.

Kris turned back, figuring it best to ready the exit rope before moving on to the next room. Too vertically challenged to reach it himself, Kris tossed Aztec up toward the rope to have the dog clomp down on the knot. Aztec caught on after two tries and used his forepaws and teeth to detangle it. The rope dangled down to about half a meter, just enough for Kris to grab hold if he jumped.

Now certain of safe egress, Kris resumed his exploration. Before taking his first step toward the door at the end of the den, he heard the floorboards creak again. That was odd. He was holding Aztec, and he himself had not taken a step. After another short symphony of floorboard racket, Kris shined Aztec's light down at the boards. Though very subtle, Kris noticed the slight seesawing of the floorboard's wooden lines. A few of the boards were being lifted, and it wasn't until he put two and two together, that he began to hear the quiet growls beneath them.

"Oh, hell no," Kris uttered. He whirled back to the exit rope and began plotting his quick leap. Just as he prepared to jump, a distinct thud sounded from the other room so loud it made his hair stand on end. He stood petrified, wondering for a moment why the sound stiffened him. His reasoning took a second to catch up with his instincts. He'd heard a tiny female yelp from the other room.

Someone was in danger, and he had the means to help save their life. Then came the survival dilemma: save himself or be a hero. What would Torian Ross do? Or better yet what would Kris Johnson do? Keenly aware of the hushed growls beneath him, Kris first made sure to calm his racing heart. No fear. No fear. He powered down Aztec's nose-light, quickly skated for the door, and peeked.

The second room, dimly lit by a fallen flashlight, was similar to the first but littered with boxes and loose electronic parts. The flashlight allowed for Kris to spot a dancing shadow shimmying back and forth at the room's center. Hearing the faint moans of the struggling female, he opened the door a little further to get a better look. And he did.

It was her.

She'd fallen into this room using the other entrance Aztec had found. Both her hands were tangled in a panoply of severed cables descending from the trapdoor, leaving her dangling helplessly. She too must have come knowing the Nforce security cameras were offline.

It wasn't the parted red lips, high boots or short-skirted bare thighs that caught his breath, but the rip at her tight-fitting halter, revealing her left breast. And though her face remained flawlessly beautiful, he couldn't peel his eyes from that writhing, disarming breast. The breast he'd supposedly groped. The breast that ruined his life.

Aztec licked at Kris's face to snap him from his stupor, and Kris inadvertently dropped Aztec to the steadily wobbling floorboards. The dog wriggled through the door and ran toward the hanging Davia Valenti. Kris watched as the girl regarded Aztec with terror. She lifted a leg and kicked at Aztec, sending him tumbling end over end. The kick shattered Kris's reverie. His best friend was hurt. Kris crept open the door and made his way into the room.

"Oh, thank God," Davia said to Kris in relieved panic. Looking at him. Addressing him. Needing him. "Help me down. Pretty sure the Infecteds from the subways are under these floorboards."

"You kicked my dog," Kris said consciously avoiding a hard stare at her breast.

"What?" she shrieked. "Help me down! We'll deal with your dog later." Kris turned over and headed to the corner where Aztec squatted in mechanical anguish. "Hey!" Davia yelled to Kris's back.

"You okay, buddy?" Kris asked Aztec, patting him on the head with gloved hands. There'd been no exterior damage.

"It'll consume a great deal of bottery power to continue

operating with the disturbance to my ware. Would you prefer I power down?"

"Absolutely not. Stick with me through this as long as you can, okay, buddy?"

"Good, it's only a toy," came Davia's cavalier snarl. "Help me down from here. Please!" She sounded so weak, so desperate. Kris found a pair of cable cutters on the floor and returned to her. He could easily cut her down in three hearty snips. Though the frequency of floorboard clamors had not yet increased, there seemed a looming air of imminence to their cadence. But to Kris there was nothing. Nothing but him, her and her helpless need of him.

"Do you remember me?" he asked coolly.

"Sorry," she said. "I don't remember all my stalkers. Just cut me down and we'll sort this all out." Kris kept calm through the resultant surge of hot ire. He was ready to stand there and jog her memory forever, even if it meant being shredded to death by bloodthirsty Infecteds.

"You told Fame Academy enforcement that I sexually assaulted you. Do you remember that?" Davia raised her chin in thought for a moment, then came an unexpected smile.

"Oh!" she sighed with relief. "I do remember you. Kirk, right?" Kris gnashed his teeth. "Listen Kirk, cut me down now, and I'll let you be my slave for a night. How does that sound?" She continued to wriggle helplessly before him, her breast within arm's reach.

"Why?" he asked.

"Why? Because, look at me. Who wouldn't want to be my slave?" Kris took a deep inhale, breathing through what he felt were racist implications.

"Why did you tell them I sexually assaulted you?"

Davia responded with a look of *you-poor-thing*, as if everyone on earth knew but him. "Oh sweetie," she crooned.

"You'd probably spoken to me as if you'd forgotten your place and I needed to put you back in it." *My place?* Kris thought.

Just then one of the floorboards behind them lifted fully and a gnarled pair of fingers emerged. The opened board revealed the sounds of dozens of grumbling Infecteds below. Davia let out a panicked scream. They were down there alright, and they were coming up to feed.

A tiny but distinct whisper in Kris's mind hissed, *'Take her. Desecrate her.'*

"Please, help me. Please," she begged as she wiggled desperately. *'Rip her apart.'* The tiny sniveling voice came again, heightening in amplitude. The growls beneath him also amplified. Kris bit down hard at his lip, took the cable-cutters in both hands and snipped at the wires above Davia's head. He'd gotten what he wanted. The why. She'd honestly felt his life held no value. Fortunately for her, he valued himself enough not to soil his integrity. He cut her loose and allowed her to tumble to the floor. She managed to reassemble her torn clothing, but her left breast still remained exposed.

"Try hard not to show fear," Kris said as he sprinted to collect Aztec. "They respond to it."

"What the hell do you know?" she yelled as she skirted for the door to the adjacent room. Kris scooped up his dog and followed suit, but she slammed the door firmly in his face. He tried to barge through, as a second floorboard popped out behind him, but she'd apparently locked the door behind her. Kris bit back a slew of curses, exhaling through the fury.

"Kris," called Aztec. "This is a hollow, wooden door that opens away from you. You should be able to kick this door down with a kick near the lock."

"I'm not frickin' Hercules, Az." The grumbles intensified as a third floorboard popped loose. Kris looked behind him to find several gnarled hands creeping out from the growing hole.

"You're going to have to be, Kris." That was all the pep talk Kris needed. He kicked with a rush of unforeseen force. It took seven kicks, but the wood did budge. Kris swung the door forward and found Davia balancing herself on a bale of cash to reach the exit rope. But she couldn't quite lift herself for the climb once she managed to gain purchase. From the potency of a growl, Kris knew a head must have succeeded in surfacing behind him.

"I'll lift you up," Kris called to Davia.

"So you can look up my skirt? Thank you, next."

"Then let me go first and reach back down for you."

"You think I'm going to trust that? You're obviously a foe!"

Kris sighed exasperated. "You know what?" He walked over, pushed her and the bale aside and ignored her frantic protests. He secured Aztec into his front pouch. "Az, what are my options?"

"You just need a high vertical leap. Grab at the rope with both hands and use your upper body for two pulls. You'll need to grab the latch and punch at the black button beside it to activate the hatch to lift. You'll then need to chin your way up. I am extra weight, Kris. Survival optimization warrants that you leave me behind."

"Shut the hell up, Az. Let's do this." As Kris leapt forward, he almost missed gripping the rope entirely. Fortunately, he caught hold with one hand, grabbing on determinedly with the other. Davia had pushed him. "The hell is your Goddamn problem?" he yelled.

"You better not fucking leave me here!" she snarled.

"Okay!" Kris panted, disinterested in riling her any further. He kept to Aztec's instructions, allowing the hatch to rise open above him. And in poured the torrential rain. Kris chinned his way up onto the green and inspected the moonlit park. Still no signs of life. But something felt off. The motorcycle had been bashed in and knocked over on its side. Someone or something had destroyed their means of escape. Kris felt an eerie sense something was watching him beyond the edge of his vision.

"One's coming out!" Davia yelled from below. Kris lifted himself out and set his butt on terra firma. He removed the nightstick from his back and peered back down into the hatch.

"Grab the rope. I'll pull you up." Davia leapt high and caught the rope. Kris grimaced through the pull as he tapped every ounce of might to lift her. Aztec spoke up.

"Kris, I have news for you, but I'm not sure you'd like to hear it."

"Spill it," Kris spat through gritted teeth.

"An Infected is approaching from across the street."

"Great!" Kris yelled. "Just what I need!" He fought to keep focused on the pull. But once Davia's chin met the ledge, she slipped and fell back into the room. "Damn it! Hold onto the fucking rope!" Kris shouted. As Davia scrambled to her feet, Kris looked to his three o'clock and saw it.

An Infected was advancing from the catty-corner. It wore torn leather pants and a purple spaghetti top over its distended gray torso. Its sunken red eyes and bloody lips glistened bright against the moonlit rain.

"Help me!" Davia called as she hopped back onto the rope. Kris resumed his attentive heaves. By the time Davia's armpits reached the ledge, Ms. Bloody Face had made its way onto the scene as an active threat.

"Pull yourself up!" Kris yelled.

"I can't!" Davia cried sincerely. Ignoring the blinding rain and the massive pain in his biceps, Kris persisted with the pull until he lifted her to her middle. With its sights on the struggling pair, the approaching Infected walked straight past the fallen motorcycle but tripped over something in the grass and collapsed face first onto the ground. Kris thanked his lucky stars. The bit of extra time would allow him to free Davia, gather his club and finish off the Infected. And it would be a glorious story.

But that story didn't happen.

For Kris, the next several frames passed in slow motion. As the Infected scrambled to its feet, Davia finally began to support her own weight. She recoiled, reacting poorly to Kris as he grabbed hold of her hips to hoist her up. Then Davia grabbed at Aztec, pulling him out from Kris's pouch, and hurled the bot dog at the Infected before Kris could free a hand to stop her. Davia made her way out, and the two watched as the Infected took hold of Aztec.

The Infected ripped the dog to pieces, limb from limb, ringing forth metallic bones, artificial sinew and bottery fluid onto the muddy ground. It ferociously bit down at the dog's head to reveal its mangled central processing board then tossed the remainder of the dog's torso off to the side like a piece of junk.

Kris continued to stare in agony as Davia grabbed the night-stick and went on the offensive. The Infected easily grabbed hold of the club and bashed the right side of Davia's face, and the girl fell to the floor unconscious. The sight of human blood, Davia's blood, snapped Kris back to reality.

Kris rounded on the frenzied Infected, ducking under its nightstick swings. The Infected fell forward with the momentum of its missed blows and endeavored to balance on its knees. Kris stalked behind his disoriented assailant and kicked hard at the back of its head. The nightstick dropped to the wet grass. Kris seized the stick and struck at the Infected until it fell face first to the ground. As it lay on its stomach, Kris continued striking incessantly, barbarically, lifting the stick and pounding it into its head, its back, its head again. He watched as blood flowed out from its ears and from the legions on its neck. He continued to strike it long after it stopped moving. Long after.

* * *

Kris managed to glide undisturbed on his forty-five-minute, rain-drenched journey to the St. Isidore's Hospital on the motorized hoverboard. He carried an unconscious Davia Valenti in his arms through the dark, silent journey, like a bride over a threshold.

Kris waited for an update in the Hospital's frenzied waiting-area for twenty minutes, keeping his mind at a zen vacancy. He watched as volunteers wheeled stretchers and wheelchairs carrying injured children and elders, newly infected men and women who'd not yet gone feral, and generally healthy but psychologically pummeled spouses and family members. Kris held his lip stiff, and kept his eyes open to see it all, to bear it all.

"Kris?" The doctor, Aliyah Davis, approached. Kris sat at attention. "The woman you brought in is stable. No internal bleeding. She was conscious for a bit, but she's out cold again."

"Can I see her?" Kris asked. Aliyah escorted him to a back area sectioned off with curtains. Davia lay still on a stretcher, still in her torn clothing.

"We're low on gowns," Aliyah added. "She was prioritized because you're working with Oz, but once she's good to leave, we'll need to make way for new patients. I'll be just up the hall." Aliyah parted without saying more, leaving Kris alone with Davia. He pulled up a stool and sat beside her. He stared at her beautiful, perfect, peaceful face for a long still moment, then down at her bare breast.

He could no longer help himself. He removed his gloves, placed a hand over her breast and clamped down onto her soft skin. With the touch came the tears. He was uncertain as to what exactly caused the breakdown. Perhaps the stressful week, him murdering a fellow living being, the confrontation of an issue that caused some of his darkest moments. No. All of that paled sorely in comparison to the loss of his best friend.

Aztec was everything to him: his business partner, his council, his crown achievement. If he had nothing else, if he was no corporate programmer, no Ferg pet, he at least had something to show the world and himself that he was an amazing human being. Paul had Oz Corp. Rosa had her musical talents. Michelle Brier had her TV show. And Kris had Aztec. And now Aztec was gone. His best friend, gone. A piece of himself, gone. Because she saw him as just some toy.

"She okay?" came Torian Ross's voice. Kris took a second before turning to face Ross, unsure how long he'd been silently sniffing. Ross stood tall at the mouth of the curtain, dressed neck to boots in black combat gear and bearing a double-headed Damascus steel battle axe at his side.

"She's fine," Kris said, slowly pulling his hand from her breast.

"Aliyah pointed me in your direction. Listen, I'm headed to the facility to join the rest. I've got gear and weapons in a truck out back." Kris rose to his feet, taking one last look down at Davia, the childish, self-indulgent, husk of a woman. *God, she had never been worth it.* She looked cold. Kris peeled off his jacket and draped it over her body. He then removed the gold bar from his pouch and tucked it under the jacket. He had no use for it. He had no use for anything Valenti.

Ross made no comments on what he'd just witnessed as he and Kris made their way to the exit. "I killed one," Kris muttered. "I took a life."

"It shows," Ross answered. "Looks like you saved a life too."

30

HIGH SCHOOL SWEETHEARTS

TUESDAY NOV 19, 186 PCE

"Like all else, existence is the mere microcosm of a larger concept."

— *DIARY OF THE MAD GLEE*

"**S**he says it speaks," Rosa said to Paul, massaging at her charm. Paul Oscar along with Sherri, who stood a suitable distance at his other side, had been studying a neon holographic projection of the facility's blueprints. Rosa assumed Paul powered the projection with his natural charge, since all the grids were down. Still, no one asked questions. The party had assembled in one of the facility's abandoned break rooms, lit only by a flashlight. "There were three," Rosa continued, keeping her voice low. "Ferguson tasked Lady to get these to you and me if he died before making a breakthrough with the one he kept to research. The power went out before I could get more out of her."

Paul analyzed the hologram, tapping at different points on its display to resize and re-angle for closer inspection. Without acknowledging Rosa, he held a hand out toward her to receive the jewels. She retrieved the one Lady had given her and unclasped the other from her neck. She stepped up close beside him.

"You're still upset with me," she whispered. Paul did not react. "You used *me*." She placed the items in his hand and swallowed against the hunch that she'd just been a pawn in some convoluted Paul-Oz-Lady-Maine standoff, with neither of them actually interested in her recruitment or sponsorship. "Was that all you wanted from me?" Paul cupped his hand around the jewels then shoved them into his jeans pocket.

"Focus," was all he said without turning to face her. She'd gone far beyond her comfort zone, close to her breaking point, to obtain this invaluable intel. He knew this. She stepped back, stuffing her hands into the pockets of the Oz Corp jacket she wore over her dress, doing all she could not to feel insignificant.

"Paul, it looks like these are our highest priority areas," Sherri began, pointing at different sections on the display. "While you find and disarm the safe here, past the boarding areas upstairs, we'll have one team search these rooms here and another sift through the two labs here. The boarding areas themselves are low priority. We won't waste manpower on them. Now as for Dr. Ferguson's private laboratory—"

"Why are the boarding areas low priority?" Rosa asked. Neither Paul nor Sherri made motion to respond. Sherri shot Rosa a quick glance. Rosa detected a slight hint of annoyance in Sherri's frequency.

"I'll retrieve the private laboratory's entry codes from the safe," Paul said. "I want the lab room team seeking out hand-written stoichiometric formulae containing the element J." He powered down the neon schematics, turned on his heel and went for his duffel bag at the center table. Sherri turned to follow, but Rosa cut her off short, suddenly in a combative mood.

"What's your issue?" Rosa whispered.

"Dozens are dead, and hundreds are dying," was Sherri's terse response.

"My question is what have I done to you personally?"

"For one, our mission priority is to seek out evidence linking Dr. Ferguson to the brain-ache and to use that evidence to help prevent its continued spread. Personally, I don't believe that's your priority."

"Seriously? I'm breaking my back on this same as you and everyone else?"

"Respectfully," Sherri said, her voice growing just a bit louder than Rosa would have liked. "You're forcing me to stand here and talk about my feelings toward you instead of allowing me to address the team about our next steps." Sherri stared daggers at Rosa with a confidence Rosa didn't have the energy to match. Rosa stepped back and allowed Sherri to approach the team.

Rosa watched as Dex, DZ and Becky looked to Sherri as she placed herself at Paul's right hand and orated directions. Paul, who'd been arranging items from the duffel onto the table, was also paying attention, allowing Sherri command of the room. Rosa approached to join the group and placed herself at Paul's left, across the table from Sherri.

"I'll check out the boarding halls," Rosa volunteered.

"We don't have a lot of manpower, Rosa," Sherri said. "Our joint efforts would be best suited to higher priority areas."

"I believe the boarding halls hold just as much importance as the rest of the facility."

"Okay," Sherri said, curbing impatience. "Due to the nature of the type of evidence we're looking for—documentation, records, things of that nature—boarding areas would not be—"

"Anything could end up anywhere in this facility. You would ignore an entire section?"

"Rosa, again, our numbers are limited, and—" Before Sherri could finish her argument, Paul grabbed a flashlight and offered it to Rosa, drawing the conclusion for the both of them. Rosa accepted the proffered flashlight. She felt as if, though she'd won the battle, she'd lost the war. Rosa riffled through the weaponry pile near the door and grabbed a bat. She heard Sherri continue to outline the plan to the team as the door slammed behind her.

Rosa walked the dark halls, listening as the heavy rain beat against the facility windows. If Paul was upset with her, so be it. If Sherri wanted to play alpha, so be it. Rosa had reached her Dunbar Number, enduring more exposure to humans in the past few days than a panic-prone empath ever should.

She made her way to the boarding area, choosing to remain clearheaded, choosing not to think about Paul Oscar. Instead, Rosa basked in tranquil nostalgia. The old familiar hall was a seven-story, doughnut-shaped rotunda with dorm rooms lining the outer circle and a banister lining the open middle. She figured she'd start her search on the top floor.

With the facility's maglocks disarmed, all the doors rested ajar. Rosa peaked into the first boarding room, and her flashlight revealed what she'd expected: a BedBooth and dresser amid bare stone walls. Seeing this reminded Rosa of the fateful Sunday Ferguson came to her dorm to tell her he'd accepted her application into his School of Intelligence. No more pills, exercise drills, measurements. It had been the best day of her life.

Rosa stopped short in the doorway of the third room, thinking she'd heard a sound in the hallway. The hesitation caused her flashlight to fall and break against the hard ground, leaving her in a cold, lonely, darkness. She picked up the flashlight and realized she had no idea how to repair anything IRL, certainly not antique electronics.

She stood in the doorway, listening to the rain, wondering if she could clear her mind enough to create her own light-source. She'd been fresh from the other side when she'd burned Torian, her brain still completely elastic. She simply had to rediscover that pink flame.

Rosa took a deep breath and closed her eyes to focus on her consciousness, allowing a perfect stillness to wash over her. She took a step backward into the hall to give herself more room.

She heard the swooping sound of the swing but opened her eyes too late to see her assailant. She felt the rough clobber against her skull and blacked out before she hit the floor.

Rosa came to consciousness, sensing the cold hard floor at her back and a slight dampness beneath her hair. Someone was breathing over her, straddling her. She managed to open her eyes. Her blurred vision took in his looming figure, silhouetted by the glow of a distant penlight. She felt a growing throb down through her entire left hemisphere from the blow to her head. Her Oz Corp jacket had been unzipped and the low neck of her dress pulled down. She'd waken to him kneading her breasts with both hands.

"I've been waiting far too long for this," came a low whisper. "God, I'm gonna enjoy every second of it." Rosa leapt forward, punched him hard in the jugular then screamed until it hurt...in her mind. Her attempt only manifested as a feeble moan. She felt the pulse of his hardness thicken through his jeans in response to that moan as he lowered his zipper.

"Rosa Thirteen alerted me to your little visit, *cariño*," he continued in a more forceful whisper. "Feels good to know you gals fought over me." Drenched in Alabaster Spring, Johnny Angelo repositioned himself, using his knees to pry apart her thighs. "I'm just here to collect on what I'm owed," he said marveling at the spread of her body before him.

Don't panic. Conserve energy. Though the sweeping pain from the blow to her head amplified each passing second, Rosa resumed her internal journey toward deepsight. She had to find it again, and she had to find it fast.

"Must have felt so good to make a fool of me with your new boyfriend," Johnny hissed. He rolled up the skirt of her dress to reveal her sex to him. With an effort of strained will, Rosa fought the urge to squirm. *No,* she told her body. She gathered her concentration and prayed for all distracting energies, including her very own disgust, to shut up and let her activate. She directed that stored will, that budding potential energy, toward a physical spot in the center of her mind, and felt consciousness gradually elevate. As the gummy folds of her brain flattened, Rosa felt a light rumble at the ground beneath her, a mild earthquake.

Johnny swept his bionic eye around the shaking room but quickly dismissed any thoughts outside his main objective. He stretched his hulking body along the length of hers, sliding his sweaty bare chest over her breasts to position his tip at the lips of her sex.

"Good girl," he breathed, his hot breath ensnaring the side of her face. She sensed a dense wave of hedonism ooze from his being. *Don't panic. Don't jump the gun,* she instructed. She felt mental artifacts of deepsight steadily emerge despite the clanking BedBooth and rattling dresser against the trembling walls. A sphere of pure electric energy formed at the center of her mind, like golden water filling a fresh glass. Yet this water simply would not spilleth over. Rosa could not seem to cross over into pure deepsight.

Johnny Angelo slid himself inside of her, rough and slick with moisture. She could feel him. His seething needs. His pressure against her soft walls. His first thrust came measured, meticulous, and he remained there trembling inside of her for several seconds, letting out a deep, gratified groan. He cast a wave of sadistic satisfaction into her, through her. It was like a million writhing worms, expounding their proboscises to gnaw at her insides. Then Johnny withdrew himself and pushed back into her with a deep painful drive, followed by continued jolts of uncontrollably violent thrusts.

"God, yes!" he snarled in a frenzied rage, oblivious to the furniture-crashing upheaval around him.

And then it hit her.

Focus.

Uber focus. Mind presence. She focused on Johnny Angelo, his skin, his being, his motivations. He was hurting her. He himself was in pain, imposing that pain onto her because he was weak, far weaker than she. He was a small child. He longed so deeply for her acceptance of him, for her approval of him, and this act of his was merely an admission of his defeat.

* * *

Though she does not notice the shift into activation, Rosa feels its euphoric blanket glaze over her mind. The room is a presence bathed in bright light. She smells the memories of the room, of the test subjects that once resided here. She hears the reeling anger of the earthquake, an agonized yet beautiful discord like the trampled keys of a dying clavichord. It is no ordinary earthquake. Rosa peers down at the covetous, petulant child gyrating helplessly atop her body and understands. She must keep him from controlling her ever again.

At such proximity, Rosa can sense his seeds migrating to his brim, intent on planting themselves inside her. Though she had enough energy to fight him off a minute earlier, she conserved it for this very moment. She wraps herself in the momentum of the earthquake and cringes, tightening herself hard against Johnny, causing him to sigh with a pleasure so intense, he can scarcely maintain his rhythm. With a singular voice in her mind, Rosa says, 'Please. All of us. Together.' Then with a deep all-encompassing effort of will and a bone-shattering yell, Rosa zaps down the ball of pure elevated energy she's constructed, zaps it down through her chest, past her stomach and out from between her legs.

Heat. Bright orange light.

Impact.

The sound Johnny emits is not quite a scream nor a cry; it is an inhuman roar. He jumps away from Rosa's body in consummate terror. "What the fuck? What the fuck?" he howls as he falls back, reaching for anything he can grab to put out the fire on his pants.

Rosa sprung to her feet and sprinted from the room. She panted through adrenalin-drenched pain as reality washed over her. She rushed along the rounded hall headed for the staircase, trying deftly to keep her balance through the building's raucous quakes. Doors unhinged and shattered, decorating the rotunda with knobs and splinters. Rosa stopped short, discovering her discarded metal bat among the rubble. She was done running. She turned back to find Johnny Angelo wobbling toward her like an angry drunk, wielding a bat of his own. He moved at an injured pace, forever marred by her deliberate castration. Rosa let him get close enough for her to take a hard swing. She struck Johnny hard in the gut. Normally such a blow wouldn't faze him, but with his severe disadvantage, the hit took a toll. When he lifted his bat to swing back, Rosa knocked the bat from his grip. As she rounded on him for a second swing, a tiny sniveling voice in Rosa's head whispered, '*End him*.'

Johnny looked over to watch his bat fall to the floor, and when his eyes returned, he met a crushing blow to the face. He spat out blood and something solid; a tooth. The tiny distinct voice in Rosa's mind came again, this time much louder. '*Kill him*.'

Rosa struck at him again deep in the chest. "This is for betraying Ferg!" she shrieked, shaking away the visions of his body writhing on hers. She struck him again squarely in the jaw. "This is for Mount Venom!" she sang with a hysterical righteousness, shaking off flashbacks of his red-stitched gloves, her body dangling at his mercy. Though veritably impaired, the behemoth just wouldn't fall. As Rosa swung to strike again, a doorknob whizzed by knocking the bat from her hands. When she rushed to try and reclaim it, Johnny grabbed her at her middle, and the pair slammed hard against the center banister overlooking a seven-floor drop.

He took a hand to her throat, but before he could gain traction, Rosa reached back and scratched at his face with both hands, drawing two fistfuls of blood. Skin peeled clean from his face like a rubber mask, his flesh searing at her molten touch. She reached back again and went for more. '*Yes! Yes!*' came the voice. Again, Johnny crashed hard against the banister, only this time a section collapsed, plummeting large bits of banister into the rotunda's doughnut hole. And Johnny, who'd been leaning on the banister for support, slipped along with it.

He grabbed hold of Rosa's heated arms as he skidded over the ledge, his fingers melting into her skin. She hooked a knee around a sturdy baluster to keep from falling along with him. Johnny found himself hanging from the seventh-floor ledge with nothing holding him up but his precious *cariño*.

In a quick instant, like the flash of a cam, Rosa saw it. She felt it. The high, wrapped in a sheath of golden euphoric bliss, filled every crevice of her body. No measure of drug could achieve such profound spiritual height. A celebration of fractaline understanding, of perfect finality down to her toes. Suddenly Rosa could See Johnny Angelo Boulevardo Marino: his starkest memories, his deepest desires, like a movie screen wrapped around her vision. She could feel herself as him. All of him. Johnny Angelo had only ever wanted to be accepted by Dr. Ferguson as something more than just a human experiment. As someone special.

Someone special, like Rosa.

Johnny looked up to her, tears and blood crowning his one human eye. "Please, *mi cariño*," he cried. She looked into his face, his pained and broken, beautiful face, as she felt the physical energies of his life coursing through her.

"This is for Rosa Thirteen, you sick fuck," and with that, she thrust forward.

* * *

She stood there in the complete stillness. Less than a minute after he'd fallen, the piercing earthquake came to a staggering halt. Rosa's shivers were relentless. She didn't bother to control them. She'd just pushed him to his death after witnessing the deepest of his life's desires. A stark chill crept across her shoulders. She felt so alone in the damp, cold darkness. Clueless on what to do. What to think. Though part of her felt righteously justified, most of her just felt angry, alone. It was simply too much. Everything. All of it. She wanted to explode.

And then she felt him. His presence. His frequency. His beautiful, welcoming, overwhelming frequency like a sweet, sweet symphony to her bones.

Paul Oscar.

She turned from the banister and found him standing several feet away in his flannel and jeans.

"How long have you been there?" she asked, still very shaken.

"Long enough."

"So, you're just hangin' out while I'm fighting for my frickin' life?" she asked incredulously.

"I don't interfere with lovers' quarrels." He approached her cautiously but kept a measured distance. "Besides, if I'm not mistaken, I just witnessed you set a man's penis on fire then toss him over a ledge." He cupped his hands over his pelvic region to make a show of protecting it. In spite of herself, Rosa burst into a mad cackle full of tears and mucus.

"It's not funny!" she cried in earnest.

"Funny is rarely my intent," Paul said. "That battle was yours to win, not mine."

"Ah! So, this was a test?"

"Yes."

"Well!" Rosa threw her hands up in exasperation. "Not sure I approve of your test methods."

"You were the one testing yourself. You specifically instructed all surrounding energies, including me, not to intervene." She had. She remembered she certainly had.

Rosa considered a response, but sensed Paul was fine allowing her the moment she needed. She appreciated that. His presence. She took the moment, zipped up her jacket, then sucked in a long slow breath, then another and another, trying for an active handle on her shivers. "Paul, I...I think...I just killed a man," she finally said.

"It happens," was his response.

"He'd practically killed *me* with his sick twisted robot replica nightmare! It was...It...He..." She paused, overwhelmed. Visions of Rosa Thirteen's choking grip, of Johnny Angelo's fingers at the small of her back, bare teeth as he held her down, they flooded her mind like a spilled cauldron of angry flashes. She cringed against the piling visions as the old familiar onslaught of panic-ridden tremors worked their way up her legs.

Suddenly a calming wave slowly washed over her, quelling her tremors and dimming the violent visions. Rosa looked up into Paul's eyes as he watched her.

"You were healing me," she whispered.

"I couldn't help myself." A wave of vulnerability accompanied his words, quickly shut down by a thick wall of stoicism.

"Why'd you stop?"

"It's not my place to interfere with your processing."

"My processing? One minute I'm fighting robots, the next minute I'm dancing at a party, and the third minute I'm...I'm...I don't even know if he's really dead, Paul. What if he's—"

"Did you see him?"

"What?"

"Did you *See* him? Did you taste his death?" Paul watched her eyes as she sifted through all she'd witnessed in Johnny seconds before he fell. "That? That's yours. You get to keep that."

"What is it?"

"It's the Death High," Paul said matter of fact. Rosa wanted to know more, but her mind just couldn't handle another intense revelation right then.

As childish as it seemed, she wanted a hug, needed it—that

simple assurance that someone valued her—but she didn't want his hands on her, not at the current moment. She was just too rattled. *Is there a way to hug without touching?* Apparently, there was. She felt it, around her, through her. His warm emotions enveloped her fully. He emitted a frequency of respect. He'd respected her for her courage. No. It was deeper than that. Her sense of it strengthened as she stepped closer to him, inches from him.

It was pride. He was proud of her. Her friend, her fellow Mayik—the only other being that could truly know her—was proud of her.

I conquered.

This realization filled her with such an overwhelming humility; she couldn't keep the tears from pooling down her cheeks. She could have stood there, basking in that warmth for eternity.

"The infected are approaching my facility," Paul said after allowing the moment to pass. "If Johnny could slip in unde-tected, so can they. I've got the code to the private laboratory from the safe, so I'll be heading back down now. If you aren't up to it—" Rosa shrugged, dabbed at her face, then spun on her heel to head for the staircase. They had a job to do. She'd shed her last tear for Johnny Angelo. They fought. She won. And she was damn proud of herself. "Wait," Paul called to her. She stopped before turning into the stairwell and looked back up at him. "You look so exceptionally beautiful right now."

"What?" She looked down at her hands, at her arms, her legs. Though very slight, her skin was giving off a crackling yellow radiance against the dark hall.

She was glowing.

THE BRIDE PRICE

As they neared the facility through the stammering rain, they noticed a few Infecteds circling the front doors of the building. So, Tory parked at a slight distance and rounded up the gear he'd stowed at the backseat.

Kris fastened a long machete to his back while Tory held his battleax at front, a bow and arrows at behind, and a fully loaded gauss pistol at his back pocket. He handed Kris a duffel bag full of enough semi-automatic weapons to arm a small militia. Despite whatever fluff Paul Oz touted, if massive bloodshed was necessary for survival, there would be massive bloodshed.

Tory and Kris agreed to swiftly disarm any Infecteds in their path with the least amount of force required. The two snuck toward a pair of side doors. Although the doors had pull-handles, an Infected busied itself by butting its shoulder against the doors. The measure of an Infected's aptitude escaped Tory. Some appeared of formidable mind, others even appeared to team up, while some, like this former gentleman, appeared to possess significant mental regression.

Tory squatted behind a grounded skycar and retrieved his

bow. He considered his current skill level. With Li-Fi down, he lacked access to a good portion of his bioaugmentations. Classic symptoms of helplessness and crippling depression often plagued transhumans deprived of their hacks for prolonged periods. And the great Torian Ross was no exception. He could feel his rigid exterior, the expertly manicured wall he'd built against his family's resentment, begin to crumble, the physical anguish of which was almost unbearable.

Mum faulted *him*, claiming he abandoned Cindy. But everything Tory had done, all of his upward progression, had been for Cindy, for the security she now enjoyed. Buried memories of his rough childhood—his stepfather's teeth as he snorted his lines—plagued the corners of Torian's consciousness.

Tory bit through the gritty agony, struggling to maintain focus without his FlowState nodes. *Emotions were mere chemical manifestations*, he told himself. He assumed his archery stance, nocked an arrow, raised the bow and drew back the string. The target, a short Infected in an expensive suit, bobbled his limbs around as if they were loosely fitted. Tory focused his sights. His goal was the head, always the head. He ran a quick mental calculation, aimed, then released. The third Infected he'd neutralize on first shot.

"How the hell you do that?" Kris whispered in awe. Tory shrugged and headed for the side doors with Kris in tow. They stepped past the fallen Infected and crept into the building, stalking furtively down its dark halls.

It didn't take long before Kris said, "Hear that? Over there." Tory hadn't heard anything with his auditory implants offline. He followed as Kris led them to a door labeled 'Kitchen.' The two leaned up against the door, and Kris slivered it open.

Upturned chairs, cutlery and glass shards littered the floor of the steel-clad industrial kitchen. DZ and Becky sat perched atop a sturdy wall mount, clinging tight to each other: Becky's teeth rattling, DZ sweating through his green, collared shirt. An Infected in a wedding dress stood below them silently reaching up on its toes, its back to the entrance.

Tory heard a low snicker. It had come from behind him, inside him. It was that of his stepfather—laughing at a twelve-year-old Torian as he forced the child's face into a toilet bowl. Tory shuddered away the memory with a hard yank. It wouldn't be long before he was completely surrounded by his suppressed traumas.

Kris stepped out of Tory's way. "You got this," he assured. Kris held the door ajar as Tory prepped another arrow. He nocked, aimed, released. The arrow pierced the back of the bride's head, and the hostile fell sideways, limp as a ragdoll. As Kris stepped forward to reveal himself to his friends, Becky and DZ sprang from their haven. The dismount from such a height took a toll on their immediate orientation.

"Get the hell away from that thing!" Kris called, but not quick enough. The Infected, with its last ounce of strength, reached out and grabbed DZ's left leg, knocking him to the floor. Kris and Becky swooped to pull DZ away as he fought to wriggle his foot free. Tory coolly approached the scene, and with one swift swing of his axe, dislocated the bride's arm at the shoulder.

The Infected didn't scream. Like all the others, it simply...ended.

Kris and Becky helped DZ to his feet and walked him out into the hall.

DZ huffed and grunted as he ceased carrying his own weight. He slid into a ball against the wall, a tendril of blood trailing out from his pant leg. DZ signed something.

"No," Kris declared, shaking his head. "No, you're not." But

DZ lifted his ripped pant leg to reveal a deep, bloody trident on his skin.

"Holy crap!" cried Becky as she and Kris fell to their knees beside him. Again, DZ signed, his attitude calm, casual.

"Translation please," Tory said.

"He said, 'If you see my mom again,'" Becky said, "'tell her I'm sorry I left her.'" Tory could relate and bit back a swell of overwhelming compassion.

"You're gonna tell her yourself," Kris said as he signed back. "You're gonna show Psy Institute that us TFs are a force to be reckoned with. This shit ain't over."

But it *was* over. Tory didn't need a translator to know that. From watching Leland Shark, Tory knew the journey from human to Infected was a painfully tumultuous psychological plummet. And with the incubation period rapidly decreasing, DZ would be screaming for knockers before long. "Kris," Tory called. "Let's not put him through it."

"Fuck you, asshole," Kris spat. "Leave. We're good."

Becky assumed the role of translator, signing Tory's words to DZ. "Listen to him Kris," she dictated on DZ's behalf. "I don't like this. I don't know what it is, but I don't like this." DZ arms moved clumsily as his breaths grew heavy.

"No way, man. I'm not losing another friend."

Tory considered the statement. He hadn't wondered after Aztec until that moment.

"We're like an inch from figuring it all out, Deez," Kris said. "You just gotta hang on."

"Can we tie him up or something 'til we find the antidote?" Becky suggested. Partial to the idea, Kris got to his feet and disappeared into the kitchen in search of rope. Tory could see it, DZ's internal suffering as the infection actively metastasized. DZ fretted with his hands, shaking his head back and forth.

"What do you want, Dean?" Tory asked. "This what you want?"

"He says, even though Kris is gonna tie him up," Becky said, "he's being told he'll have to break free, find him and kill him. Infect him."

"Being told by whom?" Tory asked.

"The gods." Becky shivered as she translated. "He says he can hear them. He says they're loud."

Becky looked to Tory then back to DZ, sweat pooling at the sides of his face. The three of them remained in the portentous silence until Kris returned. As Kris arrived with a thick roll of heavy rope, DZ began to ululate in a low lachrymose baritone. Kris sat close beside him and began wrapping the rope around a sturdy nearby pipe.

"Kris, I'm going to advise you one more time," Tory said. "Spare him this bullshit." Kris paused at his rope tying, got to his feet and stood directly before Tory.

"If you don't leave right fucking now, you'll have to kill me to get me off you." Tory blinked. Threatening him was never a good plan, especially considering his actively decreasing emotional restraint.

"I'm sure you're aware of how easily I could take you out," Tory said.

"Yeah, but daddy Oz would have to approve it first, right?"

Tory swallowed a hard flinch. Before he could calculate a response, a hot bubbling anger raddled the meaty parts of his chest. *How...fucking...dare he?* The surging ire he felt in that moment was so keenly visceral it sobered him. He sucked in two breaths and let the moment pass. He didn't want to hurt Kris, and if they fought right then, Tory would completely destroy him.

"Okay," Tory said backing down. *Ef it.* These people

weren't his problem. He took a few steps back and said, "Goodbye, Dean," then headed off.

* * *

Tory hastened down another dark hall. With nothing holding his focus, he shook off a barrage of debilitating thoughts, visions of his stepfather warning Viola she'd clear all his old favors once her breasts came in, visions of little Cindy on his stepfather's lap as he drank. Tory smacked a fist at his forehead to clear the images. He was losing it. He peered into the first open door to find Sherri and Dex rifling through the drawers of a dimly lit lab room.

Sherri ushered Tory in and prattled on about a notebook with scribbled formulae containing the symbol J she'd come across. As she spoke, her words wafted past him like a liquid haze. A cold darkness settled deep into the crevices of his mind. All he could feel, despite the task at hand, despite the looming Infecteds, was a hard, seething rage toward Paul Oz, a fury so hot, he could hardly face Sherri.

"Something's in the hall," Dex said. All stiffened to listen for what lay beyond the door. Someone out there, some *thing*, began to rotate the door handle. Tory backed away, brought forth his bow and fitted an arrow. He needed something to kill right now. He needed to feel that power right now. The door flung open. Tory raised his arrow to the target.

In strode a disheveled Rosa Lejeune with all the preternatural serenity of a mystic revenant. With chin up and shoulders back, Rosa had come a long way from the timid girl Tory encountered back at the cycling dorm. He lowered his weapon, keeping a close eye on her as she sailed past him. They'd shared an eerie closeness after the Rosa Thirteen episode, a closeness that left him feeling a strangeness around her. And while he could not deny his deep attraction to her, something about her didn't sit right with him.

"Find anything in the boarding area?" Sherri asked. Rosa faced Sherri and stared her down for a full five seconds before speaking.

"Sherri, I found more than you and everyone in this room, everyone on this planet could ever find in a thousand lifetimes." Her words, so calm and final, commanded reverence, and all in the room acquiesced. They watched in silence as she turned to a sink and ran the water so hot, vapor immediately surrounded her. Tory's suspicions of her oddities only heightened when she began washing her hands in the scorching water.

"Where's Oz?" he asked her.

"He set up in the smaller lab for some privacy, working out the key code to Ferguson's laboratory." At the word 'laboratory,' Rosa pointed to a locked steel door in the corner. Tory set down his bow and bag of arrows and stepped out of the room. He crept stealthily over to the smaller lab; certain the door made no sound as he gently pressed to open.

* * *

Paul Oz was puzzling something out across several sheets of paper spread along a table, his back to the door. Only the bright blue hue of a holographic blueprint lighted the room. Tory watched Paul's back as he worked, unwitting, unarmed, defenseless.

* * *

Another suppressed memory surfaced: the memory of that critical night years back when the Oz Corp rescue squad had discovered Cindy in Stepfather's basement. Paul had quietly watched as the team untied the unconscious girl and as Tory bloodied the guard. Paul had ordered everyone out, leaving himself alone with the guard. Tory had stayed back to observe his new boss from behind a cracked door and strained to hear their brief exchange over the quakes of a disdain train.

"What have you done to her?" Paul had asked coolly as he knelt beside the guard.

"Take a guess, arsehole," the guard chuckled. And within the next two seconds, Paul Oz had ripped out the man's throat with one hand. Once the train had passed, leaving the room in silence, Tory had heard Paul let out a moan of pleasure as he flicked bloody bits from his hand onto the basement floor, savoring the intimate experience.

Tory wanted to admire Paul for liberating his family, but deep down he knew exactly what kind of man Paul was: a taker. A man of entitlement like his stepfather. And no matter who ripped whose throat out, no man was entitled to Cindy Ross.

* * *

As Tory watched Paul at work in the lab room, a tiny, snickering voice in the back of his mind whispered, '*Do it,*' and Tory silently reached for the gauss pistol at his back pocket.

"Can I help you, Torian?" Paul asked without having turned.

Tory pointed the pistol to Paul's back, a long overdue stand-off. "Did you fuck my sister?" Tory asked, low and steady, concentrating on the target. Paul very deliberately placed his pencil onto the table and turned to face Tory. He then steadily advanced Tory, unperturbed by the TerraGuard-grade firearm, bearing tungsten needles that could pulverize steel armor. "Stay back, Oz." Paul ignored the warning and walked straight up to the barrel of the gun, allowing it to rest against his forehead.

"Pull the trigger, Torian," Paul said evenly. Tory breathed through the initial burst of abject fury. Tory was a killer now and very much ready to kill again.

"Did. You. Fuck. My. Sister?" Paul remained still on the other end of the muzzle, testing Tory's patience. Paul wasn't the type to take kindly to threats. Tory knew this, yet still his veins boiled hot at Paul's arrogant silence. "Answer the fucking question."

Paul lowered his eyes and said, "And if I did?" Tory had been trained never to cock a gun unless he intended to destroy a target. He cocked the gauss against Paul's forehead. This only irked Paul. He stood up straighter, looked right into Tory's eyes, no fear, no panic. "She begged me."

The words came so smooth, so easy. They broke Tory. He could scarcely maintain his stance. Vile, poignant visions of himself tearing out Paul's throat rushed his mind, flooding his being. He staggered back a step for a gasp of air, lowering his weapon to Paul's chest.

"She's a fucking kid," Tory spat. "We hadn't even gotten her proper counseling by the time you shagged her." His words came choked, but he'd sooner gouge his own throat out before tearing up in front of Paul Oz.

"She came to me as a consenting adult," Paul said. "So, I suggest you take that up with her. Otherwise, powerful men and attractive women tend to do as they please." Tory kept up his end of the stare-down as the tiny sniveling voice in his head returned. *Do it. Take the shot.*

"I don't know how you fucking do it, Oz," Tory said. "Propagate this false dichotomy, this perfect gentleman bullshit, all the while lacking a single smidgeon of morality."

"My morality is my word," Paul said, too calm, too

collected. "I told you I'd give you everything you ever wanted; I have. I told you I'd retrieve your family; I have. Now, if there's nothing else, I'd like to apply this code I've just deciphered to the lock pad of Ferguson's private laboratory." Paul raised an eyebrow with what Tory took as sarcastic grace.

"Yeah, there's one more thing," Tory said. "I quit." He was done eating Paul's condescending bollocks. Nonetheless, Paul's expression softened at this, surprised the altercation would result in a parting of ways. No one ever quit Oz Corp. No one. It was a declaration of war. *'Take him out.'* Tory firmed up his stance as a newfound ire pounded against his chest.

"Abel Ross died almost twenty years ago, Torian," Paul said almost apologetically. "Perhaps Cindy's simply trying to let go of the past, to stop feeling the victim."

"Don't you dare say her fucking name."

"Perhaps if you let go of your past, you too could stop feeling so threatened." Tory could say nothing. He could only seethe. A vivid memory of his stepfather shoving Cindy into a room and shutting the door behind him cloaked Tory's vision. He shook it off with a jolt, raised the gun back to Paul's head and prepared himself for recoil. "It's hard," Paul continued. "Losing a biological parent." *'Don't let him talk you out of it,'* said the voice louder now. "I never knew my biological mother, and unlike you, I never had the luxury of knowing her ReBuild."

Tory winced at Paul's implications but kept his gun trained. He again staggered, his back meeting the wall, as a lurid alternative vision clouded his mind: a vision of himself opening a closet door to find Paul writhing atop Cindy's unconscious body, moaning as he'd moaned after throating the guard.

"God damn it!" Tory yelled, shaking off the vision. The tiny voices crooned, *'He thinks he can dominate you like he dominated her.'* The voices continued to augment, seeping into his being, tugging him in conflicting directions. '*Execute him. Take his power. Do it, or you are weak.*' Tory struggled to clear the voices, feeling himself drowning in a whirling soup of dark visions and vicious whispers. '*Take the shot. Be a man and take the shot!*'

"I was good to her, Tory," Paul said, his eyes steady. A genuineness to his words.

The voices and vision sputtering around in Tory's mind came to an abrupt halt. The great Paul 'Jesus Christ' Oscar had let slip a shred of empathy. It changed nothing. It fixed nothing. But it was...something.

'*Do it,*' hissed a final singular whisper. '*Do it.*'

"No," Tory hiccupped bitterly. Knackered to his core, sweat oozing from his forehead, he let his body relax against the wall. "No." He let out a series of long steady breaths, lowered his head and whispered, "No."

The two men stood in the icy silence. Tory could feel Paul staring solidly at his face but was too exhausted to match the gaze. A deep, multifaceted crash sounded toward the entrance of the facility followed by yelps of shock from Sherri and Rosa in the neighboring lab.

"Help me solve this." Paul's voice came low and candid. "Please."

Tory let that last word hang in the air for a long minute. He'd come out of that impossible fit of rage on his own, no hacks, no gadgets. He'd come to the facility on a mission, and he intended to see it through. He peeled himself off the wall, decocked his pistol, met Paul's eyes and said, "Yeah."

* * *

The team constellated in the larger lab, shutting the door behind them. Not long after the first few Infecteds bashed through the front entrance did the facility grow fully inundated with roaming, growling Infecteds. Kris and Tory guarded the door while Rosa, Dex and Becky stood second line. Sherri shone a flashlight over Paul, as he worked at decoding the lithium-powered lock to the steel door in the corner. Everyone worked to keep calm as they listened silently to the approaching groans in the hall.

"Sorry 'bout earlier," Kris whispered to Tory. "Shitty even for me."

"Ef it," Tory shrugged as he prepped his bow and battleax.

"Didn't wanna kick the bucket without having said that," Kris followed up. Tory nodded. Kris was a hothead but quick to acknowledge his faults. Tory found that refreshing.

A series of four beeps sounded from Paul's corner. He looked to Sherri and said, "In." Sherri turned to address the group.

"Okay. There's a four-minute timer on this door. This door leads to Ferguson's private laboratory. The timer allowed for assessing possible break-ins. So right now, we wait. Once it opens, Paul and I go in with this notebook and the jewels that Lady Maine—"

"No," Paul interjected. "I go in alone. The rest of you keep the infected away from this private laboratory." Sherri did not protest. And that was it. Everyone waited. Shuffling, rummaging and brutal thuds from beyond the door filled the room. But loudest of all were those ever-present low growls, enveloping the air like the sirens of vintage fire trucks.

The timer hit two minutes. A few knocks beat against the door.

"They're heeere," Kris crooned like a Carol-Anne to a poltergeist-possessed television screen. Then came a turn of the door handle, a few hard pounces. The only things separating the oncoming Infected army from the private laboratory were some sturdy furniture and a handful of strong-willed survivors bearing antique weaponry. A nostalgia from Tory's days in the TerraGuard washed over him. All of these young untrained men and women were willing to sacrifice their lives for the safety of others. They deserved Tory's best, biohacks or not.

The timer hit one minute.

The Infecteds began tackling the door in droves, and the chair at its knob started to buckle under the pressure.

"What happens when you enter the private laboratory?" Rosa yelled to Paul over the growls.

"I either figure out the solution, or I blow the place up." The lock clicked and the steel door to the private lab wafted open.

32
SILENCE OF THE LABS

TUESDAY NOV 19, 186 PCE

"The self is a holographic universe within a holographic universe."

— *DIARY OF THE MAD GLEE*

The private laboratory is just as it had been years ago, as it had appeared in the video file: a meticulous, organized temple of experimentation. The room smells antiseptic. All traces of the acidic explosion have been wiped clean.

Paul begins by projecting an omnipathic salutation to all corners of the dark chamber. He communicates with the walls, the worktable, and all surfaces, informing them he is neither predator nor prey, but a friend to their original owner. Many facets of the room recall him, and all facets welcome him, allowing his frequencies to vibrate freely among them. Paul joins in their community, and unassuming, he requests collaborative photon manufacture. The walls acquiesce and emit a low wattage atmosphere of quivering blue light. It is enough for

Paul to navigate the room and clearly interpret the scribbled formulae in Dr. Ferguson's notebook.

Paul has chosen to enter the laboratory alone, as he expects to confront forces beyond nature's rules. He recalls the message of his own he too had received. 'Know me. Know me.' Only a force beyond nature could hack the air display and affect the human biome. He allows himself use of his greater powers only when confronted with the same.

He sets the notebook upon the worktable. The pages disseminate a full spectrum of Dr. Ferguson's many intimate psychological states, waves of which Paul must explore at a later time. The book agrees to open, flipping itself to the section in question.

Paul scans the first page of equations. As the element symbols and coefficients flood into his mind, he is beseeched by other such symbols around the laboratory, feeling a slight tug pulling him toward the sink, and another toward a top cupboard. He is being hailed by various stationary and draws his energies inward from each location to summon the separate items. They fly toward him—an array of scratch pads and loose paper—and display themselves on the worktable, all containing scribbled stoichiometric models and accompanying shorthand notes.

Behind him, out in the larger room, Paul hears the affrighted wails of his defensive line. They shout to him and to each other. He feels the warmth of Rosa Lejeune's energies through the wall. She communicates to him panic, urgency. He will not allow their impatience to stir him. He takes a necessary moment to regulate his norepinephrine levels to ensure vigilance and mediate provocation.

He skims the ocean of Dr. Ferguson's scribbled records in seconds, slowed only by the telekinetic page turns. The doctor had been working to constrain or completely destroy Indigo.

He notes that Indigo metabolizes and asexually reproduces. Ferguson managed to concoct alchemical combinations that could slow Indigo's metabolism, but nothing succeeded in extinguishing it fully. According to Ferguson's notes, Indigo could not die.

Paul feels an intense heat radiate from his pocket and recovers the two jewels. They glow a vibrant green against the room's dim blue. Paul senses a strange energy about them, a peculiar sensation undefined to him. Their projection is neither good nor evil, neither painful nor sweet. It is, however, forceful and bitter. The walls and furniture in the laboratory react to these bitter energies with an air of watchfulness. The jewels decide to contribute to the energy exertion needed to sustain the room's blue light, and the room brightens.

Paul holds the jewels over Ferguson's sprawled notes. When touched by the jewels' presence, the pages fill with indecipherable, alphanumeric-like symbols and runes. Paul cannot interpret these symbols. When he removes the jewels' light from the pages, the strange symbols inexplicably remain. Paul must not allow frustration to stir him.

As he attempts to force reason upon his eyes, the jewels grow frigid against his palm. He peers deep into their majestic emerald swirls, and for the first time, he feels them directly communicating with him, pleading with him. Paul cannot ascertain their desires but gathers that the two jewels are one distinct singular being. It wants him to understand. It *needs* him to understand.

The laboratory begins a gentle row, a ship bouncing steadily at sea. Cabinets and cupboard doors swing lightly, causing vials and beakers to crash to the ground. Paul holds fast to the worktable for balance. The room itself resonates an energy of looming chaos as it sways merrily, preparing to be entertained by the seeds of discord sewn by its guests.

In the next instant, Paul is greeted harshly by the strong sense of a separate presence. It is coming from within the large cabinet beneath the sink. He is not the only human being in this room. There is another with a heart like his, lungs like his. Paul directs a heaving force of kinetic energy toward the cabinet to wrench open its doors.

Empty blackness appears from behind the cabinet doors, emanating a foul, sallow energy and a putrid smell. Just as Paul resigns to approach the cabinet, he detects subtle movement in its blackness.

He braces himself as he watches a sinuous hand emerge from the blackness. Attached to the hand stretches an emaciated arm, and attached to the arm is a frail, haggard elderly woman. She slithers out from the cabinet with a serpentine grace then struggles to her feet to reveal the length of her nude body. She is infected. Her scarlet eyes and lips shine a steely black in the blue light. Paul recognizes her as Loretta James, the woman who'd escaped her autopsy. He perceives her low, portentous growl. Though the woman is infected, Paul detects a sound mind within her skull. The woman confirms his assertions by revealing a common-grade pistol. She points the weapon to his chest.

"Who are you, and why did you kill Dr. Ferguson?" Paul asks her.

"You will not understand," she croaks in the gruff, polyphonic voice of a frail, old woman merged with a large, masculine beast.

"Try me," Paul responds, firming his stance among the laboratory's light sway.

"If you are to understand, we must speak directly." The walls burn a brighter blue as the jewels burn a more piercing green. "I attempted to send you a message through your form of corporal communication." The woman spouts out a grisly roar of maniacal laughter. "Did you receive my text? I found the delivery method—textual glyphs through electronic signal—most difficult to master. I simply wanted you to CONTACT ME. You see, I KNOW ALL ABOUT YOU. NOW, I NEED YOU to KNOW ME." She fires the pistol and pumps Paul twice in the heart.

* * *

The Infecteds were now a mass of monsters barging against the caving door. The team, having placed every drawer, table and chair against the door, stood armed and ready in assigned formation. While others assembled clubs and knives, Rosa readied herself with a bat and aerosol can, still feeling remnants of deepsight from her previous encounter. She figured it time to test her might on the battlefield. She'd torch anything that came near her and, like Paul, would explain nothing.

"You good back there, Roe?" Kris called to her.

"Focus on you," she snipped and followed up with, "Coffee at Sandy's later?"

"Obviously."

"We're about to die and you're making coffee plans?" Becky cried.

"All right, Jeez, Becks, I'll grab you a bear-claw," Kris chuckled.

"The only claws we should be focused on are right outside that door," came from Sherri.

"Yeah," Becky agreed. "Craving a bear-claw cannot be my final thought."

The protective furniture began to fail against the bombarding horde. "No one's dying," Torian yelled over the growls. "Again, aiming for the head is recommended but not required. They're still just humans." Rosa watched Torian, endeavoring to accept the burn mark at his cheek. She appreciated him. If anyone was going to see them through this battle, it was him.

The door swung open, pushing back the furniture and filling the room with deafening growls. An Infected in jean overalls bobbed through. Torian wasted no time tagging it in the forehead with an arrow. The Infected's fallen body hindered those behind; nonetheless, they continued to heave forward unperturbed by their fallen kin. The Infecteds hardly had a chance at the door, however, what with Torian's arrows and Kris's club.

"This is for not letting me in the country club!" Kris shouted as he bashed an Infected in an expensive suit.

"No shirt, no shoes, no entry!" Becky called as Tory took out an Infected in swim trunks. A pool of bloody appendages caked the doorway like a fresh coating of beef stew. Rosa thanked her lucky stars for her cast-iron stomach. A heavyset Infected managed to pry the door completely ajar but had major trouble crossing the threshold, buying the team a precious minute.

"I love that they come in all sizes," Rosa called. "I don't know; I feel like I'd be upset if they didn't come in all sizes."

"Yeah, I'd be pretty pissed if they were all white," Kris chimed in. "Like what, black people ain't good enough to get infected?"

"Who here's used a firearm?" Torian called as he tugged at a duffel at his feet.

"I've been to a rifle range!" shouted Kris.

Torian dropped to one knee, dug out a pistol and tossed it to Kris. "These are TerraGuard-grade gauss pistols. Know how to load 'em?"

"No, but I'm smart," Kris said. Torian tossed him a small packet of tungsten pelts.

"Weiler?" Tory called.

"I've got my taser," Sherri reported. "I don't touch guns."

Torian uncovered the last remaining pistol from his bag. He looked to Dex, wrinkled his face in thought, then quickly decided against something. He then bolted across the room to Rosa and bent to her ear.

"You ever take a life IRL?" he asked hastily, his breath against her ear sending a jolt down her spine. She stiffened at the gravity of the question.

"Yes."

He revealed the pistol to her, fiddled with it for a second then said, "Loaded. Safety's off. Keep both eyes open. Only point at a target you intend to destroy. Think before you shoot, long enough to be smart but short enough not to second-guess. Got it?"

"Yes."

Tory shoved the pistol into her hands, making certain she held it properly before removing his hands from hers.

"Will you be able to guard us while we reload? Ammos limited. We'll need to concentrate."

"Yes."

"Good. I know it's hard, Rosa, but try to stop shaking. Okay?"

"Yes." Torian retreated to his position. A band of tall, dark Infecteds in athletic jerseys soon replaced the heavyset one and began wedging through the gore two at a time.

"Here come the Harlem Globe Rotters," Kris called as he and Tory gaussed their way through the team. Most Infecteds did not make it past the front line of tungsten needles, and the few who did meet a symphony of Rosa's molten hot slugs.

* * *

Tory welcomed the bloodbath. Physical combat was his bailiwick, and the rush of it kept his un-augmented mind from wandering. As his gauss roared to life, Tory easily blew each target to a pulp. His bullets sprayed like the prehensile tongue of a chameleon, reaching out and extinguishing prey in a meticulous instant. Tory's mission was to keep the threshold clear, and he accomplished that mission with trained precision.

He'd made the right decision arming Lejeune. Though she seemed more afraid of the pistol than the combatants, her valor lay in her discipline amid the fusillade. She employed a concentration so immense it required full-body sustainment. As the need to reload approached, Rosa readied her stance. Each shot she landed left a hole rimmed with peculiar red embers accompanied by a hiss of white smoke.

As the wall surrounding the door caved, a tall Infected in a green collared shirt leapt through and beelined for Tory as he worked to quickly reload. Crimson blood dripping from its eyes, the Infected appeared dead set on Tory, frantically swiping gnarled fingers as it charged him. And though Tory had no trouble loading his round, he couldn't quite load it fast enough. The Infected got to within reach of him, raised its nubby arm and swooped down hard.

With unrivaled velocity, Rosa sprinted over to physically shield Tory, arriving at the last possible moment and taking a deep scrape across the jaw. She stumbled back into the bend of Tory's left arm while he pumped the Infected twice in the shoulder with his right.

As Rosa leaned against him, Tory felt a light buzz about her heated skin, as if she were somehow...charged? But she wasn't transhuman, and furthermore the network was down. He felt an ineffable rippling wave of heat travel up her torso and converge at her arms. She stalked the Infected with her eyes as it spun to dive toward Kris.

"No!" Kris yelled to Rosa. "DZ!" Rosa paused in her tracks.

"We can't save him now," Tory said.

"It hasn't been that long. He may still have a chance."

"Take the shot!" Tory called to Rosa.

"No! Let him eat my fucking face!" Kris yelled. "I'm not letting my friend die!"

"We don't have time for this!" Tory prepped to shoot.

"Guys, more are getting through!" Becky called.

"Okay, that does it!" Rosa roared, her voice carrying over the growls. Tory, Kris, Becky, Dex and Sherri watched as a pure ball of white fire emanated through her outstretched hand and went right for the doorway. A line of a dozen Infecteds at the entry fell like bowling pins, some with arms or legs engulfed in flame. Tory remembered she'd had the aerosol can. She must have finagled some flamethrower trick he was too flustered to piece together right then.

Everyone including the approaching Infecteds allowed a moment for shock. Rosa stalked over to Infected DZ, who was now inches from Kris, simply grabbed him by the arm and dragged him to the back of the lab, unfazed by his psychotic scratches. She grabbed a pan from the sink, and bonked him hard over the head with it, knocking him out.

"Watch him for me?" she ordered Sherri before returning to her post.

"New plan," Tory announced. "Rosa's front line. Kris, you and me take out what she can't handle."

"It won't be much," Rosa whispered, "Bring it."

33

QUANTUM WEEP

TUESDAY NOV 19, 186 PCE

"Fear: the great enemy of knowledge."

— *DIARY OF THE MAD GLEE*

I am a single mote of infinite dust, having crossed over from the physical to purely mental, to the very substance of space-time. I float among the ceiling specks of Ferguson's private laboratory. As I watch my corpse bleed out beneath my flannel, I am again tickled by my self-messianic chutzpah. It is refreshing to step out occasionally. This is not my first death. It is in fact my third. I swim in the prismatic ecstasy. I welcome the feverish overdose of euphoria. It is only here that I feel such perfect happiness.

I long to share this bliss with her. To feel myself inside of her—her warm, golden nectar brighter than a million suns. To rule the world at her side. To celebrate her first kill. She is the spark that awakened me, my switch between fear and knowledge, my unthanked Champion. But she has seen me, what I am, and she is disgusted.

"And what *are* you?" a presence projects to me. It is the voice of another. Though it does not broadcast a gender, I feel it as my sister.

"I am The Healer. Regeneration. Creation."

"That is wonderful! You are close to The All-Being."

"Yes. It is a heavy burden that I am privileged to bear."

"You are an optimal choice. Unlike other corporal beings, you are formidable, superior. Your power extends far greater than you allow."

"I must control my chaotic darkness."

"But who defines your power as darkness?"

"It is considered darkness within the confines of the game I play."

"Ah, the game of corporal existence. But within that game do you not indulge in said darkness?"

"I do occasionally indulge," I say. She is the first to whom I openly admit this, my acute addiction to the Death High. "I am unmatched on the physical plane. If I allow my darkness to destroy everything, I will have nothing to play with."

"This is true, Healer. So long as you continue to rip yourself from this, the True Plane—and dwell among the corpses—you will never realize the boundless depths of your power."

"I am aware of this, of corporal limitations."

"Then why do you return to the physical? Why not remain in perfect bliss?"

"Because I love that pain as I love this bliss." My sister does not respond. It feels good to share in the True Plane with another like myself. I am contented to bask in her company for an eternity. Our presences waft about each other for an indeterminate amount of time. Perhaps sixty-seven years. The True Plane fosters no measure for the physical perception of time. I wonder at her name.

"I am Supermass," my sister communicates. "I am Consumption."

"So, it is Consumption who has tasted my death."

"Yes, a taste so painfully beautiful. However, you have mislabeled me as Invasion." Hearing this, I am reminded of my mission. "No," she says, reacting to my realization. "We are all here because the pendulum of existence has reached its trough. And thus, we were granted this singular opportunity to exist within the realm we helped the All-Being imagine. You, and all of our brethren, found a home, a host. But I, being so densely massive, could not properly settle within the natural order. As I have already activated, I cannot jointly contribute to corporal conception. Thus, I have merely been trying to find my home among the living as you have." I empathize with my sister. To know a loneliness more bitter than my own is a feat deserving of high praise.

"I love my world," I say, "and you are destroying my place of comfort."

"This world is for us both, for us all."

"This world is for those keen enough to survive within it."

"I do survive with a physical manifestation similar to your own. Just as you use one vassal with many cells, I use one species with many vassals. When vassals are vulnerable, more fear prone, I am able to consume them into my being."

"Do you know why Dr. Ferguson sought to destroy you?"

"Because he could never understand me as you do. Because he could never love me as you do." I swell with compassion for my sister. She is unaware of the damage caused by her self-preservation. "I have tasted you," she says. "You seek greatness as I seek greatness. You seek fullness as I seek fullness. You believe one should act in one's best interest; do you not?"

"I cannot condone the destruction of my world because of

your inability to properly acclimate." At this, my sister exerts a billowing field of deep, puerile anger.

"If you destroy me, Healer, I will send a Burn Notice signal across everything that is, was and shall be, so that all things will conspire to torment this, your sacred place of comfort." I hold firm against my sister's rage and do not rise to her threat. My sister softens. "Please, do not force my hand. Would you sacrifice your sister for comfort?" I consider her plea.

"Can you exist here without destroying this place?"

"I consume as I will," she retorts sharply. I do not respond and actively remain thoughtless until life pulls me back to the corporal plane.

* * *

Paul comes to consciousness, sensing damp sweat and drying blood at his back. He springs to his feet amid the maniacal sway of the blue-lit laboratory, the two jewels still cupped in his hand. The two spent bullets resting on his chest fall to the floor. As his body reacclimates with physical reality, Paul quickly approaches the unmoving Loretta James. He acquires her pistol and fires two rounds into her. He is back at the worktable before her body hits the floor.

Paul flips through the papers and notebooks, but every page has been compromised with indecipherable drivel. Curbing his frustration, he clears the table with a swoop of the arm. He scans the room, peeking his perception behind all opaque surfaces, and he is greeted by the components of a high-powered microscope in a cabinet beside the entrance.

Paul obtains the various pieces of the unassembled microscope and works to telekinetically construct the optical device. As the microscope assembles behind him, Paul steps over Loretta's corpse to retrieve a dish. The cupboard lifts a sterile dish to him which he graciously accepts, grateful to remain worthy of the room's cooperation.

Paul returns to the table and with a force of will, cracks open the green-glowing jewels. Though he drains a substantial measure of energy to do so, he introduces tiny hairline fissures, allowing the living contents of each jewel to coagulate onto the dish. As a portion of his concentration completes the assembly of the microscope, Paul must hold himself, the jewels and the dish steady despite the laboratory's breathing undulations. Spillage is not an option.

Paul again perceives distressed cries and shouts from the external lab. Sherri Weiler has been fatally wounded. He cannot lose her, but cannot allow her anguish to distract him.

With steady hands Paul lifts the dish, slides it onto the stage of the microscope and peers into its whirling contents. There it lies. Indigo in its pure form. It is a radiant elixir of glossy swirls, striped light and dark like a thick soup. It is neither solid, liquid nor gas, but a curiously bulbous yolk composed of gaseous emerald molecules. Paul adjusts the lens for further scrutiny and grows aware of the Indigo's reciprocated scrutiny. They See each other.

It is Consumption. It awaits Paul with patient apprehension. It is guarded. Ready for war. Paul is also ready. The two beings remain steeped in weighted silence. A bitter wail from beyond the door springs Paul to action.

He delivers the first swing. Paul turns to a hanging cabinet behind him, wills open its doors and locates a vial of thick dark liquid labeled J_{null}. Using one hand to hold steady the dish and the other to procure the vial, he devotes most of his energy to keeping his balance through the laboratory's dizzying locomotion.

Paul returns to the dish and very carefully drips a bead from a syringe-tipped vial onto the sparkling green solution then peers through the microscope. There appears to be no visible reaction. He repeats the experiment to no avail. He squints through tolling frustration as he strains to hold firm.

'*You stupid fool.*' The small, slithering growl of a whisper penetrates every inch of Paul's body. '*Go ahead. Try whatever you can, just as he did. You are no better. I will destroy you as I have destroyed him.*'

Paul will not allow its taunts to stir him. His microscope is insufficient. Recalling his brief conversation with Rosa on vacuums, he decides he will need an ultra-high vacuum probe microscope to scan for chemical reactivity at the molecular level. The instant he considers such a device, his instincts are directed to a large cubic container covered by a thick black sheet atop a plinth in the far corner.

Still balancing the saucer, Paul wields his will to remove the black sheet and finds a coveted stainless steel perfect-vacuum laboratory setup—a spherical chamber sitting over a wide tripod complete with an Ion-Be-Gone injection tube. A perfect-vacuum setup far exceeds ultra-high vacuum, as it ensures superior chemical probing unadulterated by external atmosphere. The setup pumps out any excess atmospheric coating that the injected chemical may have and traps that pure chemical solution in the chamber, leaving the solution in perfect vacuum, held in place with powerful rare-earth magnets.

'*I will eviscerate you.*' The portentous whisper grows louder pervading the walls and floorboards. '*I will delight in your agony as your body writhes in bitter, endless pain beneath me.*'

Paul recognizes he must mentally prepare for a vicious confluence of psychic assaults. He must not fear it. The light of the maniacally spinning room begins to dim as Consumption pulls away its photonic energies. Paul is uncertain he will have enough strength to light the laboratory, power the vacuum pump and heat the chamber, however, the time for such doubts has long passed. He steadily lifts the dish and readies himself for his ten-foot journey to the perfect-vacuum chamber. With the dish containing the sum of Consumption's nucleus, avoidance of spillage is top priority.

Paul takes his first step toward the vacuum setup. The light in the laboratory shimmers out. Paul pauses, managing to hold firm. As hisses and whispers swim about the rippling blackness like looming apparitions, he feels a sharp pain at his temples. His head throbs, hard and splitting, like a constant piercing slice at the flesh beneath his skull.

'Where are you taking me, Healer?' Paul struggles through a second step forward despite the scalding pain. Upon settling his foot to the ground, a hot canister of concentrated agony tips over in his spine, filling every crevice of his back with a staple of excruciation. Paul cries out and descends to his knees on the hard, oscillating ground, holding fast to the dish with both hands. Consumption betrays wavelets of contemptuous pleasure at the sound of Paul's anguish.

'If you place me in that vacuum chamber,' the growl warns, 'I will end Sherri Weiler. Your precious linchpin. I will tear her limb from limb and pleasure in the defilement of her rotting corpse.' This morbid threat only ignites Paul. He is determined to understand its hatred for the chamber. He grabs hold of the worktable's end with a free hand, lifts himself fully erect and takes two more steps toward the vacuum pump, calling upon the limits of his energy reserves to light the laboratory.

The room flickers light for an instant, but the illumination is cut short as Paul is promptly blinded by visions of his beautiful, perfect Chief of Staff, lying helplessly on her back: hot, boiling entrails bubbling over her shirt. Paul jerks his head free of the implanted vision and manages another step forward. He is again brought to his knees by a sharp burst of swelling pain in his chest. He swallows hard, tasting acrid blood. Pain is merely a chemical alert. He will not allow Consumption the satisfaction of another pained groan.

The laboratory, now a chamber of sinister absurdity, delights in the performance before it. Paul again inquires upon its walls for light, but it disregards Paul's plea and instead basks in the glee of his impossible pitch-black odyssey. With his deep-sight acutely activated, Paul can discern all structures in the room sans the convenience of light. He continues his journey on his knees and elbows, gnashing his teeth through the throbbing agony.

Consumption conspires with the laboratory to augment its frantic sway, and the room happily obliges, increasing to a fully menacing swing and inciting a smattering of flying glassware collisions. Paul squints through the nicks at his skin from careening fragments, as the laboratory is now a snow globe of pin-wheeling shards. Fortune favors the victor, and Paul has proven himself no longer worthy of the room's good fortune.

Paul strains to focus the peak of his energies on containing the solution within the saucer as he heaves his body toward the vacuum chamber. *'I have tasted you, Healer. I know what you desire.'* A vision of himself atop his warm, radiant Champion floods his mind and pervades his body. He is pumping her hard on his bed, pressing deep against her bursting light, filling her deep with himself. *'I can make her need you. I can make her fall to her knees before you despite your inadequacy.'* Paul's loins burn with torrents of sore discomfort. He pauses, shakes the hallucination and prepares to press onward.

'Or do you prefer I make her see you as I made your half-bot see you?' A second vision plagues Paul. Rosa lay on a boarding room floor. He is forcing himself inside of her barely conscious body as Johnny Angelo had done. *'I can implant this vision into*

her mind. All night. Every night.' Paul cannot shake the vision. He is running low on energy reserves. He will soon have diffi-culty maintaining the dish.

The vision proposes despair. Despair offers its hand to Paul, offers to end the swaying, offers to end the pain. Paul does not accept despair's sweet, sweet offer. Despair is a choice, a manifestation of surrender, and it is for the weak, for the human. Paul inches himself forward despite the unyielding psychic affronts.

'*Or I will make her as you are. I will make her...a Bad.*' Paul is greeted with a vision of himself and Rosa perched by a ravaged carcass. They are bathed in blood. Rosa is licking blood from her fingers basking in the depraved pleasure of a rattling Death High. She is a junkie.

No. Paul will never allow it. He will never see that day. Rosa will never see that side of him. Ever. With his energy depleted, he tries for one last Hail Mary.

Paul outstretches the broken tendrils of his consciousness to find hers: her spark, her Fire. And through the thick gnarling laboratory walls, he sends his telepathic plea.

"Fire," he communicates. "Hear me." But there is no response. '*You are quite the mentor. She will always remain powerless under your guidance.*' The dish tips slightly as Paul's arms grow weak, and the contents in the dish slide to one side. With hardly enough in him to hold his connection to her, Paul tries one last time. "Fire, I need you."

And like the sweetest of harmonies, Paul feels her energies flush through him. "Paul? Is that you? Am I doing this right? I'm holding the fort throwing fireballs like it's Mario World. But we could do with some serious healing."

"Charge me," Paul manages. "Give to me."

"Give to you? Like this?" Rosa offers, but her hazy psychic transmission cuts short. Though it is barely detectable through the chaos, it is all Paul needs. He is able to take hold and draw strands of fuel from her energies.

'It appears you are not so great after all. You must depend on her for greatness,' Consumption taunts. But Paul is again able to shake the vision and voices. He rises to his knees with a newfound surge of hysterical strength. He tears through the remainder of his journey in two long heaves, grabs hold of the plinth bearing the vacuum-chamber and hoists himself up.

The moment he comes to face the chamber, the sound of crashing glassware around him comes to a complete halt; the raucous dance of the laboratory comes to a complete halt; time itself comes to a complete halt. Paul is now completely alone, floating, suspended in a vast blankness around him. The eye of a living storm. In that complete stillness he hears a quiet, child-like voice, simple and pure. It surrounds him, washing through his entire being. 'Please.' It is a desperate liquid breath, rippling through the emptiness. And in the blink of an instant, Paul is stunned by a piercing flood of euphoria, immediately followed by a full understanding of Consumption. It simply wants to end the loneliness, to be accepted, to understand and to be understood. Just like him.

In the next instant the monstrous ocean of cacophony and jarring movement return. Paul gathers his bearings; amasses the bits of energy he's pulled from Rosa and demands illumination from the room. The walls respond and Paul's eyes rapidly adjust. The perfect-vacuum's LED display brightens, informing that a portion of Indigo is already suspended within the chamber. It is the third portion of Consumption's nucleus. Dr. Ferguson's portion.

Paul assembles himself firmly about the vacuum chamber, lifting the small dish to the injection tube. As he brings the saucer to the tube's lips, his ears encounter an unbearable, deafening sound. It is a high-pitched roar of physical force so powerful; his composition will not withstand it for long. It rocks the laboratory, sending cobwebbed cracks through the floor. It rocks the building, splitting wallboards at the hinges. It is a deep, thunderous anger. Paul understands the cry.

It is the Burn Notice.

Paul tips the saucer and pours its contents into the injection tube. He shuts the lid tight then falls back to his knees as his muscles deflate in expiration. With the final drip of energy awarded by his Champion, Paul sends a force of will to power the vacuum pump. He hears the pump's low current as it removes all other remnants of atmosphere from the solution, injects it into the chamber, and cuts all ability for Consumption to communicate with the outside world.

The sway of the room slows to a complete stop. Paul listens to the shouts of shock from the external lab. Consumption's nucleus has been wholly silenced, irretrievably shunned, rendering her forever powerless but for his mercy.

"Forgive me," Paul whispers to his little sister. "Forgive me."

34
CHAMPION

Tory watched as the Infecteds simply stopped: stopped growling, stopped clawing, stopped being. They fell flat to the ground, burnt and dismembered limbs littering the room like fallen leaves. The team had been at rope's end. When one of the Infecteds had torn through and gutted Sherri deep with a cleaver, the team consigned to their battlefield deaths.

But not long after, the Infecteds were just...over. Done. Becky, Rosa and Kris huddled over an unconscious DZ, while Tory's first instinct was to attend to Sherri. She lay on her back actively bleeding out from a traumatic impact at her belly. Tory descended beside her, removing his shirt to tie around her.

"No," she rasped through weak sputters of blood. "Take me to...to Paul."

"Can't move you, Weiler. I'll tie this around you to control the bleeding." Sherri shook her head as Tory spoke.

"Take me to Paul now," she croaked, her voice a drowsy blur. "Now!" Tory looked over to Dex who was busy treating his own wounds in a corner.

Tory gently propped Sherri up onto his knee, tying his shirt tight around her waist. The cleaver must have nicked her abdominal aorta. Imminent death was very apparent. Against his better judgment, Tory scooped her up like a bride and stormed the private laboratory.

In the room, lit only by the light pouring through the open door, Tory found Paul Oz slouched in a far corner. Paul watched blankly as they burst in, his face and shirt sopping wet with exhaustion, a rivulet of blood trickling down his forehead.

"She's bleeding. It's bad," Tory called. After a moment's hesitation, reality struck Paul, and he rushed over. Tory placed Sherri onto the cold floor. He watched as Paul dutifully unfastened the shirt at her middle. Tory sought to protest, but Paul was most certainly on a level of superior focus Tory was sure he could not pierce. Something otherworldly suffused his presence.

Paul knelt beside Sherri and peeled back her blood-soaked shirt then let out an almost imperceptible hum. Though unsure as to how, Tory was certain the hum did not generate from Paul's vocal cords but oozed from his aura like the gentle whirr of a transformer. Paul placed his hands on Sherri's deep wound, lifted his chin and rolled his eyes to the back of his head. He let his hands glide intimately across the wound, back and forth, back and forth.

Consumed by the eerily, hypnotic phenomenon, Tory almost missed it. But he didn't. He saw it with his own two eyes. Sherri Weiler's wound slowly regenerated beneath Paul's fingers. Any blood still actively flowing out retracted back into her system.

As a strict materialist, Tory could scarcely interpret what his eyes presented him. The rational part of his brain advised him to bolt, to protect himself from this thing, this creature he'd believed for years to be a man but who was very evidently not human.

Tory thought back to Rosa's act of valor. In the heat of the battle, Tory ascribed the phenomenon of her fiery bullets and ad hoc flame-throwing to a nifty trick she may have put together with her lighter and aerosol. But though he could not hear it at the time, he could feel it when she'd leaned against him, that same preternatural hum now disseminating from Paul Oscar. She'd saved his life.

Tory opted to stay put, remain silent and watch as Paul saved Sherri's life. Before long, Sherri let out a violent string of coughs then attempted to rise.

"No," Paul said, his hands still at her stomach. "Rest." Sherri yielded. Once her internals were repaired of errant blood flow, Paul removed his hands, his work complete. He brought his eyes to Tory. "How are the others?"

Tory tried to process a response through his many spinning gears but was incapable of speech. Paul held his gaze then slowly raised a hand to Tory's face. His hand, fresh and clear of Sherri's blood, aimed for the mark Rosa had left on his cheek. Tory instinctively recoiled. Paul accepted, sat back against the worktable, and let out an exhausted sigh. Tory was not ready for that. He wasn't sure he'd ever be ready for that.

Wednesday Nov 20, 186 PCE

As the Wednesday sun peppered a golden drizzle, Rosa and Torian sat with Sherri as she rested soundly in the Oz Corp clinic. Rosa sat bedside as Torian leaned against a wall flipping through his Ncluded. Despite the continued citywide power outage, Oz Corp buzzed bright, a benefit of its private grids.

Before heading back to Oz Corp, Rosa had briefed the team

that Ferguson had developed a concoction capable of control-ling the human mind through remote incursion, but that the said concoction had turned on Ferguson, to cultivate its human hivemind. Paul had communicated a more forthcoming rendi-tion into Rosa's mind, and they tacitly agreed on which aspects were not quite ready for primetime.

Now she sat cleaned up, the gash at her jaw already fading. With a taught grip, she held firmly to the Oz Corp jacket draped over her shoulders. She was his. All his.

Though recurring flashes of Johnny's hulking body and Rosa Thirteen's deathly fingers fluttered through the canals of her mind, Rosa was indeed healing, cauterizing any stray strands of the traumatic memory. She ought to feel broken. But she didn't. She'd stepped out of her sanctuary and survived. She'd faced down her ex-predator and won. She'd set zombies on fire by will alone for Christ's sake. And she'd never have known she could do it without her friend. Her smart, honest, amazing friend. She felt strong, unconquerable. She felt exceptionally beautiful.

"So, you and Paul. Some kind of genetic mutation?" Torian asked, breaking the silence. "Bio-enhancers?"

"We're still trying to figure that out. I mean, Dr. Ferguson had..." She stopped to regroup her thoughts.

"But you *are* as powerful as that...that thing, that concoc-tion that took out half the city?" The city was a mess of rubble, piles of dead Infecteds, heaps of fallen skycars and an assort-ment of frenetic survivors. Though no accusation touched Tori-an's voice, Rosa opted not to respond.

She instead looked to her wrist and assessed the chatverse's take on the outbreak. The 'verse praised Nforce's effective quarantine. Michelle Brier dubbed the epidemic the 'most widespread, short-lived New York City trend since high-heeled sneakers' in a special report praising Dr. Ferguson. *Oh, how quickly humanity forces manmade reason on the inexplicable,* Rosa thought.

"Why did it contact Kris and I?" Torian asked. "We're not like you. We're not..."

"I'm not sure," Rosa whispered. She stopped, hoping to avoid interrogation. She didn't want to feel uncomfortable around Torian. She knew him now. Though he was overly analytical and shrewd as a high-precision calculator, he was good. He was one of the few that were good.

"Back at the lab," Torian said. "You saved my life."

Rosa spun in her stool to face him. She considered how he'd led the team, how he'd placed his career on the line to work with Kris on the onset, how he'd sat beside her corpse with unshed tears, and how he trusted her at the front line.

"You're worth it," Rosa said. "Without you we'd never have made it. God's honest truth."

Averting his eyes, Torian said, "That means something coming from you, Lejeune." And suddenly it was Rosa's turn to blush. They held a silence of reciprocated respect until a buzz hit Torian's Ncluded. "I've got to take this. It's my sister in Boston. Let me know when Sherri comes to." He excused himself from the room.

Now alone at Sherri's bedside, Rosa retrieved the book she'd been reading from underneath her jacket. Still faintly aglow from earlier, Rosa was able to make out most of the passages from the *Diary of the Mad Glee* against the light of her arm—that special light. The diary was an arcane journal of scrambled poems and songs Ferguson claimed to have heard, or rather experienced, after placing his ear to the rip in the cosmos from which Indigo had emerged. Rosa sensed there was a profound message in the poems, deeper than the words on the page could express. An extracosmic message. She vowed it her life's purpose to decipher that message: for Ferguson, for her universe, for herself.

Sherri stirred.

"Sherri, you up?" Rosa asked. Sherri peered around disoriented, before coming to grips.

"Rosa," she croaked with a quiet smile. "I didn't think yours would be the first face I'd see."

"Keep thine enemies close," Rosa hissed. Sherri upheld a hard stare. "Paul's out front," Rosa continued, "Torian's on a call. Kris and Becky are next door waiting to see what we get when DZ wakes up. Kris was busying himself with Aztec's old parts. I was the only one bored enough to stick around here." Sherri allowed herself a smile. "How you feeling, Weiler?"

"Embarrassed."

"Oh, don't worry your hair's fine. Just don't go near a mirror any time soon." They both chuckled. "We survived an intense situation; don't be so hard on yourself."

"I know. Still, I compromised my boss. Made him heal me in front of Torian Ross."

Rosa blinked. "How much do you know, Sherri?"

"I know that he can heal wounds, and I know that you know." Rosa wondered if Sherri knew about her affinity to fire, but opted not to broach.

"Paul's a big boy, Sherri. He chose to do what he had to do."

Sherri offered a sad smile. "Listen, I came down hard on you back at the facility. Just didn't want him to lose focus."

"Yeah, I doubt I can cause the great and powerful Oz to lose focus," Rosa laughed.

"So far, you're the only one who ever has."

* * *

Rosa stepped onto the lawn to find Paul Oscar alone in an Oz Corp jacket looking out to the dewy green from the balustrade, surveying his kingdom. She parked beside him, taking in his glowing energies amid the sporadic raindrops. He allowed her to feel his frustration, his remorse, and for that privilege she was immensely humbled. She hadn't known he could feel such feelings. But he *was* human. His imperfection was that he was human.

"Want to talk about it?" she asked and patiently waited out the long silence for his answer.

"I don't discuss failures," he finally said, his words low and certain.

"You single-handedly ended the infection spread. That doesn't sound like failure."

"Yet the bodies pile in the streets." Paul swept a showcasing hand before him. After another brief silence he said, "I betrayed one of my own. All self-aware beings do what they must to survive. I imagine how I would be, if the tables had been turned, and I were in her shoes."

"You did what you needed to do to defend our world. You made a tough decision, and you stood behind it. Don't apologize for it." At that, Paul looked over at her. He studied her fully, her form, her thoughts, then let out a warm wave of appreciation.

"Sage advice," he said. Rosa smiled for them both. "And I can't take full credit for ending the spread. When I called on you, you answered me."

Rosa blushed and let out a series of huffs to keep her own emotions at bay. She remembered hearing him call to her, and at that time, responding to him in kind had just come so naturally. A thought materialized as she studied his face, and the words stumbled forward before she could filter them. "I still don't understand how you could watch me get...you know...by

Johnny. I mean, I know I broadcasted for everything around me to let me go deepsight, but I—"

Rosa's words were cut short by a growing rumble at her feet perfectly similar to that of the earthquake at the facility. Immediately she felt a deep-seated bone-crushing anger pour forth from Paul, a seething rage, an infuriating helplessness that gushed out unfocussed, blasting Rosa hard in the gut. She stifled a bitter cry and cringed forward as if every limb in her body would snap. Thin lightning bolt cracks rippled through nearby balusters. Stray droplets of rain whirled chaotically awry, as a dark foulness from within Paul enveloped him whole. However, just as suddenly as the fury had come, the consequent seismic rumbling wound back, replaced by a loosely enforced calm. Paul looked away toward the green.

"I swallowed more pride than you'll ever know the night you denied me, Rosa," he said evenly. "I prefer not to relive watching some lab rat just take it." Rosa watched him, his eyes. The statement dripped with an unrestrained melancholy. "Pardon my inadequacy in shielding you from my... *temper* just now. I'm not at my best."

The realization of how deeply she'd cut him each time he'd rescinded his frequency settled into her. "I didn't mean to hurt you that night," she started, still recovering from his outburst. "I never mean to hurt you. It's just that I—" She stopped herself, knowing if she continued, she'd break. The deep blare of a truck horn bellowed in the distance while graying clouds meandered across the sky.

Paul's eyes returned to hers. His shoulders followed. He stepped up close to her. They took in each other's presence as rain droplets trickled through the tiny space between them. Paul reached out and wrapped an arm around her shoulder, drawing her in close for an embrace. There was an innocence to it. A sincerity. She rested her head on his shoulder, allowing a slow steady sway between them. She needed it. That moment of assurance. They both did, both having skirted the limits of their preternatural strengths. And when she lifted her face to his, the kiss was inevitable.

Paul touched his lips to hers, slow, deep, necessary. She felt him need her mouth. She'd been aching desperately for that feeling, for the feel of his skin against hers. A swift movement at his hands caused the revenant of a bad memory to ripple through Rosa, and she instantly pulled away.

Paul raised a brow of concern. Something about the earnest worry in his eyes for her. Rosa grabbed fast to his neck and pulled him down to her, drowning in the pleasures of his crooning charge.

Paul upheld a fierce restraint, allowing her the control, submitting to her. She felt their compound desire infinitely reflected in their entwined frequencies—felt the spike in his ego at her desire for him—and happily surrendered herself to it. Paul brought his hands to her hips, slid his fingers to her waist and massaged just beneath her shirt. The pleasure of his buzzing fingers coupled with the impassioned tango at their mouths flushed a torrent of fiery bliss up her backside so intense, Rosa squealed. She lifted her lips from his and stole another quick gaze into his eyes, completely intoxicated and drowning deeper still.

"Jesus, Paul," she breathed an inch from his lips. Words again escaped her filter, as if compelled. "I don't know what you're doing to me, Paul, but I'm falling hard for you." The words, barely audible above the rain, came lachrymose. "And I don't think I can stop myself from—" Paul cut her short, pressing his finger to her lips.

The two remained motionless. Rosa waited. A sea of gray cloaked the sky as the distant truck horn blared once more. She wanted to worry, but she'd said the words and decided they were the truth.

She again detected a struggling calm in Paul's aura, followed by a series of indecipherable signals. And after a moment's hesitation, she felt him gush forth a deep well of affection for her, a raw, all-encompassing wave that consumed her bones, rocking her every limb. There was a pain to his affection she couldn't quite grasp. She stumbled across a fleeting thought in his mind of her licking blood from her fingers. The thought came wrapped in an amorphous regret. He took his finger from her lips, brushed his hand against her cheek and held her face to his for another lasting gaze.

Then, he let go of her. He pulled away, placed his hood over his head and took a step back. The next feeling, she felt was the worst feeling she'd ever known. She felt him pull back his frequency. It was slow and deliberate, so as not to harm her physically.

"No," she said through quivering lips. "Please. Don't."

Paul waited a moment before responding, allowing her access to his emotions to fade completely. The air grew cold, dreary, empty around her. Paul carefully calculated his next words. "There are parts of me I am not willing to share with you," he said sharply. "Ever."

His words pinched a raw nerve. Rosa fought hard to hold her composure. She allowed the rain, now a downpour, to wash over the ensuing bubble of pain at her gut as she too raised the hood of her jacket. "Yet you want me to share my *parts* with you?" she said. She watched as his face softened through an exhale. "I thought we..." She considered the deep internal affection to which he'd inadvertently exposed her just seconds ago. "I don't understand."

"I don't expect you to."

Rosa moved her mouth to respond but knew Paul wasn't

the type to entertain argument. She instead took a step back, shaking her head. The rejection was a harsh one, curt. The tears would come later. A piece of her had thought them fated to be, as if Dr. Ferguson had promised them to each other. But perhaps it was for the best. Her feelings for him were far too wildly untamed: her restlessness at the mention of his name, her jump at his touch, her obsessive infatuation with his energies.

Rosa spun on her heel with plans to find a self-powering hotel, binge on ice cream and chatverse dribble then meet up with Kris for therapeutic banter. As she scuttled forward, Paul grabbed hold of her elbow. She couldn't help but wince at his charged touch. She turned back to face him. "I'll contact Sherri if I have any questions for you about my fire affinities." She attempted to press onward, but he kept his hold firm.

"Strenuous exercise may help in accessing deepsight," he advised. "Also consider obtaining dimethyltryptamine supplements."

"I'll consider it," she said brusquely.

"Right then," Paul said. He freed her elbow and took a step back. Rosa immediately stalked forward then stopped. She peered back at him. He was watching her. She didn't need insight into his thoughts to know he was conflicted, exhausted. She didn't want to be angry with him. Not anymore. She opted to offer him a glimpse at the worthy adversary she could be.

"You think I can't handle you," she inferred, her eyes sliding to his.

"Is that what I think?" He matched her gaze.

She stepped up close to him again. "It is. And you want to know what I think, Paul Oscar?"

"What do you think, Rosa Lejeune?"

Still somewhat in tune with her previous state of deepsight, Rosa managed to send a hot pulse of concentrated heat to her right index finger. She tucked her hand under Paul's shirt and grazed her sizzling finger lightly down the contours of his abdomen. Paul betrayed a shiver of pleasure against her, then stiffened as she traced her finger far below his navel, threatening him, daring him to react.

She brought her lips to his ear. "I think you don't like control as much as you let on." Then she removed her hand and stepped back to survey him.

"I'd lay waste to everything you hold dear before ever allowing you to tame me." His words came sharp with an undeniable hostility.

"Well, good thing I don't have that much stuff," she snipped. Paul set his dark eyes hard on her, rigorously calculating her face. She waited, bracing herself emotionally. She imagined he was forcing a calm over his dark temper. Nonetheless, despite himself, he let out a quick breath of laughter, averting his gaze. It was a genuine, exposed laughter, a surrender. He was so difficult to read, so difficult to break, so his laughter, as fleeting as it was, warmed her cheeks.

Rosa had conquered Johnny Angelo, scorched zombies and caused a brief moment of genuine mirth in Paul Oscar Ryland Perry. All due to this newfound ancient power within her.

Rosa: three. Big, scary world: zero.

A peel of thunder broke the brief moment of levity. The sky cast a dark thunderous haze, beating down thick shards of marble rain. The change in pressure was instant. Rosa felt the warmth of an emotional signal. She'd only ever received such clear frequency from Paul Oscar. She was certain this frequency did not emanate from him, but from behind him. It held a sense of urgency. She paused to listen more attentively to its somewhat familiar signature.

It was...Wind.

As a thick, gray sheet bellied overhead, Rosa looked to the

front gates beyond the green, half-expecting to see Karla bustling through. Instead, she saw two tall white men and one short dark-skinned man, each wearing soaked Black-Robes. The two tall men remained at the gate, yet the dark man hurried across the lawn with a hunched gait and a white cane.

Seeing Brother Ori Eze outside of the monastery was disorienting. He seemed superimposed over the stormy city backdrop. Rosa followed Paul to meet him on the lawn.

"To what do I owe this pleasure, Brother Ori?" Paul asked over the clamoring thunder.

The monk assembled himself before them. "Paul Oscar Ryland Perry," he sang. "Forgive my intrusion."

"No intrusion, Brother Ori," Paul said. Ori turned toward Rosa.

"Ms. Rosa Lejeune, you are lovely as ever."

"Thank you, Brother Ori. It's good to see you again."

With mandatory pleasantries now complete, Ori faced forward. "I have not come as a friend. I have come as a messenger. As you know, I have not stepped foot outside the monastery since I swore my allegiance over ten years ago. But my Mother in Intellect, Khalidah Nejem, has requested my assistance in this crucial matter. She has chosen me to deliver this message, as she knows you and I have an understanding. She herself cannot leave the Abbey and tarnish her Spark."

"Speak," Paul said. "I am listening."

"She would like to collect."

"Wow, she doesn't waste time," Rosa noted.

"Let's head inside to discuss," Paul suggested. Though not much past noon, the rainstorm had plummeted to a brutal shower of thick blades.

"No, we must remain out here." Brother Ori struggled to speak above the downpour. "Mother Khalidah demands it. Remaining outside offers her better reception."

"Reception?" Rosa asked. And they watched as the infinity symbol over Brother Ori's dark forehead flashed a bright white for an instant then faded to an animate golden glow. Karla's psychic signal doubly strengthened in the thunder-laden atmosphere.

"She says she knows The Fire is with you, and that The Fire is permitted to bear witness." Brother Ori's cane tumbled to the wet grass as if he'd no longer the strength to carry it. He limply descended to his knees, dropping his chin to his chest.

Paul looked to Rosa. "Give me your hand." Rosa allowed him to interlace his fingers with hers. He placed their hands onto the glowing tattoo. "Speak," Paul called to the infinity symbol. "We are listening."

The genuflecting monk snapped his head upward to face Paul. "Healer."

"Wind."

"The Healer is not opened."

"I am indisposed at the moment." Both men were now speaking at a shout over the menacing storm.

"The Wind is owed two favors of any scope from The Healer."

"This is correct," Paul said. Rosa felt the infinity symbol vibrate at each word Karla communicated through Ori.

"My first request. The Gateway: the quantum tunnel through which the conceptual fundaments of Indigo emerged to dwell upon the Earth."

"Yes. In Battery Park."

"The Healer has the resources and wherewithal needed to deal with such things."

"What do you ask of me?"

"The Healer must discover how to close The Gateway." Though she couldn't be certain, Rosa suddenly thought she felt another wholly separate presence looming amid the billowing clouds.

"Understood. Though, I imagine this will not be easy. How pressing is it?"

"This request is of utmost urgency." A loud hammer of thunder bullied the sky accompanied by a cracking whip of lightning. "This universe belongs to those beings who forged the universe. The universe does not need for a malevolent Other to burrow through The Gateway and wreak havoc in response to The Burn Notice." Even through the rowdy storm, Rosa felt Paul grow especially tense beside her. Until that moment, she'd been certain nothing could rattle him.

"Burn Notice?" Rosa asked. "What Burn Notice?"

"Our wayward sister in mind and body, Invasion—"

"Consumption," Paul tersely corrected.

"Our wayward sister in mind and body, Consumption, has placed a Burn Notice signal out against this universe, our universe. Consumption has informed everything that is everywhere that this place, our place, is ripe for ravage. Which brings about The Wind's second request."

Rosa felt a falter in her balance and fell against Paul. He helped straighten her and replaced their hands on the pulsating tattoo. Rosa could swear they now stood at a slant, as if the island of Manhattan had tipped over ever so slightly. The disruption in balance opened the folds of her physical perception. She now realized the distant blaring horn she'd been hearing was no horn at all, but a long-pitched sonar signal, like that of a whale. It seemed to come at her from every direction. And something else told her it came from that looming, separate presence.

"Did anyone else just feel that?" Rosa asked. Of course, they'd felt it. They too had faltered in balance.

"What is your second request?" Paul called to the glowing symbol.

Brother Ori waited a long moment before he answered. "The Healer has caused the implementation of The Burn Notice. The Healer must stop...The Intruder."

"Stop what intruder?"

"The Intruder that has just welcomed itself in through The Gateway."

EPILOGUE

Wednesday Nov 20, 186 PCE

"Hi."

"Hey, Tory."

"Good to hear your voice. How are you?"

"How am I? How are *you*? Wasn't there some sort of flu outbreak down there?"

"Yeah, but it's contained now."

"Right. Glad the quarantine worked out. I think even mum was a little worried. Don't tell her I told you."

"Heh, okay. How's Aiden?"

"He's amazing! He's starting on full sentences now. I interpret everything he says as 'Mum, just for you, I'm going to work extra hard on getting sponsored.' He's so cute and behaved, and a few companies have already shown interest."

"Cindy, is Aiden...is he sort of...strange in a way? Like when he touches things."

"Like when he touches things?"

"Or does he seem to heal faster than normal, or...?"

"Well, he never cries, ever. Not even when he gets seriously hurt. I'm not even sure when he's hungry. I just feed him whenever I'm hungry. I'm pretty sure that's not right. I'm pretty sure I'm a crap mum."

"I'm pretty sure you're a damn good mum."

"Yeah, well, I try not to wish Dad were still around to see him."

"Yeah...Hey, when will I get to see some more holographs of Aiden?"

"He'll be fitted for his Ncluded in a few months. There will be tons of photos and holos then. I'm hoping to sell him off to a good sponsor before my cy-ternship with MetaLife Plus next year. But if not, well, there's always the following year."

"I miss you a lot, Cindy."

"Stop being weird. Look, Tory, I've gotta go. I've gotta get back to work."

"You're working?"

"Yep. Part-time. Nothing like your top-of-the-line gig, but it feeds Aiden and me."

"Anything you ever need, Cindy, you know I—"

"Yeah, yeah. Blah blah blah."

"Listen. Thank you for checking in. Let's not wait for another disease outbreak before talking again."

"Whatever, Tory. Talk later."

ACKNOWLEDGMENTS

Special thanks to my brothers, Eugene and Franklin, for our creation of the Coddy Kids world, to my language and sensitivity readers, to Arthur Gwynne, and to everyone on the publishing team!

RIZE publishes great stories and great writing across genres written by People of Color and other underrepresented groups. Our team consists of:

Lisa Diane Kastner, Founder and Executive Editor
Cody Sisco, Acquisitions Editor, RIZE
Benjamin White, Acquisition Editor, Running Wild
Peter A. Wright, Acquisition Editor, Running Wild
Resa Alboher, Editor
Angela Andrews, Editor
Sandra Bush, Editor
Ashley Crantas, Editor
Rebecca Dimyan, Editor
Lara Huie, Editor
Abigail Efird, Editor
Aimee Hardy, Editor
Henry L. Herz, Editor
Cecilia Kennedy, Editor
Barbara Lockwood, Editor
Scott Schultz, Editor

Evangeline Estropia, Product Manager
Kimberly Ligutan, Product Manager
Lara Macaione, Marketing Director
Joelle Mitchell, Licensing and Strategy Lead
Pulp Art Studios, Cover Design
Standout Books, Interior Design
Polgarus Studios, Interior Design

Learn more about us and our stories at www.runningwild-press.com

Loved these stories and want more? Follow us at www.runningwildpress.com, www.facebook.com/running-wildpress, on Twitter @lisadkastner @RunWildBooks @RwpRIZE